A NEW
CHANCE

Other Books by Kevin E. Ready:

———

All the Angels Were Jewish (2016)

Gaia Weeps - The Crisis of Global Warming (1998)

The Big One (1997)

The Holy Koran - Modern English Translation (editor) (2014)

Credit Sense: How to Borrow Money and Manage Debt (1989)

———

and with **Cap Parlier:**

TWA 800 - Accident or Incident? (1998)

———

and writing as Sarah Sarnoff

The Disambiguation of Susan (2014)

A NEW CHANCE

BY
KEVIN E. READY

SAINT GAUDENS PRESS
Phoenix, Arizona & Santa Barbara, California

See other great books available from Saint Gaudens Press
http://www.SaintGaudensPress.com

Saint Gaudens Press
Post Office Box 405
Solvang, CA 93464-0405

Saint Gaudens, Saint Gaudens Press
and the Winged Liberty colophon
are trademarks of Saint Gaudens Press

Print edition ISBN: 978-0-943039-55-8
eBook ISBN: 978-0-943039-56-5
Library of Congress Catalog Number: 2020931355

Printed in the United States of America

10 8 6 4 2 3 5 7 9 1

This is a work of fiction. No character is intended to depict any real person, living or dead. Certain entities, including business, charitable, religious and educational institutions and even some famous families, are depicted for purposes of providing a proper setting for the reader to understand, enjoy and relate to the fictional story. The policies, activities and people associated with these entities, as depicted in this story, are also fictionalized. Other names, characters and incidents are the products of the author's imagination and bear no relationship to real events, or persons living or deceased.

—

~

Acknowledgment

The author would like to acknowledge several employees of the California Department of State Hospitals and various Kern County, California government agencies for their assistance in helping the author get the real-world facts right for this work of fiction. I would also like to thank Marcia Follensbee, Cap Parlier and Anna Ready for their editorial assistance.

As this is a work of fiction, the author would like to acknowledge the very real service of members of the U.S. military whose valiant real-life exploits are mentioned in this book. The invasion of Iraq, the war in Afghanistan, and the horrendous helicopter crashes in Afghanistan in 2006 and 2011 were very real, and the author has mentioned these true exploits amongst the fictional adventures of the characters herein. Other military units, such as the 75th Army Rangers, and the 274th and 250th Forward (Resuscitative) Surgical Teams[1] (Airborne) are mentioned because their real-life service happened to be in the right place and at the right time for the author's fictional characters to be joined in their story. The characters in this book are fictional and are not meant to portray any real persons, and the story herein is not meant to tell of real events, except as mentioned above.

---

1   The US Army added "Resuscitative" to these units' names in 2019.

Part One

Chapter 1

Maricela was checking the intravenous line and catheter for the young female patient when two doctors entered the room. They moved to the other side of the bed from Maricela.

"Good evening, Doctor Hecht," Maricela said in a slight Hispanic accent.

"Good evening, Maricela. Have you met Doctor Ogilvie yet? He'll be taking over for me on second shift." Hecht handed the iPad to Ogilvie as he pulled his stethoscope to his ears and tugged the blanket off the patient's shoulders.

"Nice to meet you, Doctor Ogilvie." The nurse wiggled the blue plastic oxygen tube and mouthpiece in the girl's mouth to check that it was a snug fit. She carefully smoothed the girl's long blonde hair to clear snags under the breathing tube's elastic band. Then, she gently pinched the girl's nose around the feeding tube and bent over to listen for the gentle spurt of outgoing oxygen to be sure the pressurized breathing apparatus was working.

"And nice to meet you, too." Ogilvie smiled at the nurse, who was no longer looking at him. He moved to get a better view of the girl in the bed, and he asked, "What's the story with her. Pressurized oxygen by mouth, catheter, and feeding tube. This isn't just temporary sedation like the last room."

Dr. Hecht answered, "No, this is our Sleeping Beauty. Ms. Donnelley has been in a coma since right after she got here. Coupla months. And she is not getting better. Slow spiral downward, it seems."

"Yes, she is pretty, strikingly so. What's her story? Injury? And why is she in this kind of hospital?"

Hecht gestured to the iPad, "You should read up on her when you get a chance. Sad story. Eighteen years old. Just out of high school. She's an LPS case from the Central Valley. Napa never had a chance to do a full intake workup on her. Upon admission here, she went into severe seizures, high temp, major heart palpitations, and very shallow, slow breathing. We sent her by ambulance to the ICU at Queen of the Valley Hospital because we have no ability to deal with those kinds of acute issues. They determined she had a total bowel blockage. When the surgeons went in, they found she had ingested several baggies of various drugs, methamphetamine, oxycodone, and Psilocybin, you know, shrooms. It seems that she had swallowed a drug stash in heat-sealed baggies when she was arrested just before she was sent here, and it clogged her up inside, then poisoned her when the baggies leaked. The ICU got her stabilized and tried to flush the drug cocktail out of her system with multiple transfusions and blood filtration. She went into a coma, and they decided there was nothing further they could do for her. They shipped her back here to either come out of it or die. We contracted with a coma specialist from UC Davis Med to write a treatment protocol for her and do training for the staff here in the Skilled Nursing Unit since her situation is obviously unusual for us."

Maricela now joined in, "It is really, really sad that a beautiful girl like her got so messed up. I've been hoping that she gets better all summer. But she seems to be worse and worse. Her blood ox is way down almost to 80 again tonight, and we can't get it higher."

Hecht continued, "Yeah, even if she did come out of the coma now, there is a good chance of permanent brain damage after all those drugs and weeks of low oxygen saturation." Dr. Hecht pulled his penlight from his lab coat pocket. He gently opened the girl's eyelid with his thumb, moved the light beam across the eye, and then checked the other eye. "Very little pupillary reaction in those big green eyes. I fear she is not long with us."

Dr. Hecht took the iPad back from his colleague and started entering his notes. When he finished, he looked over at the nurse and gave a half-hearted smile.

Maricela nodded and said, "I will miss you, Dr. Hecht. It has been nice working with you every night."

Hecht nodded, "Yes, but now I actually get to go to bed when my wife goes to bed for a change."

Now Maricela laughed, "She's a lucky lady, I'm jealous."

The two doctors turned to leave. Before she followed them, Maricela put her hand on the patient's forehead and said, "God bless you, little beauty. *Vaya con Dios.*"

Maricela checked her watch just before she turned off the light. It was a few minutes after eight o'clock.

———

Mark Kelleher was driving south on the I-80 Freeway over the Carquinez Bridge south of Vallejo just after dusk had turned to darkness. All four lanes were packed, but the main rush hour was over, and traffic was moving, as usual on Bay Area freeways, slightly above the speed limit.

Mark poked the dashboard display screen of his BMW 540 to check the time. He had made an appointment for a 9:00 PM meet-up with an exciting new contact he had gotten via the dating app *Tinder*. The pretty, young woman whose posting he had responded to told him of her difficult work hours at her job down in Berkeley, so Mark had suggested they meet after she got off work near her employer. He had left his apartment in American Canyon with plenty of time to get to Berkeley, and he was still on schedule, but barely. Trying to date someone in a different corner of the vast Bay area was difficult, but the intriguing profile and attractive picture of the woman made Mark decide it was worth his effort.

As he drove, Mark reached up to tuck his light brown hair behind his ears. He would need a fresh above-the-ears haircut soon. Out of habit, he quickly alternated hands on the wheel as the other hand flicked unseen dandruff from his shoulders. He still wore the sports jacket, shirt, tie, and slacks he had worn to work, but he had stopped at home first to brush his teeth and refresh his deodorant. His date was just coming off work herself, so this outfit was fine. He could wait until a possible second date to dress a bit more impressively. Rules for Millennials dating via the *Tinder* app were liberal.

Mark was in the second lane from the right when the brake lights on an 18-wheeler truck ahead of him indicated it was slowing a bit. His lane already seemed to be going slightly slower than the lanes to his left or even the 'slow' lane to his right. Not seeing a clear opening to move to the left, he risked getting tied up with the exiting and merging traffic in the slow lane, to make a quick dash up and around the truck. Mark punched the gas and shifted lanes to the right. The BMW responded smartly, and he was quickly accelerating past the truck. He saw that the car behind him before had now followed his lead and was matching his fast lane change.

The Pomona Street exit sign, the first exit after the bridge, passed above him as he came even with the front of the truck. The two of the cars ahead of him in the slow lane signaled they were taking the Pomona Street exit ramp. Mark accelerated again to be able to take advantage of the space from the exiting cars and move up to change lanes in front of the truck.

Abruptly, the front car exiting on the ramp made a wild swerve to twist crazily back onto the highway ahead of a car in front in the slow lane. Brake lights of the three cars in his view ahead flashed on with the cars ahead of him and to the left slowing quickly. The car still in the off-ramp swerved a bit as it tried to slow for something Mark could not yet see.

Mark braked too, but he felt a thud as the car behind him failed to see the brake lights ahead. With the impact from behind at full speed, the BMW's sophisticated anti-lock brake software kicked in and instantaneously released the brakes to prevent the skid that the car's sensors thought was happening. With the release of the brakes, Mark's car was still traveling at almost the speed limit, as it had the bulk of the speeding car behind still pushing the BMW.

The 18-wheeler alongside Mark now made a great whooshing sound as the trucker's airbrakes struggled to slow for the cars stopping in both lanes ahead. The vehicle just in front of Mark had spun sideways in his lane as it hit the car that had flipped back onto the freeway from the ramp. As Mark pumped his brakes and gripped the steering wheel, he saw the car in the exit ramp abruptly maneuver onto the shoulder and hit the railing of this elevated section between bridge and off-ramp.

With the two exiting cars now clear of the exit ramp, Mark saw the danger they had scattered to avoid. Bright headlights were racing toward them, the wrong way, on the exit ramp.

Mark had only the barest instant to think of what to do. He was still trying to brake his car, but there was a wrecked car turned sideways in the lane ahead of him. The car that had swerved off the ramp was smashed against the guard rail on the shoulder. The car that had hit his rear-end was still right on his bumper. The huge truck was still beside him on the left.

As Mark quickly weighed his almost non-existent options, the air filled with the blaring blast of the trucker's airhorn bellowing a late warning. Mark had only the briefest second to recognize that the oncoming headlights were from a large white pickup highlighted in the garish orange light of the exit ramp's sodium-vapor streetlights. The pick-up was heading directly at him and showed no sign of slowing.

The pickup seemed intent on keeping to the lane of the ramp and onto the freeway, so at the last instant, Mark chose to try and avoid the most severe impact, and steer away from the pick-up, and then try to avoid the wreck on the shoulder.

It was too late. Mark's last view was of his headlights shining through the pickup's windshield at the astonished face of the drunk driver in the truck who finally recognized his error. The front driver's side of the pickup hit about midway on Mark's front grill. Then, a silvery poof of the BMW airbag covered his face simultaneously with the first pounding of the impact.

The airbag deployment blocked Mark's view. The airbag muffled sounds as his car violently spun. The car flipped counterclockwise and up. His head was snapped into the side airbag and window as the BMW slammed sideways into the wrecked car already crumpled against the railing. Everything went black as Mark's head hit.

———

Mark's first conscious sensation was the shattering and tinkling of glass pieces from the side window, having been broken by a highway patrolman's nightstick. He barely felt it as the deflated airbags were pulled away from his face, and a strong hand reached for his neck to take a pulse.

Mark heard, but did not fully comprehend the highway patrolman's shout, "This guy is alive but pinned bad. Get the Jaws and paramedics."

Mark tried to open his eyes but saw little through the pink fog of his blood. The sound of the BMW's still-playing satellite radio joined the noisy turmoil of sirens and shouts outside his car. He could not breathe through his nose that had been smashed by the steering wheel emblem with the airbag's discharge upon the truck's initial impact. As he panted to breathe through his mouth, he tasted the salt of blood. He tried to move, but the steering wheel firmly cocooned his body against the tilted seat, making breathing all the worse. Now, for the first time, he felt the gashing pain from his lower legs and feet somewhere beneath the crumpled dashboard.

Mark tried to turn his head toward the repeated bumps of someone trying to pull open his door. He tried to help push it open, but his arm did not move correctly and now gave him a stab of pain. He again tried to look around. He now recognized a multitude of flashing red and blue emergency lights all around him and a stark glare of a spotlight aimed into his car through a missing window.

The bumps on his door morphed into a steady bass thump-thump-thump of machinery, and deep rhythmic vibration felt through the stabbing pain in his arm. Even in his stupor, Mark realized they were trying to cut him free of the wreck.

After an eternity, the machinery sound ended, replaced by the screeching of metal as first-responders wrenched open the door. Strong hands tried to lift him free of the steering wheel's grasp. That effort suddenly stopped, and the hydraulic machinery thumped again, set to work down by his legs.

"Hold on, man," said someone, gripping his shoulder. "We've got you."

Work near his feet and legs continued until Mark heard another loud voice. This time it was not just a shout, but a scream, with a tone of dire urgency in it, "Get that hose back here and wash this down. This tank is leaking."

The vibration of the hydraulic jaws at his feet continued until it stopped abruptly when a flash of fierce yellow-orange light hid the red and blue twinkles in his fogged vision and even overpowered the bright spotlight. The yellow light was behind him and reflected onto his face off of the limp silver airbags hanging in front of his head.

"Get that hose over the truck," someone shouted.

In the next instant, the yellow-red light magnified a hundred-fold and lit the entire area. Searing heat and pain enveloped Mark's shoulders and neck. He smelled the burning of his shirt, his skin, and the gasoline. A thick cloud of purple fire extinguisher powder filled the air, choking Mark. Hands once again desperately yanked on his shoulder and arm. Flames returned quickly.

Mark screamed in a high-pitched, quavering yodel that bordered on something inhuman. Another powerful yank by the firefighters on his broken arm brought a momentous pain that overpowered even the pain of the burn on his back. Mark managed to scream, "My arm!" Yet, his body still barely leaned out of the door, stuck in the seat, legs pinned.

In the end, the yellow fire ballooned and filled the car. It took a second for the fire to begin its destructive work on Mark. The all-encompassing heat and flame enveloped him, and he let loose the inhuman scream, which stopped when he breathed in flames.

—

Chapter 2

The unit loudspeaker squealed a chirp of feedback before announcing, "Code Red, Room Four! Code Red, Room Four!"

Elmore Huddy dropped the bedpan that he had been spraying out into the supply room utility sink with a metallic clatter. He quickly squirted a healthy dollop of hand sanitizer on his hands from the wall dispenser. Elmore closed the door and hurriedly checked that it was locked before turning and running down the long hall in the Skilled Nursing Unit. As he ran, he rubbed the gel on his hands, and then wiped the excess sanitizer on his orderly's jumpsuit.

Code Red meant a dangerous situation with a patient. A burly orderly like Elmore was the best responder to help nurses and doctors restore control. Elmore had only been in Room Four a few times to collect full urine catheter bags left by the nurses who changed them. So, he knew very little about the patient in that room that he was running to help control.

Other patients had gathered in the hallway to see the excitement in Room Four, and Elmore had to shove them aside as he ran up to the room. In the last few steps, he could see into the room through the observation windows. He saw two nurses and two doctors already there.

Running into the room, Elmore saw the patient in the bed thrashing about wildly, kicking, and then shaking like she was in a seizure. All the while, the woman was screaming at the top of her lungs, "The fire... stop it! Help!"

The two nurses were on one side of the bed, the doctors on the other. One nurse was trying to hold down the patient's head and shoulders. The other nurse was trying to grab an arm. One doctor pressed the patient's chest onto the bed and tried to grab her other arm. The second doctor was trying to control the kicking legs. The bed blanket was off, hanging on the bed rail, and the patient's gown was up around her waist, exposing naked legs and body.

Elmore hurriedly decided the best assistance he could render would be to try and restrain the wildly kicking legs closest to him. Just as he came within reach, the woman curled into a fetal position on her back, and then kicked out with both legs together. The heel of one foot caught Elmore solidly in the nose.

Elmore thought he heard the patient scream, "Godda get o-out!" just before she kicked. He staggered backward, hand to his face. His hand came away bloody. The pain of a broken nose was obvious. Elmore took an instant to recover then jumped toward the bed again, trying to land his body across the flailing legs.

The heavy body of the former defensive lineman was enough to pin the woman's legs to the bed. Another orderly was now teaming with the doctors, and both arms were in the staff's hands.

One of the doctors shouted to someone behind them, "Ten milligrams Versed/Fentanyl intramuscular — she pulled her tubes out. STAT! Bring a second dose of five milligrams down here in case she doesn't respond."

Elmore recognized the drug cocktail of choice at Napa State Hospital to quickly sedate an out-of-control patient. He had heard those words many times.

The struggle to keep the woman down continued with six staff members wrestling with what seemed to Elmore to be a frail young woman. The woman continued to scream, mostly high-pitched howls, but Elmore thought he heard "My skin, ahhh!" and "The pain!" amongst the screams.

A red smear of blood stained the bed sheet below Elmore's face. His blood. He was able to look back to the other side of the bed as someone pushed in between him and the nurses.

He heard his friend, the nurse Maricela, ask, "Hip muscle Okay? I can't get to her arms."

One of the doctors answered, "Yes, the hip is fine. Hurry!"

"Make sure you get her hip." Elmore joked since his hip lay over the woman's now exposed thighs.

"We'll see." Maricela quipped.

In just a few seconds, the screaming stopped, and the thrashing of the body slowed to a stop. The patient took a couple of deep breaths, and then eyelids fluttered, and breathing slowed. Elmore pushed himself up and off the bed. A nurse quickly pulled the patient's gown down and replaced the blanket.

Elmore fingered his nose. Maricela saw this and reached to hand him some tissues from the nightstand. Maricela gave Elmore an empathetic wink.

For a moment, the seven Napa State Hospital staffers looked at each other and the patient.

The nurse who had been at the head cradled her thumb with her other hand and said, "She bit me."

"Bad?" asked Doctor Hecht, who Elmore now recognized was the doctor shouting orders.

"Uh? Broke the skin. Down to the bone. On the knuckle," the nurse answered.

"Go back to the desk. I'll be there in a minute to look at it," Doctor Hecht ordered.

Maricela started to check the connections and tubing that was messed up in the struggle. The other nurse was checking the patient's body for injuries to her.

Maricela asked Doctor Hecht, "Do I put the oxygen mouthpiece back in?"

"Is her oximeter working?"

"Yes, it's 94."

"Wow, a big improvement for her with a little exercise. No, keep checking blood ox; if it stays up, she won't need the forced oxygen. Give her a nose tube, though, just in case. Try to squeeze the one side into the nostril with the feeding tube. It'll be tight. And let's get her restrained and gagged in case she comes to in a rage again. Enter her restrained status on her chart and show orders for re-injection, the same dosage, if she starts this again."

Hecht turned to the other orderly and ordered, "Go get a full bed restraint and protective gag, small size. Help the nurses put it on."

The new doctor that Elmore had not met now spoke, "That was quite a show. You expect anything like that?"

Hecht said, "No, like I said, I hadn't seen her move in months. We ought to order an EEG to see how her brain activity is now. Looks like she has a spark in there after all. We need to make sure the EEG gets copied to the coma doctor at UC Davis. Too bad we had to blank her; after a coma it would have been better to keep her conscious."

"How do we order an EEG? You have a service for that."

"You email it in; there's a chart for all that at the nurses' station. You should enter them into your cellphone email contacts. Won't happen 'til morning, even with a 'Stat,' Napa doesn't have 24-7 lab support like a frontline hospital." Hecht answered as he turned to look at Elmore with the bloody tissues to his nose. "You go down to the station with Claudia. I'll look at your nose. If it's broken, we'll have to do a Workers' Comp report and send you to the clinic in town."

Elmore nodded, took a last look at the pretty, young woman now peacefully sleeping, but with the other orderly starting to lock her in restraints. Elmore turned to go.

The last thing Elmore heard in the room was the new doctor saying, "A little excitement for my first night, huh?"

Doctor Hecht answered, "Ah, actually comparatively slow. You'll be here when things really get hopping. Wait 'til you get two patients going at each other."

———

Consciousness came to the patient with a flicker, not all at once. Grogginess repressed even the urge to lift eyelids and look around. Feelings from arms and legs were also slow to come about. The failure of arms and legs to move certainly seemed to be one of those deep dreams when one's body would not move, and that sensation is the first wink of evidence that it was a dream. Hips could be shifted and flexed. Knees and shoulders could be strained to rise an inch or so from what was clearly a soft bed below. But, in this languid dream, wrists, and feet refused to budge and a barely conscious nose sniffle came with vague discomfort.

What is causing that?

Finally, a blink brought a semi-dark ceiling above the patient into fuzzy view. A fluorescent light fixture, unlit, hung above. Eyes struggled to focus. A line, a thin line, appeared in the darkness heading up and away. With a tilt of the head to look around, this line seemed to move. The closer end of this line moved with the head tilt.

This view of the line helped shun the grogginess and the sensations of face, head, and body were felt. The movement of the line came with more discomfort in the nose and an urge in the throat to gag. Then, there was discomfort in the mouth where the teeth parted with something stuffed between the teeth.

What is that? Where am I?

A mental struggle ensued to push away the last of the grogginess and figure out the where and what of things. The patient's dry tongue moved and found a soft, pliable oval hole stuffed in, separating the teeth. Breath came in through the nose, a cool flow of air, uninterrupted.

Where? What? Am I in bed? Yes, it seems. What is this dark line I see?

With a head turn to the right, a wall was seen.

Turning the head to the other side again brought profound discomfort in the nose. And, something seemed to run down into a sore, dry throat— another gagging impulse. An attempt to moan came out strangely, muted by the object between the teeth, but still strange.

But now, on this side of the darkened room, a silhouette of a pole could be seen with shapes hanging on it. The line from the nose ran to an oblong shape on the pole. Above, another shape, shimmering transparent, had a kinked twirl of the smaller line dropping toward that side of the bed. In a box attached lower on the stand, a tiny green light flashed in time with an ever-so-quiet so quiet beep.

An I.V. A pulse monitor. A hospital? I'm in a hospital.

With more consciousness came realization but more questions.

I'm a patient? Why can't I move?

With the struggle to move, consciousness improved, but memory still faltered.

The patient's wrists and ankles were firmly wrapped in something. They were secured from the outside of the bed, as movement was possible toward the edge of the bed, but not toward the middle, or to touch body or hips. There was something wrapped around the patient's midsection tightly anchoring the waist. The patient was fully restrained in some hospital bed.

What happened? Why am I in a hospital bed?

The earlier grogginess was gone now, but memory had not returned. The patient tried to concentrate, to remember.

The memory of pain was first. Then, thoughts about a struggle. Pain? A struggle?

Yes, horrible pain. A struggle amidst horrible pain? People grabbing and pulling. I remember the horrible pain!

The excitement of remembering brought fresh consciousness and more questions. With the patient's head being all that could move, chin went to the chest to look around the room. In the darkened room, closed doors seemed to be in each far corner. Two large squares on the far wall were illuminated with faint light from far away behind them. Large windows were on the wall. But, the bottom of the windows could not be seen nor most of the bed, as a blanket or something was apparently blocking the view.

The patient's head shook to dislodge the fog of memory. This was rewarded with another jerk to the nose and gagging reflex.

Memory just would not clear. The patient lay in a silent struggle to remember anything.

The strongest memories were of the pain and the struggle. Searing pain. And, strong hands pulling at arms and legs. The struggle to move, chest pinned, legs trapped. A desperate struggle amidst the pain. Flashes of memory, but incomplete.

The quest to find memories stopped with the tiniest noise of a door lock being opened. The squeak of rubber soles on the floor ended with the flick of a light. Soft, fluorescent light from above. The patient squinted to see with eyes slowly adjusting to the light. The smiling face of a chubby Hispanic woman in white looked down.

"Ahh, Good morning. Our sleeping beauty awakens," said the woman.

What?

The patient blinked and tried to speak, but the gag between the teeth and the gagging presence in the sore throat only allowed a strange-sounding garble of sound. The nurse tried to hold the struggling arms and reassure the patient, to no avail. The patient's face showed the strain of trying to force out the gag and the body shook to break free of the restraints. The gagging feeling and the poking discomfort in the nose caused the patient to gag and retch. Frustration, fear, and discomfort all combined to set the patient into a frenzy. Muffled screams came from the patient. The patient finally remembered screaming with a sound like this in the fire.

Yes, the fire! The pain was from the fire?

"Whoa, whoa! Calm down, girl. You keep this up, and I've got orders to sedate you, again."

Sedate me? What is happening? This woman is a nurse. Girl?

The strange words from the nurse made the patient's frustration worse. The bed shook as the patient fought the restraints and shouted muffled, garbled demands.

I have no idea what is happening! What is this?

The nurse shook her head sadly and left the room.

———

After the nurse left, Mark closed his eyes and tried to make sense of what was happening. He was in a hospital bed, apparently tied to the bed. He finally remembered the horrible accident and the horrendous pain of the burns. His injuries must have put him in the hospital. But, he felt no injuries—no more pain in his neck, face, feet, arm, or lungs, only the annoying twisting of his nose and the gagging presence in his throat. And, the restraints. The nurse was calling him funny things. And his sound of his voice… it was wrong.

He opened his eyes and tried to make a sound through the gag hole. "Aaahhh." His voice was not raspy and hoarse as he had thought. It was clear and even… and high.

What? I remember breathing in the flames of the wreck. Has it damaged my voice?

The squeak of the nurse's rubber soles once again brought the nurse into view. She smiled down on him. He again desperately tried to make her understand.

"Well, my little beauty. I'm glad you're finally awake. Prayer answered, huh? But, you need to get your act together. We can't keep sedating you like this. You need to try and keep calm when you wake up," the nurse almost whispered to him.

Little beauty? What is this nurse talking about?

The nurse pulled the cap off a syringe, held it up, and clicked her fingernail on the tube, squirting a little out. She reached for an I.V. connection on Mark's arm.

Mark tried one last time to be understood. With no way to his touch tongue to his teeth to make the 'n' sound, a scream of "No, no, no," came out as a plaintive, high-pitched "Ho, ho, ho."

With a curious wave of warmth, the drug quickly flowed through his body from arm to shoulder to chest to face. The flood of strange warmth only lasted a moment before there was nothing.

———

Chapter 3

As before, consciousness came with a flicker. But with the first blink in what was now a bright daytime view of the room, the memory of this room, the odd flow of warmth from the drug the nurse had given, and then even a memory of that same strange feeling once before, when... when the pain and struggling had ended with that same flow of warmth, and that flow of warmth had followed the fire. Thoughts of the pain and the struggle brought Mark to full consciousness with a rush of adrenaline.

Mark's eye went wide, taking in the view above the bed, the overhead light, the hose running from his nose, and drawing the realization that he was still lashed to a bed in a hospital room. He was overwhelmed with thoughts and memories. He closed his eyes to concentrate and try to understand. Confusing thoughts. The gag in his mouth. The helpless feeling of being unable to move. Memories. The pain. The struggle. Grabbing hands. Pressure. His screams. Then, headlights flashing on the face of the man in the pickup, screaming just like he had. The crash. The helplessness in the wreck. The fire. The pain.

The memories seemed random, not connecting with one another. And small snippets of memory and thoughts defied understanding.

Why do I feel no pain now, from the horrible burns or the broken arm?

Mark thought the accident was real. All too real.

Where is this hospital? How long have I been here? Why had the nurse said such strange things to me? Why am I gagged and bound to the bed?

Mark needed to sort through everything and carefully decide what was real. He looked around. The pale turquoise paint on the wall was real. The hose coming out of his nose, and the discomfort was real. The rubbery oval in his mouth was real. His arms and legs told him the bindings were real.

He flipped his head to the side to check if his memory of an I.V. stand and heart monitor were real. They were. But so was the soft touch of something that landed across his vision when he flipped his head. He tried to focus on what was on his face. He could make out a strand of hair had fallen across his face. It was long hair and light-colored in the sunlit room. But, it did seem real.

He turned his head back toward the ceiling, and the hair slid gently from his face and seemed to fall with a tickle on his earlobe. The odd hair seemed ever so real. How long had it been for his hair to have grown so long?

The touch of the ringlet of hair brought back the odd words of the nurse.

What did she say?

The words 'Sleeping Beauty,' 'calm down girl,' and "my little beauty" did not belong to him. But, the memory of her voice was real. She had called him that.

He was Mark Kelleher; not some girl lashed to a bed. He tried to assert this by saying his name, but all that came out was, "arkh kheyeaheh" through his gagged mouth. And, the voice that gurgled the nonsense words was again in that soprano tone. *Why has my voice been so strange? Did the flames I inhaled injure my vocal cords?* He remembered screams coming from him in that voice. But, he also remembered screams, horrible screams, in his own baritone that had merged into the final screeching howl when the worst pain had come. Both voices were real memories, as was the pain.

He had felt pain. Pain from injured feet, arm and burns, everywhere. That was a very real memory. He had been injured, burned, in a horrible wreck on the freeway. It was not just a nightmare; it was so very real. He had been pinned in the car, broken and burned. The last thing he remembered was the searing pain in shoulders, face, arms and feet, and people grabbing at him in the car. But, he also remembered people grabbing at him in bed. He remembered his own screams in two different voices.

With the painful memories, he stopped. He sucked in a deep breath. He really had been burned, with the ultimate burn having been when he breathed fire into his mouth and then his lungs.

But now, he felt no pain. If he was in a hospital, what of his injuries? The burns? And his arm, he remembered the broken arm and the crushed legs. It had been real. But, his arm and his legs were without pain; they were merely tied tight to a bed rail. He moved a bit to make sure.

Mark turned away from the memories of pain and thought of the voices. He tried to clear his throat, but a tube running down his throat prevented much clearing. Like he remembered doing when the nurse had gone for the drugs, he tried to hear the sound of his voice with another "Aaahhh."

The voice was muffled coming through the gag's opening, but it was clear and distinct, and clearly high, soprano. His mind flashed to another memory a dozen years before in Mark's real world back in Stockton, standing with the other singers in the Lincoln High School Concert Choir. Their female soloist listened to the teacher play a C Major Chord on the piano, and she responded with a rising and falling 'Ahh, ahh, ahh, ahh, ahh' hitting the three notes in the chord's triad, up then down, the third note hitting the G note above the staff precisely.

With that memory, Mark decided to check his reality and try it himself, "Ahh, ahh, ahh, ahh, ahh."

Mark had little time to be astonished at his successful soprano triad when a voice interrupted him.

"Well, Miss Donnelley has calmed down and is practicing her vocal warmups through her gag. Sounds good.," A new nurse looked down at Mark's surprised expression.

Miss Donnelley?

The nurse was an attractive, middle-aged redhead. She said, "Don't stop singing on my account. I just need a blood sample."

The nurse pulled a rolling bed table over near the bed rail and set a plastic tray on it, taking two glass tubes with colored plugs and a needle from the tray. She thumped Mark's inner elbow with her index finger and smeared an alcohol wipe. "A little pinch… ."

Mark felt the needle go in and tried to speak to the nurse, "Hruh irgru huhuh."

The nurse slid the first tube into the needle's sleeve and motioned with her finger to her lips for Mark to shush. "Don't try to talk and get yourself worked up. I can't understand a word you say. Really."

The nurse pulled the tube of blood out and shook it, exchanging it for the other tube, which she inserted. This tube took a bit longer.

The nurse finished, used another wipe, and set a ball of cotton on the needle hole. She wrapped Mark's arm with a stretchy gauze wrap. "I guess it doesn't make sense for me to tell you to press your finger on the cotton, huh?" She laughed at her own joke and taped the gauze.

"Rhuha ghagh hrou," Mark pleaded.

The nurse smiled, "Oh, I got that one. You want the gag out. Sorry, that is above my paygrade. Doctor Dharma will be here soon. She's running late this morning. She's got her whole gaggle of interns waddling behind her. I'll let her know you've calmed down, seem to sing beautifully, and want the gag out."

The nurse smiled and left Mark blinking at her back.

Despite the good news about the gag, Mark strained at his bound arms and shook his head in a panic attack of confusion. His nose protested. Mark's confusion raced. He tried to think of what was happening. This nurse's naming of him as "Miss Donnelley" compounded his confusion. There were far too many bizarre, disconnected thoughts and memories. Suddenly he thought of perhaps one more test of this bizarre reality in which he found himself.

He dipped his chin to his chest to look toward his feet. He was shocked to see a rather sad looking, old woman in a hospital gown staring at him through one of the windows. He looked at her a moment, and then chose to ignore her. He looked to each edge of the bed, bending his hands back at the wrist, reaching up with his fingers. Despite the wrist restraints, he was able to poke his fingers up, so he could see his fingertips were poking the blanket up on both sides.

His thumb did not touch the blanket, but he could pinch a fold of the blanket with his first two fingers. He took a pinch of the blanket with each hand, and held it while he straightened his hand out and flat on the bed. The blanket moved on his belly, but not the top that he wanted to move. He tried again. And again.

On the third pull, he felt the blanket pull away from his throat. A few tugs later, he could see at the very bottom of his view, his hospital gown with a light blue zig-zag pattern appear on his upper chest. He had to stop for a minute to rest, as the bending of his throat to his chest caused whatever was in his throat and nose to hurt. He continued.

The blanket was now taut across his body, so each tug moved it a good distance. Now, he did the last pull, and the blanket flopped over the rise of his chest and on to his stomach. The view was unobstructed.

Mark blinked in utter astonishment. He could see the hospital gown was draped on his chest over two mounds, roughly the size of orange halves. This nightmare was getting even more bizarre.

———

Mark's bewildering discovery about his physique was interrupted by a loud voice, with a hint of South Asian accent, entering the room.

"This patient will give you something totally different to review." A short woman with black-gray hair was talking and walking toward him, followed by three other women.

The three women took their places of Mark's left and the older woman on his right. He quickly looked at each one. The three were all young women in white lab coats, two Anglo, one Asian. They each had clipboards in hand and stethoscopes around their necks. The older woman also had a stethoscope but held an iPad computer tablet. She had a red *bindi* spot just above the center of her eyebrows.

A Hindu doctor. This is Doctor Dharma, who the nurse mentioned.

This doctor gave Mark the briefest of smiles before she resumed talking. "I trust you all will remember that when we last visited this unit, this patient was in a full coma."

As the Hindu doctor spoke, Mark looked at each of the younger women, supposedly the interns the nurse had mentioned. The intern closest to Mark, a nice-looking young woman with a blonde pageboy haircut, was staring intently at Mark's face.

Doctor Dharma flicked her forefinger on the iPad screen, scrolling text as she spoke, "Yesterday evening, the patient awoke from the two-and-a-half-month coma, went into seizures, and had an apparent psychotic episode. She was shaking uncontrollably, fighting with staffers trying to control her and screaming quite loudly about some hallucinated injury. Shouting about pain, burns, and fire. It took six or seven staff members to restrain her."

Mark heard the Hindu doctor speak half-truths about him. The pain and the fire were very real, but the rest was nonsense to him, including the pronoun she used.

"Uh ruh!" Mark gurgled.

"Quiet dear, you'll get your chance." The doctor patted Mark's hip as she spoke.

"The patient was physically restrained and administered ten milligrams of our normal Versed/Fentanyl mix intramuscularly." The doctor scrolled the iPad again.

Mark looked back at the three interns and found the closest one still staring at him, almost hypnotically looking into his eyes.

"The drug was, as usual, immediately effective in stopping the seizure and psychotic activity. Full restraints were ordered to prevent the patient from harming herself or staff. The patient awoke in seven hours and was still considerably agitated and disturbed." Another scroll.

Herself? What is going on?

The intern was still staring. Mark was getting annoyed.

"Another dosage of Versed/Fentanyl was administered with similar results. A standard EEG was done mid-morning today while the patient was still sedated. The EEG was reviewed by both a staff physician and the contract coma specialist assigned to monitor this coma patient. The EEG results were found to be remarkably normal, considering the weeks of low blood oxygen and the severe drug overdose that had induced the coma."

Mark was happy to hear good news about his condition, even though he knew nothing of what the doctor spoke of regarding his case.

Drug overdose?

Dharma continued, "As you heard from Nurse Helene a few moments ago, the patient has regained consciousness, in better spirits, apparently even trying to sing a bit and asked to have the gag removed."

Mark looked from Doctor Dharma to the interns listening to her. The intern at his elbow was still staring at Mark. He could not take it. Her intense stare made him really nervous. He needed to break her stare at him. With little else at his disposal, Mark turned his head toward the young woman and quickly crossed his eyes. The young woman blinked and hurriedly jerked away from the bed a bit.

"Yes, Doctor Evans, do we have a problem?" asked Doctor Dharma sarcastically.

"Uh? Sorry. She made a face at me, and I freaked a little bit."

Doctor Dharma shook her head and pursed her lips in disapproval. "Well, Doctor Evans, if I were this dear girl and I had a googly-eyed intern staring at my misfortune as you have constantly been doing since we entered this room, I might feel like making a face at you myself. Remember, a physician must always strive to give her patients the fullest measure of respect and kindness, especially if that patient is vulnerable, in pain, or frightened. You have failed that maxim with this patient."

Dear girl?

"Sorry, doctor." The young intern looked down at the bed rail.

Dharma again patted Mark's hip, "Now Dear, let's see what we can do for you. I hear you want the gag out?"

Mark quickly nodded.

"That we can do." Dharma turned toward the interns and explained, "You never allow physical restraint of patients beyond the first sign that it is not needed. Never. Doctor Evans, please get a cup of water from the table. You three will help me do this."

Dharma moved up closer to Mark's head, looking down at him. "We are going to remove your gag and the feeding tube, since you are alert and can most likely feed yourself. Okay?"

"Ookhai," Mark said with a nod.

Doctor Dharma reached behind Mark's neck and released a Velcro strip. Straps fell loose at the side of Mark's neck. Dharma turned to the interns to say, "The gag is very stiff vinyl-coated foam rubber, and it is designed to come off with a pinch from the outside, but not a bite from the inside. Remove this hollow oval plug in the opening to allow it to compress, grab both edges of the gag like this and squeeze. Young lady, I need you to open your jaw as wide as you can."

Mark did not know if his jaw was able to open more, but he tried. He still rankled at the 'young lady.'

Dharma pressed, and Mark stretched. The brims of the gag inside Mark's top and bottom teeth slid out, and the gag was removed. Mark moved his jaw up and down, right and left.

"That better?" Dharma asked.

"Yes, a lot." Mark was amazed at the girl's voice he heard as he spoke. He tried to clear his throat, but it did not seem to change anything. His throat was obstructed. Something at the back of his nose still made him feel like gagging.

Dharma reached for the glass of water from Evans and looked down at Mark. "Okay, this next part may give you a bit of discomfort. The feeding tube in your nose goes all the way down to your stomach, and I could not find any notes that it has been removed since you were at the ICU in June. The hose has probably irritated the lower esophageal tract and the sphincter at the top of your stomach. It may be sticking to them. I need you to drink this water to lubricate everything. But, be careful as you drink because the tube may make you gag, and we don't want any water going down your windpipe."

Mark nodded and opened his mouth. He gulped a sip of water and restrained a gag reflex. Dharma nodded.

"Okay, Doctor Evans you are closest. Turn the spigot off below the feeding fluid pump and push the pump switch off, and then release the top of the tube. Hand the tube to me."

The intern obeyed.

"Doctor Watanabe, you are right-handed. Correct?"

"Yes."

"Then put on a pair of gloves from the wall dispenser and come over on this side."

Dharma moved to the side for the intern and said, "Doctor Watanabe, you are going to remove the oxygen tube and pull the adhesive tape on the feeding tube from the nose. Then, you will ask the patient to take a deep breath while you grasp the tube. When you tell her to exhale quickly, you will rapidly pull the tube forward and out, thinking about the path the tube is taking through her nose, so you don't jerk her nose up."

"Right."

The intern and Mark both performed their tasks, and the tube was free. Mark finally cleared his throat and swallowed. Dharma gave him another sip of water and then handed the cup to Evans.

Dharma motioned Watanabe to the side and took her place beside Mark again.

Dharma continued, "The chart shows the blood ox has been fine ever since the episode yesterday evening, so we can dispense with the oxygen tube. Now, we turn to the task of getting the restraints off. Usually, the doctor simply orders the removal, and an orderly or nurse finishes up. But, for training purposes, you will be doing the honors.

"But first, to be safe, you need to confirm the mental state of the patient and that the behavior that caused the restraint is at an end. Young lady, can you answer some questions?"

"Of course." Mark marveled at the sound of his voice.

"Do you know your name?"

As confusing as everything was, Mark decided to follow the hints the nurse had helped him with. He would go along with this charade for now. He knew what the doctor expected, so he said, "Donnelley."

"That's right, Naomi Donnelley."

Another clue! Naomi.

"And where are you?" Doctor Dharma scrolled the iPad as she queried Mark/Naomi.

"A hospital bed."

"Where is the hospital?"

"No clue, really, somewhere in the Bay Area?" Mark guessed.

"Close. You are at Napa State Hospital."

The mental hospital? That figures.

"And who am I?"

"Doctor Dharma."

The doctor looked a bit surprised at this, asking, "How do you know that?"

"Nurse Helene told me you were coming."

"Aha. And do you know why you are restrained?"

"Like you said, there was a struggle, and I was screaming."

Dharma smiled at this, "That's cheating. Do you remember <u>why</u> you were screaming?"

Mark knew exactly why he had been screaming, but he was beginning to realize Mark's car wreck was not what this doctor needed to hear to get the restraints off. He made up his best story, "I woke up from a really deep sleep. I was having the most realistic nightmare, like ever. My car had wrecked, and I was trapped in the wreck. Policemen were trying to pull me out by my legs and arms. There was a fire, and I dreamed I was burning. I screamed about it."

Dharma thought a moment, and then said, "A nightmare you say. A very odd nightmare where you broke an orderly's nose and bit a nurse?"

Mark was surprised at this information, but thought quickly, "Well, sometimes when you first wake up, it's hard to know where the dreams left off and the real world kicks in."

Doctor Dharma raised her eyebrows and shrugged, in a gesture of possible acceptance of the story. Then she asked, "But, when the nurse came back in the middle of the night, you were not asleep. Yet, you still were so agitated that she decided you needed to be sedated, again. No?"

Mark shook his head, he said, "I woke up in a darkened room, bound hand and foot in a bed. My mouth had a gag in it. The last thing I remembered was the nightmare. I was afraid. I had worked myself up a lot, just laying there, ya know, struggling with the bindings and, like, not knowing where I was. When the nurse came in, she couldn't understand me, sort of made fun of my situation and I got frustrated. I was really still afraid. Not angry, jus' <u>really</u> afraid."

Mark was still amazed by his voice.

"That sounds reasonable." Dharma turned to the interns, "The patient seems lucid and understanding of her situation. Now, we make sure of her current condition."

Dharma turned away from the bed, pulled a cell phone from her lab coat pocket, and made a quick call that Mark could not hear.

Turning back, Dharma asked Mark, "How do you feel now?"

"I'm really glad to get that I got that gag out. Looking forward to getting the restraints off."

"But, how do you feel? Any discomfort? Are you still afraid?"

"No, nothing. Maybe a little sore throat."

"Are you angry or frustrated?"

Mark gave a little smile, "Maybe a little with Doctor Evans, but you already took a bite out of her for me, so I'm cool."

Dharma gave a little laugh, "Well, sense of humor restored, but there is no checkbox on your chart to mark that. Okay, thank you."

Mark noticed a large black man in a blue jumpsuit come in the room. He carried what looked like a large red carry-on bag.

Dharma handed her iPad across the bed to Evans and said, "Put this on the table for me. You other two, get on either side of the bed, at the feet."

Doctor Dharma walked down to the foot of the bed, putting out her hand to the orderly. He handed her a small blue object.

Dharma started her instructions to the interns, "You might be familiar with the normal Velcro restraint straps. This is the modern white vinyl system we try to use. Safer, cleaner, more effective. It requires this pin release key and cannot be ripped off, as old Velcro might. It is also much more comfortable. So, they say. Maybe later we can try it on one of you, for some hands-on experience." She smiled at this.

Dharma flipped up the blanket off the feet and onto Mark's legs and proceeded to show the interns how to remove the restraints by releasing one leg. Then, she had them move up from feet to abdomen and finally, to Mark's hands.

"For now, just flip the restraints through the bed rail, and Elmore will collect them when we leave."

Dharma came back up beside the bed and asked, "Is that better, Naomi?"

Since he had no idea what was going on, Mark decided, for now, to accept being called this new name. In a sweet Naomi voice, he answered, "Very much. Thank you."

Dharma nodded, "Okay, you should be feeling much better now. I will have the nurse give you something to calm you. Much less powerful than what we used before. It will help you rest and recover from this traumatic experience. I don't want you to get out of bed. You haven't been on your feet in months. You might think you can, but don't try to walk. It's almost lunchtime, and I will order you a meal. Your stomach isn't used to real food. You also haven't eaten in months. You will get a soft and liquid meal. Eat whatever you can. Ask for seconds if you have room. You need to get some of your bodyweight back. If you tolerate lunch well, the nurse will be able to give you a regular meal for supper. Follow orders, and we'll have you up and around shortly. Does that sound good?"

Mark, or was it Naomi, gave a thumbs-up sign with a newly free left hand. Long fingernails touched the palm of Mark's hand as he did.

As she retrieved her iPad and turned to leave, Doctor Dharma saw an old man in green pajamas peeking at them through the observation window. She quickly pulled a blue striped curtain over the windows. The interns followed Dharma out of the room. They did seem to waddle after her.

The big, black orderly set the red bag beside the bed and started to remove the restraints from the bed frame. Dharma had called him Elmore. Naomi scooted up in bed, lifting up on her elbows to watch.

As Elmore moved up to take the arm restraint off, Mark noticed he was wearing a silver aluminum "X" brace taped onto his nose."

"Elmore, did I do that?" Mark asked, pointing to the orderly's nose.

He glanced at her, nodded, and said, "Um-hmm."

"Gosh, I'm really sorry. I never meant to do that. I was having a bad nightmare and…."

"Some nightmare. But it was my fault; I shouldna put my face where you could get a clean shot."

"Well, I am sorry," Mark said, and lifted both hips to let Elmore take the stomach strap out. "But wait, if you were working last night and its almost noon, why are you still here? That's a long time to be at work."

"I usually work a 4-10 shift; four days on, ten-hour shift, 6 PM to early morning, but I got sent to the clinic for this nose early last night. And, when I called in, they told me to come in for day shifts the rest of the week. So here I am."

"I see, I just want you to know I'm sorry."

"Hey, girl, I get it, sorry it is. Atchully, I should thank you. Gettin' day shift is a blessin'. And, it's not my first busted nose."

Mark smiled and fluffed the blanket.

Elmore finished his task and left with his bag, closing and locking the door behind him. Mark was alone, in private. Or, was it Naomi who was alone?

The confusing thoughts and memories were still there. But, some hard to believe facts had been revealed. Mark was in a mental hospital, but he obviously was not Mark, he seemed to be Naomi. It was Naomi's slim hands that lifted up to feel her face and grab a strand of hair to inspect. *Yes, long blonde hair, kind of dirty and oily, it seems to have some gooey stuff in it. What has happened to me? Am I still Mark? Or, have I become someone else? Am I crazy?*

A touch of both hands to his chest and hips confirmed what he had seen when he peeked under the hospital gown down. *Naomi has curves. No, I have curves.* Down the sides of his chest, Mark felt a washboard of ribs. *I am skinny.* Dharma had said Naomi needed to gain weight. *Months in a coma probably did that.*

Mark's fingers and hands lifted the blanket and collar of the gown to look down. There was a young woman's body under the gown.

"Ah-hmm! Are you taking inventory? Everything where you expect it to be?" the nurse had come back into the room.

Mark quickly dropped the blanket and probably blushed. Not knowing what to say, he smiled briefly.

The nurse, Helene, smiled and said, "I have a little happy juice for you, and then we get to pull some more tubes. You seem to be much more comfortable than a while ago."

"You cannot believe," was Mark's honest answer, in Naomi's voice.

The nurse prepared a hypodermic needle and injected something in the injection port above the I.V. fitting taped to Naomi's arm. There was no flow of warmth like the earlier shots. Helene capped the needle and dropped it into the red plastic sharps container on the wall. She clicked a valve on the I.V. drain tube and twisted the hose free from the arm.

"I'll leave the I.V. connection in for now, in case you show any dehydration. I'll put the water bottle and cup where you can reach it. You need to drink a bit every time you think about it. You really can't drink too much after coming off an I.V. for so long. And, we have some Gatorade for just that purpose. We'll get one of those for you." The nurse hung the I.V. hose on the hook on the stand and bent to do something lower on the stand. Mark peeked through the bed rail to see what she was doing. The nurse clicked a plastic valve near what looked like a bag of pale urine.

The nurse stood, opened an alcohol pad, and said, "Now the fun one."

The nurse folded the blanket up from the foot of the bed to lay it on Naomi's belly. There was an odd sensation of tugging as the nurse moved a thin tube, also filled with urine. There was another tube unknown to Mark, or Naomi. The nurse clicked another valve closed and applied the alcohol pad to Naomi around where a urinary catheter entered her body. The cool swipes of the alcohol pad confirmed that everything between the legs belonged to Naomi, not Mark. The catheter deflated and slid free. Helene hung it on the stand and covered Naomi up.

Helene, as promised, rolled the bed table over where Naomi could reach it, pushing the water bottle, cup and tissues over within reach. She hung a call button in a loop on the bed rail. She collected the used needle and said,

"Someone will be right in with your meal. Yummy green Jello, chicken broth, and apple juice for Naomi."

The nurse hurried out, leaving the patient to contemplate whatever had happened to her, or him or... whatever.

—

Chapter 4

Mark tried to take in all that had happened and this bizarre situation. He, or was it she, was in a mental hospital, his self-image and memories conflicted radically with the body that he was obviously in. *Is this what insanity is?*

He found he had no memories whatsoever from Naomi Donnelley. Yet, he thought about the way he had spoken to Doctor Dharma in the slightly sassy accent used by young girls, the Valley Girls, so to speak. *Am I really an insane young woman who thinks she is Mark?*

Mark read the wrist band on Naomi's slender wrist. 'PATIENT — Napa State Hospital, Napa, CA, Name: DONNELLEY, Naomi Lynne, Age:18, Blood Type:O-Pos, Status: LPS/Kern, Unit: A-4/SNF.' He did not understand the last two entries, but the wrist band served as very real evidence of who the world thought he, or she, was.

Since he had no memories as Naomi, Mark studied his memories as Mark. They seemed full and complete, not the ravings and creations of a crazy girl. His memories of being Mark and Mark's life were as clear as... as before the wreck. With the vivid memories of the wreck—the wreck on a Friday evening, August 23rd, came new questions. With that, he had a reference point. Doctor Dharma had said Naomi had been admitted here in June and had been in a coma for two and a half months. *What day is it now? How long ago did the wreck happen? Did the wreck really happen? Are my memories real or just an intricate symptom?*

The sound of a key in the hospital room door announced the arrival of Elmore, with a big smile and a tray. He maneuvered the bed table across, in front of Naomi, sat down the food tray, and used the electrical controls to elevate the head of the bed a bit more.

As he surveyed the tray, Mark asked, "Elmore, what day is it?"

"Saturday."

"Date?"

He pulled a cell phone from his pocket and said, "August 24th."

Naomi's face showed surprise. Then she asked, "So, my little 'performance' last night happened right at 8 o'clock, on Friday, August 23rd. Right?"

"Well, more like 8:15 or so. But, yeah, that's about right. Why?"

Mark thought for a moment, before giving a little smile and saying, "I just think that might be really important in my life and I wanted to remember everything about it."

"Okay, bone appetite." Elmore's French was dismal. He left the room, locking the door.

Mark, or perhaps it was Naomi, surveyed the tray; a covered plastic bowl of golden broth, a little cup of apple juice, green Jello, a packet of plump, soft Gummi bears, and a bottle of yellow Gatorade. Someone had done a good job of making the bland food colorful and interesting.

Naomi's hands shook the bottle of apple juice as she marveled at how the very first memories she had as Naomi must have precisely coincided with the final moment of Mark's life. At least, it could be assumed Mark was dead.

A fire like I remember must have been fatal. If so, I can no longer be Mark. If Mark is dead, then it is Naomi in this bed. But, I still have Mark's memories, yet this is clearly Naomi's body, not mine, and Naomi thinking like this. Am I now Naomi?

Naomi opened the apple juice, then set it back down. She closed her eyes and thought about what she had just done. She had just declared in her mind that Mark's body was dead and that she was this young woman, hungrily yearning for food. She opened her eyes and raised the juice cup to her lips. *Good juice.*

As she picked up the covered bowl of golden chicken broth, she noticed the fingernails on her hand. They were long, maybe a half-inch or more beyond the end of her finger. And she could see an oval of pale silvery pink at the tip and clear unpolished nail below that. Naomi had worn nail polish when she went into the coma, and nobody had clipped her nails since. *Shouldn't someone have done that for me?*

While she was trying to pry the lid off the chicken broth bowl, the sound of the lock announced another visitor. Naomi was surprised by this visitor. It was the young intern, Doctor Evans.

"Coming to check up on me?" she asked Evans.

"No, coming to apologize and try to start over." Doctor Evans was still carrying her clipboard and a stack of papers, or something.

"Apologize?"

"Yes, I apologize for staring at you and causing you discomfort."

"No apology needed, But, I apologize for getting you in trouble with Dharma."

Evans smiled and shook her head. "She was right. I deserved that, but I wanted to explain why I did that."

Naomi waited and looked attentively at Evans. She took another sip of juice.

Evans pressed her lips together and spoke, "As I stood there looking at you, I realized you and I are much alike. You're prettier, and I'm a little older, but we could be sisters. My mind couldn't get over how you must feel to be... like that. All bound in a bed, unable to talk or explain anything. I tried to picture how I would act in your situation. Frankly, it blew my mind. Until you spooked me out of it."

"I understand. I still am having trouble believing it myself. And I had a ringside seat." Naomi smiled at Doctor Evans.

Evans shifted the clipboard to her other hand and said, "Let's start this again. Hi, I'm Lindsey Evans." She put out her hand to shake Naomi's hand.

Naomi said, for the very first time, "I'm Naomi Donnelley. Pleased to meet you."

Wow, I really just said that.

They shook hands and smiled at each other.

Evans continued, "I brought a peace offering. I know you're stuck in this bed, and in this room for a while, without anything to do, I thought you might be going stir crazy... ." She stopped speaking suddenly and said, "Oops, that's on our forbidden words list here. Hmm, I thought you might be getting <u>cabin fever</u>. So, when I was over in the Doctor's Lounge for lunch, I saw they had quite a stack of new magazines. Much better than the old, worn-out copies of *People* they have here on the unit in the Day Room. So, I brought you a few magazines. I tried to get a selection. I hope they are okay with you. At least something to read to pass your time."

Naomi accepted the pile of magazines across the bed table. She quickly looked at them, a thick Back-to-School issue of *Vogue*, a *Martha Stewart Living*, a *Vanity Fair*, and a copy of *American Nurse Today*, still in the plastic mailing bag with the subscriber's address blacked out. "Wow, thanks."

"It's the least I could do. I'll be spending the next couple of weeks here until my residency in San Fran starts in September. If you need anything, anything at all, have them call me. I sure hope everything works out for you. Really."

Naomi had to lift her eyebrows up to restrain a tear.

I can't believe I'm reacting like this.

Naomi smiled and said, "Thanks, Lindsey."

"Okay, 'til later," Doctor Evans gave a little fingertip wave to Naomi and turned to leave.

I wonder if Naomi has a real sister.

———

Chapter 5

Mark spent the afternoon alternating between thoughts of whether he was really insane or living a *Twilight Zone* episode. This was interspersed with racking his brain to see if he could find any meaning, spiritual, scientific or otherwise, for what seemed to have happened to her. He concluded something supernatural was obviously at work. But supernatural events belonged in books and movies, and not in the center of one's life. Whether she was really Naomi with Mark's memories, insane Naomi with delusions of being Mark, or Mark's soul moved over to Naomi, she was, to the world, Naomi Lynne Donnelley.

Were those the choices? A memory switch, insanity, or soul transfer? None of those choices had any explanation.

None of this made any sense to Mark. What is a person? Is it their memories, some soul or spirit within them? Is their identity who they think they are or who everyone else thinks they are?

What makes this person me?

Is there a difference between a person's memories and their soul? A person who has amnesia has not lost their soul. They just are missing some memories. A person with Alzheimers Disease does not stop being the person they have always been. But, if a person's memories switched, are they a different person? Are a person's memories tied in to who they are?

Mark had no reason to doubt that his mind and his soul were still his. He felt like the same person. He just looked like a stranger. His body's gender and identity was out of kilter with his thoughts and memories. Those memories were truly his. And those memories could not be the imagination of this inmate in an insane asylum.

Who was or is this person that I have become? Why was she in this mental hospital? Should I start thinking about myself as Naomi?

Elmore had taken her food tray and replaced her empty Gatorade bottle with a blue one. She started to open the nursing magazine to continue reading when she heard her stomach growl and felt…. She grabbed the nurse's call button and pressed it anxiously.

"Yes?" came a voice.

"I <u>really</u> need to go to the bathroom, and Doctor Dharma told me not to walk." Naomi's voice conveyed the urgency of her plea, "Please, hurry!"

"I'll be right down." It sounded like Helene on the speaker.

The nurse unlocked the door a moment later and hurried in. She saw the anxious look on Naomi's face. "I'm sorry, Honey. We should have thought of this."

Helene ran over to the bathroom door in the corner and unlocked it with a key on her wrist band, scurrying back to lower the bed rail.

"My bathroom is locked up?" Naomi asked as she turned her legs over the edge of the bed.

"Some patients can get in trouble in a bathroom without supervision. It is standard to leave them locked until…. Here lean on me. Can you stand?"

Naomi's feet hit the cold floor, and she put her weight on her legs. She did not seem to have any trouble. She was weak, but her weight seemed so light she took a step with ease.

A wave of dizziness hit Naomi, and Helene felt it in her grip on Naomi. "You okay?"

"Yeah, fine, it's been a long time. I guess. Hurry!"

Helene helped her across the room, pushed the door open, and directed Naomi into the small bathroom. She held Naomi's shoulder as Naomi turned to take a seat on the toilet.

"This is one of the only times those open-backed hospital gowns are a blessing," Helene said, as she bunched the gown in front for Naomi to sit.

When Helene did not leave, Naomi asked, "You gonna watch?"

"Uh, no, sometimes we have to," Helene backed out of the door and pushed the door mostly closed.

From outside the door, Helene continued, "Like I said, we should have thought of this. When you are in a coma you usually excrete involuntarily, but you aren't eating any solids so it isn't much—makes a real mess in bed, but often the bilirubin and the like builds up inside the gut and comes out like gangbusters after the stomach and gut become active again."

"Yeah, I see." Naomi did not explain. And then added, "Hey, I have a metal mirror in here!"

"Yes? So? That's normal, for here at Napa."

"Never mind. Ugh."

Helene opened the door after she heard the flush. Naomi was at the sink, turning on the water without looking, as she had her nose almost on the shiny, stainless-steel mirror, inspecting her face. She wiped her hands on a towel on the bar without looking at it. She put her hands up to her face and hair. Her mouth hung open a little.

"You okay?" Helene asked.

"I've never seen myself… uhh…." Naomi paused a moment before realizing she had to add something, "…Never seen myself looking like a vampire who hasn't sucked blood in ages."

Mark realized that he was hiding her mental identity predicament from the staff but resolved to let someone know and ask for help, at some point. *Not now.*

Mark also realized that he was thinking about himself as Mark, but about the girl in the mirror as Naomi. *That is not right. I cannot be thinking I am someone different from who my body is. That really is crazy.*

"Yes, you are pretty thin, but isn't that look what the runway models strive for?" Helene said, and then added, "You are very pretty, just need some meat on your bones."

"I think gaunt is the word for this. I look positively starved."

"A good trim of that hair and a little make-up, you could turn a few heads."

"This place doesn't seem like the place for doing makeovers."

"Oh, you're wrong. They've got a Wellness and Recovery Planning program, they call it WRP, here at Napa, you know, life enhancement, to get people back on their feet. They bring in volunteers to help people pull themselves together and get ready for the world again. Barbers for the men and some good beauticians volunteer for just this purpose—Even donated clothes and toiletries. You gonna keep staring at yourself or come back to bed?"

The girl in the mirror checked her teeth before turning to get help to walk back to bed. Her teeth were straight and white; Naomi's drug scene must have been short-lived. *Didn't Meth users always have bad teeth and skin sores? Maybe they are wrong about what they say about Naomi, or me.*

Helene got Naomi back in bed and said, "I don't think they do the beautician route here in Skilled Nursing, but when you get to an Intermediate Care Unit, you really need to take advantage of that service. A girl with your looks needs to... you know."

"Thanks for the help. Are you going to leave that unlocked now?" She pointed to the bathroom.

"Yes, sure. But if you can, you should call us first for help, until you get used to walking. Unfortunately, I still have to lock your outside door. You don't have Unit privileges yet, until your assigned psychotherapist clears you."

"Who is my assigned psychotherapist? Doctor Dharma?"

"No, she's a GP, in charge of general medical issues on a couple of units. I read your chart, and you are assigned to Doctor Partridge."

"When do I see him? What's he like?"

"Oh, he is a real gem. Downright nice guy. Really. And gorgeous, at least to me. But he's probably just an 'old guy' to a girl your age. You'll probably see him real quick, now that you are awake, that is."

"Can't wait; I've got a lot to talk to him about." *Perhaps he will be the right one to confide this bizarre identity switch with. How can I possibly tell someone about this? It makes me sound totally crazy. Am I?*

"I'll bet. I'm going off shift now. See you tomorrow. Have a nice evening."

"You, too."

Mark went back to the thoughts he had before his trip to the bathroom. He could not get away from the many questions. He had no information about this Naomi Donnelley. It seemed that her identity was a big part of his mystery. If he was in her body, where was she? Is she gone? Had she been insane?

My memories are too clear to be the ravings of an insane girl. A crazy girl could not make up the details of my life, Mark's life, that I know to be true.

While she was thinking, Mark broke the 'no walking by yourself' rule and went back into the bathroom. The metal mirror was not a perfect reflection, but he marveled at the pretty girl who stared back at him—this gaunt, yet pretty girl in a hospital gown staring out of the mental hospital safety mirror. He had the awkward, yet enlightening feeling that this was him, looking back from out of the mirror. No, not him, he was her... she was her. *God!*

Without any clear answers, the only thing he firmly resolved was that he really needed to start thinking of himself as Naomi, not Mark, because it just seemed right. It was mentally awkward to think of himself as Mark anymore. This person staring at him was not a 'himself,' she was a 'herself.' Her mind was the mind of Mark Kelleher, but it was clear the body was Naomi Donnelley's. She really needed to find out more about Naomi.

Tired by the hours of deep thought, Naomi needed to get her mind off this bizarre mystery. *It's enough to drive you crazy. Ha!* Naomi went back to sit on the bed and picked up the *American Nurse Today* magazine and turned to the dog ear she had left on one article about problems nurses face with various types of difficult patients. She seemed to be having a bit of trouble reading the magazine's small print. She found the magazine interesting, even aside from her current circumstances.

———

They had given Naomi a sleeping pill that worked, but with a problem. She slept through the night, but she was troubled by several nightmares of fiery crashes.

Naomi's breakfast was not exactly bad; it could probably best be described as 'ordinary.' Like the Salisbury Steak and mashed potatoes the previous evening, it was uninspiring—bland, rubbery scrambled eggs folded into a square, cold wheat toast with margarine, and semi-warm sausage patties. However, Naomi quite literally cleaned her plastic dishes in her hunger. She had not had Malt-o-Meal since she was a kid, well, since Mark was a kid. Naomi's second regular meal at Napa State Hospital had disappeared without a trace.

Naomi drained the apple juice cup and set it down when she heard the door lock. A new nurse, a tall black woman with corn-row hair, came in with a smile, a couple of bags of what looked like khaki clothing, and a pair of rubber sandals.

"Good morning, Naomi. I'm Laetitia. Are you all done with breakfast?"

"Yes, all gone. But Doctor Dharma said I should ask for seconds if I could handle it, to get some weight back on. I could use another toast and apple juice."

"I'll try to set aside another tray for your brunch, but it will have to wait." Laetitia held up the two packages of clothing. "First, we need to get you dressed to go for your doctor's appointment. We can't have you gallivanting between buildings in that flimsy gown."

Laetitia rolled the bed service table to the side and stuck her finger into the first plastic bag. She took out and shook a pair of khaki pants. The pants were somewhere between pajamas and medical scrubs. She then pressed the release on the bed rail and flipped the blanket down for Naomi.

Naomi took the pants the nurse handed her. The pants were heavy cotton, soft, but a little stiff in their newness.

Laetitia kept talking as she opened the other bag, "I managed to get a set of new ones for you, not rewashed."

"They're not the best in fashion, but better than the gown," Naomi said, holding up the pants.

"These are the general issue outfits, like the patients in high security are forced to wear, but in orange. You're an LPS patient so that you can wear your own clothes, if you have any," Laetitia shook out the folds in the shirt.

Naomi did not know what an 'LPS' patient was, but she hoped it would be made clear as she went on. She remembered the "LPS" on her wristband.

"And how would I get my own?"

"Whatever you brought with you from home, or what you can buy here or buy through mail order. Didn't they tell you all that when you were admitted?"

"As near as I can tell, I went into seizures right when I was admitted and only woke up the night before last, like three months later. I know nothing about this place. I have no idea what came with me."

"I'll call the Wellness and Recovery Planning Team while you're gone and tell them your problem. You want to put these on in bed or turn around and step into the legs?"

Naomi answered by sitting up and turning her legs over the edge of the bed.

"You need help?"

"No, I got it," Naomi said, while she put her feet into the pants and pulled them up. "You said a doctor's appointment. Is that with… uh… Partridge, I think that was his name."

Naomi pulled the elastic band to her thighs up under her gown, jerked the pants' cuff over her feet, and stood up to pull them all the way up, elastic band around her belly. They were big on her thin waist.

"Yes, Partridge. I was a bit surprised one of the senior psychiatrists came in for an office visit on a Sunday morning, but they do have a hospital rule of giving a full evaluation by the assigned psych therapist within 12 hours of admission and, as you said, you are something like three months overdue for that." Laetitia had the shirt out and held the sleeve open toward Naomi. "These new tops have Velcro front openings, so you don't have to pull them off over your head and do a striptease to get dressed. Here let me untie your back knots on the gown."

Laetitia helped Naomi remove one gown sleeve and put one shirt sleeve on, and then the other, finally closing the front for her. Laetitia handed the black rubber sandals to Naomi, who put them on. Then, the nurse crumpled the plastics bags on the food tray and picked it up to go.

"Okay, Naomi, you sit here on the bed, and an orderly will be in shortly to wheel you to the doctor's office."

"I have to go in a wheelchair?"

"Oh yeah, rules are rules."

When the nurse left the room, she pushed the wide door to its fully open position, where it stayed. For the first time, Naomi was not locked in her room.

Naomi took her stack of magazines from the bed serving table and put them in the upper drawer of the nightstand. She didn't want anyone taking them while she was gone. She looked around for anything else that was needed to be done before she left and realized the four magazines were all she had, here or elsewhere. She was alone, penniless, and confined in a mental hospital. The good part was she was neither dying in a coma nor dead, anymore.

The orderly who arrived was not Elmore. It was a pimply-faced young man who entered without any greeting or announcement and rolled a wheelchair over next to the bed. He locked the wheels, and then came around to reach toward Naomi without saying anything.

Naomi lifted her hands to signal him to stop and said, "No, I'm good." Then she stood and sat in the chair.

The orderly reached down and lifted a wide leather strap laying at the side of the seat, along Naomi's leg. Then, in his first words to Naomi, he said, "Lift your arms, please."

Seeing that he intended to put the strap around her, Naomi said, "I don't need that. I won't fall out."

"It isn't just for safety. It's to keep you from getting up and running away when I get you outside the Unit."

"Really?"

"Yup, really."

Naomi lifted her arms and the strap went around her stomach. A little tug came when a buckle was cinched tight and snapped shut behind the chair back.

The silent orderly rolled Naomi out into the hall. They passed a couple of other patient rooms before they entered an open area with food service tables and benches on one side, and a recreation area with couches and chairs on the other. The recreation area was unremarkable, except the television that was showing a golf match seemed to be in a cage so that the patients could not reach it, and much of the furniture was clearly bolted to the floor with small metal brackets. A dozen or so patients were watching television, reading and standing around the room. Some were wearing khaki outfits like Naomi wore and many were in regular clothes. Two were playing chess with oversize foam chess pieces at one of the food service tables that had the chessboard painted onto it. Virtually every one of the patients stopped and turned to watch Naomi roll by. She was obviously the new kid on the block, and everyone wanted to get a good view. Naomi stared back as they were a very motley assemblage, many of them elderly, both men and women, many with a look about them that announced the primary specialty of Napa State Hospital.

One middle-aged man who fit into the 'crazy-look' group stood with his arms akimbo, angrily scowling at the wheelchair passing by. As they passed close by him, Naomi noticed the man was frowning at the orderly, not Naomi.

Naomi saw Laetitia and a couple of other nurses sitting in what must be the nurses' station. It was visible through several thick windows that had an access window with a round peephole opening and a small pass-thru port like a movie ticket office has. The windows had a foggy quality that indicated they were thick Plexiglas, not glass. Napa State Hospital had multiple indications that some patients had a dangerous or destructive streak.

The orderly spun around and walked the wheelchair backward toward the door near the nurses' station. A loud buzzer went off, releasing the magnetic door lock, and the orderly opened the door with his hips and pulled Naomi through.

As Naomi was spun again, she saw Laetitia wave to her over the counter on this side of the nurses' station. She waved back.

A security guard in the small lobby nodded at the orderly.

The guard buzzed them through another door. Naomi had expected to be leaving a building, but she found herself in a covered walkway. The covered walkway had multiple entrances on the left into units like she had just left as well as exits on the right to the outside. Numerous people were walking to and from many entrances and exits.

Outside open windows on her right, she could see a two-story brick and stucco building with a red tile roof. As she passed on, she saw the view to the other building was the back of a building, labeled with a sign 'Administration.' As they went on, Naomi noticed that the exits from the walkway to the outside were guarded as her unit door had been, but some of the entrances to building on her left were not. A couple buildings had bars on windows. Each entrance had a sign designating the Unit, A-4, A-7, and so on. Different buildings seemed to have different rules and operations, but all fed off this one guarded walkway.

One of the people they passed in the covered walkway was a priest in full Sunday regalia and a four-cornered hat with a fuzzy tassel ball on top. The elderly priest gave Naomi a broad smile, which Naomi returned.

At one of the building entrances, the orderly took a turn, and they arrived at a sign "Medical Staff Offices & Unit A-1."

At this entrance, there was a square, aluminum, handicapped access button down low next to the door. The orderly stepped forward and kicked at it. There was no guard inside this door to a small lobby. A closed-door showed a sign 'Unit A-1" directly ahead. The orderly turned to an elevator door and took Naomi up an old-style, slow elevator. On the upper floor, the orderly moved her down a carpeted hallway, nicely decorated with wallpaper and pictures and paintings. Naomi noticed the paintings had no glass in them and little brackets screwing them tightly to the walls. A few people, both medical staff in lab coats and scrubs, and a couple of patients, came and went down the hall. One older woman strapped into a wheelchair, just like Naomi, was being rolled the other way. This woman with ferociously unkempt hair was intently looking down at her hands folded in her lap and slowly shaking her head.

The orderly rolled Naomi up close beside a counter she could not see over. He looked at a paper in his hand and said, "I've got Donnelley for Doctor Partridge."

"You're early. He's just finished with his previous patient. Leave her there for now," came from a woman somewhere beyond the counter.

"Okay. So, you've got her, right? I can go?"

"Yeah, I've got her."

The orderly turned without any explanation to Naomi and left. Naomi was left in the hallway, watching people watch her as they passed by.

———

Chapter 6

'Lawrence Partridge, M.D. (Psychiatry)' announced the engraved sign next to the door. The nurse who had come around the counter to get Naomi, rolled her in the open door, and placed the wheelchair before a large mahogany desk with many file folders and a computer screen on it. The nurse left without a word to Naomi, firmly flipping the wheel locks on the wheelchair.

The room was nicely decorated, but in an old-fashioned way, wood-paneled, with several bookcases lined with thick books and several framed certificates on the wall behind the desk. A black leather couch and two matching overstuffed chairs faced each other on the far wall. There was no doctor, however.

As Naomi squinted to try and read the diplomas on the wall, the sound of a toilet flushing could be heard behind the door in the corner of the room. A man came out, drying his hands on a paper towel. Seeing Naomi, he wadded up the towel and tossed it back into the bathroom.

"Oh, you're here," he said, giving a quick disapproving look in the direction where the nurse had disappeared. "I wasn't expecting you quite yet. I wanted to read your records first."

Naomi did not know what to say to this, so she gave him a tiny smile. He returned the smile and walked over to her, holding out his hand. They shook hands.

"Good morning, I'm Doctor Lawrence Partridge. I'm your psychiatrist."

"I'm Naomi Donnelley. I'm glad to get to talk to you finally."

As he went back around to sit at his desk, Naomi took stock of Partridge. He was quite tall, light blonde-haired, tending toward gray, and had a trim, athletic build. Naomi understood why Helene had described him as gorgeous. He had boyish good looks that defied his obvious middle-age. He was in a white shirt and a red tie. His white lab coat and a suit coat matching his gray slacks hung on the oak coat tree next to the diplomas.

"It is quite odd for us to have our first talk three months after your admission. I recall I was on my way over to Unit A-9 to meet you when you had your first seizure back in June. It was me who sent you to the ICU at Queen of the Valley." He paused and looked at Naomi, as if he expected a response.

"I really don't remember anything about any of that."

"I don't suppose you would. I was quite surprised and delighted to get the text message Friday evening that you had come around, so to speak."

"I do remember some of that."

"Doctor Hecht called me later and described events. It seems quite unusual for someone to come out of a three-month-long coma with quite your... uhh,... level of exuberance."

"Yes, I was able to apologize to the orderly whose nose I broke, but the nurse I bit has not risked meeting up with me again."

"Oh, really? I hadn't heard of the broken nose. Hecht did tell me it took seven staffers to get you under control. And two full sedations over the next eight hours."

"Let's just say I was really excited."

"So, it seems. Give me a moment, so I can read your file and background, then we can talk to get acquainted."

"Sure."

Partridge continued scrolling through files on the computer. He took some notes on a yellow lined tablet as he went. Naomi busied herself, trying to read his diplomas and certificates on the wall. She was squinting her eyes to read the large Old English and Roman lettering, and she could make out very little of the printing. That seemed odd. She rubbed her eyes.

At risk of interrupting the doctor's reading, she asked, "You Mormon?"

Partridge looked at her over the top of his computer reading glasses, "Yes, I am. You're inferring that from reading my Brigham Young University diploma?"

"Yes."

"You know, there are non-Mormons who go to the 'Y.'"

"Yeah, like maybe one percent, if that. It's as Mormon as the Tabernacle Choir."

"And how would you know that? Are you a Latter-Day Saint?"

"No, I'm not," Naomi said, and since she couldn't tell him how she knew that, yet, she finished, "I had a good friend who told me about it."

"I see." Partridge went back to reading.

Naomi continued to look around the office. She tried to read some of the titles on his books, but with a few exceptions, she could not make them out. She rubbed her eyes and tried to focus on the books, without luck. Partridge was intent on reading the screen and scrolling with the computer mouse.

A thought popped into Naomi's head, and she blurted it out, "I guess I should thank you for coming in on a Sunday to see me. The nurse told me it is unusual for a senior psychiatrist to do Sunday office hours."

Partridge looked at her with the barest hint of annoyance, "Well, since you mentioned the LDS church. I can tell you I had an early meeting this morning, and then several hours off until Sacrament Meeting and Sunday

School in the afternoon. I told my wife I would meet her at the church later, and I came in here to meet two patients that I needed to talk to sooner rather than later."

"Okay, sorry to interrupt. I haven't been able to sit and talk to anyone in a long time. Sorry."

"I understand. I'm almost done. Then I'll explain what I've found, and you can fire away with whatever you want to talk about. Okay?'

Naomi just nodded.

Partridge finally moved away from the computer, turned his pad of paper to the first page, and faced Naomi. "Well, Naomi. I've been able to read through a few of your records, your LPS commitment order, an evaluation from the drug and mental health center, and a couple of police reports from your juvenile arrests last spring, and the two arrests in May and June that got you committed. Plus, your recent medical files."

"What's LPS?"

"The Lanterman, Petris, and Short Law, LPS for short, is the name of the California law that the courts use to create a conservatorship for an adult who is thought to be a danger to themselves or others due to mental illness. The Superior Court judge back home in Kern County committed you to our care after they put you under an LPS order."

"Kern. I'm from Kern County? I did see Kern on my wrist band."

"Yes, Kern County. You don't remember being from Kern County? Bakersfield?"

"That is part of why I need to talk to you. I don't remember much of anything from Naomi's life before Friday night."

"Naomi's life? That's an odd way to say that. What do you remember?"

"Other stuff. I've been thinking of how to explain all this to someone like you. I've thought of nothing else since I woke up yesterday. I think it would be better if I let you finish, and then I can explain."

"Okay, sounds good." Partridge turned the page back to review his notes and continued, "Kern Social Services and Juvenile authorities had multiple interactions with you starting with an incident last August in which you and your mother were victims of domestic abuse by your stepfather. I don't have that file, but I can get it. They paraphrased that incident in their later report when you started having trouble, including criminal and drug-related issues, and what they saw as increasing mental problems, throughout your senior year in high school. They mentioned they suspected drug use by your stepfather and a lack of supervision by your mother due to her health issues. You were finally expelled from school in late Spring due to a couple of bizarre incidents at school, which included an arrest and detention at Juvenile Hall. Your mother died in early May, your stepfather was already in jail on a case unrelated to but arising out of his assault of you and your mother. They found an old court order from Nevada ordering your real father to stay away from you and your mother. So, Social Services and Mental Health had to try and find a place for you when you got out of Juvey since they did not want you living alone in the apartment you had lived in with your mother. You walked away from a residential care home; then, you were diagnosed with a possible schizoid disorder, psychotic related hallucinations, and severe drug problems. They had already started the LPS process since you had become an adult on your 18th birthday in May, and then you escaped from a low-security wing of a Bakersfield mental health facility. You had one final arrest when they found you at the residence of a drug dealer where you had locked yourself in a bathroom. You were a busy girl last May.

"They combined your Juvenile criminal case, the other criminal file, and the LPS case and when the Superior Court judge saw your mental health report, the history of abuse of both drugs and alcohol throughout your teen years, he dismissed the criminal cases and ordered the commitment to the hospital. It just happened that Napa had an opening for an LPS patient, and you were sent here a day or two after your last arrest."

Partridge turned to another page of notes. "You arrived here in restraints, clearly exhibiting psychotic behavior. But while still doing intake in our unit that does admissions, that is, waiting to see me, your assigned psychiatrist, you went into seizures, and I sent you to Queen of the Valley Hospital here in Napa in an ambulance. Those doctors found you had a serious, full bowel blockage. When they opened you up in the operating room, they found one baggy of shrooms, that is, hallucinogenic mushrooms, one small bag of opioids, and one small bag of methamphetamine. All the bags were stuck inside you and leaking to one extent or the other. They speculated that the opioids had anesthetized your small intestine to cause the blockage. The shrooms were leaking just enough to cause the psychotic behavior. And the meth had caused the seizures, but also counteracted, for a while, the effect of the massive levels of opioids that were easily enough to knock you out and kill you. You were a walking chemistry set with the drugs fighting each other and killing you.

"The surgeons were able to get the drugs and blockage out of you and they gave you emergency dialysis and massive transfusions. The report from Queen of the Valley says they were amazed you were still alive at all and wouldn't have been for much longer, but they could not get you out of the coma that ensued. They tried all their tricks for the coma and got an expert from UC Davis Med to look at you. They had nothing they could do for you, and since you were our patient, they sent you back here to be our problem. We retained the same UC Davis doctor to help us design a protocol to deal with you in our skilled nursing facility. You didn't improve and, in fact, got worse. Just last Friday night before your incident, our doctor made notes that your blood oxygen level was falling, and he did not expect you would live much longer. Then, you went into seizures, awoke, and..."

Partridge turned the page. "You started screaming about pain, fire, and people hurting you, again and again. When staff tried to restrain you, you screamed that they were hurting you, pulling your arms, legs, and skin off. Then you screamed about burning again. You thrashed about, tried to jump from the bed, had more seizures, and kept screaming in what they described as a full psychotic break. You were so violent physically that it took seven staff members and a full dosage of our most potent sedation med to get you down from it.

"Then, after seven hours of sedation and restraint, you woke up, and the nurse found you angry, violent, screaming incoherently, and trying to break out of the restraints. She followed previous doctor's orders and re-sedated you. You woke up again, just before noon yesterday, calm, trying to sing something, even with the gag, in a reported lovely voice and pleading to get the gag out of your mouth. The staff physician decided to remove the restraints, and you have been fine since. Your electroencephalogram, EEG, yesterday morning, showed brain activity was remarkably normal for someone who had been nearly brain dead the night before, had months of low oxygen to her brain and had suffered a massive triple-drug overdose."

Partridge turned to a fresh page in his tablet and looked to Naomi, "That's what I have. Do you need any further explanation, or would you like to talk now?"

Naomi took a deep breath and said, "Wow, that is quite a history. I'll try to explain what I know. But, first, I have two questions for you to cogitate on while I talk."

Partridge interrupted, "Cogitate, aye. That is a good psychiatrist's word. I like it."

"I thought you might. Let's see. My questions have to do with the very last time I was sedated yesterday morning as your report described it, I think, angry, violent, screaming incoherently, and trying to break out of the restraints. The questions I have for you are: First, have you ever seen anybody with a huge rubber psych restraint gag in their mouth who said anything that wasn't incoherent, be it screaming or otherwise? Second, imagine if you woke up in a darkened room, with the last thing you remember being the most horrible memory of your life. You find you are in that darkened room bound tightly, hands, legs, and body, and you have a gag in your mouth. You have no idea what has happened or why you are like that. You lay for maybe a half-hour like that, with those horrible memories in your head and frightened beyond belief about what is still happening to you lashed to that bed. Then, an unknown woman comes who cannot understand you, doesn't even try, makes fun of your situation, or so it seems, and threatens to drug you if you don't obey her. The second question is, what would you do in that situation?"

Partridge interrupted Naomi before she could continue, "As to your two questions, I see your point. No cogitation needed."

"Thank you." Naomi cleared her throat and continued, "Before I go on, I want to let you know that for the last day I have thought about little else than what I could say to you or someone in your position. My story is admittedly so far out there that nobody in their right mind would believe it, especially a psychiatrist in a mental hospital. Except, I have one little piece of undisputed fact, a connection to reality, that only you out of everyone else who might hear my story in the future can use to find out if my unbelievable tale is true. I need you to go with me on this. I am telling you my true story, and I need to get you to see the spark that proves it true.

"Next, I'll go back to the beginning of your report. As I said, I have no memories of anything you mentioned there, before the incident night before last in the hospital. I don't remember anything about a domestic violence incident; I don't remember my stepfather or my mother for that matter. I don't remember what you said about high school. I don't remember anything about those problems you say I had. I don't remember Juvenile Hall or any judge, or even coming here.

"And when I say I don't remember; I am not saying the memory is vague or incomplete. I mean, it is absolutely zero, zilch, nada. No memories of that at all. In fact, I have no memories at all of ever being…," Naomi fingered her wrist band for dramatic effect, reading, "Naomi Lynne Donnelley. But, that lack of memory is not simple amnesia, it goes to that unbelievable story I need you to believe.

"Let me skip back to your report about what happened Friday night here in the hospital because I do remember that, and I can explain exactly why I was screaming. What was in my mind that was not psychotic hallucinations, at least not any psychosis you will find in your books over on the wall.

"Everything you told me about Friday night is absolutely true. Let me tell you what I experienced and remember. Wait, I forgot something.

"I need you to understand that I have been locked in a hospital room in Unit A-4 continuously since Friday night, either totally sedated or constantly drugged to calm me down with no access to TV or any other news, right?"

"Is this a complaint?" Partridge asked.

"No, it is a presentation of an essential fact that I need to make sure you know before I ask you to believe my impossible story."

"Agreed, you have been locked by yourself in a room in a mental ward, *incommunicado*, since your incident Friday night." He straightened in his chair and leaned forward, paying close attention to what Naomi was saying.

"Thank you, Doctor Partridge. Continuing… What I experienced and remember from Friday night and what I was screaming about and fighting against was this…. I remember being in a car on the I-80 Freeway, driving down to Berkeley. A wrong-way driver came up an on-ramp at me, I tried to avoid him, but could not. There was a horrible wreck. My car was crushed. I was pinned in the wreck. First responders tried to cut me free, but they couldn't finish before a fire started. I was burned in the fire, a little at first, burns to my neck and shoulders, the firefighters tried to put out the fire and yank me from the car, pulling on my broken arm and yanking at me while my legs were still pinned in the wreckage. Then, the fire blew up and consumed the car with me inside. My last act was to scream in horrible pain, but my screams were cut short when I inhaled the fire."

Naomi paused and looked at Partridge.

He asked, "And you are telling me that is not a horrible hallucination?"

"That's right; it is not a hallucination; it is a memory. It is the first thing I remember as Naomi. But, it is the memory of someone else."

She paused again.

Partridge waited, and then asked, "Are you going to tell who that someone else is and why you think you remember it?"

"No, you are going to do that," Naomi appeared confident, as she pointed Partridge to his computer. "I want you to pull up your browser and go to the search engine, either Google or Bing, doesn't matter which. Please, Doctor?"

Partridge turned to his computer, clicked the mouse several times to close windows, and then once to open the internet browser. He typed and waited a moment, then saying, "Google.com. They have a cute cartoon about a scientist this morning."

"Doc, just a reminder of what you know about where I've been since Friday night."

Partridge nodded.

Naomi directed, "Please do a search for the name, Mark Kelleher. M-A-R-K, space, K-E-L-L-E-H-E-R. Probably using Google's 'News' tab would be best."

Partridge clicked the mouse once, and then typed the name. He waited.

Partridge furrowed his brow and looked sideways at Naomi, before he read, "There are several entries. The first one is a video blog from ABC7News, titled, 'One Dead, Seven Injured in Wrong-Way Driving Accident Near Vallejo.' What…?"

"Let's read it before we talk. Bring it up and read it out loud, maybe watch the video, whatever they have. Compare it to what I just told you I was screaming about Friday evening." Naomi was clearly excited.

Partridge clicked again and waited, "There's a video window, looks like an aerial shot from the still picture they have. The story below it reads:

> Intoxicated driving is suspected after a wrong-way crash at the south end of the Carquinez Bridge on the I-80 Freeway near Vallejo left one man dead and seven others injured, one critically, early Friday evening, authorities said.

> One man was pronounced dead at the scene of the 8:02 p.m. crash in the southbound lanes of the I-80 Freeway at the Pomona Street off-ramp, the California Highway Patrol said. The decedent was Mark Kelleher of American Canyon, the driver and sole occupant of a BMW who was hit by a suspected drunk driver in the wrong-way vehicle, described as a late model Ford 4x4 truck.

> The BMW was headed south on the outside lane of the freeway when it slammed into the Ford truck coming the wrong way onto the freeway up the exit ramp, officials said. The deceased was pinned in the wreckage of the BMW, and the Jaws of Life was used to attempt a rescue. However, a fire broke out and consumed the wreck before the driver could be extricated.

> An 18-year-old Richmond woman, Lydia Needham, who was riding as a passenger in another car involved in the seven-car wreck was hospitalized with major injuries and is still in critical condition, according to the CHP. Five other persons were hospitalized, including the suspected drunk driver, who had minor injuries. The drunk driver's name was withheld until the Contra Costa County District Attorney completes their review.

> After the collision, southbound lanes of the Carquinez Bridge on the I-80 were closed, creating a traffic backup on both the I-80 and 29 freeways. All lanes were reopened by midnight."

When Partridge finished reading, Naomi said, "You can watch the video if you want, it is probably just the view from the news chopper of the wreckage after the fact. If so, you might be able to see my car catch fire."

"You want to see the video, too?" Partridge asked.

"No. I'll pass. I saw the real thing. Up close." Naomi said.

Partridge frowned at Naomi, and then clicked his mouse. He watched for a minute or two, before rolling his eyes up, and then closing them. He opened his eyes and clicked the mouse again. He turned toward Naomi and sat silently, thinking. He put his elbows on the desk and the fingers of both hands to his chin, staring at Naomi. He was silent for at least a minute, as was Naomi. Naomi stared at Partridge unblinking; her expression was resolute.

Partridge swallowed and spoke, "So, with the recognition that you could not possibly know about that wreck from where you have been, you're telling me you somehow channeled that guy's memories of the wreck and the injuries, which caused your incident here in the hospital? That wreck was about fifteen miles south of this hospital."

"Fifteen miles. Sounds about right. But no, I am not telling you that I 'somehow channeled' his memories of that wreck. I have every one of Mark Kelleher's memories. That is, all his thoughts, memories, knowledge, doubts, fears, dreams, for his entire life, right up until the accident. From my viewpoint sitting here in front of you, I can't tell you anything, except that I am Mark Kelleher. His very soul seems to be inside this body we can see is really Naomi Donnelley. And the kicker is that I have none of Naomi's memories. Absolutely none, until a little bit after 8 p.m. on Friday. The exact moment Mark Kelleher died. I don't think this is channeling memories like you said. It is my sense that I, my soul, is Mark Kelleher."

Partridge started to speak, but Naomi cut him off, "Jus' a sec, Doc. One more thing on that last thing I said about not having Naomi's memories. There have been a couple things about me that seem to be Naomi's and not Mark's, besides the body. Weird little things, you know. First, I noticed that when I was speaking to Doctor Dharma yesterday, I distinctly caught myself talking in, like, Valley Girl accent. There I did it again, ya see. That has got to be Naomi; Mark Kelleher is an articulate, college-educated man. In fact, Mark, that is… I… graduated from BYU, like you, with a major in Bioinformatics. That's how I knew the 'Y' is almost wall to wall Mormons. Mark, or that is, I, was not Mormon. The next weird thing I've noticed is that when one of the interns did something really sweet and unexpected, to help me out yesterday, I got all teary-eyed, like a girl would, not like Mark would. Then, when I ate my food yesterday and this morning, I found myself using my left hand for all the utensils and to open all the packages, like I was left-handed. Mark was right-handed. Everything I did was backward, to my way of thinking. But, the left-handedness worked correctly."

Doctor Partridge nodded his head to indicate he was considering what Naomi had said. "That is something else interesting to consider." He paused and thought. "But… Okay. Let's see."

Partridge picked up his pad of paper and pen and came around the desk. He moved a chair near the wheelchair out of the way and pulled a wooden writing leaf extension from the front of the desk and set the paper and pen on it. He drew two lines across the page, one at the top of the page and one below that. "I have been wondering how I could use these writing leaves since I got this desk. Finally, we can."

Partridge rolled Naomi's wheelchair over in a position to write on the pad. He handed her the pen.

"Naomi, first, I want you to write your signature with your right hand. On the top line."

"Mark's signature or Naomi's?"

Partridge smiled at this question, "Naomi's."

Naomi picked up the pen in her right hand and, with some difficulty, started to write. The 'Naomi Donnelley' signature came out scrawled and wiggly, like a very elderly person had written it. It was almost illegible.

"Long fingernails," Partridge remarked.

"Yeah, I guess nobody bothered to clip them while I was in the coma. I figure that's three months' worth."

"Switch hands and do it again, on the other line."

Naomi moved the pen to her left hand and tilted the paper to the right. The 'Naomi Donnelley' came out smooth, flowing, rounded, and distinctly feminine. With the last stroke of the signature, Naomi drew a small circle over the 'i' in her first name, instead of just a dot over it.

"Lit! I have her signature," Naomi said.

Partridge took the pen and paper and moved Naomi's wheelchair back a bit, shoving in the writing leaf.

"What does that mean, Doc?"

Partridge sat back in his chair, waited a moment, and then spoke, "Well, after a bit of thought, it really tells us next to nothing about what your main claim is, that you are really this guy, Mark, and not Naomi. What it does tell us, in fact, what all three 'weird things' you mentioned tell us, is that the brain you are using is Naomi's brain. Unconscious accent in language, emotional reactions, and basic manual dexterity using one hand or the other, predominantly, are things that are semi-hardwired into the brain, like the subconscious. You have to train yourself to unlearn those uses, to change your accent, to hide emotion, or learn to use the other hand. I have never studied signatures that much, but from what I know, the way one does their signature is a somewhat autonomic thing, you must learn to do it differently and train yourself. That is a basic principle of modern handwriting analysis. An expert can tell someone's handwriting by their reflex action of writing even if they try to write like someone else. And the emotional reaction with the intern is also probably just Naomi's way of reacting. I am afraid all you have proven is that your brain is Naomi's female brain that is pre-programmed to do the things you have tried to do. It may be of some comfort to you in the circumstance you think you are in to realize that you are reacting in the way this young woman should or would. But, it doesn't mean anything in relation to your claim that you have someone else's soul."

Naomi frowned, "You said, 'the circumstance you <u>think</u> you are in.' Do you think this is all a hallucination in my insane brain? After all I have shown you?"

Seeing Naomi was possibly ready to cry, Partridge quickly said, "No, no, I understand that you have proven you couldn't have known all of what you had me find out. But, you have to realize I am a man of science and a man of faith. What you have come to me with is not answered by what I know in either science or religion. As your psychiatrist, my first duty is to find a medical answer to your, well…situation."

"But, isn't the man of faith supposed to believe in miracles, those things that occur that can only be accepted on faith and not by mere knowledge?"

This stopped Partridge and required some thought. At last, he said, "Yes, that is true. *The power of God works miracles, Alma 23:6.* And, *It is by faith that miracles are wrought, Moroni 7:37.*"

Naomi smiled and said, "You went Mormon on me there, but I think that is what I said. Doctor Partridge, you have to realize that from where I stand, with a dead guy's memory and thoughts, but a young girl's body and now you tell me her subconscious, that this being a miracle is my best bet, because my only other answer is that I really belong in this mental hospital, for certain."

Partridge nodded his head and kept nodding it slowly as he closed his eyes in thought. He was broken out of his thoughts by a knock on the door.

"Yes."

The nurse stuck her head in the door, "Larry, look at the time. Any idea how long we will be?"

Partridge looked at the wall clock and shook his head. "I'm sorry, Becca, this is serious, and I need you here to cover the co-ed rule. Do you need to get someplace?

The nurse shook her head, "No, I am fine, nothing to do except read a textbook today, lazy Sunday planned, and I've got my book here. I don't mind getting paid to read it. I just wanted you to know that with the problems we stayed late for Wednesday and Thursday, that I am about to go into double-time for this pay period, and you will have to answer to the Big Lady over budget-busting."

"Thanks. What is she going to do, take away my birthday? Stay around here this morning, and I'll see if I can cut you free a bit early this next week."

"Sure thing. Let me know if you need anything." The nurse closed the door, leaving it open a crack.

Naomi asked, "What's the co-ed rule?"

"Hospital rule that any time a member of staff is alone with a patient of the opposite sex in a closed area, there has to be an opposite-sex staff member nearby. To protect the patient from abuse and the hospital from claims of abuse. Becca has to stay close enough to hear if there is a problem, but far enough away to allow confidentiality."

"Ah. Good idea; it seems."

"Yes, now, where was I? Oh yes, I wanted to check one more thing on our 'non-proof but interesting' discovery about you and your brain."

He turned back to the computer and clicked a couple of boxes; then, he scrolled with the mouse until he found what he wanted. He pressed his lips together and nodded as though he had found something he thought was important. He clicked a couple more times and said, "I'm printing something down at the nurses' station. Don't move while I'm gone."

"You're kidding, right? What have I done to make you think I would cause trouble?"

"Right, sorry. I was on automatic there." He went out and left the door open.

Partridge came back in a minute or two. He had a single piece of paper.

He went to his desk and picked up the pad of paper. He looked at the papers and gave a satisfied smile when he came over to show them to Naomi.

"This is mostly for your benefit, but I do find it interesting. This should help your comfort zone that you are acting like Naomi should be acting. This is a paper from the court file from Naomi's first conservatorship hearing in late May, where she was asked to acknowledge that she understood her rights under the law. Naomi signed the court document. Look."

Partridge held the bottom of the court paper copy above the signature Naomi had done with her left hand. Partridge explained, "Naomi's signature in May and yours today are identical, same flowery script, little circle above the 'i' and the same slight leftward tilt of a left-handed person doing their signature. It doesn't prove anything about your memories, but it does show my worried patient that she is behaving on a subconscious level the way her apparent identity would be expected to act."

"So, what's next? Naomi asked.

"Let me think a minute and maybe ask some questions. I think I may be able to add some other proof to your 'I was locked up ever since it happened' argument." Partridge leaned back in his chair and looked at the ceiling.

Naomi waited quite a while before saying to him, "Doctor Partridge, admit it, you are enjoying this little mystery I have dumped in your lap."

He looked over at her without straightening up in his chair, "I will admit it is interesting, and you are much more pleasant to work with than many of my patients. I am probably enjoying it quite a bit more than you are."

"Oh, Doctor Partridge, if you can help me figure out what happened to me, explain any of this or prove to me I am not insane, I will enjoy that tremendously."

"Let me ask some questions so that I can formulate a plan of attack." Partridge turned his pad to another blank page, "Why was Mark driving to Berkeley?"

"I had a 9:00 p.m. first date with a girl. Whoa, that sounds too weird. I should have followed your lead and used 'Mark.' Make that, Mark had a first date with a girl."

Partridge smiled at this and wrote something else down before asking, "And how did Mark get that date, where'd he meet her."

"Hadn't met her. He answered her Tinder.com App posting."

"Does Naomi know Mark's Tinder.com username and password?"

"Yes, of course." Naomi smiled. "I see where you're going there."

"How does Mark send work emails?"

"He has an account at work. In fact, one of his additional duties is, or was, that he runs the IT desk at his employer."

"And can Mark, or could Mark, sign into that work email at home or here?"

"You bet he could." Naomi mimed shooting a 'bingo' pistol at Partridge.

"What does Mark use for private personal emails? How would he email Miss Berkeley to set up a second date?"

"Well, emailing for a second date would be uncool, he would call her. But, he has an email account at Google, Gmail.com. That is how he wrote to her to get the phone number to set up the first date. After he got her email from Tinder."

"Good, that's three. Should be enough." Partridge stood and looked at the computer. He turned the flat screen monitor around to face Naomi, and then picked up the keyboard and mouse, and set them at the front of the desk. He came around and pulled out the writing leaf on that corner of his desk. He set the keyboard and mouse on the leaf and maneuvered Naomi's wheelchair in front of it. He leaned in to maximize the browser window and stepped back, with his pad and pen in hand to take notes.

He smiled at Naomi and said, "Naomi, can we get Mark Kelleher to sign into his Tinder.com account?"

"Yes, sir."

Naomi typed the website name, Tinder.com, and then stopped to say, "Kinda hard to type with these nails."

"Your nurse can help you with that."

Naomi then clicked the mouse, typed a username, and then clicked the password box, and typed a complicated password with multiple symbols and numbers. After a moment, a 'Welcome Back, Mark' screen appeared with a frame showing Mark's picture, his profile and a list of usernames with pictures of women, new inquiries responding to Mark's posting. Naomi proudly turned to Doctor Partridge with a '*Voilà*' flip of her hand. He was already smiling at her.

"Mark was a handsome guy, huh?" Partridge asked.

"Yeah, he was. Naomi would have liked to meet him. But, he's prob'ly a little old for her. Maybe not."

Partridge smiled at this and wrote something down on the pad.

"Very good, try the next one. Work email." Partridge urged Naomi on.

Naomi typed the company website, HeptImun.com, and explained, "Mark was IT manager for a biotech company over in Fairfield. I can do better than just the email. It is still the first weekend. They probably haven't changed anything since they won't know about Mark's tragic end until maybe Monday when Mark's mother or somebody calls…"

Naomi suddenly got very quiet and dropped her hands from the keyboard.

Partridge asked, "You thought about your mother, right?"

"Yeah, my Mom and Dad probably had a California Highway Patrol officer visit them on Saturday down in Stockton. I think that is how they do that." She thought for a moment and said, "Nothing much I can do about any of that. It's not like Naomi could say anything to them, even if she weren't locked in a looney bin."

Naomi paused again, and then continued, "As I said, I can do better than log into his email. Mark was the webmaster for HeptImun, Inc. Watch this."

Naomi typed additional address code after the website name, then a user name, and another password. A page appeared that read 'Website Control Panel—Heptimun Inc.—Powered by Drupal.'

Naomi turned to Partridge and said, "We're into the inner workings of the company website. We can change anything from here."

"Let's not. Naomi Donnelley hacking into a company's website is probably illegal."

"Oh, yeah, a felony! Go, Naomi!" Naomi had obviously bypassed the sadness of thinking about her parents' grief, or rather Mark's parents' grief.

"Okay, Naomi, one last one. Probably not needed, but let's call it the third strike. Log out of that site and open Mark's private email account."

Naomi went to the Google.com page, clicked on the Gmail tab, and then typed in 'Mark.R.Kelleher@Gmail.com.'

She started to type the password and turned to Partridge to say, "This is kind of cheating, cuz Mark used the same password for Tinder as he used for Gmail."

Partridge smiled, "You get a bonus point for knowing how to cheat on Mark's accounts."

"Right!"

Naomi finished the password, hit enter, and Mark's Gmail message log filled the screen. She showed Partridge.

He said, "Alright, sign off. Let's talk about this."

"Just a sec. Can I look at these?" Naomi pointed to the emails.

"Of course." Partridge backed away to give her some privacy.

Naomi clicked a couple of times. "A couple of Mark's friends trying to reach him." She clicked again and said, "Uh oh!"

"What?"

"It's from Denise in Berkeley. She is really upset Mark stood her up, didn't call and won't answer his cell when she calls. Too bad. She was a sweet girl, so it seemed."

"Anything you can do to explain things to her?" Partridge was using his psychiatrist's counseling voice.

"Yeah, there is. Is this tab the TV news screen?" Naomi pointed to a tab on the browser.

"Yes."

Naomi went to the ABC7News.com site, highlighted, and copied the webpage URL address of the wreck video. She flipped to the Gmail tab, clicked reply to Denise's email, and then typed a message and copied the address of the news story. She hit send.

Partridge said, "What did you say? I wasn't watching. If you don't mind telling me."

"Pretty simple. I told her I was a friend of Mark. I told her I knew he had been looking forward to meeting her, but she should look at the news link I gave her to see why he had not returned her call or met her."

"Now, let's talk," Partridge said

He started to reach for Naomi's wheelchair when she said, "I got this." She grabbed the wheels and rolled herself back, centered in front of the desk.

Partridge replaced his computer and sat in his chair, "So, we now have four pretty good chunks of evidence in favor of your contention that you have Mark's memories spinning around in Naomi's blonde head. You say your conscious thoughts are Mark's, not Naomi's. Meanwhile, my learned psychiatrist and wise scholar's head is spinning from the implications of that."

Naomi joined in, "My worries about being a raving lunatic are somewhat tempered down, and your scripture quotes about miracles are looking like a good answer. But we haven't done anything to rule out demonic possession, yet."

Partridge smiled, "Let's not add to the problem with new issues."

"It's not new to me. I was totally thinking *The Exorcist* for a while after I woke up tied to a bed and speaking in a strange voice."

Partridge started to say something, and then realized Naomi was toying with him. Maybe she was toying with him, her quip about the movie made as much sense as any of this did.

"Okay, Naomi, you say you are really Mark Kelleher. If I am going to help you with this, I need to know more about who you say you are. I have no idea how, but it might help us find out what happened to you."

Naomi thought for a minute, then said, "Mark Robert Kelleher was born and raised in Stockton, California. His folks were ordinary, working-class people. He had one older sister. When Mark was little, his parents got the idea that his mother's experience as a fry cook might let them run their own restaurant. They borrowed to buy a greasy spoon sort of place where the owner was retiring. Mark's folks running that little restaurant near the freeway is what his main memory of childhood was. Mark went to public schools and graduated from Lincoln High in Stockton. He was kind of a geek, but he did letter in both swimming and water polo in high school. When he graduated, the Recession had hit, and Stockton took the brunt of it. Even the city government there went bankrupt. His folks held on, but there wasn't any money to pay for college. They barely kept his older sister in community college.

"That didn't matter much since Mark had grown up in the post 9/11 world, and he felt the right thing for him to do was join the service. He enlisted in the Army, thinking that a basic enlistment would get him in the infantry, to go over to Iraq or Afghanistan to do his part. That didn't happen. With decent scores on the Army's aptitude test in mechanical and technical subjects, Mark got sent to heavy equipment school. Then he got assigned to an Army transportation company that was scheduled to deploy to Afghanistan. Instead of heavy equipment, Mark found himself driving a five-ton truck and an occasional big rig. He went to Afghanistan, did a good job, and came home with a couple of medals on his chest, one for valor in combat, and the GI Bill to help pay for college.

"Mark came back and started at the junior college in Stockton, where he went back to his swimming and managed to win two individual events at an NJCAA level swim meet. He got offers from a couple of four-year universities to transfer there after junior college. The best offer was from Brigham Young University, even though Mark was not Mormon. He followed his geeky interests and got a degree in Bioinformatics at BYU and survived two years there with his non-Mormon-ness intact despite the efforts of more than one Mormon coed.

"Mark looked for jobs that matched his degree in the Bay area, near home, and took a job with a biotech company that had just gotten good investment capital and a big government contract, HeptImun, in Fairfield. That job paid for Mark's rented condo in American Canyon and a nice BMW sports sedan. As a single 27-year-old man with a good job, Mark decided he needed to find a wife, which brought him to the I-80 southbound last Friday evening, with the results you know about."

Partridge listened to Naomi finish telling about Mark, and then said, "I'm not sure if that helps me understand anything. Sounds like a really nice guy, an All-American boy."

Naomi agreed, "Yeah, although my opinion is a bit prejudiced, I think 'nice guy' is a pretty good description of Mark Kelleher. His life was a far cry from what you told me about Naomi. You know it is getting really weird talking about myself in the third person, whether it is Mark or Naomi."

"I'm guessing that is not the weirdest thing you're are having to deal with."

"Very true. I seem to be the grand prize winner in the Really Weird Life contest."

Partridge leaned forward and held up a finger, as though he had an idea, "You know, uh, Naomi, we may never get any clear signposts to help us reach a firm conclusion on what this is that has happened to you. But, maybe there is something to the fact that, as you said, Mark's life was the antithesis of Naomi's. Mark was a nice guy, a war hero, a hard worker, an athlete, a young man on the way up when he was struck down by a senseless act of a drunk driver. Naomi was the opposite. She had thrown away her life in drug and alcohol use, crime, and the rest. Last Friday, she was just about as far down as she could get, ready to die in her drug-induced coma, having pretty much wasted her beauty, her potential, and her life. Could it be that the really nice guy was given a second chance at life, a new chance, using what little was left of Naomi's life?"

Naomi sat blinking at Partridge, finally saying, "Wow, just maybe you are right. What was that quote you told me? 'The power of God works miracles?' I suppose it would be ungrateful of me to say that if God was going to give Mark a miracle, he might come up with something other than locking him up in an insane asylum."

"Ahh, wait on that thought, Naomi," Partridge was nodding as he said, "Maybe the miracle of a second chance at life for Mark is also a new chance for the life that was Naomi's. Naomi's life had no way to go but up, and maybe that nice guy is meant to make something miraculous out of this strange new chance he has been given. Miracles would not be miracles if they were easily understood or easy to handle."

Naomi's blonde hair flipped from side to side as she slowly shook her head in wonderment. "This is all pretty heavy stuff. I think I need some time to… ahh… cogitate on this."

Partridge smiled and nodded, "You are right. Let's be happy to contemplate the truths we have uncovered today. It is a lot for either of us to deal with. We can talk again tomorrow. I'm going to clear you for full Unit privileges, so you aren't locked in your room, and first thing tomorrow, I will do some more checking, and then drop by A-4 to talk to you again. I'll start the process to get you transferred from Skilled Nursing in A-4, down here to Intermediate Care in A-1, we've got openings. You don't need skilled medical care anymore. Sound good?"

Naomi smiled, "Sounds like a plan."

Partridge started to push Naomi to the door when she put up her hand to get him to stop. "Any chance you can do something about me not being trusted to walk around without being strapped in this chair?"

"You think you can walk? You just came out of a full coma not even 48 hours ago," he asked.

"I feel great. I'd like to try."

"Okay. If you think you can." Partridge bent to fiddle with the strap buckle behind Naomi's back. It came free, and he walked around to help get the strap from around her and offer Naomi a hand up.

Naomi stood, and then shifted her balance from side to side, flexed her knees, took two steps, then flashed a big smile. "I'm great."

Partridge smiled back, pointing to the door, "Okay, ladies first."

When they got to the nurses' counter, Partridge said, "Becca, could you please call Unit A-4 to tell them that I'll be bringing Miss Donnelley back to the Unit myself. She wants to get some exercise."

Becca looked perplexed, "You're taking her back yourself. Uh, okay, I'll call them."

"And that's all for this morning. You can go when you lock your area up. I'll be back in a few minutes to finish up some things in my office. I hope the rest of your Sunday is nice."

They went down to the ground floor in the elevator. Naomi pushed the outside door open, held it for Partridge to roll the wheelchair through, and stepped out into the walkway on her own two feet.

Halfway up the walkway, Naomi and Partridge passed the same priest going the other way. The priest smiled again, but this time, he gave Naomi an "Okay" sign with his hand. Naomi glanced over and saw Doctor Partridge smiling. It seemed that graduating from being strapped in a wheelchair to walking on your own was cause for congratulations around here.

———

Leyla, a new nurse on night shift, gave Naomi a mint green capsule to help her sleep. "Sweet dreams. This should put you to sleep in just a few minutes."

"Do you have a pill for sleep without dreams. The nightmares I had last night were freaky. Like reliving the worst moment of my life in high definition 3D."

"I can't guarantee no nightmares. That's something to talk to your doc about. Good night."

Naomi nodded.

The nurse's estimate of sleep in a few minutes was wrong. Naomi lay awake for a long time, drowsy from the pill but with thoughts and questions churning in her head. This bizarre situation she found herself in defied reality itself and led to a myriad of thoughts, none of which had any answers or explanation.

———

Chapter 7

Naomi was sitting, lotus style, on her bed, devouring her breakfast on her third full day at Napa State Hospital. Her third conscious day, that is. She had just shoved the last of her muffin into her mouth when a young woman in a business suit walked into her room, through the now open door.

"Oh, if you're still eating, I can come back," said the woman.

Naomi held up a finger to indicate the woman should wait and pointed to her mouth. Naomi quickly chewed and swallowed the muffin.

"I'm finished," Naomi announced, as she wiped her mouth with a napkin and pushed the bed table away.

The young woman shifted the large bundle of things in her hands and reached to Naomi to shake hands, "Good morning, Naomi. I'm Clarissa Rodriguez, the social worker on your Wellness and Recovery Planning Team."

"Naomi Donnelley, but I guess you know that," Naomi said as she shook hands. "I didn't know I had a, uh, 'whatever' Team."

"Wellness and Recovery — that's the team of social workers and other staff members who help plan your program here at Napa help to prepare for future release."

"Sounds good, a worthy goal from my perspective."

Rodriguez was looking around for someplace to set the things in her arms. Naomi patted the bed beside her and moved to sit on the edge of the bed.

"It is rather odd to be doing your admissions interview so long after arrival, but you were indisposed," Rodriguez said. She sat in the chair that an orderly had brought into Naomi's room earlier since Naomi had been upgraded to a non-risk status and could have things like chairs in her room.

"Yes, Doctor Partridge said the same thing yesterday when I met with him."

"Yes, I saw that part of his report this morning. Congratulations."

"Uh, congratulations?"

"Yes, the part of his report that came to our office indicated the Doctor Partridge questioned whether your situation required hospitalization at Napa, and he put in a request for a full evaluation of that."

Naomi smiled but said nothing.

Rodriguez continued, "So, let's get on with your admissions interview. First, here is your Patient's Information Guide brochure, telling you about Napa's facilities and Program 4, which is the treatment program that LPS patients like you are involved in." Rodriguez handed Naomi a glossy brochure.

"Next, we have a list of your specific rights as an LPS patient," she said, as she handed Naomi a laminated card. "These nineteen rights apply to every LPS patient at Napa, things such as basic human rights, on down through things like having the right to wear your own clothing, have your own personal possessions, your expense account, your right to communicate and have visitors, et cetera. If you feel your rights are being violated, you can contact any member of the staff, our Team, or ask to see the Patient Ombudsman."

Rodriguez now grabbed a large black vinyl bag, bulging with contents, from the pile on the bed, "And with those rights in mind... Here are your personal possessions you came with from home. The list the Property people gave me shows you have some items of clothing and shoes, your purse and its contents, a few toiletries and make-up, a hand hairdryer, some paperwork, and miscellaneous other items. Things that you don't need, like your suitcase, or are forbidden in the units, like your cellphone and metal nail file, will be kept by Property until your discharge."

Rodriguez sat the vinyl bag on the bed closer to Naomi. Then, she gave Naomi a couple slips of paper and a plastic card. "And last, but certainly not least, is the receipt for your personal funds held by our Trust Office. It shows that between the money you brought with you and an amount deposited into your patient account from a Bakersfield attorney, you have $316.00 in your account. And, along with it is a card with a barcode and account number on it. That card will allow you to buy items from the patient commissary here or through the online canteen service we provide. If you don't have your own private bank account, the Trust Office will help you get a bank debit card you can use to access your funds to make online purchases from outside vendors. That is, if you don't already have a debit card in your stuff. You can turn to the section in the Patient Information Guide I gave you for more on how to do that."

So, I'm not penniless.

Rodriguez looked at her wristwatch and said, "Do you have any questions? I see you are scheduled to move to Unit A-1 today, so the meeting with the rest of your Team will be down there later this week. If you have no questions, I have a couple more stops to make this morning."

Naomi looked at her bag of things and said, "No, Ms. Rodriguez, looks like I have some things to look through here."

"Oh, no, call me Clarissa. We want you to view your Wellness and Recovery Planning Team as your friends. Nice meeting you," Clarissa gave Naomi a quick wave of her hand, gathered the rest of her bundle on the bed, and left.

Naomi hopped off the bed and unzipped the opening of the vinyl bag. On top of the contents was a well-worn, red leather purse, which seemed like the best place to start. Instead of pawing through the purse, Naomi smoothed out the blanket on the bed and dumped the contents on the bed.

It was quite a pile.

The item on top of the pile on her bed was a bit of a surprise—a pair of women's prescription eyeglasses. Naomi picked them up to inspect. They had large, circular lenses with thin black frames with a tiny rhinestone near each hinge.

Naomi tried them on, and then alternated a few times with the glasses in place, and then without. Naomi was nearsighted. That explained the difficulty in reading Doctor Partridge's diplomas on the wall. The glasses even helped Naomi's near vision a bit, which explained her trouble reading fine print. She kept them on as she continued with the purse's contents.

The red leather wallet was Naomi's next choice for closer inspection.

The driver's license in the wallet was a California minor's provisional license that had expired on Naomi's 18th birthday last May. When she pulled the license from the clear plastic pocket to look closer, Naomi found a Renewal by Mail form folded and stuffed behind the license. She had a chore to do sometime.

The picture on the license was of a slightly younger, heavier Naomi with a bob haircut that went down to mid-neck. As driver's license pictures go, it was a fairly nice, attractive picture. Now, Naomi knew what she had looked like before the coma, and intervening problems had created the gaunt look she had seen in the mirror. The pretty girl in the picture, probably 16 years old, also had make-up on and was wearing the glasses. Naomi did not recognize the address in Bakersfield on the license. There was no reason she should. But it did give her a birthdate to start recreating Naomi's identity in her memory. There was a Wells Fargo Bank debit card in the wallet along with what looked like an attractive senior class photo of Naomi, without glasses. There was also a picture of a pretty woman in her late 30's with curly brown hair. *My mother?* At the back of the wallet was an ID card from Centennial High School in Bakersfield with another, slightly older, picture of Naomi, declaring her to be a senior. There was no money in the wallet, just a few old receipts, and a to-do list for groceries.

Naomi put the wallet back in the purse and started moving the other things back in as she sorted through them. She found a small hairbrush, a royal blue scrunchie for her hair, and breath spray. She set them aside. There was a compact with light-toned face powder, a tube of light mauve matte lipstick, eyeliner, a little plastic box with brownish kohl eyeshadow and a little wand for applying it. There were several other trinkets, of unknown use and meaning. Naomi put everything back in the purse.

Next in the bag were a pair of black patent low heels and a pair of scuffed white Nike running shoes, size 8. Naomi set the Nikes aside. There was a wrinkled pink 'California Girl' t-shirt, three plain colored t-shirts, a white cotton gypsy blouse, and a plain, white, long-sleeved, silk blouse. There were two dresses; one was a classic 'little black dress,' and one was a yellow flower print. There was a plain black wool skirt. She found two pairs of jeans, one black with stretchy thin legs and one denim with rips on the knees that appeared to be intentional. There was another pair of dressier gray slacks. The hairdryer Clarissa had mentioned looked well used and was wrapped in a pink terrycloth bathrobe. A small silver lamé make-up bag held more make-up, more scrunchies, and the pink nail polish Naomi had worn before Laetitia had helped her trim her nails yesterday afternoon. There was also a small sprayer of Chloé *Nomade* perfume. Naomi sniffed the perfume bottle. *Not bad.* Two pairs of white crew socks and two pairs of taupe pantyhose were rolled up near the bottom of the bag, along with a blue sports bra, a regular cream-colored bra, and four pairs of pastel-colored panties. In a Rite-Aid Pharmacy bag, Naomi found a bottle of shampoo, conditioner, a bar of soap, ladies' deodorant, toothbrush, toothpaste, and tampons. At the bottom of the bag, Naomi found a manila envelope with various papers in it.

Naomi surveyed her horde laying on the bed with mixed feelings. On the one hand, she liked the idea that she was not destitute and property-less. On the other hand, she had a nagging feeling that she was a voyeur going through someone else's things. Integral to that feeling of being an interloper was the fact the Naomi had no memory of personal experience using many of the items in the bag, like make-up, bra, and tampons. She hoped that Doctor Partridge's theory about her subconscious might be of some help in this. Mark's knowledge was useless in dealing with most of these items.

Naomi started repacking the things she had no current use for and thought about changing from the prisoner-like khaki hospital clothing to some regular clothes. But, the bathrobe and shampoo reminded her that she had not bathed in three months.

Naomi picked up the nurse call button and pushed it. Helene answered.

Naomi asked, "Helene, how do I go about getting a shower around here?"

"I'll be down in a few minutes to help you with that. I'll have to let you into the ladies' shower room."

Naomi sat her chosen clothes on the bed with the bathrobe and some of the Rite-aid bag contents. She put the rest of her things back in the bag. She put the envelope of papers on the bedside table to read through after her shower.

———

Naomi was feeling pretty good about herself as she sat on the edge of the bed, waiting for the expected orderly from Unit A-1 to come for her. The shower had been good for her and had let her get acquainted with her new body. Helene had brought some scissors and helped her trim her hair to the long bob length she had seen in the pictures she found in the purse. She had dried her hair, and even ventured to use a bit of eye make-up to try and achieve the same look as the pictures of Naomi she had found in her wallet. She could not figure out how to wear the shoulder-strapped bra with the wide-necked gypsy blouse, so she ignored the bra, and her outfit was a gypsy blouse, hole-y denim jeans, panties, socks, Nike shoes, and her glasses. The vinyl property bag and her four magazines were stacked on the bed next to her for the trip down to A-1.

Naomi had kept the envelope of papers out of the property bag and had it stacked with the magazines. Most of the documents were court forms from the Kern County Superior Court. There was also a letter from an attorney in Bakersfield.

The letter from the attorney was rather nice. The female attorney, Victoria Roth, had told Naomi she had been appointed Naomi's guardian *ad litem* by the Court. The attorney explained a Probate Court filing she had made on Naomi's behalf. With the death of Naomi's mother so recently before Naomi's commitment as an LPS patient, the attorney had taken on the task of settling the affairs of Naomi's deceased mother, and the judge had agreed this was a good idea. She had taken care of the property in the apartment where Naomi and her mother had lived. Apparently, the attorney's legal assistant was the one to thank for the Rite-Aid toiletry purchases Naomi had found and the selection of Naomi's personal property. The attorney wished Naomi well and said she would be in touch. The letter was dated in June.

The person to appear in Naomi's doorway was not the orderly, but Doctor Partridge. He was wearing his white lab coat and had one of the iPads all the doctors at Napa seemed to carry. He flashed a broad smile when he saw Naomi.

"Wow, Naomi cleans up nice. You look great," he said.

Naomi nodded, "Feeling pretty good, too. They brought my stuff by this morning."

"I guess it was good to see all your things again."

Naomi raised her eyebrows, "Well, not quite. It was a bit strange going through everything, since I had never seen any of it before."

"Oh. yes, I suppose that is true," Partridge had an odd look on his face as he saw his error.

"And, I found out I'm nearsighted." Naomi wiggled her glasses frame and fluttered her eyelashes. *Why did I do that? Naomi's subconscious has some cute tricks.* "I guess I should thank you for your report about me."

"How'd you hear about that?"

"The lady from the Wellness Team told me a bit."

"Yes, I went back to my office after our talk yesterday and realized that I had not seen anything in you that fit with a need to be here in a mental hospital. You obviously have a major problem and mystery to solve, and a lot of major adjustments to make. But your problems are not something that the repertoire of Napa State Hospital is not capable of dealing with, that is if anybody can understand what you told me about."

"So, what is the plan?"

"Well, I have to run over to Unit A-9 for two new admissions, and you have to get moved down to Unit A-1. I have ordered some more information from Bakersfield that may help you. At least, it will fill in gaps for you. And, when I was in my office at church yesterday afternoon, I found something else that might interest you."

"You have an office at the Mormon church?"

"Yes, I'm the bishop for one of the wards here in Napa."

"Oh." Naomi furrowed her brow at Partridge. That was something new to think about.

Partridge handed her a single piece of paper, "That is a printout of your LDS Church records online. You were baptized into the church at age 8 in St. George, Utah, by Elder David Donnelley, your father. You and your mother are shown as members of a Church ward down in Bakersfield. I changed your mother's records to show her date of death."

Naomi looked at the paper without words.

"Naomi, you get yourself settled in down in A-1. It should be a bit more comfortable than here. I will try to set aside some time maybe late this morning, so we can talk about how we can help you move on in life. Then, hopefully tomorrow, I'll have more information on your background and we can talk again." Partridge smiled and said, "See you later."

———

Chapter 8

"Here it is, Naomi. Home sweet home," Mindy, the young woman who was introduced to Naomi as the Unit A-1 social worker, said. "Don't get used to having no roommate. We rarely have one empty bed, let alone two. It's just that both prior occupants were moved out Friday. And, we are waiting to see who the next incoming patient is to see if you get paired up with her or one of our other patients. We try to make sure the age and… uhh… the condition of the roommates is a good match."

"Did those two that left get discharged?" Naomi asked.

"One did, Karina. She went to a halfway house in Hayward. The other gal we had in here went the other direction. We had to send her back to A-9 for a little bit more supervision and control than we have here in A-1," Mindy said as she patted the bed by the far wall. "Since you're first one in here, you probably want to claim the bed by the window, away from the door. A little more privacy. The window doesn't have any view, just the side of the next building, but it has sunlight. You're lucky this is a two-person room, many have four in them. Just put your things in the bureau here, the clothing that is. I see you have magazines; you can put them on the shelf on your nightstand, or wherever. It's your place. Toiletries in your bureau drawer or the bathroom. Common shower three doors down on the right. Keep anything you don't want your roommate to maybe try out in the bureau; they have a couple of drawers. The unit rule is you never get into a roommate's stuff. Oh, and this," Mindy picked up a brown teddy bear with heart-shaped eyes and pink ribbon around its neck and tossed it to Naomi, "This is a pass down from Karina. Karina said she helped her, and maybe she has some more love for the next girl."

"What's her name?"

"No idea about that."

"Well, I guess she ought to be Karina then," Naomi said, setting the bear on her bed. "Thanks for the welcome, Karina."

"So, make yourself at home. Lunch in an hour or so. You can eat in your room or in the common area. That would be a good time to meet the other women here. After lunch, a physical therapist is scheduled to take you to the gym and rehab area, they want you to get some strength therapy after your months in bed. Bye for now. Welcome to A-1," Mindy said as she turned and left without waiting for any response.

———

As he had promised, Doctor Partridge scheduled an appointment for Naomi shortly after she arrived in Unit A-1. From A-1, it was only a short elevator ride up one floor to Partridge's office. The nurse in A-1 told her she could go up by herself and check in at the counter near the doctor's office.

Partridge was seated at his desk when Becca, his nurse receptionist, showed Naomi in. He motioned Naomi into the chair in front of his desk.

"Naomi, I wanted to talk with you, get some more information and see how you are doing. Are you comfortable there, or would you like to go over there and get comfortable?" Partridge pointed to the couch and armchair on the far wall.

Naomi looked over and smiled, "Lounging on the shrink's couch? Nice touch that. But, no, I'm good here."

Partridge nodded, "I thought I'd offer. How have you been? I can't imagine what has been going on in your head, trying to take all of this in. Are you handling this alright?"

"I'm not sure what 'handling this' entails. Everything I do is somewhat weird. Every time I say something, it sounds alien. Looking in the mirror while I brush my teeth is like watching a Twilight Zone episode with some stranger mimicking my moves in the mirror. Everything keeps recycling in my brain with me trying to figure out some logical answer for where I find myself.

"Last night, the nurse gave me a sleeping pill. It didn't really work at first. I lay there for an hour or so, just thinking about all of this. Thoughts about what this thing that happened to me is, what it means, what is behind it all. Then, when I did sleep I had a horrible nightmare about the accident. I sort of knew it was a dream but I couldn't wake up. I think I had another dream about being all tied up and helpless. I finally woke up fighting with my blanket."

Partridge nodded and wrote something on a notebook. "Tell me about the thoughts you had while you were awake. Let's talk about them."

"The conversation we had yesterday kept churning in my mind, again and again. This bizarre situation I am in defies understanding. How am I supposed to deal with waking up with someone else's outward appearance and with everything I have ever worked for in my life having disappeared, except for the memories of that life?"

Naomi cleared her throat.

Partridge asked, "Can I get you a water?"

"That would be good."

Partridge went to a small office refrigerator in the corner that Naomi had not noticed before and got her a bottle of water. "Here, please continue."

Naomi took a sip and recapped the bottle, "The oddest thing is the act of simply thinking about myself. You know, a person's self-image is the central focus of most of their thoughts and ideas. The self-image I have grown used to over many years abruptly disappeared last Friday night, and this physical appearance is so new and strange to me that I have to continuously picture the view of Naomi's face in the mirror as I think about myself. And, since I have told myself I need to consider myself as being Naomi, I have this weird argument with myself, in my brain, that the face is my face, not Naomi's. Then I think, no, my face **is** Naomi's face. It is really weird having thoughts like that in your head. Arguing with myself over who I am. I have to get used to being Naomi. God, I even have to change how I think about myself. I am Naomi! Then I wonder, can I act like Naomi, too, even if my thoughts are not hers. Should I?"

Partridge said, "Given what we have learned about you, those thoughts are probably to be expected. I understand. What else?"

Naomi swallowed another sip of water and said, "All the little lessons I learned about myself as I grew up and went through life, about my capabilities, my strengths, my weaknesses are now hopelessly skewed for me as this brand-new Naomi. I keep having to double check my thoughts to make sure I am thinking correctly about myself." She tapped her temple with her finger for emphasis. "Simple things every person knows, like personal hygiene and grooming, are a mystery in this new body. I was wondering if my basic values have changed. Am I still that person I was, with a pretty solid grounding in life and basic values, or am I this young woman who got herself sent to this place?

"The life of this person I now am is so different from that I have lived. Is this Naomi's life now mine? Or, can I create my own life? Shouldn't such simple concepts and thoughts be automatic? I find them difficult to grasp. This is really confusing to me. I can't imagine what to think about the more complex things like sexuality, hopes, dreams, and life goals. I find these questions nearly impossible to even think about. Should I still feel the same way about things. Has my emotional center been ripped out and replaced along with my physical self. Things I have always taken for granted are not so certain any more. I used to know how I felt about almost everything in life. Has that changed, too? Should it change? Should I try to change it?"

As Naomi paused, Partridge sat up straighter and said, "Wow, Naomi. You make my job easier with your openness. I was trained to try and pry those insights out of a patient, and here you spill them out for me like... like you are an intern or a colleague reporting on a case."

Naomi thought for a moment and then said, "Actually, Doc, I have to disagree. I am not giving you any insights at all. All I have are questions. I'm just repeating for you everything I went over three or four times last night. Lots of questions and problems; no insights."

Partridge laughed, "I think it is a matter of terminology. In my line of work, often just knowing enough to ask the right questions is an insight as to what the problem is. In this odd problem you have presented us with, you have a unique case and you seem to have done a good job focusing on what you need to know to move forward. That makes my job as a psychiatrist easier."

Naomi frowned, "So, you are looking at this as a psychiatric problem still?"

Partridge shook his head, "No, no, not at all. It is just that I am a psychiatrist who has a patient who has an absolutely unique and mysterious event she is dealing with and I need to make sure the profound changes she is faced with don't cause any more problems for her. I feel totally incompetent to answer the question of what happened to her, but I can try to help her cope with it. That is a psychiatrist's stock in trade."

"Sounds fair," Naomi said. "And on that question, I went around and around on that last night, too, and all day today. And, I'm guessing I will be working on the question of what happened to me for a long time to come.

She continued, "There is no explanation for what happened to me. At least in my experience and knowledge. I had a comparative religion class in college. BYU let me, as a non-Mormon, take it to fulfill my religion requirement. I know that several religions include in their beliefs the concept of rebirth after death. Some believe in reincarnation. The Christianity I learned in Sunday School in Stockton is based on an act of spiritual rebirth and life after death. You, Mormons, put your twist on that by believing that every person is a spirit that existed before this world existed, comes here to an Earthly existence to live their life and then continues on in the next world with connections to the other spirits in the hereafter. I have read of other religions with ancient stories of people being taken over by other spirits, like the Catholic legends of exorcism and demonic possession. But, much of those are legends and mythology, something I don't believe in. Yet, something akin to that is now the central feature of my life."

Partridge nodded, "I have tried to make sense of what happened to you in light of my beliefs, but it goes beyond what I can explain."

Naomi continued, "Yeh, my soul, my spirit, seems to have jumped from a dead body to the body of someone else a few miles away. It is truly confounding. A quirky supernatural event has transformed my life.

"I keep thinking about the idea that you mentioned, that the person I used to be was a good person who died horribly, and perhaps before my time, while Naomi was on the last legs of a downward spiral. Thinking about what happened to me as some sort of karmic blessing somehow reassures me.

"You mentioned when we were discussing it before that this was a kind of miracle and that 'It is by faith that miracles happen.' Right?" Naomi asked.

"Yes, that is a passage from the scriptures."

"Well, in my case it looks like the miracle happened all by itself, because I cannot have faith in something when I don't even know what exactly happened. That is not a question of faith. Is it?"

Partridge answered, "What happened to you is very real, so the religious issue of needing to have faith to believe this twist your life took last Friday is not a factor. It is now your reality and you have shared it with me, so it is my reality, too. You need no faith to believe this, it really happened. However, it might be reassuring to have a glimmer of faith that there is a higher purpose behind what has happened to you. Perhaps in your case, the faith involved in your miracle is the faith to believe that it happened for a reason. You need to persevere and find out more about that reason or purpose."

Naomi smiled, "I guess that thought and hope is what separates me from insanity. When you loose your grip on reality, you must have faith that the there is a reason for the way things are."

"Yes, Naomi, while understanding how this happened to you would be rewarding to know, the real problem you face is was how to best deal with this new life you have been given. My job is to help you with that. Your faith has to be focused on your life. Your best choice will be to create as good a life for Naomi as you can."

Naomi smiled and nodded, "That seems to be a good place to start."

But what life can I create? What destiny will I face in this new life?

———

When Naomi came down after meeting with Partridge, it was lunch time. She decided to eat lunch in the A-1 common area, and it resulted in several of the current residents of the unit coming over to introduce themselves to her. The two patients who sat at the table with Naomi were older women, Barbara and Marilyn. They had been friendly and asked Naomi many questions about herself. Naomi's answers were necessarily vague. But, when Naomi returned the questions to them, she got answers that clearly exhibited why the two women were in a mental hospital. Naomi would need some further thought to digest the supposed life stories of Barbara and Marilyn.

Naomi was placing her lunch tray in the slot in the rolling cart when one of the psychiatric technicians, a young Filipino man, came up to her.

"Naomi, if you're done with lunch, Doctor Partridge has ordered some medical tests for you that you have to go over to the clinic to get done. We don't do them in this unit. There are several things, like getting an EEG while you are conscious. I guess they did one Saturday while you were sedated."

"Yes, he mentioned that. What do I need to do?"

"Well, the clinic is at the rear of the center building here. You can go there yourself, but I can take you over if you want. You just go out the back door to our unit and go left through the passageway about halfway down. You'll need to have your patient ID badge on that we gave you this morning."

"Yeah, I'd like to try getting there myself. A little freedom never hurts. Huh?"

"Okay, get your ID badge and pick up the lab request forms from the nurses' station before you go. Oh, and, since you're new here, just go to the clinic and back, no sightseeing. Them's the rules. Okay?"

"Will do. Oh, I was told I was supposed to do physical therapy after lunch."

"If Rehab stops in to get you before you get back, we'll tell them to reschedule. Both clinic and therapy are important."

———

Naomi had taken her glasses off to put her scrunchie on her ponytail before heading to the clinic, and she had forgotten to put the glasses back on. She needed to get used to wearing glasses and remembering them, as Mark had perfect eyesight. Naomi regretted not having her glasses since she was trying to find her way in a hallway filled with offices and direction signs. She thought about going back to get the glasses but continued. She had to get fairly close to read the signs. She finally found a double door marked, 'Clinic— Labs— Dental — Optician — X-ray — Phys. Rehab.

There was a counter inside the door where Naomi showed her three lab requests. The young male technician took them from her and read them.

"Okay, take this one down and sit on that third bench on the right side of the hall. They will come out for you. Come back here, and I'll give you the next one and directions," the technician handed her one of the forms.

The clinic hallway was busy with staff, patients on their own, and patients escorted by orderlies. Naomi counted the benches as she passed and sat down on a wooden bench next to a sign labeled 'EKG/EEG/Stress.' There was nobody else on her bench, but on the other side of the hallway, on either side of the women's restroom, the benches were full waiting on 'Dental' and 'Optician.'

As Naomi sat on her bench, she could not help but take notice of the people around her. The people on the benches seemed to be in a queue, getting up and moving closer to the doors they were waiting for as the closest person was called. All by herself, Naomi seemed to be on the correct end of her bench, waiting for her EEG test.

The patients sitting on the two benches in front of her were a mixed bag. Some, both men and women, were in civilian clothes like her, and others in khaki and orange patients' outfits. Two of those in orange at the front of the long Optician line had two orderlies hovering over them, watching their every move.

Directly across the hall from Naomi, at the end of the Dental line and sitting right next to the door to the women's restroom, was a patient in khaki who caught Naomi's eye. He had sat down about when Naomi had. He was watching the people passing just as Naomi was, but his eyes flitted nervously from one to the other, with his head jerking as his eyes moved. He seemed nervous and almost afraid; his hands, arms, and jaw seemed shaky. He was repeatedly pressing and squeezing his knees and thighs with his hands. He was probably in his 30's, hair in a close buzz cut, and although he had moderate height and weight for a man, he had the same gaunt, hollow cheeks Naomi had seen in her first look at herself in the mirror. When he looked her way, Naomi realized she had been staring at him and turned her head quickly to look elsewhere. Naomi remembered Doctor Evans staring at her, and she found herself feeling sorry for this man and embarrassed at her stare.

There was a noise at the Dental door, and she turned to see a young Hispanic man who must have been a dental assistant pushing a cart with the two shelves of the cart loaded with what seemed to be used dental tools, dirty metal pans, and old towels. He had bumped into a female staffer and spilled a few of the metal dental utensils on the cart onto the floor. He apologized to the woman he had bumped and picked the items up, put them on the cart, and turned to walk down the hall past Naomi.

Like the other people sitting in the hallway, Naomi watched the dental assistant pass, but right when he was even with her, she saw the odd patient in khaki jump up and snatch something from the cart with one hand. He gave a strong push in the back of the dental assistant with the other hand. The dental assistant fell, sliding down the hall to Naomi's right with the now upended cart scattering its contents clattering on the floor.

Naomi now saw that the patient in khaki was now holding a scalpel. When other people on the benches saw this, they jumped up and ran either way. The woman on the rear end of the Optician line tripped and fell to the floor at the door to the restroom directly across the hall from Naomi. The armed man was only a few feet from Naomi, and she felt if she jumped up to escape, she would be even closer to him. Instead, she shrank back against the wall, thinking about whether she could slide down or go inside the closed door next to her to escape the danger.

This part of the hallway was now empty except for the scalpel-wielding patient, the woman on the floor, and Naomi. The closest people to them were the two orderlies who had been guarding the two patients in the Dental line, and the dental assistant on the floor with his cart and its contents. These orderlies took up defensive positions, arms wide, facing the man with the scalpel.

The patient with the scalpel now kept turning nervously, trying to watch each end of the hallway. He held the scalpel out in front of him and bent his knees as though mimicking what he thought was a fighting stance. He said nothing, but his actions made his threat clear. The nervous jumpiness Naomi had seen earlier in this man was now magnified.

Seeing this man standing like this, Naomi's mind involuntarily turned to Mark's memories of his last weeks before his military deployment overseas. The Army had sent his transport company to Fort Benning for the pre-deployment weapons and combat training the truck drivers and mechanics never had before. The Army thought the additional combat training was wise before sending them into a battle zone like Afghanistan. In her memories, Naomi had a clear picture of Mark's buddies spending many hours with drill sergeants learning to fight and defend themselves.

Faced with this mental patient holding a scalpel just a few feet from her, her memory of Mark's training now focused on the hand-to-hand combat training classes, which had been taught by a short, wiry, female drill sergeant from Guam. The female sergeant had been the primary instructor for dealing with a knife or bayonet wielding enemy. She remembered the female drill sergeant flipping a fake wood and rubber Bowie knife to the burliest mechanic in Mark's company. She had told him to try and stab her, and then, when he attempted to, she had landed him on his back with the wooden knife in her hand in an instant. Each member of Mark's company had been shown the move. Then, they had gone over the move with each other time and again, until the necessary speed and three steps of the knife defense were ingrained in them.

The orderlies near the Optician desk were still standing on either side of the hallway, arms out, blocking the patient from going their direction. There was a crowd of patients and one nurse the other way, so the patient with the knife spun in that direction, still flipping his head to make sure nobody approached from either direction. His eyes flitted toward Naomi as he turned. Just as he turned, an older man in a lab coat emerged from the Dental door, probably the dentist, and he immediately turned to block the armed patient from reaching the crowd of patients behind him.

Naomi was still thinking about whether she was capable of reacting to this threat. She quickly looked down at her own somewhat frail arms, and then to the man standing in front of her. He grossly outweighed Naomi. She had even been assigned to go to physical therapy due to her months in bed in her coma. How could she think of taking on a tough physical task? But, Naomi had Mark's memory of the little female drill sergeant saying to the soldiers, 'It isn't about strength, it is about surprise, it is about speed and using your own body mass to overcome the enemy's advantages.'

Just as the armed patient took another nervous spin to watch behind him, a woman in green medical scrubs came out of the restroom door. She tripped over the patient still cowering there on the floor and stumbled toward the armed patient with his scalpel.

The patient turned and slashed at the woman. She brought her arm up in defense, and he cut her across the forearm, viciously. She staggered back against the restroom door again, stumbling on the patient on the floor. She fell on top of the other woman, bleeding profusely.

The attacker now stepped quickly sideways, away from the restroom door and the two women, which put him nearly on top of Naomi. When the patient turned his hand with the scalpel toward the two orderlies to block their advance toward him, Naomi had her chance.

In one motion, Naomi grabbed as tightly as she could to the lower forearm of the scalpel-holding hand as she rose to her full height and raised her hands above her head. As fast as she could move, Naomi planted her right foot on the floor close to the man and stepped with the other foot in between her body and the assailant, spinning in a basketball-like pivot. As she pivoted, she dropped her hands, let them follow the pivot, thus keeping the scalpel pointed toward the man, not her.

Now, the drill sergeant's magic came into play. With Naomi's body moving with the pivot, she did not have to have the strength to twist this man's arm, all she had to do was keep her grip on it, and her own body weight would twist the arm as she pivoted. By the time the man thought of using his bicep's lateral strength to stop Naomi's move, his arm was already 180 degrees around. A human arm that was twisted 180 degrees has little power of any sort, just pain.

The last piece of magic from the drill sergeant now began. With his arm twisted and pulled to the side by someone with feet planted behind him, and a firmly planted leg blocking his step back, the hostile patient lost his balance. He fell backward against Naomi's firmly planted leg and the bench, facing away from her and his free arm below him, trying to stop his fall.

Now, Naomi had the man's arm in her grip, with him in pain, off-balance, and the scalpel pointed away from both of them. At last, Naomi twisted her hands on the man's upper wrist, and his ligaments could not bear the pain. His hand reacted by flexing open, loosening the grip on the scalpel.

Instead of following the last instruction of the petite Guamanian drill sergeant to grab the weapon from the hand and stab back toward the enemy's torso or head in a killing blow, Naomi shook the partially open hand, which sent the scalpel flipping to the floor and bouncing to the feet of the dumbfounded orderlies.

The attacker shrieked in pain from his overstretched shoulder and elbow tendons. Naomi looked toward the open-mouthed orderlies for assistance, which did not immediately come.

Naomi looked the closest orderly in the eye and said, "A little help here. Maybe?"

Both orderlies now jumped in and took the patient from Naomi's grasp. The dentist and a nurse rushed forward to help the injured woman on the floor. When the nurse helped the woman away, the dentist helped the other patient off the floor, and then turned to Naomi, who had flopped herself back onto her bench, breathing hard.

"Are you alright, young lady?" the dentist asked.

Still catching her breath, Naomi just nodded her head and closed her eyes for a moment.

The dentist stuttered as he said, "That... That was utterly amazing, young lady. I have never seen anything like that."

Naomi opened her eyes, took another deep breath, and gave a meek smile to the dentist as she shrugged. Then, she modestly pulled the wide neck of the gypsy blouse back up from her arm to her shoulder.

The hallway was pandemonium. Several guards now rushed in, quite late to the dance. Two guards took the formerly armed patient off the hands of the orderlies. The dentist started to explain to a state hospital policeman in a green and khaki uniform what had happened. The policeman took notes and put the scalpel in a little evidence bag. Naomi could not hear what the dentist said to the cop in the noise of the chaotic hallway, but she saw the dentist point to her several times, shaking his head.

After talking to the dentist, the policeman came over to Naomi. Without saying anything, he bent over to read Naomi's patient ID badge, which hung around her neck on a chain. Then, he said, "Uh, Miss Donnelley, Doctor Waltham tells me you disarmed the patient with a knife?"

"No, scalpel. He had a scalpel," Naomi argued. Then, she realized this was unnecessary, as the policeman had the scalpel in a bag in his hand.

"Well, that is pretty much the same. Maybe worse," the policeman said as he probably wrote 'scalpel' in his notes. "And Doc Waltham said you used a pretty nifty martial arts move on that guy."

Naomi shrugged again.

"Jus' wondering. Where'd you learn to do a move like that against an armed man twice your size."

Naomi knew she had to lie to the policeman. She quickly thought of the most believable story for someone like her. "Rape self-defense class in high school."

"Jeesh! Where was that?"

Naomi thought for a second and said, "Bakersfield."

"Ah," said the cop, as though some mystery had been explained.

After Naomi finished answering the questions from the cop and the hallway had settled down somewhat, a technician in a lab coat walked up in front of Naomi. "What was it you were waiting for?"

Naomi looked around for the lab request form that had fallen to the floor. She retrieved it and handed it to the technician.

"EEG, that's me. Come on in. That was quite a show you put on," the technician said, pointing Naomi to his doorway.

Naomi stood and, once again, shrugged. That was the best response she had for this.

———

Naomi was in her robe, with her hair in a towel and shampoo in hand, walking back from the shower to her room. She now knew why her hair had been so gooey when she first felt it Saturday afternoon. EEG technicians plopped numerous dollops of electrical contact goo on the heads of their victims. She'd had an EEG before she awoke that first day, same as today.

When she had returned from her harrowing trip to the clinic, before she could take a shower, the physical therapist had arrived to take her to the therapy room for leg and upper body strength therapy. Naomi noted the irony there. The shower, when it finally came, was welcome.

Naomi opened the door to her room and was faced by a young woman in hospital khakis. The woman was part African, from her skin-tone, and had curly but not kinky coal black hair. Naomi guessed she was in her mid-20's. The woman was standing in the middle of the room, looking around. A small pile of possessions lay on the bed.

"Ah, a roommate," Naomi announced. Naomi stuck out her hand toward the woman and said, "Hi, I'm Naomi Donnelley."

The woman looked down at Naomi's hand for a moment as though she did not know what to do. Then, she took it and shook Naomi's hand, saying, "I'm Tiara La Forte. Sorry about that. I'm not used to a friendly greeting and handshake where I've been lately. And, sometimes I'm a little slow to get things. So, people say."

"No, prob. Where you comin' from?"

"I just got to Napa last week. They put me in A-9, then here. Before that, I was in Alameda County Jail for a long, long time."

"Yeah, I'd guess a big city jail isn't a very friendly place to be."

"Nah. Say, Naomi, I heard you are kind of a badass."

"What?" Naomi's voice broadcast her incredulity.

"The orderly told me when they brought me over here that I would be rooming with the badass gal who took a knife away from a guy, just like Bruce Lee. That true?"

Naomi shook her head, thinking. Then she said, "Well, it's true, but I sure wish they wouldn't introduce me to somebody like that."

"Well, it's not just the orderly. Everybody in A-9 was yakking about what you did. You're famous. They said the guy cut up some nurse really bad before you got him."

"Jeesh." Naomi walked around Tiara to her bed, sat down, and finished drying her hair with the blower she had left out.

Tiara sat on her bed, facing Naomi, saying, "Come on, tell me what happened. You sure don't look like a knife fighter."

—

Chapter 9

Tiara was just coming back from her first breakfast in A-1 when Naomi came out of the bathroom. Naomi had the gray slacks, white blouse, and black shoes on. She had debated the wearing of a bra, but resolved it went with fitting into the mold into which she had been cast. With a little experimenting, she had mastered the regular bra's workings and hooks. With her hair brushed, a little eye make-up on, and her glasses in place, Naomi thought she looked nice. She had tried to match the look of the girl in the pictures in her wallet.

Tiara confirmed Naomi's opinion, "Whoa, what you all dressed up for?"

"I've got a doctor's appointment this morning."

"You have to dress up to go to the doctor?"

"No, you don't. But, the word is the Doc is planning on getting me sprung from here, and I want to act and look like I don't belong here."

"Well, you've got that look pegged. I'm glad you don't have to dress for the doctor, cuz this is all I have to wear." Tiara fingered the khaki suit.

"You don't have anything coming, or maybe from family?"

Tiara laughed loudly, "Ha, not likely, everybody I know got busted along with me, and my Ma probably hopes I'm dead. She's had to deal with my problems too many times. I've been wearing those darned striped jail jumpsuits for months. They gave me this when I came here in the van. I got a laugh over the social worker telling me about my rights to wear my own clothes."

Naomi stopped brushing her hair. She looked at Tiara's hips, and then her own. She raised her eyebrows at the possibility and said, "Tiara, you want a loaner outfit. You'd have to give it back to me, okay. We're about the same size, but you're a little taller."

Tiara answered, "Uh, yeah, sure. Watcha got?"

Naomi opened the sliding door on her bureau. She handed the black stretchy jeans to Tiara and asked, "What color t-shirt you want? Green, pink, or baby blue?"

Tiara took the black jeans and said, "Green."

Naomi found the t-shirt in the drawer and turned to hand the forest green t-shirt to Tiara. She found her roommate already out of the khaki shirt and was flipping the pants toward her bed with her foot. Tiara was in a plain white sports bra and cotton panties that bespoke 'jail issue.' Naomi saw from the sports bra's heft that Tiara had her outmatched in that department.

Tiara was slipping into the t-shirt when Naomi announced, "I'll see how you look when I get back. I gotta run."

Naomi headed for the nurses' counter to check out of the Unit and head upstairs to Doctor Partridge's office.

———

Naomi waited by the receptionist's counter in the physician's office hallway, then when Becca told her to she went and knocked on Doctor Partridge's partially open door.

She heard Partridge say, "This must be her," as though talking to someone else. "Come in!"

Naomi opened the door and found herself facing both Partridge and a state hospital police officer. This policeman was a huge man, as tall as Partridge and well-muscled, with a carrot-red crew-cut. Naomi saw captain's bars on his tan uniform collar.

"This is her?" queried the cop, staring at Naomi, curiously.

"Yes, Naomi, let me introduce you to Captain Mortenson. The captain is our Napa State Hospital Police Chief. Captain, Naomi Donnelley."

Naomi's hand was lost in the huge handshake of the Police Chief.

"Let's have a seat," Partridge said, indicating Naomi should sit in the farther chair. The cop also sat, turning his chair to partly face Naomi, and Partridge went behind his desk and sat.

"Naomi, Captain Mortenson contacted me, as is our policy on talking with patients involved in an investigation. He is looking into the matter yesterday in the clinic. You may not be aware, but Napa has had some rough times involving assaults by patients on staff and other patients, including a death a few years ago. The captain needs to put together the facts from yesterday, and I told him I thought you would be happy to help out. Is that okay with you."

"Yes, sure."

The police chief turned in his chair a bit more toward Naomi. "I appreciate your helping me out with this. Now, I've read the report on this incident, including Doctor Waltham's statement and a few others. I've also seen your short statement to our officer. Oh, and I was able to watch the video from the hallway camera."

"I didn't know they had a video camera," Naomi said.

"Yes, the average patient may not be aware, but the busiest common areas are all on camera.

"So, other than the obvious problem with a technician rolling a cart of hazardous implements across in front of the open patient population at close quarters, which we will deal with… I need to address how the response to this dangerous incident fell to… pardon my description of you… to a somewhat petite

18-year-old girl, a patient, who found herself in harm's way and had to act without the aid of several NSH staff members, who apparently stood by and watched."

The police chief stopped and looked to Naomi.

Naomi said, "I didn't hear a question there."

Naomi saw Partridge give a little smile at her comment.

The cop cleared his throat, took a breath, and said, "Miss Donnelley, I need to explain how this horrible incident that resulted in a nurse getting cut very badly and could have ended in far greater tragedy was handled, and how it was mishandled. I guess my first question to you would be, how did you learn to carry out the move you made on that maniac?"

"I told your officer that I learned that in a self-defense class in high-school."

The cop laughed, "Miss Donnelley, I watched the video. The speed and surety you moved to take that guy down is not taught in any rape defense class on God's Green Earth and certainly not in Bakersfield High School. After watching your video, I am not sure that many of the men and women on my force could handle a knife-wielding attacker like that."

Naomi kept a serious face when she answered, "I didn't go to Bakersfield High. I went to Centennial High."

"So, you are sticking to that?" the police chief asked, rather gruffly.

"Yes, that's my story, and I am sticking to it." Naomi tried not to smile. "But, why does it matter? I got the weapon away and nobody else was hurt." She decided to go further. "Look, Captain Mortenson, I am quite sure that Doctor Partridge knows exactly how it is I know how to make a move like that, but I told him in strict doctor/patient confidentiality. I will consent to him assuring you that there is a very good reason I know how to take the action I did and that there is nothing untoward about my knowing how to do it. Besides, the issue of where I learned to stop that guy is not germane, that simple fact is I knew how to act, and I did."

The cop frowned at this, "'Untoward' and 'germane?' You don't talk like a typical 18-year-old girl who didn't graduate from high school and is…."

Now Naomi was mad, "Is what? Locked in an insane asylum? Is that your concern? Just say it. I think Doctor Partridge can attest to the fact that I am not your usual 18-year-old crazy girl."

Partridge and Mortenson both started talking at the same time. Naomi interrupted them both, and said, with a clear air of sarcasm, "Captain Mortenson, since you appear to be a nice guy with a difficult task, let me give you a statement that should fit well into your report and says what I think you need to say. Try this — Naomi Donnelley found herself in a near-impossible situation. The attacker with the scalpel had just seriously injured a nurse who was positioned in almost the same danger zone as Miss Donnelley was. The two orderlies and Doctor Waltham were both protecting the patients along with staff behind them. But, they had no way of getting to the three women near the attacker without further danger to the women or themselves. When the attacker came close to Miss Donnelley, she realized she had to act, as the weapon was within inches of her face. So, she acted in the best way she thought possible, following some previous personal defense training she had and managed to disarm the hostile patient. The orderlies immediately moved in to capture the now disarmed attacker. — That's my full statement. I hope it helps. Oh, and if you want, I'd be happy to do a little training session for your officers. And, if possible, I'd like a copy of that video for my YouTube channel." Naomi ended with a semi-smug smile.

Naomi now turned away from the cop and toward Partridge, signaling that she thought the interview was over.

Captain Mortenson got the message and stood, "Thank you very much. If we have anything else, we'll be in touch. And, don't hold your breath waiting for the video."

Naomi nodded and gave the cop a perfunctory smile as he turned and left.

When the cop shut the door, Naomi turned to Partridge and gave him a real, self-satisfied smile.

Partridge smiled back and said, "Wow, life around Naomi gets interesting, doesn't it?"

Naomi raised her eyebrows and said, "I wouldn't really know, it is only my fifth day on the job as Naomi, but things seem to keep my attention well enough."

Partridge now held his hands out as though presenting something, as in 'Now look at you' and said, "I guess you realize this is not the look of my normal patient visiting my office."

"I tried hard. It is kinda new to me. It made me feel a wee bit weird to be trying."

"You indeed succeeded. I guess I don't have to ask whether Mark helped you out in your move on that guy in the clinic."

"Yes, Mark was most helpful. He has a good memory and had a really great drill sergeant at Fort Benning, a female, by the way, a little smaller than Naomi. In case you hadn't noticed it, I put Mark in charge of the conversation with Captain Mortenson."

"Yes, I saw that," Partridge said, as he moved a stack of papers over in front of him. "I've received a bit more information that you probably want to know to fill in your knowledge of your identity as Naomi. But first, how are you doing? That is, other than your exploits at the clinic yesterday. You doing alright?"

Naomi pursed her lips and said, "I'm doing well. Like I said yesterday I'm, of course, feeling a bit freaked out when I have to do feminine things, like trying to present a female façade in dressing and grooming. I've got a new roommate. She's a little older than me and seems to have been on the same bad career track as the old Naomi. I'm feeling fine, eating well. Started going to physical therapy." Naomi gave a quick flexing bicep motion with a smile, "When I say I'm feeling fine, eating well, maybe overly well. I keep freaking out the other women in A-1 when I keep snarfing down double meals. Oh, I had lunch yesterday with a movie star."

Partridge gave Naomi a questioning look for a second, and then smiled, "Oh, you mean Marilyn?"

"Yeah, is that really her name?"

"No, but don't try to tell her that."

"I see. Over lunch yesterday, Marilyn gave me a rather complete rundown on her friends and boyfriends like Tab Hunter and Rock Hudson, and her ex-husband Joe Garagiola. She doesn't seem to know they are all dead now. I certainly am glad I didn't run into her before you helped me find some proof I really am me. It would have been very depressing knowing I was just another crazy female sitting around Napa, thinking I was really somebody else. Marilyn, Barbara, and Naomi all commiserating together about their imaginary identities."

"You've met Barbara, too, then."

"Yes, she thought I'd make a great actress in a forthcoming commercial for her cosmetics line."

"Since I really can't talk with you about my other patients, let's get on with reviewing the new information I have gotten about Naomi, pardon, about you, and let you know how I plan on proceeding. And, on that point, I think we ought to both get into the mode of talking about Naomi, whether you, the person sitting here or the other Naomi back in Bakersfield, as just 'you.' Because, whether we are talking about some miracle, or your cute idea of supernatural possession, or whatever happened, the fact is that you are Naomi, and you are going to have to deal with her history and put her life back together. Agreed?"

"Good. Agreed, I am already doing that in my head. At least most of the time. I find myself thinking of the girl back in Bakersfield, as somebody else. But, this person here, in this body, is me. Sometimes Mark is asking himself what Naomi would do in this situation. And other times, I am thinking about what I, this girl, should be doing. And, I'm trying to act the way I think she would act, as well as dress and groom myself as she would, which is kinda weird, for now. But, it seems to be more natural than I would have thought."

Doctor Partridge nodded, wrote something down on his pad, and continued, "Kern County was really prompt in getting me what I asked for. It seems the Social Services and Mental Health offices had gathered most everything to put together their LPS petition for you. Fortunately, most of the evidence they used to justify a finding that you were mentally impaired was situational evidence, not a clear face-to-face diagnosis by a professional. For example, the clinical psychologist who did the main report on you used reports from the school about you talking to people who weren't there, and police reports of your arrests talking about your condition with delusions and irrational fears to make the diagnosis. In any normal circumstance, that might be a valid basis for a professional opinion. However, with the clear evidence of long-term drug use and the rather unique medical situation you had with the multi-drug intestinal blockage, I think I can make a good argument that your mental problems seem to be based solely on the drug use and not on any organic psychiatric malady."

"And that will get me out of here?"

"Slow down, Naomi. That diagnosis will be the foundation of what will get you out of here. Unfortunately, Napa State Hospital is a state government bureaucracy, and there are procedures we must follow for everything. Since two doctors in Bakersfield and a judge in a long black robe have all declared you mentally incompetent, it is going to take two of us here to declare you restored to competency with a report to send back to Bakersfield, so the judge will agree, and get you on your way back to life and freedom. The process is not overnight. If everything goes right for you, it could still be weeks before you see results."

"So, I have to tell my bizarre story to one of your colleagues and get somebody else to believe me?" Naomi sounded despondent as she said this.

"No, no. Not exactly. Frankly, I am not a big fan of my trying to explain your 'miracle' to anyone. What you and I need to do is convince one of my colleagues that the Naomi standing in front of them is clearly mentally competent and has a record of problems that can be explained by drug or alcohol use. I think I, or we, can do that. But, I also have a problem that I cannot ethically counsel my patient to try and lie to my medical colleague."

"I can see that, so what do we do?"

"That is why I asked for as complete a dossier on Naomi Donnelley as I could. I have your school records, the full report on your stepfather's assault on you and your mother, all the arrest and a mental health records on you, a synopsis of your mother's health record upon her death last Spring. And, I pulled a good number of tidbits from the Internet on the life and times of Naomi Donnelley. What I plan on doing is making sure you have enough information about your life so that when I send you over to Dr. Karen Richards for a second opinion, you can present yourself, in all honesty, as the bright and positive young lady I see in front of me. You need to be someone who knows all about her life and plans on correcting her past drug problems and moving on with life. I see nothing about you that signals a mental disorder, and Dr. Richards will not either. She specializes in drug-related disorders, which is perfect for you. And, you and I will keep your 'miracle' to ourselves."

Naomi's joy was apparent as she said, "Sounds good. When do we start?"

Doctor Partridge put his hand on the large stack of papers before him and said, "I have cleared my calendar for this morning, and I assume you don't have any prior commitments, we can start your education on yourself right now."

"Aye, professor, Naomi 101 it is."

——

Naomi left the doctors' floor and pushed the down button in the elevator with both a sense of excitement and a good helping of depression. The potential of release from this mental hospital brought excitement. Spending an hour or more with Doctor Partridge saying things like "You were expelled from high school after assaulting a girl in art class," and "The arresting deputy said you were muttering incoherently and threw up on him when he was questioning you" was depressing. To think of herself as this Naomi with so many dire problems bordered on shocking. But, the Naomi 101 class had been a success, Naomi felt she knew enough about herself to tell the psychologist about her drug problem and tough life back home. And, she had copies of most of Partridge's 'Naomi dossier' to study.

A few steps from her room door in A-1, Naomi saw Tiara come out. Tiara had Naomi's black pants and green t-shirt on.

"Looking good, Tiara."

"Thanks, I appreciate the loan," Tiara quickly turned away, heading for the back door.

Naomi said, "You're in a hurry. Where ya going?"

"I found out there is a library. Mindy said she would take me over. Ya wanna come?"

Naomi started to think to herself that Tiara did not seem the book-loving type, when Tiara explained, "These old women here are obsessed with soap operas and talk shows on the one television, and I really will be crazy if I have to endure that torture. I figure almost any book to read will be better."

It sounded good to Naomi; she had gone through all of her four magazines a couple of times. She said, "Hold on, let me get rid of my papers. I'll go, too."

Mindy escorted Tiara, Naomi, and a quiet older woman who did not introduce herself down the back hallway past the clinic. Mindy took a seat on a bench by the door and motioned the three patients into the library.

A silver-haired, very elderly woman with a 'Volunteer' badge came over to welcome them, "Welcome to the Library. Have you ladies been here before?"

The older woman nodded yes and went her way. Tiara and Naomi waited for the woman to continue.

"Everything on the shelves and on the back wall, and over there are books for checking out. You can check out a book for three weeks and renew it twice. The books over on the table and in the boxes behind the table are donations that we didn't think would be popular for lending purposes. So, if you want any of those, they will be yours to keep, and I'll put your name in them as your property. Any questions?"

Tiara and Naomi followed the older patient back to the shelves to look around.

Naomi quickly discovered it was a library in name only, quite disorganized. Everything was grouped only by book type and genre. The biggest selection was in romances, action-adventure, and sci-fi paperbacks. There was a smattering of fiction and non-fiction hardcovers, but they were all well-used to the point of being borderline worn out.

Naomi decided to give the donated books a try. Many of the books on the table were obviously donations of private persons' self-help and non-fiction books. There were a couple income tax guides from previous years, many self-help guides on dieting, marital dysfunction, and the like. Seeing nothing of interest on the table, Naomi started digging into the boxes.

In the second box she scrounged in, something caught her eye. It was a large, very thick, hardcover book with a bright pink and gold cover, titled "Lippincott Manual of Nursing, 10th Edition." It looked almost unread, but Naomi checked the copyright date, and it was a few years old. Inside the front cover, she found an owner's name label announcing the book belonged to 'Rikki Janssen, R.N.' Right below the nursing book was a nearly new copy of Van de Graaf & Fox's human anatomy textbook. It had the same name in the front. After thumbing through the pages of the two books a bit, Naomi decided these were her choices. She had enjoyed the nursing magazine Doctor Evans had given her, and these two books were much the same, only more technical. Having something technical to read enthused the old Mark part of her that had a university bio-science degree.

Naomi took the books to the volunteer librarian and told her, "These are from the donated books by the table."

The librarian looked at the two massive books, and then looked at Naomi. "Yes, I saw these two. I think the 11th edition is out, and this is the 10th edition, but it still should be useful. The anatomy book is nice, too. I'm glad we have someone who can use them."

She checked inside the front covers and put two white Napa State Hospital labels over Rikki Janssen's name and asked, "Your name, Miss?"

Naomi told her, spelling it out. The librarian wrote the name in black felt-tip in the books and handed them to Naomi, "All yours. Enjoy."

"Thank you very much," Naomi said, and looking at the woman's name tag added, "Mrs. Waverly."

As Naomi was turning away to go sit by Mindy at the door, Mrs. Waverly added, "You are most welcome. We don't get many staff in here."

Naomi wondered what Mrs. Waverly was talking about. When she sat next to Mindy on the bench and opened her new possessions, she found out what Mrs. Waverly's confusion was. She had covered up the previous owner's name, but not her title. The books were now declared to be the property of 'Naomi Donnelley, R.N.,' and the little 'Napa State Hospital' imprint on each label gave the ownership a hint of authority. Naomi's outfit, demeanor, and book choice had faked the old woman out, and Naomi kind of liked that.

———

Chapter 10

Naomi sat at one of the foodservice tables in A-1. As was usual, she was the last to finish breakfast, both because of her affinity for seconds and because she had brought her Nursing Manual with her to read. In the days since she got the book, she had read well into the Nursing Practice and Process Section, skipping at times to the Psychiatric Nursing Section. She nibbled on her bagel and cream cheese as she read.

"Are you Naomi?" came a question in a woman's voice from slightly behind her.

Naomi turned to look. Seeing a woman in a lab coat, she answered, "That's me."

"Oh, I walked right by you a sec ago. I saw a nicely dressed woman reading a Lippincott's and thought you were staff," said the woman in her late 30's with dark brown well-coiffed hair and distinctive make-up.

"I get that a lot. You recognized my book?"

"Yes. A huge pink book like that is pretty easy to recognize. I had one just like it in grad school."

"And you are?" Naomi asked.

"Oh, I'm sorry, how rude of me. I'm Karen Richards, Doctor Richards. I'm the clinical psychologist that Doctor Partridge wanted to talk to you."

"That's great. He mentioned you, and I've been waiting to hear from you."

"May I sit down?"

"Sure, but you want to talk here?"

"Oh, no. Just to get to know each other. I'll find an office we can use, and we can talk about details later this morning or this afternoon." Richards sat across the table from Naomi.

"You don't have an office?" Naomi asked. "Sorry if that is a weird question, I just thought…."

Richards laughed, "Oh, I have an office, but my main patient load is in the Secure Area, not here in Program 4. You really would not want to go to my usual office. It is basically behind bars. I do drug and alcohol counseling of the criminal commitments, you know, Forensic cases."

"I'm sorry, I really don't know anything about that. I've heard there is a secure prison area somewhere around here."

"Yes, most of Napa State Hospital is behind bars, and barbed wire fences, your area here is nothing like that."

"I see."

"So, I've gotten Larry's… sorry, Doctor Partridge's report that he wants me to compare notes on. He seems to think that you don't belong here and that my expertise in substance abuse may hold the key to that opinion."

"That's what I understand. And, if I am allowed an opinion, I agree with him." Naomi smiled.

"Well, if first impressions are any guide, it would seem there may be something to Doctor Partridge's diagnosis. I'll get word to you when and where we can talk; that should be today, though."

As they had spoken, the pages of Naomi's book had flipped closed, but the cover remained open, exposing the owner's name inside the cover. As Doctor Richards finished speaking, she reached across the table and fingered the name, questioning, "Naomi Donnelley, R.N.?"

"Yeah, when I picked up my books, the lady thought I was a nurse and put my name like that."

"Well, I sort of had that same problem just now, didn't I? I guess a secret identity is nothing unusual for Supergirl."

"Uh, pardon?" Naomi gave a confused look.

"Oh, you hadn't heard that. It seems the guy you took down in the clinic was sent over to the criminal lock-up area due to his armed assault and battery of a nurse, and he told everyone about the blonde gal who had moved like lightning and took away his knife before he knew what happened. He made you famous over there. The men in the Program 3 section are telling stories about the beautiful, blonde Supergirl in the LPS Program."

"Yeah, I've kinda made a name for myself over here too, but not Supergirl."

"You know, Naomi, there are worse things people could be saying about you." Richards smiled, "See you later."

———

Naomi looked around the staff meeting room she had been brought to for the doctor's interview while Doctor Richards typed something on her laptop. There was not much of interest to see, just a bulletin board with Worker's Compensation notices, workplace harassment warning and safety posters and a 'Roommate Wanted - Female' Post-it.

Richards now continued, "We are getting toward the end here. I need to hear from you what you expect to be doing when you get released. Where will you stay, and what are your plans?"

Naomi tried to think of something positive to say, but she recognized that Doctor Richards was an expert at determining when a patient was just telling a story or trying to cover something up. So, Naomi's answer was, "I want to get my high school credits finished up, and I have really been thinking about some kind of nursing training, if I can, given my background. But, with my mother deceased and my stepfather in prison, I don't really have anybody to help me get settled. My attorney in Bakersfield wrote to me that she had settled my mother's estate and put our family stuff in storage. She mentioned a small insurance policy from her work on my mother's estate, but I am not sure how far that will go to get me settled."

"I'm glad to hear that you have thought about those things. I …."

Naomi interrupted, "Doctor Richards, since your question was about what I would do 'when' I am released, you know, is that an indication of, well…."

Richards smiled, "… of what I plan on recommending for you. Well, yes, it is. I plan to second Doctor Partridge's diagnosis and recommendation. I don't see any indication whatsoever of any organic mental disorder, or any current indication that you ever did have a mental problem that would justify commitment to a mental hospital. But, I have to tell you, that with your history of substance abuse, I am not pleased with the prospect of you going back to Bakersfield without any support structure in place. According to the reports, although you don't seem to remember much about it, you have been abusing alcohol since your early teens, and over the last year, you have moved on to some really hard drugs, and a mix of them at that. You have exhibited a fantastic attitude toward dealing with that. Still, Doctor Partridge and I need to talk about what can be put in place to support your good attitude with some infrastructure of support. That is mostly a problem for the Kern County people, but we need to address it in our report to them."

Naomi responded, "That makes sense. Anything I can do?"

"Not really," Richards said as she pushed her laptop closed. "Doctor Partridge will be calling you in to talk about your options. Maybe he has some ideas. My usual patients in Napa's criminal lockup are never in quite the situation you present. But, I only have one more piece of parting advice…."

Naomi waited and said, "Yes?"

"The next time some guy pulls out a knife, back off and let someone else handle it. You really aren't Supergirl."

———

"Come in," came a voice from inside the partially open door to the office.

Naomi entered and saw Doctor Partridge hanging his lab coat up on the coat tree.

"Naomi, welcome," Partridge said cheerfully as he saw her. "Ah, 'California Girl' shirt and a ponytail, looking like a teenager. That's a good look, too."

Naomi had been in her hole-y, distressed blue jeans, and pink California girl t-shirt when she got the message to come to visit Partridge. She did a fashion show type pirouette to show off the outfit and sat in her usual chair.

Partridge sat down at his desk and asked, "How are you doing? Any problems?"

"No, nothi…," Naomi started to answer, and then stopped.

"What?"

Naomi looked at the floor and said, "I kinda got in a fight… no, an altercation, with a couple of staff members. One was a cop."

"What?" Partridge sounded shocked. "Explain."

Naomi sighed and started, "I was sitting in one of the armchairs in the unit dayroom, reading my book. These three staff members come through. It was some security consultant, with a female security guard and a hospital police officer.

"Anyway, they were apparently on some kind of security survey to look for dangerous conditions in hospital common areas. I noticed them, but paid no attention, just reading my book. The female guard came over to me and demanded I give her my book. I asked why. She said the security consultant had pointed out that there is some regulation that patients are not allowed any heavy or dangerous objects that can be used as weapons. Apparently, anything over five pounds is forbidden, since it could be used to injure someone if you hit them with it. She said my book looked much heavier than that, and I needed to surrender it. I refused."

Partridge interrupted, "What book are we talking about?"

"Lippincott's Manual of Nursing. It is a big pink book, probably well over five pounds. I have one. It is my property."

"I'm familiar with it. Go on."

"Well, when I refused to give it to her, the guard tried to pull it out of my hands. I wouldn't let go. I thought that declaring a book a dangerous object was stupid. We got into a tugging match over my book, and the cop stepped in to help the guard. Then, the head nurse for our unit saw the commotion of me fighting with a cop and a guard, and she ran over. The nurse screamed for everyone to stop. We did.

"I held on tight to my book while the cop and this security consultant explained the rule to the nurse. The nurse thought for a minute, and then told the cop that my reading the nursing manual was part of my Wellness and Recovery Planning Program, you know, preparation for a career. And, she said it was my personal property and within my LPS Patients' Bill of Rights to have. The head nurse said if they didn't leave me alone, she was going to turn them into the hospital director for interfering with my treatment and violation of my Patients' Rights. She basically told the security consultant that he could put his security regulation where the sun doesn't shine."

Partridge could not refrain from smiling at Naomi. "Another nice calm day around Naomi, huh?"

Naomi shrugged.

"I didn't know that anyone had actually done a WR Plan on you," Partridge said.

"Well, I don't think there is any written plan, as such, but Doctor Richards knows about my nursing manual, and I've talked about going into nursing with that head nurse and Clarissa, who's the social worker on my Wellness Team thingy. The head nurse was kind of winging it when she told the cop to back off."

"I'm supposed to be the leader of your Wellness Team 'thingy,' and although reading a two-thousand-page medical treatise is not a usual part of a Wellness and Recovery Plan, I'm glad that nurse took your side."

"1800 pages," Naomi clarified.

Partridge did not take Naomi's bait about the pages and continued, "What I asked you in for today is some good news for you and some serious advice."

Naomi smiled at the 'good news.'

"As I think Doctor Richards talked to you about, she and I have prepared our reports that conclude you have no true mental disorder caused by any physical or psychological dysfunction. Instead, we are concluding your problems are primarily drug and alcohol addiction, and use. Now, those addictions can have both physical and psychological reasons, but they are not something that needs to be treated as mental disorders, like the supposed 'possible schizoid disorder, psychotic related hallucinations' diagnosis the county mental health people put in your LPS commitment order."

"Thank you."

"You're welcome, but it wasn't us doing you a favor, it was the truth. But, Doctor Richards mentioned she talked to you about her concerns about sending a drug addict and alcohol abuser back into society without some kind of support structure."

Naomi interrupted, "But, you and I both know that I am not the same person as that addict who came in here."

Partridge nodded, "Two things on that. Regardless of what you and I may know about 'Naomi's miracle,' the fact remains that Doctor Richards has outlined her concerns for this patient, and the officials in Kern probably will have the same concerns. Sending an 18-year-old drug addict back on the streets requires the professionals involved to do some planning. And on that exact point, there is something about Naomi's weaknesses and addictions that the 'Mark' in you may be powerless to handle given what you and I have discovered about this 'miracle.'"

"Huh?"

"I am going way out on the limb here, being that I am diagnosing a condition that has never been known in science, nor even any metaphysics or religion I know of. Having watched you and listened to you from the first day we met, I have noticed some indications that in spite of you sincerely and probably correctly believing you have all of Mark's thoughts, memories, and even his soul, that there are still some distinctive parts of the original Naomi hanging around, besides her physical body. Let me explain.

"During our first conversation, you mentioned to me three things you, yourself, had noticed. You mentioned the odd vocal accents and voice inflections that seemed to be Naomi's and not Mark's. You said you noticed yourself reacting emotionally 'like a girl.' And then, you talked about suddenly becoming left-handed like Naomi had been, and we determined that you signed your signature identically to the way the original Naomi did.

"During that first meeting, I also noticed a couple of things I did not discuss with you at the time that play into this diagnosis or advice I am giving you now. And also, there have been other indications of what I am going to say next I have seen in your actions since then. What I am talking about here is that when we looked at Mark's picture, you indicated that you, as Naomi, thought he was attractive, and you might have liked to meet him. Then, you were openly embarrassed to have said something about you going on a date with a girl. Those are both decent indications that our 'new' Naomi is acting and thinking like a typical 18-year-old heterosexual girl who is attracted to the opposite sex, not Mark's old attraction focus. Added to that is your actions in the intervening weeks, you have adopted the dress, grooming, and habits that real Naomi would have. That attractive, well-groomed young woman who walked into our meeting with Captain Mortenson was not some geeky male masquerading as a female; it was a real young woman who knew how to look proper."

"I get it, Doctor. And I agree. I have noticed myself doing things that were certainly not natural to what Mark would have done. But, what is the point of that regarding my addictions?"

"I'll get to that in a second. I have one more; I just learned about."

Naomi flipped her hands open toward Partridge, inviting him to finish.

"Our old Mark was a university-trained computer science and biotechnology professional, happy with his career choice and apparently fairly good at it. The young 'California Girl' in front of me has apparently, all on her own, decided she wants to choose a career of nursing. The empathy and care-giving mentality that would lead you to want to be a nurse are, I think, something coming from the Naomi in you, not from Mark."

Naomi nodded, "Agreed, I have thought of that same thing. But, nursing is what I decided I wanted to do, from my heart." Naomi slapped her hand over her heart to emphasize this.

"Exactly, and whether we say these last pieces of Naomi that keep popping up, or shining through, are said to come from the heart, or the subconscious or the wiring of Naomi's female brain, these are what I think I need to warn you about."

"Warn me?" Naomi furrowed her brow.

"Yes, warn you to be wary of as you head into this new life. All those interesting indications that some of Naomi still exists inside you have been either really unique and exciting, kind of cute, or sometimes really positive for your life. But if I am correct in my guess about this unusual case you have presented me, you have also been saddled with the brain and subconscious you inherited from the old Naomi.

"The brain chemical serotonin is directly affected through drug and alcohol addiction. The levels of serotonin become erratic through the process of addiction, and this can change the way the brain tells the body to act. Neuroscience is finding out more about addiction and how it influences the brain all the time. That is Doctor Richards' area of expertise. How the mind is affected by substances is a key factor in drug and alcohol dependency. It starts with incentive sensitization, a reward system with the brain. It results in the body becoming dependent on the drug to regulate the chemistry in the brain. If you and I are right, and you are stuck with Naomi's brain and subconscious, you need to be as cautious of getting back into the addiction cycle as if you were our old Naomi. Mark's good attitude and memories won't matter, if Naomi makes a mistake, and lets drugs and alcohol back in her life from here on out."

Naomi sat quietly, thinking, watching Partridge, "I understand, and I think I agree. What do I need to do?"

"Well, your three-month coma provided the best drying out, cold-turkey session a person could have, So, there is not any current physical dependence. But, if your 'wiring' is prone to addiction, I think you need to be sure you never, ever, use any kind of drug or alcohol again, not even to test the theory. I would also add normal things into that, like opioid-based painkillers and strong cough medications, which have the same kind of serotonin cycle problem."

"So, absolute abstinence, huh?" Naomi asked. Then, she gave Partridge a smile and added, "And, you're sure this is cutting-edge psychiatric advice and not the advice from the Mormon bishop?"

Partridge laughed, "*Touché*. Good question. Rest assured, it is the sage advice from both Doctor Larry and Bishop Partridge."

"Ok, that will be my plan. My old buddy Mark was not much into drinking and had no interest in drugs. He had survived two years without alcohol at the 'Y' and was the usual designated driver with his Army buddies."

"Good, now a little bit more good news. Since our report and recommendation are going to your judge back in Bakersfield, you are entitled to a copy," he handed Naomi several pages stapled together. "As I said, we are recommending your immediate release from both this hospital and any domiciliary setting in Kern County. We have sent this up the chain of command for approval, and we usually get approval in a week or two."

"Chain of command? You mean two doctors don't have enough say to get me released? Why?"

"As I once said, we are part of a state bureaucracy. A few years back, the state hospitals were in a real overcrowding situation, and they got a reputation, whether deserved or otherwise, of releasing patients before they were ready, just to solve the overcrowding. A review process was put in place to oversee that possibility."

"So, some bureaucrat gets to have the final say on my freedom, not my doctors?"

"Not exactly. Our doctors' union blew its top when we heard what was proposed. We threatened to report the state hospitals to the national hospital accrediting commission for allowing a non-doctor to be making a medical decision. The state relented and hired a doctor to make the final call. They offered me the job, and I refused. The good news is that the reviewing doctor who has the job is a straight shooter and a member of our doctors' union. Your release is as good as done. And, the judges back home in the patients' home jurisdictions almost always follow our advice."

Before Naomi could say anything, Partridge continued, "I have good news to answer Doctor Richards concerns about a support program for you. And, I think this will answer any questions the local Kern County judge and mental health people have, too. Since you and your mother have been on the records as members of a Latter-Day Saint Church ward there, my alter-ego Bishop Partridge called the LDS Stake President of the Bakersfield South Stake, who just happened to have been in the mission field as young men with Elder Partridge. The Stake President, President Sandoval, found a perfect place for you to get the support and roof over your head that Doctor Richards demanded. It seems a middle-aged couple in the Stake lost their only daughter to a drunk driver last year, and they have a perfect spot for you in their home and a willingness to provide whatever support you need. It's perfect!"

Naomi sat with a wrinkle in her forehead.

"What's wrong? I think this is a great answer for you. Right?" Partridge asked.

"Yes, don't get me wrong. I appreciate the offer, and I don't have much choice other than accepting it. But, don't you think the level of odd circumstances in all this is a bit too much?"

"I don't understand," said Partridge sincerely.

"Okay, here. Mark is killed by a drunk driver. He gets a miraculous chance to come back to life in the body of a comatose Mormon girl, Naomi. Naomi's doctor just happens to be a Mormon bishop who manages to arrange for Naomi to go back home and fill in for another Mormon girl, who was killed by a drunk driver, just like Mark," Naomi stopped and looked at Partridge.

"Naomi, I see your point, but this is the best thing for you. And, as I said before, miracles would not be miracles if they were easily understood."

"So, who are these people I'm going to stay with?"

"Ray and Janet Morrison. President Sandoval sent me a picture of them for you." Partridge handed her a computer-printed picture.

"They seem nice, like a happy version of 'American Gothic.' If Ray had a pitchfork, it would be a perfect Grant Wood painting."

———

Dozens of cars are racing through the gray metal archways and shapes in a darkened landscape. Vehicles start to skew and slide chaotically. I fear what I know will happen, but I can do nothing to stop it. I control nothing. I reach for the seat belt ahead of time this once, but my arms are caught on something and cannot reach the seatbelt. I struggle, but cannot free my hands from the layers of cloth that restrict them. Horrors are coming at me. Faces of the vehicle drivers scream out at me as though this is my fault. Suddenly fire comes from nowhere. The flames, pain and fear envelope me. I scream out in agony. Unseen people grab at me, inflicting more pain. In the last instant, I break free and try to jump out of the burning vehicle. A highway patrol officer is shouting at me in a strange voice.

"Hey, girl. Stop! Stop! Wake up. Naomi wake up," said the voice.

When Naomi recognized Tiara's voice, she remembered that she was Naomi now, not Mark.

Naomi sat upright in her bed; her flannel pajamas plastered with sweat to her body.

"Naomi, these dreams are freaking even me out now. Ain't there something they can give you?"

"No, Tiara. I tried to take a sleeping pill, and I still had the nightmare, I just couldn't wake up from it, which was worse."

"Is this car wreck and fire you scream about something out of your memory? You really seem to be reliving it," Tiara asked.

Naomi smiled at Tiara in the darkened room, "Tiara, if you only knew...."

———

"It's almost 10 o'clock; ya wanna go watch *The View* with me?" Tiara shouted to Naomi from the door of their room.

"*The View?* I thought you were the one who hated talk shows."

"*The View* has Whoopi Goldberg. I love Whoopi."

Naomi smiled, "Sure, I've been reading too long anyway." Naomi got up, put a Kleenex as a bookmark in her book, and joined Tiara.

They had just found seats by the television in the dayroom, when Mindy ran up to Naomi, "There you are. We just got word you need to be in Room 122 of the Admin Building in fifteen minutes, and you need to be dressed nicely."

"Dressed nicely? What for?" Naomi stood as Mindy started pulling her arm toward her room. Naomi broke free of Mindy's grasp. She was not good about her arms being pulled on.

"No idea. We've never got a call like that before. Sounded important. What do you have to wear? I'll help you get ready," Mindy said.

"Wait up. I'll help, too," Tiara said, trailing the other two down the hall.

In their room, Naomi slid the bureau door open, and while she showed each of the women her clothes, she said, "I have two dresses, black and multi-color print. I have a silk blouse. I can wear it with either gray business slacks or black wool skirt."

"Little black dress might work, but this isn't a cocktail party or funeral, so I'd go with the silk blouse and wool skirt," Mindy surmised.

"I agree. Black skirt and white blouse. You got shoes and stockings?" Tiara asked.

"Yes, in the drawer. Bottom drawer," Naomi said, as she slipped out of the blue t-shirt.

"Ok, you strip and lose the ponytail." Mindy seemed to be giving orders. "Tiara, go get her make-up."

"Whoa, blue sports bra won't work under a white blouse. You got another?" Mindy ordered when Naomi pulled up her t-shirt.

"Yes, same drawer."

Mindy had Naomi dressed when Tiara came back with Naomi's silver make-up bag. Naomi reached for it, but Mindy grabbed it away.

"I can do my own make-up." Naomi insisted.

"No way. I have orders to get you dressed up, and I have a secret fantasy of doing costuming and make-up on a movie set, and this is the closest I'm ever gonna come. Take your glasses off and close your eyes."

Naomi huffed but obeyed.

When Naomi realized Mindy was using more make-up than she ever had, including a full coat of the mauve lipstick, she said, "That's too much...."

"Sssshhhhhhh! I know what I'm doing."

When Mindy was done, she asked Tiara, "What you think?"

Tiara looked at Naomi, nibbled on her bottom lip, and said, "That'll do. Pretty decent paint job for a social worker."

"I gotta see." Naomi ran into the bathroom to look in the mirror, putting on her glasses.

When she came out of the bathroom, Naomi said, "Not bad, not my usual look, but not bad at all."

"Can you lose the glasses?" Mindy asked.

"Nope, I can't see without them."

Mindy nodded. "Okay, I hereby declare you nicely dressed. But, don't forget your ID badge, you need that to get through the guard to go outside. I'll have to clear you through the guard and walk you over?"

"Do you have to do that? I can see the Admin building right across the street," Naomi protested. "I would kind of like to be free on my own for the first time in ages."

"Admin asked for you to come over, but you're my responsibility. I'll walk you over. Hurry, times a wastin'."

———

"Excuse me. Where's Room 122?" Naomi asked the receptionist.

"Are you Ms. Donnelley?"

"Yes."

"Down the right-hand hallway, all the way to the end. They are expecting you. They asked me to call you over."

Naomi and Mindy walked past many office doors with signs announcing names and various job titles. At the end of the hallway, they found 'Room 122 – Executive Meeting and Staff Training Room.' Naomi stopped, wondering if she should knock.

Mindy said, "The receptionist had said they were expecting you, whoever 'they' are."

So, Mindy opened the door and Naomi entered.

As Naomi stepped inside the room, she stopped short. She found herself interrupting a meeting of perhaps fifty people, all in suits, medical uniforms, and, in a couple of cases, uniformed police officers and guards. They were all in chairs facing a podium at the front of the room where a heavy-set woman with long, straight, wheat blonde hair was speaking. Behind the speaker was a large decorative seal of Napa State Hospital and California and U.S., flags.

Many of the people in the room turned to see Naomi enter. The woman at the podium stopped talking and looked toward Naomi, who tried to close the door as quietly as she could behind her.

The woman at the podium said, apparently through a microphone, "Did you bring her?"

Naomi had to speak loudly to be heard in the front of the room, "Did I bring whom?"

The woman said, "The patient, Naomi Donnelley."

"Uh, I am Naomi Donnelley."

The woman said, "Oh, my goodness…" as she left the podium to hurry toward Naomi.

As the woman got near Naomi, she put out her hand to shake and introduced herself, with her voice still coming out of the PA system, "Miss Donnelley, I'm Christine Bachmann, the hospital director. I apologize for my confusion. I thought you were one of our new staff assistants. I didn't think you were a patient."

"I was told to dress nicely."

"And, you have succeeded. Please come with me to the front."

As she and the director turned the corner to stand by the podium, Naomi saw Doctor Partridge and Doctor Richards sitting together in the front row. She now recognized Captain Mortenson as one of the policemen she had noticed from the door.

As she stood next to the podium, a young man in a polo shirt walked up and clipped a small microphone on her blouse collar, explaining, "You need this so everybody can hear you." He tapped the little microphone and the auditorium speakers thumped.

Naomi gave a nervous smile to Doctor Partridge. He smiled back.

"Well. Miss Donnelley, I guess you know why you are here today."

"Truthfully, ma'am, I don't have a clue why I'm here. When I walked in, I got pretty nervous because the last time I had to appear before this many people, it was a courtroom, but I'm guessing I'm not in trouble this time," Naomi improvised for the sake of apparently successful humor, as everyone in the room laughed.

When the laughter died down, Director Bachmann said, "No, dear, you are not in trouble, just the opposite. We got the word you were being discharged soon, and we wanted to recognize you for your bravery and quick thinking in the knife attack incident. We really don't have any method of recognizing a patient for heroic actions such as yours, but if an employee had taken similar action in an emergency, we would have recognized their bravery. So, we decided we should do the same for you."

The director moved some papers on the podium and picked up an engraved plaque and an envelope. "The California Department of State Hospitals has a program of awarding an employee who goes above and beyond their expected duties with a Meritorious Service Award, and sometimes that award is supplemented with a modest monetary stipend, particularly in the act of bravery or lifesaving, both of which your deed was.

"On behalf of the men and women of Napa State Hospital, both patients and staff, I want to honor you for your bravery and quick-wittedness, in stopping a dangerous attack and preventing further bloodshed. Please accept this the plaque and this check as our token of gratitude for your actions."

The crowd of senior hospital staffers erupted in applause, then they all stood, still applauding. As Naomi felt her eyes tear up, she realized that old Naomi's emotions were in charge of her at the moment. So, she did not even try to resist the urge to walk over to Doctor Partridge in the front row and hug him. A tearful hug.

—

Chapter 11

Naomi yawned as she finished dressing in her blouse and gray slacks. She was in the bathroom, brushing her hair and checking her make-up. She heard someone enter the room as she collected her make-up bag from the bathroom. The mid-shift nurse had come in with a dark blue suitcase.

The nurse spoke quietly, "Property brought over your suitcase, cellphone, and a couple of other things you couldn't have on the unit. You can finish packing. I'll be back with your discharge paperwork."

Tiara awoke in the semi-dark room and complained, "What time is it? What is going on?"

Naomi explained, "It is a bit after six o'clock, I think. They woke me up about a half-hour ago to tell me a van heading to Bakersfield will be here to pick me up at 6:30. I'm getting sprung!"

Tiara quickly sat up in bed, "Really?"

"Yeah. I'm glad you are up now. I can turn on the lights to pack."

"Okay."

Naomi turned on the lights. She went over to her bed, where she already had most of her things in piles. She opened the suitcase and found an older iPhone with no charge and a plastic bag with the phone charger and a couple other items in it.

"Tiara, here. I want you to have the other two colored t-shirts. You can use them, and I can get more stuff now that I'm out. And, I left all my shampoo, soap and stuff in the bathroom. Oh, and here's Karina. I told you about her. She's a good luck pass down in this room. She's all yours now." Naomi handed the t-shirts and teddy bear to Tiara.

"I'll miss you, Naomi."

"I'll miss you, too. But, I won't miss this place. I'll try to give you a call occasionally to see how you're doing."

"Yeah, that would be nice."

Naomi finished her clothes packing. She carefully put her big nursing manual, the anatomy book, and the award plaque on top of the suitcase contents. She looked at the magazines, then turned, and gave three of them to Tiara, too. She kept the nursing magazine.

The nurse came in with several papers she handed to Naomi, "These are your copies. You'll have to give this pink one to the guy at the Out-Processing desk. They'll pick you up there. I'll take you over if you're ready."

"Who is 'they'?" Naomi asked.

"Officials from Kern County. Probably either Mental Health workers or deputy sheriffs."

Naomi put the papers into her important paper folder in her suitcase and snapped it shut. She looked around and could not see anything else she had forgotten. She turned to Tiara and opened her arms, "Hug?"

Tiara jumped up, and they had a lengthy hug. Then, Tiara held Naomi out at arm's length and said, "Girl, you are looking mighty fine this morning. Make us proud out there, 'kay?"

Naomi nodded and mouthed 'Bye.'

Naomi picked up her suitcase and purse and followed the nurse out. Her sojourn at Napa State Hospital was at an end.

———

The guard at the Napa State Hospital's Out-Processing desk had a space heater running behind the counter, but it did little for Naomi, where she stood waiting near the automatic sliding door to the outside. She could see a faint hint of sunrise in the sky, but the clouds and rain hid most of the dawn light. Naomi shivered a bit as she waited.

An over-sized, white van with an official seal on the door and an emergency light bar on the top drove up outside and stopped. A man in a dark green uniform jacket got out of the passenger's seat in the van and entered, passing Naomi with a sideways glance. Naomi saw a gold star on the jacket.

Naomi turned to watch as the man went up to the counter and announced, "Kern County." The man's shiny green parka announced 'SHERIFF' in bold, yellow letters across his back shoulders. Naomi noticed the sheriff's deputy had several stout, white, nylon ties, the kind used for prisoner restraint in his hand.

The guard handed a clipboard to the deputy and announced, "You won't need those ties. Her paperwork says, 'No Restraints.'"

The deputy looked at the clipboard where the guard was pointing and acknowledged, "Hmmpf, the first time I've seen that. Okay."

With the paperwork finished, the sheriff deputy came over to Naomi and said, "Let's go."

When Naomi bent to pick up her suitcase, the deputy reached for it and said, "I've got that."

"Can I keep my purse?" she asked.

"That's not the norm, but I guess so, since you are not restrained. I need to look inside though."

Naomi opened the purse and the deputy gave the purse's contents a cursory search.

They went out to the van, which Naomi saw had 'Kern County Sheriff' and a seven-pointed sheriff's star on the door. The deputy opened and slammed the front passenger door shut to make sure it was closed. Then, he opened the sliding door and told Naomi, "Sit anywhere you want, except the front center seat. Buckle up!"

Naomi got in and sat half-way down on the far side. All the seats were arranged around the outer edge of the cab, instead of the rows of bench seats in a typical passenger van. Naomi noticed that each position had a thick steel loop welded to the floor in front of the seat, obviously to attached leg restraints. She heard the deputy put her suitcase into the back of the van, behind a grid of sheet metal and wire mesh separating the passenger area from the back storage area. Another panel of heavy wire grid separated the passenger area from the driver and front seat.

The deputy got in and slid the door closed, sitting in the front seat in the passenger area, facing Naomi. As he buckled up, he rapped his knuckles on the partition and told the driver, "Let's go!"

The deputy looked over at Naomi and asked, "You buckled in?"

Naomi lifted and waved the strap of her seatbelt to show him.

Naomi saw that the deputy had his name and rank embroidered above the right pocket of his jacket, Senior Deputy Buehler.

The deputy nodded and said, "I'd usually be buckling you in myself and attaching your feet to the floor with the manacles. How is it you're going back from Napa and not restrained? Even the people coming back for release are restrained until the judge rules on their cases."

Naomi gave a little laugh and answered, "It might have something to do with the fact that I kinda flunked out of Napa State Hospital. They have this silly rule that their patients actually have to be mentally ill. The doctors here kicked me out when they decided I wasn't crazy."

"So, what was your problem? If you don't mind me asking."

"Substance abuse is the best answer I can give."

"How old are you?"

"Eighteen, nineteen next May."

"Kinda young to be getting sent to a state hospital for substance abuse."

"I didn't know they had a minimum age for that."

The deputy met Naomi's eyes and gave a knowing nod.

Naomi continued, "The other reason they might have nixed the restraints is that the hospital sort of owes me a favor."

Buehler gave a curious glance and asked, "How so?"

Naomi gave the deputy a short recount of the scalpel incident and the award she had gotten for her actions.

"So, how big was this guy?"

"About your size, but a lot thinner."

The deputy shook his head and smiled at Naomi.

Naomi finished up with, "So, I'm guessing the hospital folks thought it would be bad form to give someone an award for heroism, and then send them home in handcuffs and shackles."

Naomi finished her story, put her purse on her lap, and crossed her arms, grabbing her elbows with her hands to keep warm.

Deputy Buehler turned toward the driver and said, "Hey Cory, can you crank up the heater. It's cold back here."

"It's all the way up. This old van has never had good heat. I took it to Truckee last week and froze my ass going over Donner Pass."

The deputy asked Naomi, "Do you have a coat or sweater in your suitcase? We can stop so that you can get it on."

Naomi shook her head, "Nope, they brought me here in June. No October weather clothes at all."

Buehler frowned.

Naomi saw that they were taking Highway 29 down through American Canyon, where Mark's condo had been. As they drove on, she rubbed her forearms for warmth, and then stopped when she noticed the deputy watching her.

As they approached the built-up area, the deputy sitting with Naomi turned to the driver and said, "Cory, I think I remember a Walmart up ahead. Take a left at the first light. I want to get something."

"Okay,"

A few minutes later, the driver took the turn, and then another, stopping in a 'No Parking' zone near the Walmart entrance.

Buehler told the driver, "I'll just be a coupla minutes."

"Yeah, sure."

Naomi waited; a bit embarrassed as the early morning shoppers all stared at the woman in the back of the sheriff's prisoner van. This was probably the place where the local police picked up shoplifting suspects from the store.

True to his word, Deputy Buehler shortly emerged from Walmart and took something out of a shopping bag, stuffing the bag in a trash can. Then, he yanked at something attached to his purchase, then did so again, putting something in the trash each time. Buehler slid open the door and got in. As he took his seat, he handed Naomi a bright red quilted ladies' parka, lightweight nylon, but warm. "There you go," he said.

"I, uh…." Naomi sputtered, "Thank you very much. You didn't have to. Can I pay you for this?"

The deputy expressed mock anger at this, "Naw, you're gonna ruin it if you do that."

"Ruin what?"

"That feeling a guy gets when he does somethin' nice for a beautiful damsel in distress, that's what."

"Oh, that. Well, thanks anyways," Naomi unbuckled for a second to be able to put the jacket on.

"Fits perfectly," she said.

"Yeah, I figured you were the same size as my daughter."

"How old's she?"

"Seventeen. Goes to Centennial High."

Naomi remembered her school ID in her purse, so she said, "I went to Centennial until last spring...."

"What do your folks do?" the deputy asked.

"My Mom died last May; my stepdad is in prison."

Neither Naomi nor the deputy said much else for a while.

———

Naomi was watching the scenery go by in silence. It was familiar territory in Mark's memory.

"Are you taking Highway 4 all the way across. Seems like going down to the 580 Interstate would be quicker to Bakersfield," Naomi said as she took notice of where they were, heading toward Discovery Bay.

Buehler looked over at her and said, "Thank you for that advice, young lady. You're correct, except we have another pickup to make at San Joaquin County Jail. You aren't our only passenger today.

"Oh."

After a moment, Naomi asked, "Do you ever stop to eat?"

"Yes, we do, but lunch isn't for a couple of hours."

"Lunch? I never had breakfast," Naomi said. "You picked me up just before six-thirty, our breakfast is at seven o'clock."

"No breakfast, gosh, I'm sorry. Not feeding prisoners is a no-no."

When Naomi laughed at this, the deputy said, "Technically, you are a prisoner, regardless of your restraint status. We'll get you something to eat, soon as we can."

"Would this be sit down food, or just carry out?"

"Well, since you aren't in restraints, we could do sit down, if we do it before we pick up the other passenger. We have time."

Naomi could not believe she might have this opportunity, "If that's the case, can I make a suggestion. There is a great little restaurant, 'Ma and Pa' type place, right off the 5 freeway on the west edge of Stockton. It's right on your way to the San Joaquin Jail just south of there. They have great food."

"Okay, sure, sounds good. Tell Cory how to get there."

Naomi told him how to exit the freeway in west Stockton.. She could get them to this restaurant with her eyes closed. Some of her earliest and best memories were in that restaurant.

———

It was raining hard as Naomi and the two deputies ran into the restaurant. It was not very crowded mid-morning but had a decent number of customers.

A new waitress who Naomi had never seen before took them to a booth and gave them menus. "You can order from either the breakfast page on the back or the lunch section. I'll be back to get your order."

"You guys gonna eat, or is this just me?" Naomi asked.

The younger deputy, Cory, said, "I can pretty much eat any time. Especially since Senior Deputy Buehler has the county credit card." He picked up his menu.

Buehler said, "I'll have a coffee and some pie. You have whatever you want. Kern County is paying for you while you are 'in custody,' so to speak."

Naomi looked around the restaurant. It was the same as always. She did not see who she was looking for. Then, the swinging door to the back room and kitchen came open, and a woman in late middle age came out wearing a white cook's apron and carrying two stacked trays of coffee mugs over to the coffee pot area.

The waitress came back, and Naomi told the deputies to order first while she thought about what she should order and what she could do....

When it was her turn, Naomi said, "I'll have the pastrami on rye special, and could you tell Mrs. Kelleher that I want an ice cream float Mark's way."

"Pardon?" the waitress was confused.

"Give me a pastrami special, and please tell Mrs. Kelleher that someone is here who wants an ice cream float the way Mark always asked for it. She'll know what I mean."

"Okay, whatever," The waitress took the order but looked suspiciously at Naomi.

When the waitress left, Deputy Buehler asked, "What was that?"

Naomi put her finger to her lips, "Just a second, wait."

Naomi saw the waitress talk to the woman in the apron. The woman looked over toward their table, and then went to the prep counter and did something. As she turned to walk toward them, Naomi saw the woman had a large milkshake goblet full of brown liquid and topped with whipped cream and cherries.

As the woman in the apron approached the table, Naomi folded her napkin on the table and stood up. The woman came directly in front of Naomi and held the glass up, "You ordered this?"

As Naomi nodded, she felt the tears begin to form in her eyes. She looked at the glass and said, with a slight crack in her voice, "Yes. Root beer, Rocky Road ice cream, whipped cream, and five cherries. Looks perfect."

"Do I know you?" the woman asked.

"No, Mrs. Kelleher. But, I knew Mark very well. He told me how he used to sit at that counter doing his homework after school, and you would make him one of these."

At this point, tears were freely flowing from Naomi, and Mrs. Kelleher was starting, too.

Naomi's voice was wavering as she said, "He also told me about the wonderful party you threw for him here in the restaurant when he came home from Afghanistan. He told me how much he loved you and his father. I am really sorry for your loss."

Naomi was now sobbing, so Mrs. Kelleher sat the float glass on the table and took Naomi in her arms. They hugged for a moment, and then separated. When they did, Deputy Buehler handed each woman a paper napkin.

"So, you were a friend of Mark's, from up North?" his mother asked.

Naomi knew she needed to give a little white lie here, so she said, "Yes, it is a long story. But yes, really good friends. Seems like we were kind of soulmates, we got along so well. His death hit me hard."

Naomi was amazed at how none of that was untrue. She also realized that Mrs. Kelleher's tears were tears of sorrow, but hers were tears of joy and remembrance.

"Are you in town for a while? Mark's father is out right now. He'd like to meet a friend of Mark's, too."

"Uh, no. The deputies and I have quite a tough schedule to meet. Maybe I can come back sometime, when I have time to talk. My name is Naomi Donnelley."

"That would be wonderful. I'd like to hear about you and Mark. Yes, come back; you're always welcome."

Mrs. Kelleher gave Naomi another short hug and disappeared into the swinging doors, wiping her tears.

As Naomi sat down, Deputy Buehler said, "Seems this place has a bit more than just good food."

Naomi smiled as she wiped her eyes with the napkin. Seeing the kohl eye shadow smudge on the napkin, she asked, "Is it okay if I go to the ladies' room and deal with my raccoon eyes?"

Deputy Buehler smiled, saw the restroom doors on the nearby wall, and waved for Naomi to feel free and leave the table.

The food was at the table when Naomi came back. They ate in silence for a while until Buehler asked, "You gonna fill me in on any of what just happened?"

"Not unless you want me to start crying again. What you saw is pretty much it. Her son died in August, killed by a drunk driver. She and I really miss him. End of story."

Buehler nodded, and they finished eating.

When the waitress came to clear the dishes, Buehler asked for the check.

The waitress said, "No check. Mrs. Kelleher told me the deputies and Mark's girlfriend eat free."

Naomi had to smile at her promotion to a full-fledged girlfriend. She wondered if those were the words of the waitress or Mark's mother.

She saw Buehler slide a five-dollar tip under the empty coffee cup.

———

The trip from Stockton to Bakersfield was in near silence. The prisoner they had picked up from the San Joaquin County Jail south of Stockton was a surly, mean-looking man in his 30's. Deputy Buehler had asked Naomi to get out of the van when he put the prisoner in. Buehler secured the man's leg shackles to the floor of the van in the far back seat. Then, he directed Naomi to sit in the far front, closest to the deputy's chair. Naomi was happy to do so. The prisoner was nobody she wanted to talk to or look at. However, the opposite was not true. For most of the trip south, the prisoner was leering at Naomi.

Around noon, Cory took an exit off the 99 freeway south of Visalia, and they went to a McDonald's to buy lunch, take-out. Buehler smiled when Naomi again ordered food. Buehler had Cory come around and stand by the sliding door as Buehler went inside to buy everyone's food, since the lightbar on the Sheriff's van was too high for the drive-through lane.

When they got to Bakersfield, the van was admitted through a guarded gate behind the Kern County Jail downtown. When Deputy Buehler started to get out, Naomi asked if this was her stop. He said it was not, but he asked her to get out of the van while he got the male prisoner out. Apparently, Buehler was hesitant to let the prisoner, even though handcuffed and shackled, to get within reaching distance of Naomi.

When Buehler got back in, Naomi asked, "Where am I going?"

"You have a 1:30 court hearing. We're supposed to deliver you to County Mental Health first, and then escort you to Court. Mental Health is right next door to the branch Superior Court Building out on the Eastside."

"I have a court hearing today?" Naomi asked.

"Yes, that's why the early wake-up was necessary. You're going before the judge this afternoon." Buehler said, then he smiled and added, "Unless, of course, you want to be locked up overnight...."

"Oh no, today's fine." She opened her purse to pull out her compact. "I probably look horrible after my episode in Stockton."

"Nope. You look better than anybody I have ever seen in court. Women lawyers included."

"What'll I do with my suitcase when I go to court?"

"We'll figure that out. The person handling your case from Mental Health can help you with that."

—

Part Two

Chapter 12

Senior Deputy Buehler had helped Naomi find Ms. Alice Minnifee at the Mental Health Center. Minnifee stored Naomi's suitcase in her office, as they hurried to the scheduled court hearing. Buehler walked with them across the street and the parking lot between Alice's office and the stark, white Superior Court building. When they passed the Sheriff's van out front of the building, Buehler told the Cory to go ahead to the motor pool, Buehler would get a ride from the bailiffs after court.

Naomi now had her red purse over her shoulder, the shoulder of the red jacket Deputy Buehler had bought for her. The young mental health worker was dressed in a gray business suit with a raincoat and had several heavy file folders.

"So, what should I expect in court now? I really can't remember what happened last time," Naomi said.

"Yeah, as I recall, you seemed pretty blitzed last time in June."

"I don't remember anything, but the doctors told me I had three baggies of hard drugs in my intestine, just waiting to pop, or maybe had already."

"They faxed me your file yesterday afternoon. You had yourself quite a summer."

"So? In court…?"

"Yeah, I'm only involved in your LPS case about your mental health. The doctors at Napa pretty much answered the issues on mental health, saying they think everything was a substance abuse issue. We have no reason to discount that. Looking at you, you seem fine, standing here today."

"What else is there, besides the LPS case?"

"Well, you had two juvenile criminal cases and those last two criminal cases that got you arrested before the last court appearance. As I recall, the judge dismissed those adult cases, but they are on the court docket for hearing this afternoon. Your attorney is probably around here somewhere, you should speak to her, if you have questions on those cases or anything else for that matter. I can't advise you on legal issues."

They entered the Court's lobby and went through the magnetic screening booth and property inspection. Buehler, in his uniform with his sidearm, walked around the screening area.

Naomi was gathering her purse from the conveyor belt when an older short-haired black woman in a blue business suit, with slacks, came up to Alice Minnifee and asked, "Alice, this is Naomi, right?"

"Yes, that's her," Alice said. "Naomi, this is your attorney, Victoria Roth."

"Actually, we've met before. Last June, very briefly. I didn't recognize you now, big change," Roth said. She offered her hand to Naomi, who noticed Buehler back away when the attorney came up, apparently to not be eavesdropping on them.

"I'm sorry, I don't remember." Naomi said, "But Hi!"

"Yes, little doubt that you don't remember me. The judge had already decided your case when he called me up to the podium and appointed me guardian *ad litem* as they hauled you out of the room, screaming that you didn't know what was happening."

"I remember none of that. I did get your letter, though, and everything you sent me. Thank you for all of that help."

"That's okay. That's my job. We need to get inside. They are already calling cases. Do you have any questions?"

"I have nothing but questions." Naomi said, "I really still don't know what to expect."

"I actually haven't been able to read through all the new stuff faxed from Napa. Let me look through that, and if I need to ask you anything, we can ask for a bit of delay to talk. Just follow my lead and don't say anything unless you are asked something directly." Deputy Buehler opened the courtroom door for the three women. Naomi sat with Roth in the front row. Alice went to the other side and talked with some other people sitting there. Buehler went over, said hello to, and sat near the court bailiff. Naomi took off her jacket and folded it on her lap with her purse.

While Roth read through papers, Naomi looked around the courtroom.

Three people were sitting in what must be a jury box, a low-walled cubicle with fourteen theater-like seats in two elevated rows. Two men were in orange jail jumpsuits like the prisoner in the van that morning had worn. The other person in the jury box was a woman in her 20's with dirty, stringy brown hair in a khaki suit like was worn in Napa. She had a vacant look about her, staring up at the courtroom lights with her mouth open a bit. A female officer in a gray Probation Department uniform sat right behind this woman with a hand on the woman's chair. A deputy, in a uniform like Buehler and Cory wore, stood near the three in the jury box. Another sheriff's deputy sat with Buehler on the other side of the courtroom at a small podium that was marked 'Bailiff.' A female judge with gray hair was on the judge's bench, and a clerk and court reporter sat nearby. Probably twenty people sat either at the two tables in front of the judge or in nearby chairs. Maybe ten people watched from the audience. The courtroom seemed very new.

As Naomi looked at the audience, she caught the eye of a woman sitting with a man in the back row. It was the 'American Gothic' couple, Mr. and Mrs.

Morrison, from the picture Doctor Partridge had given her. They had come to her court hearing. When the woman smiled at Naomi, Naomi smiled, too, and gave a little wave. The woman seemed nice.

One by one, the people in the jury box were called up before the judge. Various attorneys and officials in the room entered their appearances in each case, and the judge made quick rulings. Naomi did not understand what was happening in these cases, but it seemed that everything was routine, as none of the attorneys argued, and the judge made quick decisions on what to do in each case.

The last case was that of the woman in khaki. The female probation officer had to lead the woman by her arm up to the podium. The case was announced as "In re the Conservatorship of Priscilla Bender." As near as Naomi could tell this woman was being sent to a fifteen-day hold in a Bakersfield mental hospital to determine if she was 'gravely disabled.'

One of the lawyers was appointed as her attorney, and then the judge asked the woman if she understood her rights. After a poke in the shoulder by the probation officer, the woman answered, "Not guilty, your Honor."

The judge shook her head in frustration, and said, "Counselor, please make sure your client is informed of her rights, and the nature of this case, as best you can."

"Yes, your Honor," said one of the attorneys at the right-hand table.

The judge read her order sending Priscilla Bender to the local mental hospital and closed that case.

As the three in the jury box were escorted out a rear door by the deputy, Naomi saw Ms. Roth getting her papers gathered up on her lap. Roth whispered to Naomi, "We're next."

Sure enough, the judge said, "Calling the case of, 'In Re the Conservatorship of Naomi Lynne Donnelley,' Case number 4758329 and two related juvenile cases, numbers ending in 0293 and 0294, and two criminal matters numbers ending in 4657 and 4689. Make your appearances."

Naomi followed her attorney through the swinging gates as Roth announced, "Victoria Roth, guardian *ad litem* and attorney for the conservatee and defendant, Naomi Donnelley."

"Heather Monfort, Deputy District Attorney, for the People, your Honor."

Several other people, including Alice, announced themselves, the others were from Social Services, Probation/Juvenile Services, and some deputy something from somewhere else Naomi could not understand.

The judge said, "The court notes for the record that the Conservatee and Defendant is present in court, apparently out of custody. Is that correct?"

Deputy Buehler quickly stood up, "Your Honor, Miss Donnelley is in custody. She's just not under restraint per the written orders of the State Hospital."

The judge nodded, "Thank you, Deputy."

The judge turned toward Naomi and continued, "Well, that is interesting. The court notes that the primary purpose of this hearing is to review the reports of Napa State Hospital as to the Conservatee and make appropriate orders. The two juvenile cases and the two criminal cases were docketed by the court after looking at the record of Judge Hawkins' orders last June, and my preliminary reading of the report from Napa. Apparently, Judge Hawkins dismissed the adult criminal charges last June, but kept them associated with the primary LPS case in case any further orders, such as Penal Code 851.8, might be appropriate."

"Miss Donnelley…" the judge called her name, and Naomi's attorney nudged her to stand up to talk to the judge.

"Yes, your Honor."

"Miss Donnelley, I read through your file over lunch. I, of course, found it intriguing. In a couple of decades as an attorney, and then as a judge in mental health cases, I have read many recommendations from state psychiatrists regarding the mental state of a patient, but I have never before seen a letter of recommendation from a director of the State Hospital sent to a judge about a mental patient. Tell me, is all of that in the letter true?"

"Uh, your Honor, I have not actually read all of that letter, but I can say that the director of Napa State Hospital seemed to me to be a good person when she gave me the award. I would have to give her the benefit of the doubt as to her opinion about me."

The judge laughed at this and said, "And, you really took a scalpel away from a deranged man who had already attacked a nurse?"

"Yes, your Honor. I can't say myself he was deranged, but he was really angry and scary looking."

"And, the Department of State Hospitals gave you a Meritorious Service Award and a monetary stipend for your effort."

"Yes, your Honor."

"How much was that stipend?"

"Five hundred dollars, your Honor, I have the check in my purse if you would like to see it."

"That won't be necessary," the judge said, smiling. "Now, let's get to the medical issues. Shall we?

"Napa has sent two rather lengthy medical analyses, by Doctors Lawrence Partridge and Karen L. Richards. The Court notes for the record that Doctor

Richards is a renowned expert in the treatment of substance abuse cases and taught a professional education program last January for California Superior Court judges on the handling of substance abuse cases in the courts. I attended that course given by Doctor Richards, and I was impressed by her knowledge and expertise.

"The reports of both Doctor Richards and Doctor Partridge are in agreement that they see no evidence of any organic mental illness. Instead, they attribute the entirety of Miss Donnelley's problems, last winter, and spring, with long-standing and untreated substance abuse. The reports go into some detail about the dire circumstances Miss Donnelley faced in a comatose condition for much of the summer months, brought about by the ingestion of large quantities of multiple drugs. A condition that was caused by something that was fully possible for our mental health and medical people here in Kern County to assess, but which was not discovered until Miss Donnelley nearly died at Napa."

The judge now stopped and turned some pages.

"Miss Donnelley, do you have anything to say about this finding that your problems are substance abuse related."

"Your Honor, I have no current memory of the period of time when I was reported to be abusing drugs. Doctor Partridge talked to me about it, and he says my lack of memory could be either a result of the massive levels of drugs I both used and was poisoned by when the baggies leaked in my intestine, or the memory loss could be because of the lengthy coma I was in from early June through late August. Doctor Partridge says that the lengthy comatose period I was in probably served to cleanse my system of the drugs in the same way a long-term drug rehab would. But, Doctor Partridge warned me that I can never, ever use alcohol or drugs in any amount without once again risking my life. I fully understand that and plan to follow that advice."

"Thank you, Miss Donnelley, and I must say I am impressed by your ability to express yourself to the court, especially given Judge Hawkins' findings of your condition when you last appeared in this court last June."

Naomi smiled at the judge.

"I have one more area I need to address before final ruling in these cases. Both Doctor Richards and Doctor Partridge express their firm belief that Miss Donnelley needs some sort of support infrastructure in order to succeed upon release. But, besides just voicing his opinion that the support is needed, Doctor Partridge seems to have done something about it. He includes information that he has contacted the leadership of Miss Donnelley's church she is a member of here in Bakersfield, and the church has arranged for Miss Donnelley to stay with a couple, church members, who have offered to provide a home and support for Miss Donnelley, given that her own mother is deceased. Is that correct, Miss Donnelley."

"Yes, your Honor, and those people, Mr. and Mrs. Morrison, are here in court, too."

"Are they? Oh, yes, I see them. Please come forward," the judge requested.

Naomi turned to see the Morrisons walk up to the swinging gate and stop.

"Oh, my goodness, Janet. It's been a long time. Let the record reflect that Janet Morrison and I attended high school together," the judge said. "Mr. and Mrs. Morrison, you have heard what I read from Doctor Partridge's letter. Is it correct that you will provide a place to stay and support for Miss Donnelley, as she gets back into putting her life together?"

Mr. Morrison answered with his wife rapidly nodding her head, "Yes, your Honor, we hope to do anything we can for Naomi."

"Thank you; you can sit back down. If neither counsel has any objections…," the judge started to speak when she saw the young female deputy district attorney begin to rise and to say something.

The older man next to the deputy DA, obviously her superior, touched her hand and slowly shook his head. The deputy district attorney frowned, and then she said, "The People have no objection."

The judge, in a slightly officious tone, bordering on sarcastic, said, "Thank you. DDA Monfort."

The judge took a breath and continued, "As I was saying… Without objection, the Court finds for good cause shown that the conservatorship previously ordered for Naomi Lynne Donnelley is dissolved, and the case is provisionally dismissed pending a report by Miss Minnifee of County Mental Health not later than 90 days from this date *in re* the success of Miss Donnelley's efforts on her own. If that report is satisfactory, this LPS case will be closed and sealed, *nunc pro tunc* to today's date. No further appearances by the conservatee or her counsel will be necessary. The Clerk will draft appropriate orders thereto.

"Furthermore, the Court finds overwhelming medical evidence that the alleged criminal conduct in both the juvenile justice cases, and the adult criminal charges were the result of profound drug use and substance abuse. The court further finds that in accordance with the prevailing direction as well as operational credo of Drug Courts in California that this is a perfect case to adopt the findings and rulings in conformity with the Drug Court credo. It is in the best interest of both the public and the defendant that the juvenile cases be dismissed with prejudice, and the matters sealed in accordance with standard procedure in such juvenile cases. Further, in the two adult criminal cases, this court agrees with the previous ruling by Judge Hawkins that the criminal charges are dismissed with prejudice, and the cases and arrests are hereby expunged per

California Penal Code 851.8. The Office of the District Attorney will ensure the Bakersfield Police and Kern County Sheriff are so notified, and the CalDOJ arrest database is duly expunged. DDA Monfort will report back to the court to ensure those matters are dealt with in accordance with the governing statute within thirty days. So ordered. This matter is calendared five weeks out for review of that report by the DA.

"Miss Donnelley, go and have a great life, you have a fine opportunity for a new chance at getting your life in order. The Court will be in recess for fifteen minutes after which the remainder of the Juvenile and Civil calendars will be called."

The judge banged her gavel.

Naomi started to follow Ms. Roth out of the courtroom but saw Deputy Buehler stand up across the room. She walked over to him.

Naomi walked up close to him and spoke softly, "I wanted to thank you for your kindness." She patted her red parka.

Buehler smiled and pulled a business card from his shirt pocket. "Here's my card, if you ever need help, anything at all, give me a call. Congratulations on the outcome here today. I think you are going to do fine from here on out. And oh, leave the knife-wielding crazies to somebody else from now on."

Naomi leaned close to him, "Is it ok to give you a thank-you hug?"

"Nothing in the rule book about that. Frankly, it never came up before, that I know." Buehler smiled.

Naomi stepped up and gave the sheriff's deputy a hug, and she said, "Your daughter is a lucky girl. I wish I had a father like you."

Naomi turned and walked away. Deputy DA Heather Monfort had watched the exchange between the defendant and the deputy in disbelief.

At the door, Naomi introduced herself to the Morrison couple and shook their hands. It seemed a new phase was beginning for Naomi.

—

Chapter 13

Ray and Janet Morrison were waiting for Naomi as she hurried across the parking lot from the Mental Health Building. When Ray saw her carrying a suitcase, he got out and opened the rear hatch of the late-model Buick SUV.

Seeing Janet Morrison in the front seat, Naomi sat in the rear.

As soon as Naomi was in her seat, Janet handed a business card over the car seat to her. "That black lady, your attorney, had to run to another court case. She gave me her business card for you, and said you should call her after 3:30 this afternoon to talk and make arrangements about your things that are in storage."

"Thank you," said Naomi. "I have to say how thankful I am that you folks have decided to help me out. You heard how important the judge thought your help was to me. I'm not sure I can ever repay you."

Ray shook his head and objected, "It is not a matter of something to be repaid. We heard about your need and your mother dying. We just wanted to do the right thing."

"Well, before this is over, you are probably going to get tired of me thanking you. I will probably get sort of annoying." Naomi unsnapped her new jacket in the Buick's heated interior, the first time she had been warm all day.

"Looks like the rain is stopping a bit," Naomi said. "Where do you live?"

Again, it was Ray who answered, "We have an older place out on Johnson Road, beyond Renfro. Ya know, just north of the Westside Parkway."

"Oh, yeah," Naomi said, pretending she understood Bakersfield geography.

Janet now asked, "Where did you live? You know, before your mother died, and all of your, uh, troubles?"

Naomi had to think fast on an answer. She couldn't remember the address on her driver's license, so she said, "We had a place near Centennial High School."

"Oh, that's fairly close. Our daughter went to Liberty High," Janet said with obvious sadness in her voice.

Naomi had to say something since the subject had come up, "Doctor Partridge told me your daughter had passed away. I'm sorry for your loss."

Both Ray and Janet nodded their heads. Ray finally filled in some details, "Yes, last March. A drunk driver hit Belinda and her boyfriend up on the 99."

The three were silent for a while, until Naomi thought of a question, "Is there a Wells Fargo bank on the way? I need to deposit this check."

Ray answered, "Yes, I can take the Rosedale Highway out. Wells Fargo is right on our way, then."

Janet now asked, "Yes, Naomi about the check, what was that the judge was talking about, with the deranged guy and the knife, and this reward you got?"

So, Naomi, once again, had to tell the story. She was getting good at it. The Morrisons listened with rapt attention.

"My goodness, Naomi," Janet said, "that was a brave thing for a girl like you to do."

"Hmmph? Not just brave, downright crazy if you ask me," Ray added.

Naomi was opening her purse to make sure she had her debit card and check ready when she heard Ray's faux pas about her.

Ray immediately realized his mistake in his word choice, especially when his wife slapped him on the arm. He quickly added, "I'm sorry, Naomi, I didn't mean 'crazy' crazy, just kind of a scary thing for us to hear."

Naomi tried to make her voice light-hearted to make Ray feel better, "No, Ray, you are probably right with 'crazy.' More than one person has told me I wasn't just brave, but also very lucky. Could have turned out bad. Fortunately for me, that is not the kind of crazy they keep you in the hospital for."

———

Ray pulled in their driveway and parked the Buick next to a huge, white Ford Super Duty pickup truck. Naomi recognized the truck was the same model of vehicle that had hit the BMW in the accident.

The Morrison residence was a large, old Craftsman-type home that looked like an addition had been added to it. There were a couple of large outbuildings behind it.

"Wow, nice place. Those buildings yours, too?" Naomi asked Ray when he opened the door to get her suitcase.

"Yes, this was the homestead for a half section of land. My parents sold off the rest when I was a kid. All those new houses over yonder are built on what used to be Morrison land."

"You're still living in the house you grew up in?" Naomi asked.

"Yup, boring, huh?" Ray said.

Naomi shook her head, "Not boring at all. I don't know what to call it, but boring isn't it. Having connections like that to your family must feel good."

Ray would not let Naomi carry her suitcase. He took it and waved her ahead.

Janet joined in, "It has been a good home for us. Raised a son and a daughter here, well mostly. Now, it is a good place for us and hopefully a good place for you, too."

"I didn't know you have a son," Naomi said.

Janet smiled, "Yes, Ray, Jr., his wife, and kids live in Colorado. He works for the U.S. Bureau of Land Management. We have pictures inside. Proud grandparents, us Morrisons."

They went in the back door and into the kitchen. Naomi looked around the kitchen. The interior of the kitchen did not match the age of the house. The kitchen was modern in décor and appliances.

"I'll put your bag in your room," Ray told Naomi.

"Put your coat on the hook here to dry out, Naomi. I'll show you around the house," Janet said, hanging her raincoat next to Ray's jacket.

The rest of the Morrison home matched the kitchen in updated, modern décor. Janet Morrison seemed to be meticulous around her house.

"This will be your room," Janet said. Naomi could see her suitcase on the bed. "It used to be Belinda's, and I never really pushed myself to move her stuff out. Then, we didn't have much notice you were coming, and we didn't know if you had any of your own things, so we left her stuff in the closet and in those boxes over there in the corner. Since it seems you have your own things with your attorney, you may not want to bother. But, as near as I can tell you are the same size as Belinda, and she may have something that will work for you. Keep anything you want, put the rest back in the boxes, and we will donate it."

"Thank you. I'm not sure what the attorney saved from my mother's apartment. I may need some of Belinda's things," Naomi said, looking around the room.

"Belinda's things are really pretty nice. She was a snappy dresser; she worked at Macy's in the mall her senior year and last year when she was in junior college. She took full advantage of the employee discount. And on the little desk, we have the laptop; the password is on the sticky note on the keyboard. We have wi-fi."

"Great, I've missed having access to the Internet up in Napa."

"You didn't have Internet?"

"Well, they had a couple computers for like thirty women. And, they were set up to only retrieve information from certain sites, so the patients couldn't, you know, cause mischief by sending out stuff from the hospital. It was pretty restrictive, but by necessity; you don't want crazy people loose on the Internet."

"I'd like to hear more about the hospital, that is, if you want to, some time," Janet spoke gently, not wanting to perturb Naomi.

"Sure, we can do that. But, most of my time there, as you heard, was lying in bed in a coma. I was only conscious since late August."

"My goodness, what a horrible experience."

Naomi thought of how she could delay or limit having to talk about the hospital, and her non-knowledge of life in Bakersfield before then, "The doctor said I should try to get myself oriented to the future, not dwell on the past too much."

"Certainly, dear, that makes sense," Janet put her hand on Naomi's shoulder and added, "You can get settled here. Remember, you need to call your attorney after 3:30. The phone is in the living room. Most of the dresser drawers are empty for your stuff. The ones that aren't empty are for you to go through. You have your own bathroom and full bath through that door. Let me know if you need anything, okay?"

Janet seemed ready to leave when a large gray cat jumped up on the bed in Naomi's new room.

"Who is this?" Naomi asked, as she reached to pet the cat.

"That is Oodles," Janet answered. Then with a little crack to her voice, she added, "He was Belinda's cat."

Oodles reacted to Naomi's petting by purring loudly and butting his head against her hand, asking for more affection. Then, he flipped on the bed and offered his belly to Naomi to rub.

Janet said, "Looks like Oodles is welcoming Naomi, too."

Naomi nodded, and Janet's hand to the shoulder turned into a full hug, and she whispered in Naomi's ear, "Welcome to our home, Naomi, consider it your home, too."

—

"The young lady who works for your attorney dropped some keys and paperwork off while you were in the bath," Janet said, as Naomi came into the kitchen. "Supper is almost ready. I try to have supper ready for the table when Ray gets home."

"Ms. Roth said she would send her assistant out. So, I can try to get into the storage area and pick up my Mom's car tomorrow," Naomi said, as she took the keys Janet handed her. "So, Ray went back to work? I hadn't seen him around."

"Yes, Ray was changing his clothes and left, while you and I were going around the house. Fridays are a big day for Ray; he needs to get all the fieldwork scheduled for the crews that come in over the weekend. Working a farm that big is a seven day a week job. You have a car? That's nice to have. Where is it?" Janet asked.

"She said it was on South H Street. The same place where my mother's stuff, well, my stuff, is in storage. They have an auto storage service, too. But, I suppose before I pick up the car, I'd better get to the DMV, 'cuz my driver's license expired on my birthday last May. I should have a current license to pick up the car."

"Let's see what Ray has on his schedule tomorrow. Either he or I can drive you to the DMV, and then get your stuff."

"Anything I can help with for supper?" Naomi asked.

"Nothin' much left. Oh, you could set the table. Everyday dishes are in the cupboard over the toaster. We'll eat here in the kitchen, not the dining room."

"Okay, will do," Naomi said, as she headed over to the cupboard.

Janet looked at Naomi and commented, "I'm glad you were able to find something from Belinda's stuff for you. Those skinny jeans seem to be a perfect fit."

"Yes, I tried several things on, and I do seem to be her size, maybe a bit skinnier. I only had two pants at the hospital, and they could use laundering."

"Anything that needs washing just put it in the laundry hamper, here off the kitchen," Janet pointed. "Monday is washing day. Any dry cleaning goes in the bag on the hook behind the laundry room door."

"Ahh."

—

Janet had the food on the table by the time Ray got back from washing up and changing out of his khaki work clothes into jeans and a Dodgers t-shirt. Naomi followed the Morrisons lead and took the third seat behind the table.

Naomi already had the serving spoon in the mashed potatoes when she heard Ray start off, "Our Heavenly Father…."

Naomi quietly replaced the spoon and followed the Morrisons in bowing her head.

Ray continued, "…we give thanks for the bounty on the table before us, and for this beautiful day we have had. Today, we give special thanks for the presence of Naomi in our home. We thank you for thy blessings and guidance in her life to have allowed her to overcome the turmoil and tribulations she has faced, and we thank you for the miracles that have brought her safely back home to Bakersfield. We give thanks and ask your continued presence with our family, including Naomi, as we enjoy the blessings and miracles thou hast in store for us. In the name of Jesus Christ. Amen."

"Amen," Janet added.

"Amen," Naomi said, appreciative of the line about miracles in Rays' blessing.

Naomi finally got a spoonful of the potatoes and passed them to Ray.

"How was your afternoon, dear?" Janet asked.

Ray shook his head, "Fairly normal. I was gone, what, three hours? And when I got back there, everyone had something different that they thought was my priority to do in the two hours we had left of the day. Even Eli, you'd think I was the owner, not him."

Janet laughed, "Like I often say, Ray. Keep them thinking they can't do without you."

"If that is what I'm judged on, I'm a success," Ray said, as he poured brown gravy over everything on his plate. "How's everything here. Naomi getting settled in?

Naomi started to answer, but Janet got in first, "Naomi's doing great. Her attorney sent over some keys to the storage place and to Naomi's mother's car there. If you don't have any plans tomorrow, you could help get Naomi to the DMV for her license renewal, and then down to South H Street for the storage."

"Sure, I had to get some things from Home Depot, and I can go to the Home Depot on Ming instead," Ray seemed to accept the chore list from Janet as standard procedure, "What kind of car, Naomi?"

"Toyota Prius. My attorney told me she sold the Camry that was parked at the apartment for scrap. It seems the damage my stepfather caused when he was running from the police last year wasn't repairable. So, she junked it. All I have left is the Prius."

Ray asked, "Your stepfather?"

Naomi now realized this was guaranteed to require a story from her, and all she knew was what Doctor Partridge had found out for her. She recited much of the police report, and Internet clipping Partridge had given her and embellished the story a bit. "My stepfather assaulted both my mother and me the August before last. It wasn't his first time doing that. But, that time, we had to go to the ER, which caused a police report on him. Then, when he heard the police were after him for domestic abuse, he ran, headed north, in the Camry. He drove into Sequoia National Park and tried to hide in one of the campgrounds, but a National Park Ranger saw he didn't have a tag for the national park on the Camry and started to question him. My stepfather assaulted the Ranger, who is a federal officer, and made a run for it. Dumb move, as there are only two ways out of Sequoia. A SWAT team was waiting for him at the south entrance, and he crashed and got caught. He is in federal prison over in Lompoc, for assault on a federal officer, the Park Ranger. He managed to turn a simple domestic abuse case into a federal offense."

"Oh, my dear," Janet could think of nothing else to say.

Wanting to change the subject, Naomi quickly asked Ray, "Ray, if the Prius has been in storage for several months, shouldn't I get an oil change or something. I heard that was recommended."

"Depends on what condition the oil was in going into storage. If it was old or low, then yes, change it. But, if it was fresh, shouldn't need it for a few months in lay-up. I'll check it for you when you get it."

"Thanks, I'd appreciate it. Can I have some more pot roast?" Naomi smiled and reached toward the pot roast, hoping there were no more questions about her past.

———

"We try to leave for sacrament meeting at twenty 'til," Janet called through the closed bedroom door. "So, you've got about fifteen minutes until we leave."

"Okay," was all Naomi could think to say.

Naomi had been forewarned over Sunday breakfast that the Morrisons expected, without asking her, that Naomi would be going to church with them. She could not blame them. Here, they had opened their home to her, offering her the property of their deceased daughter, Ray had spent all day yesterday driving her around, helping Naomi at the storage area, lugging boxes back in his truck for her to go through back at the Morrison home and a dozen other acts of kindness. Not to mention the action of the two Mormon leaders, Partridge and his old mission buddy, who had arranged for Naomi to have the support everybody said she needed to put her life back together. Naomi realized that it was entirely fair for her to go to church with the Morrisons and whatever else was needed to repay them for their kindness. So, Naomi stood at the sliding door to the closet now filled with both Naomi's and Belinda's clothing, wondering what was proper for an 18-year-old girl, or was it woman, to wear to a Latter-Day Saint Sacrament Meeting on a rainy, chilly Sunday morning in October.

Fortunately, Mark had gone to church several times with his roommates at BYU, so Naomi knew pretty much what to expect at the church, it was just that she was still getting used to female fashion and whatnot, something which Mark's old memories were of no help. In the end, Naomi decided to wear the same print dress she had from up at the hospital, coupled with a pair of yellow flats courtesy of Belinda and a gray raincoat that could have been either Naomi's or her mother's coat. She had no idea whose coat it was, as most of the things in the storage were comingled by whomever had cleared out the old Donnelley apartment for Ms. Roth. But, it fit her.

So, Naomi dressed and went to the bathroom mirror to check hair and make-up. Putting on make-up was still a particular problem for Naomi. Her recollection via Mark was that the Mormon girls in Provo had been well-groomed, but Naomi now questioned whether that was just the matrimonially inclined social focus of the Mormon college's lifestyle. She figured the worst that could happen would be she was over-groomed for this first Bakersfield church meeting and would be better informed for the future church adventures she was sure would be forthcoming.

Naomi checked herself in the dresser mirror and thought she looked nice. The outfit, hair, and make-up seemed right, so she turned to leave. Then, before she left the bedroom, she stopped. She had done it again. She needed to get used to being Naomi. She went into the bathroom and retrieved her very essential eyeglasses.

—

Chapter 14

Naomi survived the Sacrament Meeting without much trouble. Her only problem was that the toddler in the row in front of where Naomi and the Morrisons sat had politely shared several pieces of the Cheerios his mother gave him to keep quiet. Naomi had dutifully accepted the offering. She had thought about getting rid of her handful of Cheerios in the sacrament tray's used cup hole when it was passed by her but decided against it as possibly being irreverent. Seeing that everyone was ending the meeting with handshakes, Naomi put her Cheerios presents in her purse and smiled at her toddler friend.

As they stood up, Naomi whispered to Janet. "Where do we go now?"

Janet whispered back, "Under the new schedule, we have priesthood and Relief Society on the 1st and 3rd Sunday, and Sunday School on 2nd and 4th. Since our ward is so close to Cal State Bakersfield, we have a pretty active YSA Relief Society for women your age. I'll show you where they meet on my way to the main Relief Society Room. Ray goes to the High Priests' Quorum."

Naomi nodded as though she understood that and tried to remember what YSA was. She had heard it before in Provo. She followed Janet and Ray out of the sanctuary.

Just before they got to the lobby door, a large male hand was thrust in front of her, and she looked up to find a very tall young man smiling down at her.

"Naomi isn't it? I don't know if you remember me, we had Sophomore English together," the unknown young man continued to smile at her.

"Hi, yes, I'm Naomi, Naomi Donnelley. Remind me of your name." She took his hand.

"Nate, Nate Hoskins."

"Ah, yes, Nate," Naomi was getting good about little white lies to cover up her vacant memory.

"So, you've moved over from our old ward, too. You going to CSUB, too?"

"Uh, no, I'm living with the Morrisons; they live over here."

"Well, it's nice to see you again. I hope to see you at the Young Singles dances. Almost every Friday, one place or another around town."

"Sure, that might be nice," Naomi said, getting another long handshake when Nate left her side.

Janet leaned back and whispered, "Who was that?"

"Nate Hoskins, we went to high school together," Naomi said, hoping there were no questions to follow up.

"Really handsome guy. Tall," Janet commented.

With Nate's comment about the dances, Naomi remembered what 'YSA' stood for, "Young Single Adult." Naomi remembered that Mark had felt like a hunted creature when faced by the coeds at BYU who attended YSA events. So, this YSA Relief Society meeting Naomi was headed for was a meeting of young, unmarried, LDS women. Naomi wondered if there was any excuse she could make to get her out of having to manage her introduction to that group. What could she say when asked to introduce herself to such a group? She needed to make up some standard tale about where she had been for nearly six months.

She had little time to plan, as Janet soon said, "Here you go," pointed her to a classroom and disappeared, assuming Naomi knew what to do.

Naomi went in and folded her raincoat over a chair in the far back row, sat and watched people come in. One point in Naomi's favor was that she seemed to be perfectly dressed and groomed, based upon the young women who entered. Now, her biggest concern seemed to be how many of these young women would have known Naomi, as Nate had, and how she should introduce herself, as she expected to be asked.

Maybe twenty or more young women came in and sat down or milled around. Nobody seemed to notice Naomi until....

"Naomi!" came a high-pitched cry, almost a squeal, from a girl in the doorway. "I can't believe it's you."

The young woman was Naomi's age and a pretty brunette. She charged toward Naomi down the row of chairs, obviously intent on a hug. Naomi stood to accept the inevitable. Naomi was a hugger, too, but not with people she did not know.

"Oh, Naomi, I was so sorry to hear about your mom. And then, you dropped out of sight. How you been?"

"I'm fine. Back in town. Living with the Morrisons out here."

"Yes, you did a good job of disappearing; I never got to talk to you and tell you...."

"What?"

"Well, how much I missed having you around and that you were my hero."

"Your hero?" Naomi was intrigued, even if she did not know with whom she was talking.

"Yeah, the way you finally stuck it to Little Miss Perfect in Everything, Mary Anne Malloy. When I heard you had poured a jar of red paint down her blouse, I was truly inspired, none of the rest of us who had been that bully's pawns since middle school had the nerve. But you, you were perfect."

Naomi now realized this girl was talking about the art class assault that Doctor Partridge had told her had resulted in the first juvenile charge against her and had ultimately gotten her expelled from Centennial High. Before they could say anything else, a slightly older woman had stood up front and said, "Okay, ladies. Time to start."

Naomi's exuberant fan club member took a seat right next to Naomi and lovingly patted Naomi's hand. Apparently, Naomi had at least one dear friend, Whats-her-name.

The YSA Relief Society from this ward was apparently scheduled to host an area-wide Halloween Party and dance in two weeks, and duties were being handed out. A large chart of needed functions was put onto an easel. Naomi was thankful that nobody knew her except the one person at her side.

Unfortunately, her enthusiastic friend figured volunteering for both herself and her old friend was an excellent way to get back in touch with each other. When two large pans of Halloween cupcakes came up on the duties list, the girl next to Naomi raised her hand.

"Sister Allred?" the leader said, giving Naomi a first clue.

"Yes, I can handle the cupcakes. And, let me introduce my old friend, Naomi Donnelley. We go back to 6th grade together. She has just moved back to town. Maybe Naomi and I could do the cupcakes together. Huh?" She turned to Naomi.

"Uh, sure, that sounds great," Naomi was concerned that this probably also required her to go to the Halloween Party and Dance.

Naomi's concern was offset by the knowledge the volunteering gave her. The group's leader now filled in the names next to 'Cupcakes' on the duties poster with 'Kendra Allred' and 'Naomi Donnelley.'

Naomi recognized Kendra's name as having been on the list of contacts she had found on Naomi's old cellphone when she had finally charged it Friday evening.

After the Halloween duties were doled out, the agenda moved on, and Naomi discovered Kendra had saved her from introducing herself by already having done so. The meeting concluded with a profoundly boring lesson on 'A Woman's Duty of Civic Awareness.' Naomi acknowledged that the instructor's heart was in the right place, but her ability to inspire class response was sorely missing.

After class, Kendra and Naomi walked together back to the lobby. Naomi got brave and decided to ask Kendra an open-ended question, "So, Kendra, what are you doing this year?"

"Like we always thought, I'm going to Bakersfield College. Just started, of course, so I'm in basic classes. What are your plans?"

Naomi nodded, "Much the same as you, now that I'm back. I'd thought of maybe trying nursing; I see they have a program there."

"Yeah, you'd be good at that. You always had better grades than me. You could probably get into their nursing program. Have you checked with Centennial; I didn't see your name on the graduation list last May."

"Yeah, that's on my To-Do list. I saw an old copy of my high school transcript, but it wasn't complete. I need to see what I need to do," Naomi didn't know if she should be talking like this, but Kendra seemed like a sincere friend. "And hey, let's make sure our contacts are still good."

Naomi took her cellphone out of her purse and scrolled to 'A' in contacts. She pushed Kendra's call icon, and Kendra's purse played Ingrid Michaelson's 'Soldier' song.

"So, you want to get together before we have to do the cupcakes?" Kendra asked.

"That would be nice but let me call you. My chore list is growing day by day. I have to go through all my Mom's old stuff."

"Oh, sheesh. I'm sorry. I don't know how I'd handle something like that," Kendra sounded sincerely sad. Then, as if it had been planned, she said, "Here's my Mom now."

"Mom, you remember my friend Naomi?"

"Of course, Naomi," Naomi got another hug. "I was sorry to hear about your mother. How are you doing?"

Naomi smiled, "Doing well. Back in town, staying with Janet and Ray Morrison."

"Oh, good. I was so sorry to hear about their Belinda, too. Lots of sorrow around last spring."

Naomi could only nod her head to that.

"Well. It looks like the Morrisons are waiting by the door. Nice seeing you again. And, I will call to get together and for the cupcakes," Naomi said, touching Kendra's arm.

Kendra could not resist a departing hug. Naomi thought it was kind of nice to have a friend who was an unrepentant hugger.

Naomi's only regret from today's encounter was that she had no memory of having poured red paint down her bullying nemesis' blouse. It must have been awesome.

———

"So, let me make sure I have this straight. With what the judge ordered my record is clear? Totally clear?" Naomi asked, sitting on the edge of her seat in front of Victoria Roth's modern clear glass desk.

"Yes, and both the police agencies involved in your cases, the Bakersfield PD and Kern Sheriff, have to destroy the arrest record and certify to you and the court that it has been done. That certificate should come here to my office since that is the address they have for you. And then, in mid-January, provided you keep yourself out of trouble, even the civil court file will be permanently sealed. Now, there may be some vestiges of your problems, like a medical record at the hospital and your school records, but those are confidential and aren't usually reported to anybody else," Roth looked at Naomi's smile and added, "Considering where you were a couple of months ago, you came out of this one smelling like a rose."

"I can truthfully answer an application question that I have never been arrested?"

"Yes, that is the whole point of the legislation the judge used to clear your record. The California statute actually says, 'Thereafter, the arrest shall be deemed not to have occurred and the person may answer accordingly any question relating to its occurrence.' If I were you, I would make sure I got the certificates back before I started applying for jobs or anything that requires a background check."

"How about drug use? What can I say about that?"

"Pretty much the same thing. The judge invoked the power of a Drug Court dismissal, the whole purpose of which is the get the person back on their feet without a bad record monkey on their back. Even your file out at County Mental Health will be closed and sealed after January per the judge's order."

"That's good to know. My next stop today is high school. I need to see what I need to do to get my diploma, so I can start college work," Naomi said. "Anything else you see me needing to do?"

"No, just keep on the straight and narrow, make sure Alice gives the judge a good report in January. That's it. I'll send the police and DOJ certificates when I get them."

"Do I owe you anything for all your work on this?"

"No, nothing else. I filed an expense report with the Probate case on your mother. That paid for my services in the probate matter, and the Court pays for court-appointed guardian *ad litem* costs. Your stepfather defaulted on answering the Probate Court filing, so the money in your mother's joint account with him came into her estate. The remainder of the funds from Probate and that little insurance policy from your mother's job are in your account at Wells Fargo. The Probate accounting form is in your papers there, along with a final tax filing for your mother. That money should help you get started in college. You'll have to file income tax in your own name next April, on the income from the estate after your mother's death. I'll send you a *pro forma* filing before you need to file your state and federal returns."

"Okay, thanks." Naomi gathered up her papers and purse.

"Sure, feel free to call me if you have other questions. A lot of this stuff isn't apparent to people. Good luck out there, Naomi." Victoria Roth escorted Naomi to the door, and Naomi followed Kendra's guide, by hugging her attorney.

———

Naomi had tried to find out information about Centennial High School online. She had found lists of graduation requirements and compared them with the partial transcript Doctor Partridge had retrieved from her case records. She found a list of counselors, including one who was assigned to her alphabet group, A-F. She had some questions she needed answering. For instance, the old transcript showed Naomi had taken two semesters of U.S. History in summer school one year and had received ten credits for that summer. With the 30 credits for every semester from 9th grade on, it seemed to Naomi that she had enough credits to graduate even before her expulsion from Centennial in the spring of her senior year. She had to ask someone about that.

Naomi had also found three school yearbooks in the storage area. She had brought those back to the house to look through. She, of course, did not have a yearbook for her senior year, but from the entries and signatures, Naomi seemed to have been fairly active in high school in previous years. In the junior year annual, she had found that Naomi Donnelley was the president of the Art Club. It seemed that Naomi's serious problems were not all-consuming. Besides Kendra and Nate, she could only think of one name to look up in the yearbooks, and she found a girl named Buehler. Deputy Buehler's daughter, Connie, was a year behind Naomi.

Naomi drove the Prius into the parking lot at Centennial High School. It was impressive, modern looking, and an expansive campus like you would expect for a college, with many modern buildings. She found a sign that said, "Office – All visitors must report to the office.' She parked in a visitor parking spot and got out.

A rent-a-cop hurriedly ran up to her. "Sorry, you cannot park there. That is visitor parking only. Students must park in the student parking lots. You'll have to move."

"I am not enrolled here. I am a visitor. I need to go to the office and check in like the sign says. I am pretty sure visitor parking is correct for me," Naomi walked past the rent-a-cop without any further words. She heard him mutter something but ignored him.

In the main building, she found the office. At the counter, Naomi asked, "I need to see Ms. Dawes in Counseling. Where do I go?"

The secretary looked at her like she had asked a horribly stupid question. "You should know where her office is. Students need to set an appointment before talking to a counselor. Log in to your student account to set that up."

"I'm a former student, and I have some questions regarding my transcript and diploma. I really need to speak to her," Naomi was trying to be courteous, but realized she was getting a bit short with the secretary.

The secretary frowned at her, "Go to the counter at counseling, next door. I'll tell her you need to see her. What was your name?"

"Naomi Donnelley," she answered. The secretary seemed to recognize the name.

Naomi went to the next suite of offices and waited at the counter.

In a few moments, a 30-ish woman appeared, wearing a dark print dress and eyeglasses. She said, "Well, Naomi. It's been a while. I was a bit surprised to hear you were here."

Naomi realized she was in another slippery area where she needed to cover for her lack of memory. "Hi, yes, it has been a while. What I needed was to ask some questions about my transcript and getting my diploma."

"Naomi, you were formally expelled from Centennial last April, as I recall. For not one, but two incidents. If you want to make up for your lost credits and get your diploma, you need to contact the school district adult school or one of the special admission schools. You would not be welcome to re-enroll in Centennial without a formal appeal."

"I understand that. What I need is to ask you some questions about my existing transcript. Can we do that? It seems I would need to know about my transcript from here even if I went to the adult school. Right?"

"Right. Let's go to my office. I don't have a lot of time for this, but we can print out a transcript for you." Ms. Dawes buzzed the swinging counter door open for Naomi to enter behind the counter.

In Dawes' office, Naomi took her seat in the visitor's chair in front of the cluttered desk, while Dawes entered some information in her computer. While Dawes waited for something, she said, "As I said, I was surprised to see you here. I heard you got sent away for something you did. Right?"

Naomi did not want to have to tell this woman about her life since leaving Centennial, so she just said, "Reports of my demise were premature. I'm back; I have a clean record. And, I want to get on with my life."

Ms. Dawes started to say something, but thought better and said, "Let me go get the printouts. I made two copies, so we can both see."

Dawes left the office. She came back in with two pages for each of them, "So what is your question?"

Naomi held up a finger, indicating she needed time, "Just a sec." She looked through the transcript. "Yes, that is what I wanted to know about. I see something else that I didn't have on my old copy of the transcript.

"If you look at the entry for Summer School, Semester One and Two, between my sophomore and junior year, you see I took U.S. History for both summer terms. But, it wasn't a make-up class, it was a get ahead class. I had never taken U.S. History before or after. That should be 10 credits toward graduation. Right?"

Dawes looked at the transcript, "Well, I…."

Naomi cut her off, "And now I see that although I got Incompletes for five classes the last half of my senior year, I see I got an 'A' in Studio Art. That should be 5 credits too. Right?"

Dawes was shaking her head at this new information, "Yes, that's Mrs. Lynen, she was the one faculty member who took your side in the expulsion. And, your attack on the other student was in her class. Go figure. She thought you had been bullied and were just defending yourself. But, school rules make any physical assault an offense. It looks like she gave you an 'A' for the whole semester. Which I guess is her right, in a dual enrollment college credit class for a graduating senior."

Naomi now had what she needed, "So, even without that last 5 credits from Studio Art that last semester, I had seven full load semesters of 30 credits each from 9th grade to the first half of my senior year, plus the 10 credits for those 'get ahead' summer school classes in U.S. History. That makes 220 credits, enough to graduate per the Kern High School District rules before I was expelled. If you add the 5 credits for the second semester of Studio Art, that's 225 credits, more than enough to graduate. Right?"

Ms. Dawes looked back and forth on the two pages. Then, she looked at Naomi over the rims of her glasses with her eyebrows up. "Wait here a minute. I need to check with someone." She took one copy of the transcript with her.

It was much more than 'a minute.' Naomi waited nearly ten minutes before Ms. Dawes came back in, followed by a man in a pinstriped business suit.

Dawes said, "Mr. Brundage wants to talk to you, Naomi."

The man, Brundage, now spoke, "Naomi, I understand that a few weeks after we last met for that expulsion hearing with your mother, that she passed away?"

Naomi stood up to talk to him, "Yes, she did. She died in early May."

"Well, I'm terribly sorry to hear that. You had a bad run of things last year. You have my sincere condolences on your mother's death," Brundage told Naomi.

"Thank you."

"And now, Ms. Dawes tells me you say you are back, supposedly with a clean record, and want to continue your schooling in college."

"Yes, all the charges were dropped, and the arrests expunged. I would like to start at Bakersfield College as soon as I can."

Brundage looked at the papers in his hand, "Well, Naomi, I have some good news for you then. From what Ms. Dawes has shown me, you were eligible for graduation from Centennial High prior to your expulsion; you had sufficient credits. You seem to have had a guardian angel on your side in the form of your Art teacher, who believed in you. I am directing that your records indicate that you graduated with your senior class last June. If you can give us your current address, we will send your diploma and a final official transcript as soon as it's is ready." Mr. Brundage now put out his hand to shake Naomi's, "Congratulations, Miss Donnelley, you are a Centennial High graduate. What do you plan on studying at the College? Art?"

"No, sir. I am hoping to go into nursing."

"Well, that is a switch. I wish you well."

Brundage left. Ms. Dawes gave Naomi a student enrollment data card to put her new address on it.

It was not a miracle, just a lucky set of facts uncovered, but Naomi was feeling somewhat blessed as she smiled at the rent-a-cop on her way to the car. She thought she ought to send this Ms. Lynen a thank you card. She thought of going and giving Ms. Lynen a Kendra-esque hug, but she had no idea where the art classrooms were. Besides, that would probably lead to more questions about her life, for which Naomi had few answers.

———

Naomi was in her bedroom reading the Bakersfield College website on the laptop when she heard the rumble of Ray's diesel truck drive into the driveway. She knew Janet was out shopping, so she decided she would go out and welcome Ray home from work.

Ray was already inside and hanging his jacket on his hook in the kitchen when Naomi came in.

"Evenin' Ray! Janet had to go shopping, something for the Relief Society. She already made your supper. It is in the oven. I'll get it for you. How'd work go?" Naomi was intentionally chipper, knowing Ray usually worked hard, and it was how Janet greeted him when he came home.

Ray's voice sounded tired as he said, "Work was mostly good, but right at the end... I took a spill trying to get out of the way of a forklift and dinged my arm pretty badly on the asphalt."

He held up his arm to show that his long-sleeved khaki shirt was ripped, and his elbow and arm had a serious, still dirty, and bloody abrasion.".

Naomi hurried to his side and pulled out a chair from the kitchen table. "Sit down and take your shirt off. Let me see."

Ray did as she asked. He took off his shirt and sat down in his t-shirt, lifting his arm up high, so Naomi could see it.

Naomi 'tsk-ed' and said, "Uh, nasty scrap, all the way up above your elbow. And, you've got dirt in the scrape. Let me clean it up."

Naomi pulled three sheets from the paper towel roll and opened the doors under the kitchen sink to get the sanitary wipes she had seen there. She went over and pulled another chair up behind Ray's, gently reaching to lift his arm back toward her.

She took one paper towel to brush the dirt out of the scrap. "This may hurt a bit. You've got sand in the dried blood."

Ray said nothing but rumbled a sound to tell her to go ahead.

Naomi softly brushed the scrape, refolding the towel to get a clean side. Then, she used the second towel to blot the bloody grooves of the cut. Nothing was too deep, but the scrape was wide and ugly. She opened the Lysol wipes.

"This will sting," Naomi warned.

"Yup," was Ray's response.

Naomi gently touched the wipe to the wound. Ray said nothing, but Naomi could feel his arm tense up. She gently ran the wipe down the scrapped arm and over the elbow. Most of the dried blood came off. A couple of the deeper scrape grooves now bled more. Naomi pulled another wipe out. She then wiped all around the edge of the wound and the nearby arm, seeing the sheet get brown with dusty dirt from his skin. She followed with another clean paper towel.

"Do you have some antiseptic around here? And bandages?" Naomi asked.

"Bag Balm and first-aid stuff are on the top shelf of the cabinet in the guest bathroom," Ray answered.

"Bag Balm?" Naomi said, a bit quizzically.

Ray gave a little laugh and said, "Yeah, we're farmers. We use Bag Balm to treat everything, scrapes, cuts, sunburn…. Big green box."

"Right, Bag Balm, it is." Naomi left the kitchen and headed to the guest bathroom.

In the bathroom, Naomi swung the mirror open, and she saw a big, leaf green box on the top shelf. She took the box down to inspect it.

The green metal box had somewhat antiquated graphics on it, but it was bright and shiny new. The metal lid of the container pictured a beatific-looking cow's head surrounded by red roses. One side of the box, indeed, had a circular picture of a cow's udder and a list of medicinal ingredients. But, the other side of the box had a picture of someone rubbing salve onto their hands, and wording about skin moisturizer and antiseptic.

Naomi also saw boxes of band-aids, gauze, and adhesive tape on the shelf. She took the gauze and tape. She pulled open the drawer in the cabinet under the sink and found some scissors. Naomi gathered her tools and headed for the kitchen.

She sat her pile of things on the kitchen table behind where Ray was patiently waiting.

"Find it?" he asked.

"Sure did."

She sat down behind him again and, with a bit of difficulty, popped the tight metal lid off the Bag Balm. The box was half full of golden jelly. Many fingers had scooped out Bag Balm before her.

Naomi scooped up a healthy quantity of the Bag Balm with her left forefinger and lifted it to sniff it. It had a slight menthol smell to it. Definitely mediciny. It made her think of the little, round, olive-drab tins of ointment the Army medics had dispensed to troops to treat various skin maladies. *Is this the same stuff?*

Naomi again pulled Ray's injured arm back with her right arm and gently spread the goop on the wound with her left. After several more finger scoops, she was finished. She wiped her hand with the back of one of the paper towels. Naomi reached for the gauze and opened the unused box.

Naomi considered whether she should make a square pad out of the gauze to cover just the scrap. But, the scrape was large, and she had plenty of gauze, so she decided to make a pad, but also wrap the gauze around Ray's arm from bicep to below his elbow. She wrapped the area of his elbow and below slightly looser than above.

She grabbed the scissors and cut the end of the gauze. Then, she popped the round case off the adhesive tape roll. It was unused and new. She pulled the end of the tape loose with her fingernail. She carefully pulled and snipped various lengths, and stuck them to the edge of the kitchen table. She cut enough to secure the gauze bands from separating around the top and bottom of the gauze, and careful to not tape his skin at the edges. Then, she finished up with four short vertical strips that taped the edge of the bandage to his arm and prevented it from slipping. The gauze bandage was secure and would not fall off, yet he could move his arm, and there was minimal contact of tape to his skin. It was just like she had read in the nursing manual.

"You are probably going to want to take a shower and don't want to get this wet. Can I put a piece of plastic over it, just until you take your shower?" Naomi asked.

"That would be great," came his answer.

Naomi had just started to unroll the roll of sandwich wrap when they heard the screen door spring screech, and Janet came in the back door into the kitchen. Janet stopped short as she saw her husband sitting at the table in his t-shirt, arm wrapped in white, and Naomi standing over him.

"What happened?" Janet asked, as she set the grocery bags on the counter.

"Ray got hurt at work, and I fixed him up," Naomi said, rather meekly.

"Yeah," Ray added.

Janet came over and kissed her husband on his receding hairline and bent further to inspect Naomi's work. She looked at the pile of first-aid supplies on the table, and then at Naomi and at what Naomi was holding.

"You are getting ready to put Saran Wrap over the dressing so he can take a shower?" Janet asked.

"Ah… Yes?" Naomi answered.

Janet stepped back, looked at Ray, and then at Naomi. "Well, we seem to have a real little Florence Nightingale at work here."

Naomi gave another little smile. Ray nodded.

Janet waved her hand toward the Saran Wrap roll and said, "Go ahead and finish, Naomi. You seem to have the situation under control."

With that, Janet Morrison turned away and started unpacking and putting away her purchases.

———

Naomi sat up quickly in bed. It took her a while to figure out where and who she was. Oodles complained at the interruption to his sleep. The softly purring cat was her first clue to reality. The darkened bedroom and affectionate cat in the Morrison's house were a long way from the scene of her nightmare.

She was still experiencing the nightmares of Mark Kelleher, but this one tonight was a bit different. It was still a dark dream about a bloody, horrible, burning wreck. But this time, she had dreamed of being a driver approaching a fiery wreckage. Instead of being pulled out of the flaming vehicle, she had been the person pulling on the body. This nightmare had been as real as the other version, another vestige of her past memories. As far as Naomi was concerned it was a memory that was better left alone. It had no place in her life anymore. She had resolved to forget such things.

It had come to her anyway. Her heart was pounding and she was sweating as always when the nightmares intruded. Oodles came over to offer calming assistance. This nightmare was different from the earlier ones, the ones she had often experienced ever since Napa. More correctly—ever since Vallejo. Neither this nightmare nor the others were really classic nightmares, they were memories. Only this time, instead of the wreck on the freeway in Vallejo, the memory went deeper into Mark's past, another fiery wreck, long ago and far away.

It took her a long time to get back to sleep. She tried to put all thoughts of burning wrecks out of her mind. Such things were no longer part of her life. They did not belong in Naomi's life. When she finally thought she had vanquished the memories and thoughts of burning vehicles, Oodles came over and bumped her chin with his head to get petted, just like he once had done with Belinda Morrison in this same bed. She was reminded that Belinda died in a car wreck, too, not so long ago and not so far away. It was going to be another long night.

—

Chapter 15

Naomi watched Janet work from the kitchen door. Janet was in the middle of canning the apricots, apples, and peaches from the trees in the old orchard on the Morrisons' lot. Boiling kettles were on several stove burners and rows of Mason jars, both filled and empty, lined the table and counters. The air of the kitchen was filled with warm, fruity scents. Janet seemed to be oblivious to Naomi's presence.

Naomi had helped Ray pick the fruit, but Janet had not spoken about the canning process to her. "Anything I can help with?" Naomi asked.

Janet startled a bit, "Oh, Naomi, I didn't see you there. No, I've got this. I kind of have my groove once I get the work started. But, you know what? You could run an important errand for me."

"Sure, whatever," Naomi said.

"Ray had to leave early this morning and forgot his wallet on the dresser," Janet said. "He doesn't have his license, his credit cards, or any cash to buy his lunch. If he has to come all the way back here, it will mess up his day. Can you drive it out to him?"

"Of course, I'd kinda like to see where Ray works. It would fill in the blanks for me. I hear him talk about stuff, but I don't know anything about where he is talking. But, you need to give me directions. I am not good about driving outside the city."

"It's easy to get there, just take any of the cross streets north to Highway 58 west, that's where your bank is. Take the 58 all the way west, out of town, until you hit Highway 43, quite a long way, then turn right and keep going until you see the big billboard for Kentfield Farms. It's a big place, lots of buildings, a tall grain elevator. Got that?" Janet asked. Naomi nodded her affirmation. "Then, just ask in the main office where you can find Ray."

"Left on 58 to the 43, right until the Kentfield billboard. Doesn't sound hard," Naomi said, repeating it under her breath. "Where's the wallet?"

———

Eli Kent was going over crop reports at his desk. His office manager, Mattie Heidenreich, and two of her bookkeepers were working at other desks in the office. He looked up when the buzzer sounded to indicate someone had opened the front door. A young woman walked in, approached the office counter. Eli motioned to Mattie that he would handle it.

"Yes, Hon?" Eli said, as he walked up to face the woman at the counter. 'Hon' was Eli's usual name for most women or girls he met. It kept him from having to admit he had forgotten their names, and Eli was really bad with names.

The young woman, not much more than a girl, smiled nicely and held a man's wallet up and said, "Ray Morrison forgot his wallet at home. How do I get it to him?"

Eli nodded and answered, "We've got a blown pump out in the 2-3 North-west field. Ray is supervising the work crew. You can take it right out to him."

The pretty blonde's cheery smile disappeared as she blinked and said, "I have no clue what that means." Eli noted the crisp California accent with its overemphasis of "no clue."

"No, I suppose not. Let me show you," Eli said, as he walked around the counter and went up to the big plexiglass covered map on the front wall, proudly captioned Kentfield Farms Properties. The young woman followed him across the lobby.

Eli pointed to the map and said to the girl, "Here's where we are now in the buildings on the highway. 2-3 North-west is the second quarter-section north and the third one west from here." He moved his finger along the map to show what he meant.

"I can just drive out there?" she asked. He noticed she was chomping on gum.

"Sure thing, Hon. Just keep to the graveled roads and keep out of the way of any equipment traffic you see."

"How far is that?"

"Each quarter-section is a half-mile on a side. You'll turn on the road between the first and second fields. That's a half-mile north, and a mile and a half west."

"Wow, this place is big!"

Eli smiled at the compliment to his farm, "Yes, and we have nearly 16,000 acres under irrigation here in Kern County, some owned, some leased. Even more up north."

The girl raised her eyebrows in appreciation of that and said, "Thanks much. I appreciate your help." The girl presented her hand to him to shake and gave Eli a surprisingly hearty handshake.

Eli was still smiling after the girl left, and he went back around the counter to his desk. His smile disappeared as he looked over toward his office manager and said, "Mattie, I thought Ray Morrison's daughter died last year."

Mattie looked over and answered, "She did. Car wreck on the old 99 north of town. I sent in Ray's claim on his employee's life insurance policy for a family member's death and changed his W-4 form for dependents."

Ray looked at Mattie for a moment, and then shrugged and sat down.

———

The late morning air was hot and humid as Naomi left the office and returned to the Prius. The hot Indian Summer weather was a welcome change from the cold, wet, rainy weather of her first few weeks in Bakersfield. She had parked with the sun on the driver's side, so she flipped over the old bath towel on the driver's seat to the cool side, so she would not sizzle her thighs on the vinyl seat as she sat down in the shorts she was wearing. Belinda Morrison had been a fan of shorts. Naomi had inherited her collection, and this was perfect shorts weather.

In trying to find places in her new hometown of Bakersfield from Google directions, she had found that the Prius had a remarkably accurate trip odometer that even had a decimal place indication, so she reset it to zero. She saw the gravel side road heading north along the county highway and headed out.

At precisely '0.5' miles, there was a T-intersection, and she took it to the left.

Most of the fields had crops growing. The second one to the left looked like it had recently been harvested, as she could see dying leaves and a few broken stalks of what looked like celery. She could smell onions somewhere. Everything was hot and dusty in the fields. On the far horizon to the north, the skyline shimmered in a mirage.

Naomi slowed as the odometer approached '2.0.' Ahead she could see three clusters of workers. Several work trucks and a couple of older cars were parked just off the road. She parked off the edge of the gravel road and got out.

She did not see Ray, so she approached the first two men nearest her, who seemed to be working on a metal irrigation pipe with shovels and wrenches. The two men were dark-skinned Hispanics, their denim jeans covered in dirt, and their t-shirts were soaked in sweat.

"I'm looking for Ray Morrison?" She smiled at them.

The man facing her did not seem to understand, and he poked the shoulder of the other one, pointing at Naomi, without words.

"Ray Morrison?" Naomi repeated for him.

The other man quickly nodded and pointed to a cluster of men standing between fields a short walk to the right.

Naomi thanked the two workers and turned toward the other group. As she got closer to them, the path between the two fields got wetter and wetter until by the time she was half-way down, she was hopping from dry spot to dry spot amongst mud puddles. She finally recognized Ray in his khaki work clothes, kneeling near a large piece of equipment on a cement foundation. Behind them, there was a large, vertical, brown, ceramic pipe, ten feet high, that seemed to be slowly gushing water out of the top of it. The man standing next to Ray was holding the most enormous Crescent wrench Naomi had ever seen, as big as a banjo.

As she hopped over the puddles, Naomi had a momentary thought that the side to side running movement was not unlike the rubber tire obstacle course Mark had run in Army basic training. It was a bit disconcerting to Naomi when she realized she had almost thought of Mark's experience as that of another person, even though the memory was hers.

———

Ray Morrison and the men working with him on the plugged diesel pump and irrigation standpipe noticed the approaching figure. As Ray stood, he recognized Naomi as she hopped over the puddles of standing water caused by the malfunctioning irrigation system. Naomi deftly navigated the wet path but stopped when she got to the last, larger puddle. Ray motioned that he would come to her, but Naomi raised her hand in protest, bent her knees, and swung her arms to do a leapfrog jump over the last pond. She had something in her hand.

Naomi easily cleared the distance and landed next to Ray in the dry dirt patch. Ray grabbed her shoulders to make sure she kept her balance on landing.

Naomi stood up straight and smiled up into Ray's face. "You forgot your wallet on your dresser."

Ray unnecessarily swatted his empty back pants pocket, as Naomi lifted his wallet in her hand to show him with a grin.

Ray still had his left hand on her shoulder, which he squeezed, as he said, "Thanks, Naomi, you saved my lunch hour for me."

Naomi smiled broadly, "No prob. See ya tonight."

Naomi turned to leave, but this time, instead of the leapfrog move, she did a two-step jump with her left foot to the field embankment on the far-left edge of the big puddle and another quick hop to the far side with her right foot.

Ray and his men watched appreciatively as the long-legged girl bounced her way down the muddy path to the road. Her blonde hair and the white shorts flipped from side to side with each hop.

The man next to Ray said, "Ray, your daughter is a beauty."

"She's n…," Ray quickly cut off his denial that Naomi was his daughter, and instead said, "Yes, Naomi is a real treasure."

———

Naomi had stopped in at the campus bookstore to buy a canvas tote bag with the Bakersfield College logo on it after her first stop at the Admissions Office. Now, after stops at the Career Counselor's office and the Nursing Department, her tote bag was filling with a pile of various forms, brochures, and information sheets. The path to becoming a nurse was a mix of at least four different tracks or routes to becoming an RN. Then, once you were a licensed registered nurse, there was also a move up to California State University Bakersfield to get a full bachelor's degree in nursing needed for many nurses' career paths.

With her memories from Mark's time at both junior college and university, Naomi had a leg up on many of her fellow prospective nurses, but she was in a new field, and only a little of the aid from Mark's experience was of any value. She did have one advantage due to Mark's past. It seemed the college allowed up to thirty credits to be done by the College Level Examination Program (CLEP) tests and various tests for college classes. With Mark's degree in Bioinformatics from BYU, Naomi was reasonably sure she would be able to test out of many of the necessary courses required as prerequisites for the associate degree in the nursing program. She could apply now, in October, to start classes in January. With the test credits and spring semester classes, Naomi should be eligible to apply for the nursing program next June and start next fall. That is, assuming she got into the restricted admission program. She was determined to make that happen.

After leaving the Nursing Department office, Naomi walked back across campus toward where she had parked her car by the admin building with another stop at the bookstore to see what books were needed for Nursing and the classes she thought she could test out of. On the way, she passed the gymnasium and the huge swimming pool. This gave her another idea. She would soon be a college student again and eligible for the swim team. Mark had been an award-winning swimmer. Swimming had gotten him into BYU. Naomi wondered whether she had some of that swimming prowess via that weird switch between Naomi and Mark. It might be fun to swim competitively again.

Naomi made a mental note to check out the Bakersfield College swim team online. She had not seen a swimsuit in either Naomi's or Belinda's things. Perhaps, she should buy herself a racing Speedo. Naomi had a good figure for it and the long legs needed for swimming. She would need to get herself in shape, though. She was still recovering from her time in the hospital bed.

—

Naomi loaded her Prius with the two pans of cupcakes she and Kendra had made that morning. Naomi put the wings of the costume she had purchased via the Internet next to the cupcakes. It was a short drive to the Church meetinghouse.

Kendra was waiting when Naomi drove up into the church parking lot. It took Naomi a while to figure out what Kendra's costume was. Then, as Kendra walked closer, Naomi could see that the bodice of the moderately low-cut, poof-sleeved blouse was a French flag, and the skirt was tri-color striped. Kendra was Marianne, the heroine and mascot of the French Revolution. Kendra even had a red Phrygian cap on her head. Naomi felt outclassed by Kendra's sheer imagination.

Since they had made the cupcakes in Janet Morrison's kitchen, Naomi had them in her car. She opened the hatchback and waited for Kendra to get there.

"Great outfit, Mademoiselle!" Naomi said.

"*Merci beaucoup. Pour la liberte!*" Kendra shouted dramatically.

"Can you hook me up before we get the cupcakes. I couldn't drive with my wings on," Naomi said. She pulled two fluffy, feathered wings from the hatchback and showed Kendra the catch in the back of her white floor-length angel dress to attach the wings. Naomi also donned her LED-lighted 'Halo' headband she had purchased online with the angel outfit.

"Wow, halo and new glasses, too," Kendra announced.

"Well, actually, old glasses. Luckily, I found these old, rimless, granny glasses in my stuff. My normal black-rimmed ones messed up the angel look. Made me into a bookwormy kind of angel. These little, clear ones are better. Right?"

"Much, you might even consider them full time. I like them," was Kendra's friendly advice. "It doesn't hide your face."

They split the cupcakes pans up and carried them inside.

The decorating crew of YSA women was finishing orange and black crepe paper hangings. There were some pumpkins, spooky cats, and headless horsemen decorations. There was one very lonely witch cartoon over the snack table, but it was clear witches and ghosts were not popular. Naomi noticed a large folded card on the name tag table, announcing 'No Masks! Thank you."

Naomi had to ask Kendra, "No masks allowed?"

Kendra nodded, "Yeah, I guess there was an article in *Ensign* magazine a few years back by one of the Church General Authorities who said wearing masks was contrary to Mormon tradition. The article noted that there was nothing wrong with the fun of Halloween, but we should avoid wearing masks to hide our true identity and should avoid aggrandizing evil characters and the Devil's work. I've also heard that part of the problem with masks is that Joseph Smith's murderers in Missouri wore something like Klan hoods and blackface to hide their identities.

"Ah," Naomi accepted the concept.

They deposited the cupcakes next to the matching punchbowls with orange and black punch in them. Kendra made sure the orange cupcakes and black ones were aligned with their proper punchbowl.

"Sorry, I have to try this," Naomi said, dipping a plastic cup in the black punch and very carefully tasting it. She smiled and said to Kendra, "Very dark grape. I was worried it was licorice or something."

Naomi and Kendra went back to get their name tags and wait for the party to get rolling.

At the top of the hour, Sister Dora Lampert, the YSA Relief Society president, waved to a young man standing on the stage. The fluorescent gymnasium lights dimmed to off. The stage lights that had been turned around to cover the whole gym floor went on in multicolor array, mostly blues and oranges. There was even a mirror ball hanging from one of the basketball hoops with a spotlight on it.

"Hmm, not bad," was Naomi's reaction. She now saw a DJ was setting up a table just below the stage area with a large speaker array on either side of him. The Mormon Young Single Adults seemed to know how to throw a bash.

Naomi asked Kendra, "Would you mind if we sat over in the wallflower seats by the door? My angel shoes are killing me."

Kendra looked down at Naomi's feet. Naomi explained, "The only angel white shoes I could find were full heels, and I'm not that used to them."

"Sure, that will let us get a good look at the people coming in," Kendra headed toward the chairs.

Naomi smiled to herself about her 'I'm not that used to them' line. *'Never wore high heels before in my life and spent the whole afternoon practicing walking in my bedroom'* was more accurate.

Kendra had been right about the view they had from the chairs by the front wall. The Halloween dance had been intended for YSA people in the three LDS stakes, which covered twenty-odd congregations across the southern Central Valley, and the cultural hall was filling up. There were plenty of people in fairly nice costumes and several in just normal dressy clothes. Naomi even saw several cowboy-types in tight denims, plaid shirts, and cowboy boots. Almost universally, however, the young women were either in costume or fancily dressed. Naomi noticed that Sister Dora had to ask one Batman to remove his mask, which he did under protest.

Even though the DJ had started a good round-robin of a broad selection of danceable slow and fast dance songs, the dance floor was slow to gather a crowd. This changed ever so slowly.

Naomi was on guard for someone coming up to her and renewing an acquaintance that she could not remember, as Kendra and Nate Hoskins had done at her first Sacrament Meeting. So far, this had not happened. *Thank goodness.*

Naomi did notice a couple of men come in who did not fit the mold of the others. Two tall men came in wearing military flight suits. From their swagger, Naomi assumed the suits were work clothes and not mere costumes.

She asked Kendra, indicating the two men with a point of her chin, "Is there a military base around here?"

Kendra answered, "I think the Hanford Ward is in the stakes invited tonight. There is a huge Navy fighter base just west of Hanford,

Lemoore Naval Air Station."

"Ah," Naomi stored the information. Her memories from Mark included something about the Lemoore base. But, she had little time to think about the pilots, as Nate Hoskins appeared in front of her.

"May I have a dance with an angel," Nate asked.

Naomi had been dreading this moment since she had realized she would not be able to avoid the Halloween Dance. Her miserable day trying to learn to move in the heels had only made it worse. But, she gave Nate a good trouper's smile and took his hand.

Naturally, the moderate tempo music that had been playing when Nate had come up to her ended before they were on the dance floor, and the old B. J. Thomas *Somebody Done Somebody Wrong* song was announced by the DJ. She thought she saw Nate smile a bit at the slow, romantic melody.

Naomi messed up the hand placement and had to quickly move her left hand from Nate's side to his shoulder. Nate pulled her in toward him with his hand on the small of her back and commenced to lead her. Everything was backwards from every dance she had ever danced. The only redeeming grace of the situation was that with Naomi being able to use Nate as a balance point and Nate dancing as slow and close as he could, Naomi was probably less likely to break her ankle in the high heels than if they had been dancing faster and moving more.

"I've been trying to think of some witty way to comment on both your costume and how great you look, but all the witty comments sounded really corny. So, I'll just say, 'you look beautiful, Naomi.'" Nate's head was tilted down, almost nose to nose with her as he said that.

"Thank you, Nate. It has been a long time since I danced."

"I find that hard to believe. You are delightful to dance with." Nate was full of compliments.

Naomi looked up at him and suddenly realized that with him being a good half foot taller than her, her LED lights in her halo were right in his eyes. Nate's face was illuminated as though Naomi were a spotlight.

"Just a second, Nate. Can we stop a moment?" Naomi pulled away, and Nate looked surprised.

Naomi quickly pulled the halo headband off and flicked the switch off. Then, she put it back on and put her hands back in dancing position.

"My ethereal presence was a bit much, huh?" Naomi laughed.

"Much better," Nate agreed.

No sooner than they had gotten back in step, Naomi felt one of her wings get bumped. Naomi quickly turned her head to see that her right wing had scored a hit on the man's shoulder of a nearby couple.

Nate reacted, "Oops, my bad. It's my job to steer my angel safely. I misjudged your wingspan."

They both laughed.

Naomi now noticed that they were a good match at dancing. She was being held fairly close. Then, Naomi realized she really did not mind that at all. They were in synch dancing, and it was comfortable and nice to be in his arms—his tall, handsome arms. The extended slow dance was not all that bad. But, it did bring some divergent thoughts to Naomi's mind; it was her first male/female close encounter since she had become Naomi.

I have more to get used to than just the dancing position and who leads.

When the dance finally ended, the DJ announced, "Five-minute break. When I come back, let's have everybody out there dancing. I'll put a little intermission music on for now."

"You want any refreshments. Cupcakes? Punch?" Nate asked.

"No, not really. I made the cupcakes, so I already got to eat all the mistakes. But, I think I need to sit down for a while. I'm not used to these high heels. I'm kind of a Nike girl, and three-inch heels take a little getting used to again. But, I'd love to dance again, later on."

"Sure, I'll hold you to that," Nate smiled and headed for the snack table.

When Naomi got back to her earlier chair, she noticed Kendra was also being escorted back by one of the cowboys. She sat with Kendra again.

"So, how was the cowboy?" Naomi asked.

Kendra gave a wiggly 'hand balance' gesture, "Not that bad, Mr. Ken Hotchkiss really did know how to dance well, had a recent shower, and used lots of musky cologne. Never stepped on my toes. And, introduced me to the fact that his daddy owns a big chunk of western Tulare County."

"Sounds romantic. I hear Tulare County is so nice in the spring when all the cows are birthing," Naomi smiled.

"And you, how was Nate?"

"Actually, just fine. Couldn't be better. Also, he knew how to dance and hold on tight. No noticeable smells. He was a quick learner in avoiding hitting people with my wings. And, took my hint when I wanted to sit down."

"I guess both of us could have done far worse," Kendra surmised.

"I guess."

The DJ's pleading for more dance activity seemed to have an effect, as there was a decided uptake in couples heading out when he started again. Naomi was watching this activity, and Nate heading toward her again when two large bodies appeared in front of her and Kendra. She looked up to see that both bodies wore flight suits. The Navy men seemed to be making a coordinated effort on the two of them.

The flyer in front of Naomi bent low to read Naomi's name tag and said, "Good evening, Naomi, I'm Connor Holloway. May I have this dance?" He extended his hand to her.

Naomi did not get to hear the introduction of the other flyer to Kendra, as Naomi had no sooner taken the proffered hand that she was being escorted onto the dance floor, rather hurriedly.

The music seemed to be a medley of slower show tunes, so her dance partner took her right hand in his left and spread his other hand wide on Naomi's lower ribs. Naomi got her other hand correct first time this time around. The broad shoulder under the flight suit was a firm grasping point for a lady's hand.

When they turned so the light allowed her to see it, Naomi saw the red nametag on the flight suit, "Ah, not Navy, you are a Marine. I should have known."

He smiled and said, "This is a Halloween Party. Maybe this is just a costume."

Naomi shook her head, "Nope, nice try."

"What gave me away?"

"A couple things," Naomi said. "When you reached for my hand, your big, gold Naval Academy class ring was rather obvious. Those don't come with mere costumes. Second... and don't get me wrong, I'm not complaining... the level of pheromones that are exuded by a flight suit that was obviously worn in a flight today by a naval aviator is positively overpowering my olfactory senses. My female pheromone receptors are literally screaming to me to either demurely swoon or offer to bear your children. Both of which urges I have well under control."

"There is a lot to be said for going out of control," Connor said.

"Don't let your squadron commander here you say that. I'm guessing you guys got off work and remembered the Halloween Party tonight. With the long trip down here, you figured you'd just come as you were. Actually, it is pretty cool. I did the same thing, that is, not changing out of my work clothes."

"Ah, ha! I thought you looked a little too heavenly for your outfit to be a mere costume."

"Five bonus points for the Marine."

"I should get a few more bonus points for rescuing you from that other guy who was coming back for another dance with you when I stepped in."

"Why do you think I needed rescuing from Nate?"

"That guy had a neon-lighted sign on his forehead announcing, 'I'm going on my mission soon and will expect you to wait two years for me.'"

"So, here I am dancing with a guy who has a sign on his forehead that says 'I'm going to be deployed overseas every couple years, for the next twenty years or so, and every time I leave you bad people will be trying to kill me and make you a widow.'"

Connor shrugged, "And yet, you are still here dancing with me. Smart girl."

Naomi was not exactly sure when they had switched positions, but she now saw that both her hands were on the Marine's shoulders, and both of his hands were around her back. There was no space between them as they danced.

Naomi now asked, "So, where you from, Gyrene?"

"All over. Second generation military. Probably spent as much time in North Carolina and Florida as anywhere."

"I thought I heard that. Dropping your 'ings' and long vowels everyplace you can put them."

"Well, at least you had to ask. I hear California, *like totally*, from you."

"Ah, but born and bred in Utah."

"Ninety percent of the people in this room probably have Utah somewhere in their genes."

"You?"

"Yup, my folks met at Utah State, my dad was in NROTC," Connor Holloway had a great smile. "You wanna sit down and talk for a while? We can probably hide you from 'Mission' boy, if we go sit down at the far end of the hall."

"You mean in the dark area, behind the mirror ball?"

"Yeah, good protective camouflage to hide a beautiful angel from predators."

"You mean from 'other' predators."

"Like I said."

Naomi followed First Lieutenant Connor Holloway, USMC, off the dance floor.

———

"I suppose I should be feeling really guilty right now. But I don't," Connor said.

"Guilty about what? I haven't seen any major indiscretions out of you. At least, not anything reportable to higher authorities," Naomi replied.

"I've done a pretty good job monopolizing your time, and it looks like the DJ is winding things up."

"I haven't complained, have I? And, after tonight I can claim a good knowledge of the uses and benefits of an F-35B. Not sure where I can use that knowledge, but it's there if I need it."

"See, I have bored you, huh?" Connor feigned sadness.

"Like I said, no complaints from me. And, it looks like your wingman has been doing a little monopolizing on my wing-girl, too. Kendra and I will have to compare notes tomorrow."

"I probably need to be careful about Nate, the Mission boy. He's probably waiting outside for me with a pack of his high school friends, ready for payback for hiding you from him all night."

"If you're worried, I can walk you to your car and protect you," Naomi grinned.

"Gosh, if I'd known it was that easy to get you to walk out with me, I'd not have tried so hard."

The fluorescent lights flickered on, and the DJ thanked the crowd. Naomi and Connor stood up.

"Well, you're right. Time to go." Naomi said. "Since we aren't hiding in a dark corner anymore, I can put my navigation lights back on." She took her halo off and clicked the LEDs back on, before putting it back on.

They walked back toward the main group of people. They saw Kendra and Connor's friend still standing together.

"You need to get anything. Purse, coat?" Connor asked.

"Just my cupcake pans. I left my purse in the car and have my key fob in my secret angel pocket."

"Yes, I felt the bump, but couldn't think of a polite way to ask about it."

"Yea, now I can tell my friends about the Marine who felt my bump."

Connor cleared his throat as a response to her joke.

Naomi saw Kendra wave at her, and both couples headed for the snack table.

Kendra and Naomi met up at the table, and Kendra was first to do introductions, "Naomi, may I present Lieutenant Junior Grade Dennis 'Carnivore' Smith, U.S. Navy. Dennis, meet my fellow cupcake maker, Naomi Donnelley."

Naomi shook his hand and turned to Connor, "And Kendra, please meet Connor Holloway, First Lieutenant, U.S. Marine Corps, who failed to tell me his callsign nickname. Connor, this is Kendra Allred."

Dennis cut in, as Connor took Kendra's hand, "Connor is 'Longshanks.'"

"Ah, like King Edward the First, huh?" Naomi asked.

Connor gave Naomi a quick look, as though surprised at her knowledge of English history.

Dennis laughed, "No, more like the guy who tried to fit into a regular size flight suit in flight school when he needed a tall. He looked pretty silly with a high water Nomex suit."

Naomi could not resist looking down at Connor's feet.

Connor said, "That was quite a while back, but once given a tactical call sign, it sticks like glue."

"Ah, is that what it's called?" Kendra said.

"That or just plain nickname," Dennis explained.

Naomi changed the subject, "So, looks like orange cupcakes were a hit. Not so much the black ones."

Half of the cookie sheet of black cupcakes still remained.

"You guys have any interest in taking cupcakes back to Lemoore?" Naomi asked.

"Sure, they'll disappear in the ready room tomorrow morning. Guaranteed. We'll probably have to make up a story about where all those black cupcakes came from. But, we can be creative on that." Connor reached to help Naomi with the pans.

"You have anything in the car you can put the cupcakes in?" Naomi asked.

"How about if I just take the pan for now. And, I can return it to you Saturday when I pick you up for our date?" Connor gave her a surly smile.

Naomi stood blinking at Connor, then whispered, "I saw what you did there."

"Yes, I kind of liked that myself. It preempts your ability to turn me down for the date without looking kind of silly." Connor whispered back and smiled at Naomi.

Kendra apparently did not catch the *tête-à-tête* going on between Naomi and Connor, as she asked, "Where you guys going?"

Naomi quickly said, "Connor said he would try to get tickets to some country music event here in the Valley, so I could teach him how to really dance when I'm in my boots and not in three-inch heels."

"Sounds like a great idea!" Kendra said, looking at Dennis. Then, she elbowed him gently and added, "Right, Carnivore?"

Dennis realized his goof and said, "Yes, sounds great. Double date?"

Connor whispered to Naomi, "I saw what you did there."

Naomi whispered back, "Paybacks are hell."

Connor said, "Yes, double date, but in two cars. Neither my Corvette nor Denny's 370Z have room for two couples."

"Your serve, Miss Donnelley," Connor whispered.

"Our next game will be Saturday evening. At a location to be determined." Naomi smiled.

Connor took a silver ballpoint pen out of his upper left sleeve pocket and gently pulled Naomi's name tag off her dress. He waited, pen to nametag, for Naomi to figure out what he wanted.

Naomi gave Connor her cellphone number and the Morrison's address. Connor handed the pen to Dennis, who got Kendra's information from her.

Connor picked up the empty orange cupcake pan and Dennis the half-full black pan. The two couples nodded to Sister Dora and an older guy hovering near her at the door and left the cultural hall and meetinghouse.

As they went outside, Connor did a quick 360° turn and announced, "Nope, no high school boys lying in wait for us."

"What?" both Dennis and Kendra asked at the same time.

"Never mind. Inside joke," Naomi said.

The parking lot was emptying out fast. With Naomi's Prius at one side and Kendra's car on the other, the women pointed their escorts in opposite directions.

"You guys came together? I suppose," Naomi asked after they split from the other couple.

"Yes."

"You don't need to tell me what you drove. The bright orange Corvette says, 'single pilot's car' all over it."

"It's a necessary accouterment of my station in life," Connor said.

"There are a couple other ways to say that, but I'll be nice."

"I assume the angel drives the cute little hybrid?"

"My sainted mother's car, so no wisecracks," Naomi ordered. She tugged the Toyota key fob from the hidden dress pocket and beeped her hatchback open.

Connor put the empty pan in the storage area and turned to Naomi, who had her back to him.

"You need to pull the wing tabs out of the slot on my dress. The Highway Patrol doesn't like us angels to drive while wing-ed," Naomi put her hand over her shoulder to point out the wing connection spot.

Connor chuckled to himself and said, "There has got to be a good line about an angel losing her wings, but I'm missing it right now."

"Let me help. You should have tried, in *It's a Wonderful Life,* we learn, 'Every time a bell rings an Angel gets its wings.' You should have asked me, so what do we hear when an angel loses its wings?"

"Ah, a Prius lock chirping?"

"Needs work, but good try."

Connor put the wings next to the baking tray and closed the hatch. This time when he turned, Naomi was facing him.

"I had a good time tonight," Naomi said.

"The best part is not done, yet," Connor said, taking a step toward her.

With his forefinger, Connor tipped Naomi's chin up. Then, he turned his head and bent to give her a long kiss.

As the kiss continued, Naomi felt silly with her hands at her sides. She reached up and put her hands on Connor's sides. He took the hint and put his arms around her, drawing her into him. After a quick look into Naomi's eyes, Connor gave her one more kiss. Then, he opened the driver's door for her.

As Naomi gathered the long white dress to seat herself, Connor bent into the car for one last close encounter with Naomi. He kissed her cheek and whispered in her ear, "I can't wait to see the cowgirl boots on the Bakersfield Angel."

Connor closed her door, and she watched Connor, quite literally, saunter toward his Corvette. Longshanks was, indeed, a suitable moniker for him. At the far end of the parking lot, Naomi saw Kendra with Carnivore saying good night in much the same way she and Connor had.

Naomi put the key in the ignition and closed her eyes to take stock of things. Her heart was racing, her cheeks were flushed, and she could quite easily tell Doctor Partridge that his guess about her attraction to the opposite sex had been right on. The dance with Nate had only been a prelude to her jumbled thoughts after the kiss from Connor.

Naomi would long remember her 'first kiss' this night. She now realized that the joke she had told Connor about the effect of his flight suit's pheromones on her had turned out to be all too true.

I kissed a man and I liked it. My old memories of Mark's boy-girl kisses are like a distant memory, a memory I am sort of embarrassed by. This needs a lot of thought.

———

Chapter 16

Naomi entered the offices of Kentfield Farms for the second time in as many weeks. Instead of the four people that were here last time, now there was only one older woman at one of the desks.

Naomi was wearing a much different outfit this time. The first time, when she brought Ray's wallet, she had been in shorts, tank top, and tennis shoes, now she was in black slacks and a white blouse, trying to look business-like.

Naomi heard the bell ring as she opened the door. The woman looked up as Naomi walked across the lobby.

Naomi went to the counter and said, "Is Eli around?"

The woman did not stand as she said, "No, he's out. Should be back soon, though. Can I help you?"

"I was told to talk to Eli about an extra help office job he had," Naomi said.

At this, the woman showed interest and stood up to come over to the counter.

"How'd you hear about that?" the woman asked.

"Ray Morrison told me to come in."

"Ah, thought I recognized you. You were in here a week or so ago."

"Yeah, that was me."

The woman put out her hand to Naomi, "Hi, I'm Mattie Heidenreich. I'm the office manager. If you went to work here, you'd be working for me."

"Hi, Naomi Donnelley," Naomi shook the woman's hand.

"So, you a relative of Ray's or something?"

"Uh, I'm staying with Ray and Janet. My mother died last spring, and they sort of took me in." Naomi did not exactly know how to explain her situation to a prospective employer.

"Yeah, they're good people, the Morrisons." The woman looked Naomi up and down, as far down as the counter would let her. "You're pretty young. You know anything about bookkeeping or data processing?"

Naomi knew she had no possibility of giving any real experience, as Naomi. She made up the best story she could. Her best bet was saying something that would get her foot in the door, as her knowledge of business and computers, via Mark, was more than any farm office manager could possibly hope for.

"I am really knowledgeable in bookkeeping; my mother was a bookkeeper, and I have been helping her for years. Also, I can do pretty much anything you might need in the way of data processing, all the way up to programming, if necessary." Naomi hoped that did not sound too boastful for a young girl five months out of high school. All she could hope for was to be allowed to get her hands on their system and show what she could do.

"Hmm, I learned from my mother, too," Mattie said.

Naomi gave a knowing smile as she realized she had, with blind luck, dodged the experience issue. Accountant mothers rule!

"The 'extra help' position Ray heard about turned into two positions when I lost the second of my girls helping me here in the office last Monday. It seems she went and got herself married in Fresno over the weekend. I have a big project we need to get done before the end of the year and nobody to help. How much time can you work?"

"I can work whatever you need now, through mid-January, when I want to start at the college. I am free to give you whatever you need. After January, maybe part-time, 'cuz besides college classes, I need to do some extra help work in a medical job for college. They require it."

"Well, I don't know how you know stuff like programming, but that isn't what we need. We hired the programmers already, and they gave us a new accounting system that needs our old accounting data entered into it. What I need is data entry, putting our old spreadsheets into the new accounting software in time to do end of year work using the new system. We've got vendors, and invoices and billings and wages and expenses and taxes and fund balances and …well, lots of stuff that all have to be input correctly. You think you can do that for us."

Naomi shrugged, "No problem, show me where to start."

"Okay, we pay the office staff on the same scale as the union contract we use for the ag workers. Makes things simpler, and the attorneys had some reason they liked it, too. Some equal pay for sexes rule. Starting out, you earn contract minimum, sixteen bucks an hour, time and a half over 40 hours, or over ten hours on any given day. If you're here for ninety days, we'll talk about benefits. Sit down at the third desk that'll be yours, and I'll give you all the forms to fill out. Consider yourself hired," Mattie shook Naomi's hand again, and went to a filing cabinet where she started pulling out papers and forms.

Naomi walked around the counter and put her red purse on the third desk. Naomi was employed.

———

Mattie came over and put her hand on Naomi's shoulder, looking at what Naomi was working on.

"How ya doin'?" Mattie asked.

"Just fine. But, I have a couple of questions after looking at the new accounting program," Naomi turned to look at Mattie.

"Ok, shoot." Mattie crossed her arms.

"Alright, it seems your accounting database is really a standard Microsoft Access database with a custom accounting program shell built around the basic program. And, your old bookkeeping information was kept on a simple Microsoft Excel spreadsheet program that you said you printed out and took to the CPAs to do the final accounting and taxes. Right?"

"Yes, that's is pretty much what we had. Kind of archaic, but now we've got a modern accounting program and can get rid of the old spreadsheets."

Naomi put her hand to her chin, "Okay, then I have a fairly basic question. Why are you wasting all the time doing data entry of all the old accounting data into the new accounting program when you already have it on the computer? You should be able to just export a datafile from the spreadsheets and import it into the accounting software. They are all compatible."

Mattie squinted at Naomi, "Would that be what they call 'porting?'"

"Yeah, 'porting' is a shorthand term for 'exporting and importing.'"

"Well, Eli handled all the contracts with the Ag software people in Riverside, and I believe they said they could send some people out here to do the 'porting,' but it was an add-on to the contract and would cost something like nine thousand dollars extra, beyond the software cost. They asked if we had somebody to input all of that into our new program, and he told them yes. We could do our own data input much cheaper than paying some team of contractors to drive out from Riverside to do it for us."

Naomi tried to be respectful and not laugh at this. Mattie, Eli, and Kentfield Farms were very crudely reinventing the accounting wheel by hiring those other two girls, and now Naomi, to do manual data input of accounting information that was already in usable computer formatted files.

"Mattie, I need to tell you that if you can give me a couple hours, maybe not even that long, I can probably have this entire conversion project done. I can very easily make a data template from the old spreadsheets to export the data in the same form the accounting software wants to see in the new database. And then, I just tell the accounting software to load the data into its current database."

"But, you don't want to do something and lose all our accounting information."

Naomi smiled, "Never happen! I can just make a new directory and copy all the old spreadsheet files into it. Then, I can duplicate the accounting database into that directory. I can run everything I need to run without even touching the main accounting files. If it works like I'm sure it will, I can just make my copies your main data file."

Mattie shook her head, "Naomi, that sounds too good to be true. And, you know what they say about things that are too good to be true."

Naomi smiled at Mattie, "Well, in this case, 'They' would be wrong, dead wrong. You know Mattie, you said a few minutes ago you needed to run into town at lunch to go to the bank and run some errands. Right?"

"Right, and Eli might be here before I get back, but probably not."

"So, Mattie, take your time at lunch. Give me an hour and a half, and I will totally knock your socks off. Promise."

"And, you won't screw anything up."

"The only thing I may screw up is the need for me to be employed to do the data entry job. Everything will be just fine."

"Ok, Naomi, be careful."

——

Naomi had already explained everything to Mattie when Eli finally came back after lunch and had Ray with him. Naomi had carefully shown Mattie how every spreadsheet and all of the data could now be found in the accounting software program.

"Eli, come here. You gotta see this." Mattie shouted to Eli as he came across the lobby.

"Not right now Mattie, Ray asked me to go with him to the machine shed," Eli said. "Yeah, I see you hired Ray's girl, but I'll be right back to say 'Hi' to her."

"No! Eli, you need to come see this now!" Mattie firmly ordered her boss. "Whatever Ray had can wait. What Naomi has done is downright miraculous."

Eli headed over, and Ray followed, curious about what 'Ray's girl' had done. When Eli got close to Naomi's new desk, he put out his hand to Naomi, "Welcome. Is it Naomi?"

"Yes, Mr. Kent, Naomi Donnelley."

"We can do introductions later, Eli. Naomi, you explain to him what you did." Mattie was bouncing with excitement.

For Eli's benefit, Naomi went over all of her discussion about what 'porting' was and why you did not need to do data entry for existing files. As an example, she showed him the accounting software's printout for all the checks paid to state withholding tax for the year for the farm's employees.

"So, let me get this straight, over the lunch hour you did exactly what the software company in Riverside offered to do for me for $9000? Is that right?" Eli stared at Naomi with his arms crossed in front of him.

Naomi nodded her head and said, "Well, another way to look at it was that in an hour and a half I did what you and Mattie were ready to pay two people like me to do over the next eight weeks before the end of the year. For that hour and a half, you will pay me about $24.00, whereas the two people working for 8 weeks would cost you eight to ten thousand dollars."

Eli turned to Mattie, "Is this for real?"

Mattie could only nod.

Eli looked to Naomi, back to Mattie, and then over to Ray, and back to Naomi.

"Well, Hon, I guess you're hired. Full-time, permanent. Mattie, forget about that 90-day stuff. Give her benefits and backdate her paycheck a bit to pay her some of what she saved us."

"Uh, Eli?" Naomi said with a little bit of cringing expression, she wanted to say something but was not sure how to say it.

"What?" Eli asked.

"Eli, I really appreciate the offer of a permanent job and everything. But, my plans are to start at Bakersfield College in January and try to get into their Registered Nurse program next fall. For that, they require that I do at least 300 hours of either volunteer work or employment in a medical job, like medical assistant, or practical nurse, or something like that. I can't do that if I'm working here full time." Naomi tried to use her best apologetic voice.

"Where you plan on asking for that medical job?" Eli asked.

"I have no idea," Naomi responded. "I don't know anyone in the medical profession here. I'll have to pound the pavement."

Eli thought for a moment. "I think we can do better than pound the pavement. You did me a favor. Let me see what I can do for you. You work here as long as you can, and we'll find something to fit your needs, somewhere. Sound good?"

"Sounds great!"

———

Naomi put on her old sweatpants and t-shirt to get some exercise. Janet had told her about the corner of the Morrison family tool shed where her son had set up a weight bench and treadmill when he had been attending Cal State University Bakersfield years before. Janet said that Ray had left the exercise area in place when their son left home, and except for a short aborted attempt by Belinda to "get in shape," the weight bench and treadmill had sat unused, gathering dust.

Naomi had quickly jumped at the opportunity to have a workout area. She recognized that her physique had slightly withered during her two-and-a-half-month sojourn in the coma. The girl she saw in the mirror after Napa was not the same young woman in the high school pictures. Combined with following the instructions of the doctor at Napa to add body weight, Naomi was determined to make sure the added weight was healthy, not flab.

Seeing what weight Naomi could lift and how many repetitions she could do made an interesting comparison for Naomi, to what Mark had once been able to do. It was an excellent opportunity to get to know her own body. She was, of course, weaker, yet she was also more limber than Mark had been and seemed to have good stamina. She was probably half of Mark's weight. She found with less weight she could jog on the treadmill a bit longer than Mark had once been able to. As Mark, she had used a treadmill in the extra bedroom in the condo in American Canyon. Thinking about that made her wonder what had become of all of Mark's old stuff. Naomi put that thought aside.

Naomi had done an internet search to set herself a program appropriate for the exercise of a young woman. She had found a how-to article about how an actress had gotten ready for a part in a super-hero action movie that was helpful. Naomi discovered that if she exercised in the evening, followed by a long hot shower, it made getting to sleep easier. Laying in bed, thinking about the strange life she was leading always seemed to interfere with going to sleep. And then, there were the nightmares. The exercise routine before bed short-circuited her brooding philosophical thoughts about her odd identity switch and the myriad of issues that she always thought about, both problems she was facing now and would have to face in the future. The exercise also made her feel good about herself. She was rapidly getting into excellent condition.

———

"Now, that's what I call some duds. Jan, come look at this girl!" Ray Morrison shouted to Janet in the kitchen. He seemed as excited as Naomi had ever seen him. He stood up as she came into the living room and muted his television program.

Janet came in from the kitchen, drying her hands on a dishrag, to see why Ray had called her. Janet clapped her hands together, "Wow, I guess there is a date with the pilot tonight."

Ray turned to Janet, "Pilot, what pilot?"

"Naomi found herself a Marine fighter pilot from the air station at the YSA Halloween Dance. Looks like he is taking her strutting tonight." Janet said.

Naomi blushed, "Is it too much?"

Janet shook her head, "No, dear. Nobody that looks like that is ever 'too much.' I just hope your Marine is big enough to fight off the other men."

Naomi had Belinda's red and gold fancy cowboy boots on, but her jeans, shirt, and scarf were new. Part of her first paycheck from Kentfield Farms had gone downtown to the big western wear emporium. The jeans were standard skinny-leg, boot-cut women's jeans, but they had plenty of decorative shiny rivets and rhinestones down the leg seams and on the pockets. Naomi's plaid shirt and silk scarf matched the cream, red, and gold cowboy boots' color scheme. Naomi had the shirt folded and tucked into the back of the jeans so that it looked custom-tailored. The scarlet silk scarf had a silver slide like a girl scout might wear but with a shiny, scarlet, spinel stone in it. A white cowboy hat was in one hand, and a new leather purse with a long shoulder strap was over her shoulder. She had two silver hairpins that matched the scarf slide and kept her hair away from her face a bit, showing off dark eye makeup and red lips.

"Yes, that is a real Bakersfield girl. You're looking really fine, Naomi." Ray sat back down but did not unmute his TV.

"Did you forget your glasses, dear? You don't want to do that. Remember." Janet advised.

"Nope, I didn't forget my glasses. Mattie told me my new benefits from Kentfield Farms included a vision service insurance policy, and I went downtown and got myself some soft contacts. Look!" Naomi blinked her eyes at Janet.

"Oh, my goodness, really green," Janet said.

"Let me see," Ray protested.

Naomi fluttered her eyelashes at Ray, too.

"Aha!" was all Ray could say.

"So, where you going?" Janet asked.

"Connor said something about Buck Owens' Palace."

"Oh, that's nice," Janet said.

"Gonna be really crowded on a Saturday night," Ray added.

"Connor texted me and said he had made reservations for four," Naomi explained.

"You're going with another couple?" Janet asked.

"Yeah, Kendra Allred is going with a Navy pilot. The two pilots came together to the dance and kind of zeroed in on Kendra and me."

"So, the two pilots are driving down from all the way up in Kings County? That's a long way," Janet said.

Ray shook his head. "Janet, take another look at Naomi tonight. A hundred mile drive ain't nothing to a young man with someone like Naomi waiting on the other end," Ray opined.

"I suppose you're right." Janet reached for Naomi to turn her around and see the jeans' rear pocket decoration. "How are those going to be sitting down?"

"Okay, I think. But after I bought them, I was wondering what the rhinestones will do to the leather seats in his Corvette."

"He drives a Corvette?" Ray asked, but Naomi and Janet ignored him.

"You're right about the seats. Maybe you can take one of the thick, dark blue hand towels with you to put on the seat. I'll get one for you," Janet said, heading into the hall.

"Good idea," Naomi said, taking her cellphone out of her purse to check the time.

They did not have to wait long for the double bong-bong of the front doorbell. Naomi started to get it, but Ray beat her to the door and said, "I got this."

Connor had the screen door open and entered when Naomi opened the door. Naomi noticed that his broad shoulders and height nearly filled the doorway. He had the cupcake pan under his arm. He was trying to shake hands with Ray but got side-tracked when he saw Naomi waiting for him.

Connor aimed a simple "Wow" at Naomi before turning back to Ray and introducing himself.

Janet came in and palmed the towel onto the strap of Naomi's purse. She went over to get introduced to Connor also and take possession of her baking pan.

Naomi noticed that Connor was in cowboy finery also, but nothing like her outfit. She did not see a hat, but the boots, jeans, and shirt were genuine looking.

Janet said, "Can you two hold a minute? I gotta get somethin'." She went into the kitchen and came back in with her cellphone. "Would you two mind if I got a picture?"

Naomi realized what Janet wanted from the picture, so she put her hat on and struck a pose with one hand on Connor's shoulder, the other hand on her decorated rear pocket and a slight hip twist to show off the pants' unique decor. Janet stepped forward and took the towel away for the picture.

Connor also understood, asking, "Mrs. Morrison, think I could get a copy of that pic?"

Janet smiled, "Sure thing. I'll have Naomi give me your number tomorrow. Or, she can send it to you."

Ray told them, "Hope you guys have fun. Drive safe."

Janet stuck the towel back in the purse strap and cheek-kissed Naomi.

Connor escorted Naomi to his car. He watched as she put down the towel on his seat. He helped her find the seatbelt and closed the door.

He got in and looked over at Naomi. "Will I be a horrible person if I say 'Wow' again."

"I think I can forgive your stunted vocabulary. Thanks."

"I have two things. First, it was a nice touch to bring the towel, but I doubt it is needed. And second, are you totally sure those two people inside aren't your parents? They seemed very proprietary about their Naomi. I was definitely being scoped out to see if I was worthy of taking you out."

Naomi explained the situation with Belinda and the Morrisons, and how Naomi fit into things, as Connor started on the way to downtown Bakersfield.

———

"Hey, isn't that where we're going?" Naomi turned and pointed to the huge neon guitar sign that announced 'Buck Owens' Crystal Palace.'

"Yeah, that's it. But, as a first timer here, I figured I had to do this right. I saw what was around the corner from the Palace on Google Maps," Connor said, as he took a right turn around the Palace.

"Ah, the Bakersfield sign. Should'a known." Naomi said, as they passed under the colossal arching Bakersfield sign over the roadway. She had never seen the huge archway herself but knew it was a local landmark that Naomi, as a Bakersfield semi-native, should obviously know.

A loud voice burst into the car, "Longshanks, Carnivore, what's your ETA?"

"This is Longshanks, I'm on final approach. How about you? Over," Connor answered his cellphone.

"I'm parked in about row four. It's really chockablocked. One more space next to me for you, buddy, if you hurry."

"Coming in now. Out," Connor finished.

"You guys actually have your cellphones set up as radios?" Naomi asked.

"It's an app we use. Comes in handy. We use them on base, too."

Connor pulled in next to Dennis' 370Z. Kendra was standing near the pearl white Nissan sports car.

Naomi saw that Kendra had done a pretty good job of keeping up with Naomi's western fashion statement. Only in her case, the shirt was matching blue denim to her pants, and most of the fancy decoration was on the shirt. She, too, had a white cowboy hat on. As Naomi got out and went closer, she saw Kendra had on blue and white boots. Kendra had one advantage over Naomi, though; her long, curly brown hair had a marvelous "big hair" style that billowed from under the hat. Naomi's straight blonde hair was tame by comparison.

Before anyone could say hello, Dennis said, "I gotta give you girls credit for doing a very nice job of showing your date's service colors. Navy blue and Marine red and gold is a mighty fine color scheme for you girls to have coordinated."

Naomi quickly looked at Kendra and gave a shake to her head, trying to convey, 'Don't admit we didn't do it intentionally.'

Naomi said, "We figured it was the least we could do to thank you guys for driving all the way down. You guys don't have hats?"

"We have them, but can't wear them inside so why bother," Connor said.

"Should we leave ours, too?" Kendra asked.

"No, No, different rules for cowgirls than cowboys. You can wear it anywhere. It's okay, fashionable for you. The only place inside a restaurant a cowboy can wear his hat is on the dance floor. So, it is just a hassle for us."

"I didn't know they had such hat etiquette rules," Naomi said.

"Yes, kind of the same rules as in the military. You don't wear your military hat inside unless you are under arms or in formation. And, it's kind of like the old hat etiquette for society, you know, women must wear a hat in church, but a man never can," Connor explained.

"Underarms?" Kendra asked, confused.

Dennis laughed, "Under… arms, armed, wearing a weapon; pistol, rifle, or sword. Under arms is the military term for that."

"Oh," Kendra said.

"We are going to be dancing, right?" Naomi asked.

"Of course, they have two country bands booked tonight, one early, one later. The website says they're good country dance bands. Dinner first, then dancing, that's the plan."

"Then, I kinda want my cowboy to wear his hat when he dances with me." Naomi protested.

"Yeah, me, too," Kendra added.

"Okay, whatever the ladies want," Connor announced.

Both men went into their cars and came out with cowboy hats. Dennis' was light gray, and Connor's was black with something shiny on the front of it.

Naomi turned Connor's shoulder so she could see his hat and said, "You have a U.S. Marine Corps cowboy hat with a Marine corps emblem on it. That is truly precious."

Connor gave her a broad smile, a hand salute, and said, "Semper Fi, ma'am."

———

"Say, Gyrene, you are pretty good at the Two-Step. Where'd a military brat learn to dance like that?" Naomi said to Connor, as they reclaimed their table with the Reserved marker on it after enough dancing to work up a sweat.

"Common misconception about military life is that it narrows your contact with culture. Besides, I was the guinea pig for my mother to teach my older sister to dance. They Two-Step in the Carolinas, too," Connor said, as he waved his root beer bottle at the waitress and signaled '2' with his fingers. He sat his hat in the middle of the table.

"Ah, first mention of an older sister. Tell me about her," Naomi requested.

"Holly Holloway; my Mom thought it was a great alliterative name, Holly hated it. A tall drink of water for a girl, probably within an inch of my height. I'm told we look like twins, same hair, eyes, and general features. But the similarity ends there. I went to Annapolis, she went to Brown, majored in journalism. Writes for *Atlantic* magazine, and substitutes on a cable news program as a talking head for pop culture and politics. Nice girl, probably the most liberal Mormon girl you can find. That is if you are looking for a liberal Mormon girl. That's an oxymoron." Connor moved closer to Naomi to make room as Denny and Kendra finally came back to the table.

The waitress brought the root beers and took Denny's order for another for him and a ginger ale for Kendra. Before she left, Denny asked, "Anybody want anything else to eat or snack on? Anybody work up a hunger out dancing?"

Naomi raised a finger, "You know, I'd kinda like one of those nice, big appetizer platters like they have over at that table, with lots of Ranch dressing."

"You got it," the waitress told her.

Connor got out of his seat and made a show of carefully looking over Naomi on both sides and in front. He shook his head in mock wonderment as he sat back down.

"What? You got some kind of problem, Gyrene?" Naomi asked.

"Nope, no problem, just wondering," Connor said.

"OK, I'll bite. Wondering what?" Naomi asked.

"Wondering where a hundred-pound girl with a lingerie model waist puts all of the food you've socked away tonight. You ordered the same 16-ounce Sirloin I did, the size they labeled as the 'King Ranch' cut, and then you cleaned your plate and actually finished my fries for me. I recognize that you moved your equipment rather energetically out on the dance floor, but your appetite is truly awe-inspiring. And, that's coming from a guy who normally eats in an Officer's Mess that is half full of brawny Marines."

Naomi sat quietly, drumming her fingernails on her root beer bottle.

"Longshanks, I think you hurt her feelings," Denny said.

"No, my feelings are just fine. I was just wondering myself. Wondering if, maybe, I ought to volunteer to split the check if the Gyrene is worried about the food bill I'm running up," Naomi said, sternly, and then couldn't hold her look and laughed.

"I just…," Connor started to speak when Naomi cut him off.

Naomi gave a little smile to let Connor know he was not in trouble, "No, Connor, you aren't the first one to notice my appetite. I've noticed Ray and Janet kind of eyeballing my plate at supper. Truth is I had a bit of a medical problem last June and my doctor told me I had to gain some bodyweight. I haven't weighed myself, but I'm pretty sure I'm not just a 'hundred-pound girl' anymore. I gotta be at least a hundred an' ten."

"Naomi, quit bragging, or I'm gonna stab you with my fork," Kendra said. "Connor's kind of right, if I ate like you, I'd… Well, you wouldn't see me in these skinny jeans."

"Okay, Denny, your turn. It's gang up on Naomi time," Naomi said.

"All, I have to say is… Can I have some of your hot wings?" Dennis pleaded.

"Connor, can I change the subject and ask you a question?" Naomi said.

"Sure."

"Well, it comes from your talk about being in the Officer's Mess with brawny Marines. I was wondering, with the question for both you and Denny, as Mormons in the military, is there pressure or blowback to you about the Word of Wisdom. My mind's eye of the Marines is they are a pretty hard drinking, fast living bunch. How's that impact you guys. Either Marines or Navy?" Naomi asked.

Dennis looked to Connor, and said, "Can I take a crack at that? I think when I first get into a unit, there is a bit of confusion or questioning, especially by guys who have never known a Mormon, of which there are a lot. They have these wrong stories about us, you know. That we don't dance, have a couple of wives, and they confuse us with other religions like Jehovah's Witnesses or Quakers. But then, once they get to know us, it smooths out. Once they know us, our 'weird habits' get reduced down to 'Doesn't drink, doesn't smoke and wears sorta odd underwear.'"

"Oh, yeah, I bet your temple garments aren't military issue clothing," Kendra added.

Naomi did not say anything as she really did not know much about these temple garments they were talking about were. Mark had seen the garments on some of his BYU roommates but had not been curious enough to inquire much about them. Guys don't ask about another's underwear.

Connor now added in, "Actually, the temple garments are no longer much of a problem, the Church has an order form listing which military service and uniform style you need. My Dad said it used to be a problem, but not anymore. You can even buy your underwear in the Base Exchange and send it to the Church Distribution Center in Salt Lake for putting the Temple marks in it," Connor explained.

I've got something else I need to Google.

"But, back on the main question, I've found that once they understand your commitment to not drinking, your buddies will support it. There is even a good chance you'll be invited to do stuff, where they want to make sure they have a sober designated driver. Nothing like a Mormon for a reliable designated driver," Connor said.

Kendra, Dennis, and Connor laughed; Naomi joined at the end. She was still wondering about the underwear Connor was wearing that needed to be special ordered from Salt Lake City. *Is Kendra wearing it, too? This is something I know nothing about. I didn't find anything like these undergarments in Belinda Morrison's stuff. I'll have to volunteer to do Janet's laundry and check out if the Morrison's wear these garments.*

The rest of the root beers and the big platter of finger foods arrived. Naomi took a boneless chicken tender, plunged it in Ranch dressing, and stuffed it in her mouth while staring down Connor. The next time the waitress passed by, Naomi inquired about the flavors of ice cream available. Connor got her message, 'Don't comment on Naomi's eating habits.'

———

Connor pulled the Corvette to a stop well away from the overhead lighting pole in the Morrison's large yard. He turned off the engine and looked over to Naomi.

Naomi spoke first, "Connor, I have to tell you, I have had a marvelous time tonight. More than I could have hoped for. Really!"

"Me, too, Naomi. You couldn't have been a much better date for me. Great dancer, fun, beautiful, good conversation. I really felt in synch with you, even when we were jousting."

"The jousting was part of the fun," Naomi added.

"I want to say that I had no idea when I got talked into that Halloween dance by Carnivore, that I would meet a girl who might qualify as a keeper in the grand scheme of things."

"Hmm, 'might qualify as a keeper,' huh. I'm not sure I'm anywhere near going for keeper status, but it would be interesting to know what a girl has to do to get rid of the qualifier 'might.'"

"Naomi, I actually think that is another point we may be in synch on here. My saying 'might qualify as a keeper' was a gentle way of saying I'm not sure I'm ready to find a 'keeper' no matter how beautiful, charming, and wonderful she is."

Naomi nodded and smiled, "Yes, Connor, I think we are truly in synch. I enjoy my time with you, but I have things that need to be done. You've got your degree under your belt and a career fully in the works. I'm several years behind you in that loop. But, keep doing what you're doing. You're perfect for what I need right now."

Connor smiled back, "I do need to tell you about something, though."

"What's that?" Naomi asked.

"I'm getting sent for several weeks down to Marine Corps Air Station Yuma, in Arizona. They have a joint air-ground exercise with the troops from Pendleton, and they want us to send down a flight of F-35s to augment the squadrons at Yuma. So, I will be gone for probably five or six weeks. I'll probably get back just before Christmas. There's a chance I can slip back up in between, I am flying a supersonic jet after all, and it's only a half-hour flight, but I'd need to figure out a reason to just happen to slip back up here in the middle of an exercise."

Naomi jumped in, "You know what, I didn't even get a chance to tell you. I got a full-time job, too. So, even if we have to take a break seeing each other, I'll be plenty busy, too."

"Oh, yeah. Watcha doing?" Connor asked.

"Helping out in the head office of Ray's farming company. I upgraded their accounting system and impressed them, so they're keeping me on 'til I start college in mid-January," Naomi said.

"Uh, Naomi, how does a girl just out of high school know how to 'upgrade an accounting system?'"

Naomi realized too late that she had overstepped her 18-year-old limits, so she used the same excuse as she had used on Mattie with a little bit of jousting added. "Connor, you may not have noticed, but I'm a little bit more than your typical high school graduate, and the fact that I learned from my mother, the accountant, helped too. Ray's boss liked what I did enough to give me a couple grand bonus, part of which I used to buy this cowgirl outfit for your viewing pleasure tonight. It also bought me my new forest green contacts which you have been looking into all night, maybe wondering where my glasses went."

"Wait, stop, you had me at 'viewing pleasure.'"

"Right, just take it easy on the 'high school girl' lines, okay, Gyrene?"

"Point taken. Let's keep in touch by email and phone. Let's see what we can work out after I get back, if not before. Sound good?"

"Sounds good. Five or six weeks is nothing compared to the deployments that any girl who finally wins the 'keeper' race will have to put up with in the future."

"Yes, there is that." Connor smiled. "And, I have to admit that my beautiful Corvette is probably the absolute worst car built for properly saying good night in without major gymnastic feats. So, let me walk you to the door.

Can you get in the back door? Your 'adopted parents' don't have the light on in the back."

"Spare key is over the window on the left of the back door. Should you ever have need of that information. But, I have the keys in my purse."

"Don't forget your little towel," Connor warned.

Connor and Naomi walked hand in hand toward the back door.

By the time Connor closed the screen door behind Naomi, her heart was pounding again.

That Marine is an expert at wishing a girl 'goodnight.' I wonder if I am as good at that for him. I think I am. I am not sure what I think of that.

—

Chapter 17

Naomi took her second paycheck from Kentfield Farms to the bank. Then, she headed for the big Valley Plaza Mall that she passed every time she went to sort through her family stuff in the storage area. When Eli had told her that he had spoken to the manager of a medical clinic about her need to have a medical job to put on her nursing application, Naomi figured a proper job-hunting outfit was a good idea.

What she had wound up with was an ivory/ecru pantsuit with matching blouse and flats. She figured it was business-like, but the light color was quasi-nurse-like. For job application purposes, she wore her old black-rimmed glasses. She thought they added some maturity or age to her look. At least, she hoped they did.

The location of the clinic was in a modern standalone medical building near the 99 freeway in central Bakersfield. She had looked up Kern Industrial Medicine Group on the Internet, and they had a good website, even showing a bio page about the person she was supposed to meet, Nina Deukmejian. Nina seemed, from the bio, to be both a manager and maybe a member of the family who owned the place. The woman's surname sounded familiar, but Naomi could not place it. Naomi put her leather purse over her shoulder and entered the clinic.

Naomi walked up to the counter, where a receptionist said, "I'll be with you in a minute."

After a short wait, the receptionist handed a clipboard to Naomi and cheerfully said, "Please fill this out and bring it back when you are done, along with any paperwork you brought with you. If you don't know an answer, put an X in the margin so someone can help you answer it."

"Uh, I'm not a patient. I'm here to see Ms. Deukmejian," Naomi said.

"She doesn't take sales calls. You have an appointment?" Naomi saw the stark difference between the receptionist's friendliness with a patient and her response to a possible salesperson.

"I have an appointment. I talked to her secretary yesterday."

"Your name? Do you have a business card?"

"I'm Naomi Donnelley. I don't have a card."

"Have a seat. We'll call you."

Naomi sat and waited. After several minutes, she was called back to the counter.

The receptionist said, "Nina can see you now. Admin offices are on the far left. Take the first hallway left, and then go right. Her office is the very last one."

"Thanks."

Naomi followed the instructions. When she had almost reached the last office, a man stepped out of an office right in front of her, nearly colliding with her.

The man was in late middle age, thin, balding, and wearing a white lab coat. "Sorry, Miss. My fault. Not usually much traffic in our hallway."

"No problem. I could have been watching better," Naomi said.

"Can I help you find something?" the man asked.

"No, I think I am on track," she pointed at the last door.

"You're meeting with Miss Deukmejian?" he asked.

"Yes," Naomi said with a nod.

The man stepped to the side of the hallway and gave Naomi a bullfighter's cape motion for her to proceed. Naomi smiled and went on. The doorway at the end was ajar a couple inches, so Naomi knocked on it.

"Just a minute," came a woman's voice from inside.

The door opened to show an attractive woman in her thirties. She wore a fashionable business suit of black and white houndstooth with black piping, and a complementary blouse. Naomi guessed the woman's dark-haired, brown-eyed ethnicity went with the Armenian surname she had. The woman also looked at Naomi in much the same way, noting outfit and looks.

"Miss Donnelley?" the woman said, sounding a bit surprised or curious, and looking at her outfit, again.

"Yes, Naomi Donnelley," she answered, looking down at her outfit as though she could see what was wrong with what the woman saw. "Is there a problem?"

Nina Deukmejian laughed, "No, no, sorry. I apologize. You just aren't what I was expecting. Considering who called to ask me to meet you, I was sort of expecting a farm girl."

Naomi smiled, "If it would help. I can go home and put on my jeans and a plaid shirt."

"No, you look great. You'd be surprised what people wear to job interviews around here. You just stand out from the pack. Come in; have a seat."

Before she took her seat in front of the desk, Naomi handed her resume across the desk to Nina. Naomi explained, "My resume is very light with on-the-job experience, you know about Kentfield. But, I have good grades, top computer skills, and a good attitude."

Nina looked at the resume. It did not take much time to read. She set it on the desk.

Nina looked at Naomi and said, "I understand your interest in working for us is that you want to get into the Bakersfield College Nursing program and need the 300 hours of medical work for their admission points system, right?"

"Yes, ma'am."

"I'm quite familiar with that. We've had several people here over the years who later went to Bakersfield College and came out Registered Nurses. One of our current nurse practitioners is a grad of that program, years back. But, usually, the people in that situation already have a state license for medical assistant, x-ray tech, practical nurse or something like that. Eli tells me you were fresh out of high school last year."

"Yes, I am registered at the college and will be taking classes starting in January. I was hoping to get a medical job that would let me take the classes while working. If I must, I can volunteer my time; I don't have to be paid."

"Volunteering time in a medical job is something for the hospitals and hospice type settings. If you're working here, you will be on wages. We have extended hours to cover the hourly workers who are our primary patients, so we have people working here from early morning through evenings. We should be able to work around your college schedule."

Naomi smiled at this and said, "That's great."

Nina waited a moment in silence before she spoke, "Can I be honest with you, Naomi?"

Naomi hoped her expression did not match her emotion at hearing this ominous sentence from Nina, "Please do."

Nina cleared her throat and spoke, "You should know this is not an ordinary job interview—for you or me. Unless you came in here with horns growing out of your forehead or with a crack pipe in your hand, you were going to be given a chance at working for us. Kentfield Farms and Eli Kent are one of the largest employers in central California. He has hundreds of ag employees at any given time, and for harvests and planting season, he adds hundreds, if not thousands, more. Doing occupational medicine and worker's compensation medicine means our business is focused on employers and employees. Employers in our area do not come any bigger than Eli Kent. He called me up and told me about this magnificent employee he had who did magical things with computers, who happened to be his foreman's relative, and who needed a spot to do her medical points work for college. He also made sure I knew he expected it as a favor to our biggest, by far, employer client. That is why I was so surprised when the woman who appeared seemed like a decent medical employee prospect. With that said, let's never mention any of that again. Understand?"

"Completely." Naomi made a 'zip' motion across her lips.

Nina smiled, "Now, without any experience or any license, you can't do any kind of invasive medical work, no blood tests, no x-ray, no wound management. But, it just happens that our kind of medicine requires lots of forms to be filled out. There are lots of urine samples, lots of explanations to workers who don't understand insurance and worker's comp rules. Plus, there are lots of phone calls to check on back-to-work status, set new appointments, insurance coverage, and the like. My back-office supervisor and our coverage manager are constantly complaining they need more help to do the administrative, bureaucratic end of the job. So, with your agreement to never talk about the real reason you are working here, we are going to go introduce you to your boss, who will thank me for getting him the medical assistant he has been begging me for, but which I said wasn't in the budget. Only you and I will know that Eli Kent clarified the budget issues for me. Right?"

Naomi smiled at Nina, who smiled back.

Nina walked Naomi out through the hallway and the maze of examination and treatment rooms. She introduced Naomi to the thin, balding man she had almost run into in the hallway. Ryan Poulsen was Naomi's new boss.

———

The woman behind the counter at Bakersfield College Admissions and Records Office nodded as she checked the file folder. She told Naomi, "Yes, we have the transcript for all of your dual enrollment classes in high school that give you college credit and we have the reports for all eight of the tests you took. To get course credit for almost all of these, we must have the Request for Evaluation forms approved by the department for each course you want to get credit by exam. We can either send those to the department heads, or you can hand-carry them. Carrying them around is much faster."

Naomi nodded, "Yes, I sorta need to know if I get credit on these prereqs before I finish registering for the spring semester."

"I figured as much. I'll make copies of the seven CLEP test reports that need an evaluation and give you seven forms to get approved by the departments involved. You need to hurry because with fall semester finals and the holidays coming up, the department heads may get hard to reach." The woman turned toward the copy machine.

"Thanks. I'll start right now." Naomi thumbed her cellphone to the college campus map to see where she had to go to get the signatures.

———

In the employee restroom, Naomi changed from her jeans and tank top, into the powder blue scrubs and lab coat the clinic had given her for a work uniform. Although she did not do the direct patient treatment functions of the nurses and licensed medical assistants, Naomi wore the same uniform. In the three weeks she had worked at the clinic, things had settled into a comfortable groove of what people expected from her and what she was allowed to do. The registered nurses and a couple of the doctors had learned of her plans to go to nursing school, and they called her in to explain while they did procedures and let her participate to the extent possible.

Ryan Poulsen turned out to be a nice guy. Naomi suspected he was behind the willingness of the nurses and doctors to include her in things, even though she was not licensed to perform them herself.

Naomi had spent most of this day in early December going around the Bakersfield College campus, collecting approval signatures for her hopes of getting sufficient credits by examination to have her course pre-requisites for nursing school done by June. Now, Naomi was starting at 4:00 in the afternoon and would finish out the evening at the clinic. After changing clothes, she ran to her car with the civilian clothes and came back in to find Ryan at the front counter of the clinic. She brought her canvas bag with the textbooks she had bought from the college bookstore with her, in case she had a chance to study tonight during slow times. Ryan had told her it was alright to study work-related things while on the job if no other work was needed.

"Ah, Naomi," Ryan said, "Lucinda called in sick tonight, so I am going to need you to cover the front desk. You think you are up to it?"

Naomi shrugged, "I guess so, I have been up front a couple times when they were swamped. I suppose I can handle it."

"Good. I'll try to make up for it with something a little meatier next week. You seem to like the learning situations." Ryan smiled and gestured to the front desk, "It's all yours. Call Jessica or me if there is something you don't know how to cover."

Things were slow for the first hour or so. Most patients were returning for follow-up, and all Naomi needed to do was enter them into the appointment program and call them when the back-office people were ready for them.

Just after a couple of the clinic staff left for their dinner break, Naomi noticed a man at the front door. He seemed to be having trouble opening the door. Naomi watched for a moment, and then went across the waiting room to try and help him.

She opened the door for him, and he came in.

"Thanks, my arm is not working right," the man said.

The man was cradling his right arm with his left hand. His face showed intense pain. He had a slight limp, too.

"How'd you get here?" Naomi asked.

"I took the bus, I always take the bus to work, and everyone else had left work when I got hurt. Hurt pretty bad."

"Well, come up here, and I will check you in." Naomi walked with him to the front counter.

Naomi went behind the counter and got the usual check-in paperwork on the clipboard.

"Can you write at all?" she asked.

The man shook his head. Naomi went through the questions on the form and filled the paper in for him. His employer was one of the usual names she heard at the clinic, a warehouse and light manufacturing plant that had an unusual number of workplace accidents.

"OK, Jim, can you tell me where you got hurt? Exactly," Naomi asked.

"Yes, on the loading dock, down to the west end, by the pallets," the man answered.

Naomi tried not to smile, "No, sir, where on your body did you get hurt? Just your arm or elsewhere, too."

The man got the joke, he smiled and said, "Sorry I thought you meant… Yeah, my arm is the worst, and my shoulder and the whole thing started when I jumped down after strapping a pallet, and twisted my ankle. That caused me to trip and fall on my arm."

"How far did you fall?" Naomi asked.

"The first jump was four feet, or so, then the fall was off the loading dock, which was exactly four feet, it's truck bed height."

"Can I see your arm?" Naomi peered over the counter.

The man pulled up his long-sleeved chambray shirt sleeve and showed Naomi his lower right arm was deformed in a slight "S" curve and had a bloody under-skin hematoma on the upper outside of the arm. He had a complex break of both bones in the right forearm, and it looked like the upper bones were splayed near the skin.

Naomi had been through the clinic's new employee training that emphasized the difference between what they did as a workers' comp and walk-in clinic, and what needed to go to an emergency room. That decision was for the trained medics, doctors, or RNs, not for Naomi.

When she saw the totality of the man's arm injuries, Naomi pushed the red pushbutton on the bottom of the desk phone and lifted the handset to announce, "Physician to the front desk—Stat!"

A few seconds wait brought not one, but two, doctors and an RN, plus Ryan Poulsen.

Doctor Bilbray, an elderly, retired physician who covered some evening shifts at the clinic, was the first out the door. As he headed to the counter, Naomi explained, "Patient has a compound fracture of lower right arm and hematoma. I needed to know if we can handle it or if we should refer him to the ER. A covered workplace accident, confirmed coverage for one of our contract employers."

Both doctors went around the counter to look at the man. After some whispered thoughts between the doctors, Dr. Bilbray told Naomi, "We'll do a quick x-ray, and if it doesn't require open reduction we should be able to handle it. If it requires surgery, we'll have you call an ambulance. You did right in calling us out. Finish his paperwork and bring it back when it's ready. We've got him."

The two doctors and the nurse escorted the patient back to the treatment rooms. Ryan Poulsen looked at Naomi before he followed them. Naomi got a smile, a nod, and a thumbs-up from her boss as he left.

Naomi watched Ryan leave and felt an emptiness as she stood in the vacant waiting room. The real work was happening in the back, and Naomi was stuck doing insurance paperwork and making a call to the 24-hour notice line for the employer's workers' compensation carrier. It was her work for the time being, but Naomi yearned for more.

The setting sun was shining in through the front windows. Naomi went to close the blinds. Back at the counter, after she finished Jim's insurance paperwork and took it back, then she pulled her Human Anatomy book from the canvas bag. A slow evening on the front desk was good for something.

—

Chapter 18

Naomi figured she would spare Connor the need to run Ray and Janet's gauntlet, so she watched from the front window for the Corvette to turn into the driveway. The window curtain was wide open, to show the Morrison's beautiful Christmas tree through the picture window. After much debate with herself, she had decided to wear a red dress she had found in the closet, left by Belinda. It seemed to be new, and the long sleeves and the midi length was perfect for going out to dinner in tonight's chilly air. It also was figure-hugging and very attractive. Red low heels, dark hose, and dangly gold earrings finished this pre-Christmas outfit.

Connor had notified her they were going out to a nice restaurant, and then a movie on this Thursday evening, their first date since early November. Connor had kept in touch with her by both email and phone during his weeks in Arizona. Naomi was looking forward to another evening with him. This time it would be just them, no wingmen.

When she saw the headlights turn in, Naomi took her purse and white wool coat from the chair. She shouted over her shoulder to where Ray and Janet were in the kitchen, "Here he is. I'm off."

Naomi was slipping her coat on as she crossed the front lawn when the driver's door on the Corvette opened. Connor got out, wearing a well-tailored three-piece suit.

Naomi smiled and said, "Wow! Connor in fancy civvy outfit. Sort of overdoing it for Bakersfield on a Thursday, isn't it?"

Connor kissed Naomi and answered, "First off, 'Wow' is my line. And, I kind of figured you would be looking this lovely and had to make myself a proper escort for you."

Naomi was sure she blushed at this. He opened her door for her.

When Connor got into the driver's seat, Naomi asked him, "So, what have you got planned for tonight?"

"Well, I got a suggestion from Dennis, via Kendra about the Café Med Restaurant. I thought we'd go there, and then give you your choice of movies. Which movies haven't you seen?"

Connor pulled out of the driveway, heading east.

Naomi was quiet for a moment, "Connor, I hate to say this as it will give you some clue about my usually boring life, but I haven't seen a movie in the theater for several months. Virtually anything you want to see will be great with me."

Connor seemed surprised at this. "Well, I was expecting this to be tough; you make it easy. The Navy has a decent first-run theater at Lemoore, called

Hangar 61, and it does a decent job of getting most first-run movies to us, but sometimes they often don't get the big-ticket movies until later. The new Star Wars spin-off came out this month, and I haven't seen it. It isn't your traditional 'date' movie, but would that be alright?"

Naomi clapped her hands, "Bonus points to Longshanks for a perfect suggestion. I am quite a Star Wars and Star Trek geek. I would love that."

Connor gave Naomi a surprised look, "Well, another surprise from Naomi. I would never have pegged you for a sci-fi geek. Mormon girls tend toward Jane Austen more than Gene Roddenberry."

"Uh, Connor," Naomi thought for a moment before she finished, "you probably should not assume I am anything like your typical Mormon girl. You may have met me at a dance in an LDS stake center, but Dennis got the typical Mormon girl in Kendra, you drew the anomaly—luck of the cards."

"I've had inklings of that. Not that I mind. I like my cards so far."

The Café Med was in a shopping center on the Stockdale Highway in south-central Bakersfield. By the time they arrived, Naomi had checked the theater times on her cell phone. "There's a 9:15 showing of the Star Wars movie at the Reading theater down at the mall. That's a quick trip from the restaurant."

"Sounds like a plan," Connor said, as he turned into the parking lot for the restaurant.

Connor opened the door for Naomi and reached to help her up out of the Corvette's low seating. He locked the car, and then offered Naomi his arm. She hooked her hand into his arm, and they walked into the restaurant like a couple from the Jane Austen stories Connor had mentioned.

———

Connor was carrying Naomi's coat for her as they headed out of the theater. They stopped at the theater doors, and Connor held the coat for Naomi to put on.

"So, what did our resident Star Wars geek think of the new movie?" Connor asked.

"I thought it was great! You can see the Disney touch, though, a bit different from the purest Lucas films of the past. I'm glad they weren't serious about ending the series at number 9. From the geek standpoint, they are very loyal to history and continuity. You aren't going to get any more arguments over things like whether Obi-Wan really forgot about R2-D2, or was just hinting to C3PO to keep quiet about the past," Naomi explained, as she buttoned her coat.

Connor held the door for Naomi to go outside, "I always thought that was a bogus argument since Obi Wan's line about not owning a droid was in a movie done twenty years before the prequel movie when he owned the droid."

"Yeah, it's easier to build on something than try to reconstruct a universe in the past." Naomi was becoming an expert on reconstructing facts from her unknown past.

It was quite a long walk back to the car. Naomi did her best not to click her heels on the parking structure pavement, but she failed.

"I'd offer you a trip to the ice cream shop for a nightcap, but I have to get you home and make the run back to Lemoore. I have a 6:00 AM flight briefing," Connor announced.

Naomi replied, "Probably for the best. I seem to have recovered from my need to bulk up the body weight. I have achieved equilibrium and need to start eating as you normal humans do. And, tomorrow is Friday, the busiest day at the clinic, and I have to be there at 8:00 when they open."

Connor looked over at her, "Yes, I noticed that your 'equilibrium' looked very lovely in that dress tonight. I have never heard that kind of asset called an equilibrium before, though." Connor laughed and continued, "I guess I will need to call you about when we can get together next. Things need to get back into a normal schedule now that I am back at the squadron in Lemoore. We have a bunch of new pilots that weren't there when I left, and I don't know how the duty schedule and flights over the holidays will be handled. I should have at least one of the holiday weeks off. I'll call you. Okay?"

Naomi looked over and met Connor's eyes, and then nodded. Connor helped her into the Corvette.

Things were relatively quiet as they drove Naomi home. It was not an uncomfortable silence, though; they had enjoyed a lengthy conversation at dinner to catch up on events for Naomi's work and college preparations, and Connor's flights down south. There was simply not much else to talk about this late in the evening. But, Naomi could not get her mind off the upcoming goodnight from Connor and from her to him. She was somewhat amazed at how she felt about the prospect of another goodnight kiss.

———

Naomi went through the process of removing her make-up and getting ready for bed. She took out her contacts and put them in the solution cups. Somehow, these routines that should be thought-free and automatic got her to thinking and changed her mood. She had been happy and excited after saying goodnight to Connor. The trio of activities, removing make-up, dealing with contact lenses, and slipping into a flannel nightgown were part and parcel of Naomi's life now, yet they were alien to everything in her life before the last few months. Naomi was getting along fine in this lifestyle of a young woman, but at times she slipped back into the deep reflective thoughts of what had happened to her.

Naomi turned off the bathroom light and went to turn off the bedroom light, too. At the bedroom door, she heard a scratching sound down low, near the floor. Oodles wanted in. She opened the door a bit, and the big gray cat came in and hopped onto the bed, ready to spend the night, as he usually did. Like the humans in the Morrison household, Oodles had quickly accepted Naomi as a decent replacement for the missing Belinda. Naomi left the door open a crack, so Oodles could leave if wanderlust struck him during the night. She turned off the light.

As Naomi crawled under the covers, Oodles came up to lay next to her arm with his purring motor running full speed. He nudged her hand to encourage an ear and neck rub. Oodles' loving presence in bed with Naomi only heightened her funky, reflective mood. Her old persona of Mark had been allergic to cats, but Naomi was not. One more thing to add to the list of changes.

Oodles started his rhythmic kneading of the bedspread near her arm with his paws and claws. Naomi lay awake, thinking.

It was apparent that her main thoughts and emotions this night were not merely from the feminine routines of getting ready for bed; that was just what had set her off on these mental gymnastics. At the center of things was the goodnight kiss from the handsome Marine and all that went with it.

Naomi's problem was not that the kiss and the emotions were unwelcome or felt odd, but just the opposite. Naomi felt precisely what a young woman should, and it felt good, yet she had memories and having been on the opposite side of a goodnight kiss when Mark had been equally excited about kissing the pretty girl. The juxtaposition of the powerful emotions and the changes so inapposite to her memories was beyond unsettling. Mark's memories were difficult, whether in the form of nightmares or merely thoughts of basic urges.

Naomi had been through this same quandary a hundred times since she had awoken in Napa in August. As before, she let the course of such thoughts continue, in vague hopes that something new would come to her about this strange life she had involuntarily entered. But, no new answers ever came, just a renewed sense of wonderment and disbelief. This night was no different. At length, Oodles ended his purring and kneading, and Naomi joined him in sleep. This sleep was not interrupted by the dreams, at least, not by the bad dreams.

—

"You're what?" Naomi blurted out when she heard Kendra's news.

Naomi's response was too loud for the seating area waiting for the Sunday morning sacrament meeting to start. Kendra shushed her and scooted closer to talk.

"You heard me," Kendra said. "Dennis' father is retiring, and his parents bought a house in San Diego. He asked me to come down with him to meet his parents over Christmas."

"Isn't it a little early for out-of-town trips to meet the parents? You've only been going together for two months."

"He spent Thanksgiving at my house. He met my parents. He wants me to meet his."

"It's just… It seems so fast. I just had my second date with Connor last night, and you are meeting Dennis' parents."

"Jealous, huh?" Kendra teased. "Just kidding. Dennis has been down here every week since we met. Connor has been stuck in Arizona or wherever. A lot can happen in two months."

"I guess it can," Naomi said. "Is there something pushing you guys? You gotta admit things are moving fast. Has he actually proposed to you?"

"Uh, not in so many words. But, we are talking about things in the future. What life might be like. It is pretty clear he is thinking about it. And, I guess, so am I. I'm not sure what Connor has told you, but the Navy brass is planning on setting up a couple more operational F-35 squadrons. Not just the fleet replacement squadrons like at Lemoore. One new Navy squadron and one Marine, at first. That was what Connor was doing down in Arizona, Dennis said, helping work out the operational end of things. Dennis is likely to be in the first Navy squadron. They don't know where the new Navy squadron will be stationed. Could be a place called—Whidbey Island—in Washington state, San Diego, or who knows where. Dennis could get orders as soon as February."

"You're really thinking of marrying him to go with him?"

"Maybe. I think Dennis may be my… my… forever guy."

Naomi was going to challenge this concept, but the bishop stood up at the podium, and the congregation moved to their seats and quieted. She was startled at this news from Kendra, but she had to open the hymnal and sing, instead of trying to get her friend to face reality. But then, Naomi's own reality was so bizarre she probably was not the right person to lecture another young woman on the subject. What did she know?

———

Dec22_1400PST_
From: Naomi Donnelley <NaomiDonnelley@Outlook.com>
To: Alice Minnifee <alice.minnifee@mhd.co.kern.ca.us>
Subj: Checking In
Dear Ms. Minnifee,

When we last met in October, you asked that I check in with you in time to get your 90-day status report to the Judge in January. Will this email be good enough, or do you need to meet with me to confirm things?

Things are going very well for me. I have a full-time job, actually two jobs, one full and one part-time. I am working at Kern Industrial Medicine Group as a medical office assistant. I also help out, part-time, at Kentfield Farms in their accounting department. If you need to confirm those jobs, please contact me as I wouldn't want an inquiry from County Mental Health to jeopardize my employment.

I have also registered for classes at Bakersfield College, starting in the middle of next month. The medical clinic says that they can work around my class schedule for me to take the college classes. I have finished several CLEP Tests and end-of-course exams to give me credit for basic college classes. I have always been good at multiple-choice tests, so this was a perfect opportunity for me. By the end of the Spring semester in June, I should have all of my pre-requisite classes completed.

My personal life is going well. No recurrence of the problems you are concerned with from my past. None at all. I am dating a really nice guy. He is a pilot in the Marine Corps. I am still living with the Morrisons; they have been great. They treat me like their adopted daughter. My attorney handled my mother's probate estate, and I have access to all our family "stuff" in a storage area. I also have my mother's Toyota to drive.

Lastly, my job at the clinic requires all of their employees to do monthly substance abuse tests. I have attached scans of my test results for November and December. These are the same tests the clinic does for its employer clients to test their employees for drug use, so you can confirm the test results are accurate by entering the test number at the website indicated in the report. You will get the same report confirmation an employer would get. Please keep this confidential.

So, that is my report. I assume you need to do some kind of due diligence before you report to the Judge. If so, I would be happy to come out to your office, or maybe we could go to lunch together.

Sincerely,

Naomi Donnelley

———

"Where'd you hear about this place? Seems like a great spot for New Years' Eve," Naomi said, as the coat check girl took her coat and Connor's white saucer hat. "When you told me to dress formal, and then I saw you in the dress blue uniform, I thought we would be overdressed for anything Bakersfield had to offer. But, this seems perfect. I had heard of the Petroleum Club but never been here. Some of the couples came here for Senior Prom dinner." Naomi had seen some of the pictures in the high school annuals.

"Did you go to your high school Senior Prom?" Connor asked.

Naomi had to think about how to answer this, as she hated trying to answer questions about a past she could not remember. Then, she realized she had a perfect answer, "No, my mother died the week before our prom."

Naomi left out the part about her being in jail around that time.

"I'm sorry, Naomi. Bad timing by Longshanks." Connor sounded saddened by his unfortunate question.

"That's okay. You had no way of putting that together. Life happens. My senior prom week was a low point."

Connor jumped at the chance to change the topic and grabbed Naomi's hand to spin her around to see her dress. "You sure took my suggestion to 'dress formal' to heart. That gown is stunning, or rather, you are stunning in that gown."

Naomi had a long, clingy dark gold gown with sparkling highlights in the cloth. She had bought the dress and the clutch purse to go with it right after Connor had called to tell her he wanted to go out on New Year's Eve with his 'dress formal' advice. She had even bought several *haute couture* magazines to study up on proper make-up for holiday party scenes. Naomi was slowly but surely getting a handle on what most young women would probably know by her age. When she was getting ready, she had even called Janet into her bedroom to get a second opinion on how she looked. Janet had told her she looked spectacular. Connor seemed to agree. Janet had insisted on Connor coming inside when he picked her up and taking more pictures of the couple.

Connor told the Petroleum Club's *maître d'hôtel* "I have reservations for two for the late five-course meal and the midnight party. Name is Holloway."

The *maître d'* checked a guest book, and then handed two menus to an assistant, "Very good, sir, have a wonderful evening. Table A-3."

They were taken to a table front and center to the dance floor and in the middle of everything. When the waiter came to take their drink orders, Connor told him they would be having a bottle of sparkling cider, not hard, and not the champagne. Naomi had wondered about that as she walked through the tables and saw champagne bottles on ice on nearly every table.

The waiter explained the three choices of the main course and what the other courses would be. A small dance band was playing rather quietly from the raised stage area in the middle of the dance floor.

After putting down her main course list, Naomi looked toward the windows and commented, "Quite a view from up here."

"Yeah, the website said it is the tallest building in town," Connor said.

"It doesn't take much to be the tallest building in a place like Bakersfield. Not much competition in Podunk USA," Naomi retorted.

"You are too hard on your hometown. Bakersfield is heaven compared to Yuma, Arizona, where I spent the last two months. Or, up in Lemoore and Hanford. Bakersfield is a true metropolis in comparison."

"I think you just made the worst advertisement for life in the Marines you could make when you say Bakersfield is heaven compared to two of the choices you have for your F-35 squadron being stationed. And, by the way, technically, St. George, Utah is my hometown."

"Where'd you hear about F-35 squadrons' stations being chosen?" Connor asked.

"Kendra filled me in on fleet replacement squadron concept, and how both you and Dennis will soon be going elsewhere for your permanent duty station."

"Yeah, have you heard from her this week?" Connor asked.

"Not yet, we were going to lunch on Saturday, now that she is back from San Diego."

"Well, when you do lunch with her, I assume she will be showing you her new ring."

"You're kidding!"

"Nope, it seems he got advance word he is going to the new F-35 squadron up at Whidbey Island, Washington. He asked Kendra if she wanted to go along, as Mrs. Smith. She said yes."

"Wow, she mentioned they had been talking, but…. "

"Yeah, my reaction, too. I guess Carnivore put Longshanks to shame in that competition."

"I didn't know there was *a competition*," Naomi said, a bit harshly.

Connor started to say something, and then stopped and started again, "Well, there wasn't…a competition. It's just that you have two couples who start out in the same place, and they seem to be moving along pretty fast. It's not like I hadn't considered whether you might be right for me, or that is, whether we might go well together…. This is impossible to talk about in light of what they did. I just can't…." Connor stopped talking, unable to explain himself.

"Connor, let me try to help you out," Naomi locked her eyes on Connor as she spoke. "You and I talked about what it meant for a girl to be considered a 'keeper' by you. Meaning a girl you wanted to keep forever. We both agreed that we were not ready to be deciding on forever decisions. I told you I am just 18 and want to finish my education. I also told you that Dennis had the luck of the draw in getting the girl at the Halloween dance who was a typical young Mormon girl open to early marriage and focused on being wife and mother. I also told you I was atypical in that regard."

Connor started to say something, but Naomi motioned him to wait and let her continue, "I'm not able to tell you the details, but I really think that there is something in life I have to do. Some destiny that I was meant to fulfill. Destiny with a capital D. I don't think it is just being a wife and mother, although I want that, too, I think. I had something happen to me that shook me to my core and made me realize there is more to life than just the trappings we see around us. I could never possibly explain to you what happened to me. But, believe me when I say it changed me to my very soul. I have a feeling that I need to continue my goal of being a nurse and find what it is in my future that is pulling me. That route seems to be part of that destiny I feel.

"I have to say that Connor Holloway taking me into his arms and making me feel the way you have, is special beyond belief. Maybe there is a place in that future destiny for me and a guy like Connor, but I am nowhere near ready to make that decision, or even give you a real indication that it might happen in the future.

"Connor, you are perfect for what I need right now. But, I cannot give you any assurances or even hope that there is a future for us like the one Kendra and Dennis have chosen."

Connor continued to hold Naomi's gaze. He blinked a couple of times, and then said, "That was awesome, Naomi. I don't think any guy has ever been given his walking papers with more style or grace. Did you rehearse that? It couldn't possibly be ad-libbed, too perfect."

"You think I rehearsed responding to news about Dennis' marriage proposal I didn't know about. Besides, it wasn't walking papers; it was being truthful about who I am, what I think my destiny is, or where it might be." Naomi bit her lip a bit after she finished.

"Naomi, yes, I understand it wasn't about walking papers, because I agree that you are correct about us and what we both need at this point in our lives. But, if we had been more serious about each other, or rather, if I had been more serious about you, that would have been an absolutely awesome Dear John speech. As it is, I agree we make a good couple for now, but the future is the future, and we are both free to find what is in that future and what destiny has in store for us. Both of us. Right?"

"Right." Naomi gave a slight nod. Naomi kept eye contact with Connor, but he broke it, looking toward the oncoming waiter.

Connor smiled at her, "Good. I think we just exorcized the Kendra and Dennis demon out of our relationship. I see our first course and our non-alcohol bubbles coming. Let's have fun tonight."

"Let's." Naomi reached across the table to put her hand on the back of Connor's hand.

As the waiter opened the sparkling cider bottle and filled the glasses, Naomi looked over at Connor. She was not sure whether his response to her was an agreement with her feelings that the couple were not ready for serious plans for the future, or whether it was his ego protecting itself from the disappointment that Naomi did not want to be considered by him as his 'keeper' candidate. Time would tell.

All she was sure of was that she had been honest with him. Her strange situation had no opening for being Connor's wife, at least for the moment.

—

Chapter 19

Professor Emmanuel Ballesteros closed the binder in front of him on the lectern and took his glasses off. He took a deep breath, looked around the room, and said, "Well, class, that concludes our first meeting for this semester in Human Anatomy II. I'm glad those of you who took the first semester survived my lectures and have decided to give it another go. As before, my office hours are 2:00 to 3:30 PM on Tuesdays and Thursdays in my office in Room MS 14. Call ahead if you can. If you have any questions, please ask me before your concern becomes a problem. If you have any Drop-Add slips for me to sign, please bring them up now. Let anyone you know who wants to sign up that we have a few more seats left for this semester, both in this section and the late afternoon section. Could I have Ms. Donnelley come up to talk to me, if she is here today? I'll see you all next class. Have a great Spring Semester."

Naomi put her book and notebook in her canvas bag and descended from her seat in the upper rows of the lecture hall down to the instructor's desk. There were two other students ahead of her to get the handsome young professor to sign their class change forms. She waited until the other two were done to introduce herself to the professor.

"Professor? I'm Naomi Donnelley, you asked me to see you?"

"Yes, Ms. Donnelley. When I saw a new student on my class list, I checked into your pre-reqs for the class and saw that you had been given Credit by Examination for the first-semester class. Normally that decision is made by the professor for the class. I was told you went straight to the department head."

"Uh, Professor Ballesteros, I'm sorry if that is a problem. I'm new here and that is what they told me to do. You were away for the holidays and I needed to get approval to take this Human Anatomy II class this semester to finish my required classes by June. Professor Newburgh gave me the same final exam you gave your Anatomy I class last year in December

"What was your score on my final?"

"I got a 97%."

Ballesteros looked at Naomi a long moment before saying anything else. Then he said, "That's a better score than anyone in my class got."

Naomi gave a little smile, "That is what Professor Newburgh said, too."

The professor thought again before asking, "Okay, I have a question. How did you get that score? Are you a transfer student? Credit by Examination is meant to be based upon prior work."

Naomi nodded; she had been ready to answer questions like this. She knew she had to come up with another story since Mark's studies for his Bioinformatics degree were not an answer for Naomi's knowledge of the subject. That, plus the fact she had studied Anatomy with the textbook she had gotten from the Napa Hospital library. She said, "I was hospitalized with a medical problem for a couple of months last summer. But, knowing I wanted to take Human Anatomy as one of my pre-requisites here, I studied my Human Anatomy book at length while I was laid up. It seemed to have worked for me."

Professor Ballesteros again thought for a moment, and then asked, "Indeed, so it seems. Since I was not involved in the process before, would you mind if I asked a couple of questions so that I can confirm things? I would appreciate it."

Naomi tried not to frown at being challenged on this, but she said, "Go ahead. Fire away."

Ballesteros seemed pleased that she had agreed, as if she really had a choice. He asked, "How many bones are in the human spine?"

Naomi answered, "The human spinal column is made up of 33 bones - 7 vertebrae in the cervical region, 12 in the thoracic region, 5 in the lumbar region, 5 in the sacral region and 4 in the coccygeal region. Sometimes that answer is given as 24 bones if you just count the vertebrae and not the nine small bones in the lower spine region."

"And, in which part of the body would you find the incus and stapes bones?"

"In the ear."

"Which part of the small intestine do the bile and pancreatic ducts enter?"

"They enter the duodenum."

"What is located immediately adjacent to and just forward of the pituitary gland?"

"Professor, I think the parts of the brain and nervous system are actually on the syllabus for this semester, in Human Anatomy II, but the answer is the optic nerve."

Ballesteros, once again, did his lengthy thinking pause, and then he concluded with, "You are right on both counts. Welcome to Human Anatomy II."

Before she could reply, Ballesteros added, "Can I ask, if you already know the subject matter in the syllabus for this semester. Why didn't you just test out of this class, too?"

"Because Bakersfield College has a 30-credit limit on testing out of classes, and I already maxed out."

The professor smiled at her, "Ah, I see. I look forward to having you in my class, Ms. Donnelley."

"Thank you, Professor." Naomi smiled at him as she left the room. She seemed to feel him watch her walk out of the classroom. After all, he was a human anatomy expert.

———

January 21_1417PST-
From: Connor Holloway <C.Holloway@av.usmc.mil>
To: Naomi Donnelley <NaomiDonnelley@outlook.com>
Subj: Hello
Dear Naomi,
I hope your afternoon is going well.
I am writing this from a commercial flight to Florida. No cell service in flight. My father called to tell me my mother is in the hospital. He asked me to fly back there. He said Holly is flying in, too. Sounds serious.
I will update you later. Hope all is well with you,
Fondly, Connor

———

Naomi read Connor's email after it dinged on her cellphone at work in the clinic. At first glance, the word 'fondly' drew her attention and a bit of feminine ire. Then, she realized it was actually a very good and politically correct closing for an email note, given their discussion of the future on New Year's Eve. 'Love, Connor' would have been too much from him, all considered. And, 'Fondly, Connor' at least was in the emotional vicinity.

Naomi typed a quick acknowledging email to Connor and repeated his closing phrase.

Naomi put the cellphone back in her lab coat pocket and continued to apply instruction labels to urine sample bottles. It would be a long afternoon.

———

Naomi was restocking exam room supply cabinets when her cellphone rang. Naomi did not recognize the 707 area code when she answered the call, "Hello?"

"Naomi, it's Larry Partridge, I got your email you wanted to talk with me. I had some time and thought I would just call you instead of sending you my number. Is this a good time?"

"Yes, thanks for calling, can you hold a second. I'm on duty and need to tell someone I'll be in the break room. One minute."

Naomi came back online a short time later. "Okay, Doctor Partridge, I'm here."

"It's good to hear from you, Naomi. How is everything going?"

"Great. Just Great. I've meant to get in touch with you, but life got hectic, and time flew by. I'm glad you called back."

"So, you said you were on duty. Where is that?"

"I'm working at a walk-in clinic in Bakersfield. We do mostly worker's comp cases, pre-employment physicals and that kind of stuff. I'm working as a medical assistant, but mostly admin stuff, since I'm not licensed."

"So, you stuck with the medical career idea?"

"Yes, I'm enrolled at Bakersfield College. Trying to get the pre-reqs to start the nursing program later this year."

"Oh, really," Partridge paused a bit before he continued, "And, your, a… problem won't be a worry with clearance to get into the nursing program?"

Naomi hesitated and looked up to make sure the breakroom door was closed, "I can't really talk about that here at work. But, technically there is no problem. The judge cleared everything. No record. She said she was giving me a new chance."

"Gosh, that is great. I'm happy for you," Partridge sounded jubilant. "And how is the rest of life going. Are you getting settled into the new way of things? I can't imagine what you have been going through."

"Yes, things are good. The people you put me in touch with are great. I'm still staying with them. There are lots of new things to learn and get used to in my new life. In fact, as you can guess, just about everything is new. But I think I'm doing well. Besides my job and getting ready for college, I've been dating a really nice guy. He's a jet fighter pilot with the Marines."

"Wow, a pilot. So, our Naomi got herself a guy, huh?"

"Yes, a good Mormon Marine. Bishop Partridge would be proud of Naomi. Actually, it was Bishop Partridge I needed to ask some advice from, not Doctor Partridge."

"Really, I hadn't expected that, but go ahead."

"Okay, let me give you some background first, and then the question."

"Alright."

Naomi explained to Partridge how she and Kendra had met the pilots at the LDS Halloween Party, and the way the two couples' relationships had gone since then. She concluded with, "So, now the friend who Naomi grew up with has announced she is getting married in the LDS Temple and asked that I be her maid of honor. Apparently, the maid of honor duties in a Mormon temple wedding are mostly for afterward in pictures and the reception, and to sign the witness line on the certificate. But, Kendra wants me to go with her and her family to the Temple to see the 'sealing' I think they call it. I have looked up this temple wedding and sealing up on the internet, but I really have nobody here I can level with that I have no idea what is involved in getting a 'Temple recommend,' which I supposedly need to get into the temple. I thought maybe you could help me with some answers since it was you who got me involved with the Church here."

"Well, Naomi, that is quite a bit to handle in a phone call but let me try. Given that you as the person you are have only been involved in the Church for a few months, it is frankly a lot to ask of you to be able to answer the number of questions the bishop there will have to ask to give you a Temple Recommend. There are many topics he will discuss with you. If you have been following my advice, you should be able to answer questions about drinking, drugs and following the Word of Wisdom. It doesn't sound like your current life puts you in jeopardy with other questions regarding your conduct. You have to realize that I had to level with the Stake President about your background when I got him to find a place for you, and he needs to co-sign your Recommend slip from the bishop. He may have talked to the bishop about your situation, so you may be walking into a bunch of questions about Naomi's past life that may be tough to answer. However, you could just say your life has changed, which is the truth. But, even with the conduct questions out of the way, you are still going to have to profess your firm belief and testimony of the truth of the Church of Jesus Christ of Latter-Day Saints, and authority of the leadership of the Church. Knowing what I know of you unless something radical has happened to you in the last three months, I don't know if you are ready to do that. But, I may be wrong; that is a question only you can answer."

"That is what I thought," Naomi said. "Given what you know about what happened to me, I didn't hear even you telling me there was a good answer, either inside the church or outside, for my, uh, miracle. Both you and the other people in the church I have met have been nothing short of fantastic, but I cannot say that equates to knowledge or belief in the church of the level you say I need. I had a soul-shaking spiritual or supernatural event happen to me, but I cannot say it made me feel about your church one way or the other. It sure made me believe in something beyond what we normally see, though. There is something I cannot understand at work in my life. I really feel that. It just did not give me anything, in particular, to believe about a specific church. Is that unequivocal level of faith really necessary just to go into a building?"

"Naomi, to be honest with you, I have to admit that in my years as bishop, there have been some cases where I have had people give me their answers at a temple recommend interview that were nearly unbelievable. You know, a parent who had not graced the front door of an LDS meetinghouse regularly in years suddenly professing faith and testimony in hopes of getting a temple recommend to be able to go with a daughter or a son to the temple for that child's wedding. Or, a young man who had been a pure hellion for his entire teenage years, suddenly getting his act together just in time to go on a mission to a foreign country. A bishop has to give the proper weight to the words of the person he is interviewing, and perhaps to give the benefit of the doubt to the purpose they seek for their lives and their family. That trip to the temple might be a transcendent experience for the parents watching their daughter be married or the young man going on his mission. Or, you know, it might be what Naomi needs to answer this enormous spiritual mystery in her life." Partridge paused, and then continued, "Just like when we were talking about what you should say to Doctor Richards about your 'miracle' and your memories of Naomi's past, I cannot in good conscience advise you to tell the bishop in Bakersfield anything but your heart's truth. And, only you know that. I can only tell you what he expects to hear."

"Thank you, Doctor Partridge. I guess you have confirmed what I already had figured out. Like always, I appreciate what you have done for me in this weird existence I have encountered."

"Naomi, let's make sure we keep in touch with each other. I really want to know how things go for you. I feel like I have shared something truly miraculous with you in the challenge life dumped in your lap."

"I agree. Thank you. I wouldn't have wanted to share my strange secret with anybody other than you."

—

Getting her long blonde hair into a swim cap was a task Naomi had never had to master before. But, she had watched women swimmers do it enough times to know the general method; twist, swirl, and poke. The black one-piece women's racing swimsuit was more restrictive than men's trunks, but she had come in for a couple of practice sessions, and she felt confident as she did her pre-swim washdown in the locker room and went out to the Bakersfield College pool.

Her contact with the swim team had been through a young woman, Crystal Gilbride, who was the assistant coach. Her explanation of a medical problem the summer before preventing her from enrolling in the fall had been enough to get her a chance to try out with the team on this late January day.

She saw Crystal standing with two male coaches. The rest of the women's team were standing in clusters at the end of the beautiful Olympic-size pool. Naomi walked up to Crystal.

"Ah, Naomi, glad you could come. Let me introduce you to the head coach." Crystal turned to the man next to her and said, "Jim, this is the new girl I mentioned who wants to try out. She just enrolled this semester. Naomi

Donnelley. Naomi, this is our Head Coach Jim Fentress, and our other assistant coach, Mike Mortimer."

Jim Fentress turned to face Naomi but had his hands full with a clipboard and whistle, so he did not move to shake hands. He looked Naomi up and down, and he said, "I understand you think you are a competitive swimmer."

"Yes sir," Naomi answered firmly, aware that the demeanor of the coach was not overly friendly.

"What high school did you swim with?" he asked.

"I went to Centennial High School, but I didn't swim there," Naomi said as she wiped a dribble of water that was running off her swim cap and down her nose.

"You did private club swimming?"

"No sir."

"You've never swum competitively, but you **think** you can? Huh?"

"Yes sir."

"Who taught you to swim?"

Naomi saw where this conversation was going and decided to input a little falsehood to move things along, "My stepfather was a Navy rescue diver, and he taught me to swim strong and fast."

Fentress thought about this a moment, and then asked, "What events can you swim?"

"I can swim in whatever you need, but I think I will be best in 100-Meter Freestyle and 200-Meter Individual Medley. I'll probably need some conditioning to do longer distances. I'd probably need practice to do Relay. I have never swum with teammates." The last was also a lie, Mark had been a great relay team member, but Naomi could not say that.

Fentress turned to Crystal and asked, "Who are our top three qualifiers in 100-Meter Free? Get them on the platforms, along with Naomi."

"No warm-ups?" Crystal asked.

"This'll be their warm-up. It's just a 100." Fentress was increasingly gruff.

Crystal went over and called out three names. She directed them to the first three platforms and pointed Naomi to the fourth. Crystal told them they would be doing the 100-Meter Freestyle. Coach Mortimer went to the timer box on a folding table at the corner of the pool. Fentress and Crystal moved to the near side of the pool, so they had a clear view of the start and finish.

Naomi climbed on her platform, pulled down her goggles, and swung her arms in a bird-like flap to loosen up. The other three women swimmers looked over with interest at Naomi. Mortimer ordered them to their marks, and the four bent to their starting position, grabbing the edge of the platform.

When the starting tone went off, Naomi made a long leap into her lane. Naomi dolphin-kicked through, under the water, came to the surface and started her best crawl stroke. She felt good, but in the end position, she could not see her competition until she made her turn.

At the turn, it seemed to her she was in the lead. Now that she had a view of the others as she turned her head to breathe, she saw no one was even with her, or ahead. Nevertheless, she concentrated on putting more effort into her strokes. Her biceps, shoulders, and thighs were tiring rapidly.

Naomi hit the timing panel, popped her head out of the water, and flipped her goggles up. She had just enough time to see all three of the other swimmers finish their race. Naomi grabbed the edge of the pool and pulled herself up and out of the pool.

She saw the digital display on the pole above the timer box flash '53.81.' When it flashed, the other women gave a group shout and gathered around Naomi, smiling and patting her back and shoulders.

One of the women, a tall black girl, seemed to know Naomi and said, "Naomi, I never knew you were a swimmer. Why didn't you swim with us at Centennial?"

Before Naomi could answer, Crystal wadded into the throng and grabbed Naomi's arm.

"Seems to be that's a good time?" Naomi asked.

"Within a second of the Cal state junior college record. But that is almost full two seconds slower than the USA record. You're really going to have to work on that," Crystal said with mock seriousness, and then she broke into a huge grin and hugged Naomi.

Jim Fentress walked up to Crystal and Naomi. He turned to Crystal and said, "Coach Gilbride, you need to get this young lady a white 'BC' swim cap. That plain black one looks wrong on her." Then, he turned to face Naomi, and said, "Miss Donnelley, go have a seat and rest up, maybe drink some electrolytes from the cooler. I'm going to want to see your 200-IM in about ten, fifteen minutes."

With those words, Coach Fentress turned away and walked over to talk to the other assistant coach.

Naomi turned to Crystal and raised her eyebrows, perplexed about the head coach.

Crystal Gilbride understood Naomi's unspoken question. She leaned close and whispered into Naomi's ear, "That's the way he is. That bit about your swim cap is your acceptance on the team. I think he is embarrassed he was sort of harsh with you earlier. Inside, I can guarantee you Jim is as thrilled as the rest of us to have you on the Bakersfield College swim team. Go get rested up for your next event."

Before Naomi could turn away, Crystal had another question, "Naomi, you said your stepfather was a Navy rescue swimmer, and he taught you to swim. What does he do now?"

Naomi thought for a moment and decided to add some truth to her earlier lie about her stepfather, "He's doing 8 to 12 years in federal prison for assault on the federal officer." Naomi finished with her cutest shrug and palms up gesture with the matching facial expression to indicate 'What can you do?'

All Crystal Gilbride could think to say was, "I see."

Naomi went to sit down and make sure she remembered the stroke order in the Individual Medley—Butterfly, Backstroke, Breaststroke, and then Freestyle. It had been a long time since Mark had swum that event for BYU. As she sat and thought about that, Naomi recognized Mark's strength in his strokes was, of course, far greater, but she really felt like she had flown off the platform at the start, and her female body and long legs seemed better at the initial underwater dolphin-kick stroke before she broke the surface.

She could certainly use some strength training though; Naomi's body was no match for the athletic women standing around the pool. She would work on that if she had time in this hectic schedule she had set for herself this semester. With work, school, and now swimming, it was probably good she had not heard from Connor in a while. She wondered how his mother was down in Florida.

———

When she got home from work at the clinic on the last Friday evening in January, Naomi found that Janet had set an envelope that had come in the mail onto the corner of her bed. The envelope showed a preprinted return address from Victoria Roth, Attorney-at-Law.

Inside the envelope was a letter from the attorney explaining that a confidential order from the Kern Superior Court had been received by her law office. The judge had, indeed, closed the LPS case on Naomi and sealed the record. The letter also reconfirmed the news Naomi had received in November via email that both the Kern County Sheriff and the Bakersfield Police Department had certified that their arrest records and the computer records with the California Department of Justice regarding Naomi's arrests and criminal charges had been removed and destroyed pursuant to the judge's order.

Naomi's record was clear. Victoria Roth closed the letter by wishing her client, Naomi, a bright and happy future.

—

Chapter 20

She was not yet in the Nursing Program, but Naomi was taking her first Nursing class. One of the pre-requisites she needed to have before the nursing school application process this next summer was Nursing 099, which was a two-credit introduction to the career of nursing. It was a necessary doorway to getting into the Bakersfield College registered nursing program, and her classmates were all hopeful candidates for either the 70% who got in via a points system or the 30% who got in via a lottery of otherwise qualified people.

A majority of the students in the class were women with four or five men. Listening to people talk amongst themselves before class, Naomi found that most of the men and a few women were former military medics looking for a civilian job that matched their military training. During the opening session, when the points program was explained, they learned the military people got bonus points for their military medical work. There were also weighted points for the grade point average people had received on their pre-requisite classes, various medical licenses, standardized tests, and the necessary points for medical work, like that Naomi was doing at the workers' comp clinic.

Naomi's own points would include a combination of the scores on the test by examination credits she had secured, plus the grades she got this semester. With her test credits, the extra load she was taking this semester, plus the credits she would receive from the Art and U.S. History classes she had taken at Centennial High that gave dual credit for high school and junior college, Naomi would easily cover the pre-requisites GPA and points for the nursing admission. She was not a shoo-in for the nursing program, but Naomi was confident she could do this.

She was even more confident after seeing the range of people taking the Nursing 099 course. They reminded Naomi of the words of Nina Deukmejian about the odd mix of people who applied for medical jobs in Bakersfield. There were many bright students in the class, but there were a couple Naomi hoped would never see the inside of a medical career. She assumed the stringent candidate standards for admission to the nursing program were in response to this.

There was minimal actual nursing practice in this course, but they taught it in the same classroom as the regular nursing courses. On the wall to the right of the chalkboard was a large poster listing the rules for the administration of medicine to a patient. It read:

The Five Rights of Medicine Administration

The Right Patient

The Right Time and Frequency of Administration

The Right Dose

The Right Route

The Right Drug

Seeing the poster on the wall somehow made Naomi feel good like she was really becoming a part of the career that had inserted itself in her psyche. Whether it had been brought on by the gift of the nursing magazine from young Doctor Evans up at Napa, or the big Nursing Manual that had been her near-constant companion in her weeks in the hospital, Naomi was certain this career was her part of her destiny.

Now, in her first Nursing class, Naomi paid strict attention to everything. To keep aware of the status, interests, and needs of the incoming nursing students, the chair of the Nursing Department taught this introductory class. This silver-haired woman, Professor Jenny Harkness, was weaving Naomi's future path with her words and career advice. Or, so it seemed to Naomi. Harkness would also be the person to approve her admission into the program and her future.

———

Janet Morrison had insisted on driving Naomi to the Kendra and Dennis's wedding reception at the Royal Palace Reception Center in South West Bakersfield. Since Naomi had not gone with the wedding party to the LDS Temple in Fresno for the Sealing ceremony, she would be meeting Kendra for the reception. She had been told there was a changing room at the center, but she had put on her bridesmaid dress, and done her make-up and hair at home. Janet driving Naomi in the big Buick made sense, given the full-length apricot-colored gown she was wearing.

"Valentine's Day is a perfect day for a wedding. The bride and groom will never have to try to remember the date," Naomi said after Janet finished explaining to Naomi the details of how a temple marriage was handled. Janet informed Naomi about how the temple wedding dress was usually different from the elegant dress the bride wears for the reception. Naomi had earlier explained to Janet why she had not tried to get a Temple Recommend to attend the sealing ceremony. Given what Janet knew about Naomi's history, she did not appear surprised to hear this.

"And, your Marine pilot is going to be there? Right?" Janet asked.

"Unfortunately, no. He emailed early this morning to tell me his mother died last night. He was supposed to be the best man. He went to the Fresno Temple this morning with Dennis, but flew out of there after the ceremony to be with his family in Florida," Naomi explained.

"You haven't seen much of him since the holidays, have you?"

"No, just that one quick date in January. He was busy, and then I started college. After that, he went home when his mother got sick, and now he is back there again for the funeral," Naomi said. "We were kind of both in shock about how quick our best friends moved to get married. Connor and I agreed we are nowhere near ready to take a giant step like Kendra and Dennis did."

"It would have been nice if you had been able to get pictures with him, you know, bridesmaid and best man, together at the reception." Janet lamented.

"Yes, I guess, but it is Kendra's day to shine. I'm happy for her. I'm going to miss her when they leave for Washington state," Naomi said. "I think that's the reception center, up ahead on the right."

———

After Lt(j.g.) and Mrs. Dennis Smith had done the first couple of circuits around the dance floor for their first dance as husband and wife, Naomi accepted the arm of the Navy lieutenant who was filling in for Connor Holloway as best man during the reception. The photographer took pictures of them as the best man and bridesmaid, and then they joined the bride and groom in the waltz. The two parental couples soon joined them, followed by everyone else.

"It's too bad Connor had to leave so suddenly. I feel kind of strange trying to fill in for him on short notice," Lieutenant Jordy Cameron said to Naomi.

"Yes, it is sad to hear about his mother," Naomi responded.

"Yes, too bad."

The conversation stopped on that note, and Naomi decided to try to continue it. Looking at Jordy's service ribbons and his full Lieutenant rank, she said, "You're more senior than both Connor and Dennis, and by the looks of your ribbons, you've already done a tour in the Mideast."

"Yes, I flew Super Hornets off the *Vinson*, and I'm in the transition crew moving to the F-35s," Jordy answered. "How is it that you know how to read my service ribbons? Are you a military brat like Connor?"

Naomi could not tell him the real reason for her knowledge, so she just answered, "Not a military brat, but I learned military guys seem to be impressed when a girl can interpret the meaning of pretty colored ribbons and shiny badges."

"Well, you really impressed Connor. When he came back after meeting you, he told us all about the fabulous beauty with brains he had met in Bakersfield. He has a picture of you two in your cowboy outfits on the inside of his flight gear locker. Now, I see what he was talking about. You look lovely."

Naomi smiled and thanked him. "Did you go to Fresno with Dennis?" Naomi asked.

"No, I think you have to be Mormon to go to the Temple ceremony. Don't know why that is. I was planning on coming down here anyway. I think Connor left after the ceremony in Fresno. He called me to fill in down here."

"Yes, that is what he told me in his email this morning."

Naomi noted that Connor had called Jordy, but emailed Naomi.

Jordy looked curiously at Naomi, "I thought Connor said you were Mormon. You didn't go to the Temple thing either."

Naomi shook her head, "I am a member of the Church, but I didn't go. It's kind of complicated. I'm not sure we have enough time to explain the whole religious thing to you. Only certain Mormons go into the Temple."

"Oh, okay," Jordy accepted her non-explanation.

Naomi continued, "The Temple marriage is just the ceremony. The real celebration is here at the reception."

"Yes, they certainly have this place decorated well. It really does look like a palace inside here."

Naomi nodded at this. "Are you going to be going to Whidbey Island with Dennis?"

"That's the plan. I got my orders last week. I'm looking forward to it. My kid sister is going to Gonzaga University, so it will be nice to get to see her more often."

"Yes, that's nice. Where are you from?"

"Originally from Pacific Northwest, but my folks moved to Washington, D.C., for my father's government work. You?"

"I was here for my high school and middle school years, before that in Las Vegas and Utah."

"So, you went to school with the bride?"

"Yes, from middle school on."

"And, Connor says you're studying to be a nurse?"

Naomi nodded, "Yes, hopefully starting the main nursing program next September, here at Bakersfield College."

"So, what about you and Connor, considering his move. It looks like he's headed for Miramar Air Station in San Diego. The Marine Corps orders for the new squadron came in week before last."

Naomi got quiet at this. Connor had not told her he knew where he was going next, and she did not want to admit that to his friend. So, she said, "Connor and I are just dating for now. We couldn't possibly keep up Dennis and Kendra. We're just going to see what the future holds."

The music ended, and Jordy escorted Naomi off the floor. He thanked Naomi for the dance. Naomi decided to head over to where she saw the other three women in bridal party apricot dresses gathering near the gift table. She had enough dancing for a while, and she saw that Nate Hoskins was hovering nearby. Naomi figured there was safety in numbers.

Between the annoyance at Connor having been less than candid about his plans, and the hustle and bustle of the reception, Naomi felt herself going into another of her deeply contemplative and somewhat dark moods as she stood listening to the other women in Kendra's bridesmaid group. She suddenly had the feeling she was engaging in an elaborate masquerade in this flowing satin gown, floral corsage on her wrist, nails matching her dress color, and uncomfortable high heels. Her old memories as Mark, and thoughts of how he would feel in such a situation made Naomi feel dreadfully uncomfortable. She rarely had such feelings anymore, but standing amidst this cluster of frilly femininity, she was having a bad case now.

Naomi mumbled something about the ladies' room and walked away from the others. Then, she saw Nate Hoskins walking towards her, and she turned in another direction. The last thing she needed in such a mood was a slow dance with a tall, handsome guy who knew enough about the old Naomi to make conversation difficult. She needed a spot where she was out of Nate's reach, and the restroom was only a temporary respite. Unfortunately, it would allow him to lay in wait for her to exit.

As she crossed around on the opposite side of the reception hall, she saw where Jordy Cameron was sitting with three other Navy officers at one of the circular tables. There was an open seat between Jordy and another man.

Naomi walked up and bent over to whisper in Jordy's ear, "Jordy, I'm trying to avoid dancing with one particular guy, can I insert myself in your group here for a bit of protection?"

Jordy looked up at her with a surprised look and jumped to his feet, "Certainly! Gentlemen can introduce I you to our bridesmaid, Naomi Donnelley." He gave her each man's name while pulling out the chair for Naomi to sit down. Naomi did not remember any of their quickly recited names, though. Luckily their dress blue uniforms had a little black nametag with their surname, and all four were either Navy lieutenants or lieutenants junior grade. Naomi sat between Jordy on her left and, on her right, a handsome officer who looked like he might be a Latino/African mix.

"Are you gentlemen enjoying yourselves?" Naomi asked.

They all nodded, but the man of the far right said, honestly, "It is a bit different from your normal wedding reception. Normally by this stage in the afternoon, somebody's uncle will have been totally sauced up and passed out in a corner. All the bubbly here is non-alcoholic."

Naomi laughed, "I hadn't thought about that. Champagne and an open bar are the norms for a wedding reception. Our Mormon shindig must seem rather tame."

The 'honest' guy replied, "I guess 'tame' is the right word for it."

The officer on the other end of the group now announced, "Gosh, I just figured it out. You're Longshanks' girl."

Naomi laughed again, "I'm not sure Connor gets to claim a possessory interest in me just yet, but yes, Lieutenant Holloway and I have been dating."

Jordy explained to those who might not know, "Connor flew back east on bereavement leave for his mother this morning."

A couple of the men said, "Yeah, I heard that," and "Very sad."

While she was talking to the Navy officers at the table, Naomi kept an eye out for Nate, and she saw he had asked someone else to dance. Relieved, she looked around the table for something to talk about now.

Naomi turned to the man on her right and pointed to his untouched wedding cake, "Are you going to eat that?"

He shook his head 'no,' and pushed the cake plate and fork over in front of Naomi with a smile. He also poured her a glass of water from the pitcher on the table.

After a couple of bites, Naomi turned to the cake's former owner and said, "I get all the aviators' wings at this table, but what is a guy with a 'Budweiser' on his chest doing here?"

Naomi intentionally used the slang nickname for the Navy SEAL Special Warfare Badge the officer wore.

The SEAL seemed surprised at her question, but answered, "I went to Annapolis with Dennis. We were teammates on the swim team. I drove up from our base in Coronado."

"Ah, swim team to SEAL. Finally, a useful career path for someone on a swim team," Naomi said. "I'm on the swim team here at Bakersfield College."

The SEAL's interest piqued, "Oh, really, what events do you do?"

"100 Free and 200 IM, right now, but I have been thinking of going for the longer distances once I get my stamina up," Naomi explained. Then, she added, "If you were in the same midshipman class as Dennis, you must have deployed to Afghanistan right after you finished SEAL training."

The SEAL showed surprise, "How'd you know…?"

Jordy cut into the conversation, "Ruben, don't ask, Naomi apparently has a hobby of knowing about military decorations. She pegged me right off, too."

Knowing about the Ruben's Afghanistan Campaign Medal, because it matched the one Mark had worn, gave Naomi a boost from her previous lousy mood. She may no longer be one of the guys, but she was basking in the camaraderie around this table. She just had to ignore the fact that she was a pretty blonde in a satin gown sitting amongst four men in Navy dress blues. *C'est la vie… c'est une vie étrange.*

One of the other men now asked Naomi, "So, what is a seemingly intelligent and charming girl doing dating a Marine?"

"Seeing as how I'm sitting in the middle of four squid officers, I probably need to plead the Fifth on that question. Let's just say that Connor has a very particular set of skills that I find intriguing." Naomi followed her reference to the *Taken* movie with a coquettish smile.

Her comment elicited a low murmur from a couple of the men.

Now Naomi added, "Plus, I like his orange Corvette." She lied.

Naomi's mood had definitely improved. She decided she needed to get back into the role of bridesmaid at her best friend's wedding reception. So, she asked, "Since I have already danced with Jordy, who else here is not afraid of asking a Marine's girl to dance?"

Ruben, the SEAL, had Naomi's hand in an instant. As they took their turn on the dance floor, the wedding photographer's flash lit them several times. The groom's darkly handsome old teammate and the bride's blonde BFF were striking dance partners.

———

The week after the Valentine's Day wedding, Naomi had a rare Monday off. The college was closed for President's Day, and she was not scheduled to work at the clinic. She spent her morning doing some chores and did a bit of studying.

With her college and work routine now in its second month, it was obvious she had tried to put a bit too much on her plate. With her 20-30 hours at the clinic, plus a class schedule that had required her to get clearance for more than a full load of credits, she was busy, but now that she had to fit swimming practice and swim meets into the schedule, life was hectic.

She had just thought about this hectic schedule and how she had not needed to make room for meeting up with Connor recently when her new iPhone dinged its tone that an email had arrived.

—

February 20_0912PST-

From: Connor Holloway <C.Holloway@av.usmc.mil>

To: Naomi Donnelley <NaomiDonnelley@Outlook.com>

Subj: Back in Golden State

Dear Naomi,

I am back at Lemoore. I flew in through Fresno this morning.

Things were difficult down in Florida. I did not get to fill you in on details after my first trip down there in January, so I will now.

It seems that my mother and father knew about her cancer for some time, but they were trying to keep it from us while they tried chemo. Then in January, there was that turn for the worse. Holly took it really badly, especially about not being told until very late. I tried to be the strong, stoic Marine son, but it was tough to see Dad like that. Mom was the love of his life.

We buried Mom early last week, and Holly stayed on to help Dad with things.

I found out when I got back that I have orders sending me to the new F-35 squadron they are forming at MCAS Miramar in San Diego. I will have to get my stuff down there, and perhaps stage one or two of the aircraft down there, too, next month. That will make things somewhat chaotic for the next few weeks.

I will be in touch, and we can see when we can get together again in light of the San Diego move.

BTW, how are things going with college classes and your new job? You did not put much info in your last email.

Dennis emailed me pictures from the wedding reception. You looked marvelous. I wish I could have been there.

See you soon,

Fondly, Connor

Sent from my Samsung Galaxy S20

———

    Several things were clear to Naomi. The first being the email itself and the message it sent as Connor's choice for communicating to her. Yes, to her, not with her. The email icon on a cellphone is right next to the telephone icon, and here was another email from Connor without a direct phone call. He could have just as easily called her to give her this information. For that matter, he could have called her during the week and a half he was in Florida? Actually, during either time he was in Florida.

    Next, was the fact that Connor could not know that Jordy Cameron had told Naomi that Connor knew about the orders to his new duty station well in advance of his last trip to Florida. Indicating that the transfer was news upon coming back was a lie. A gentle lie, but still untrue.

    Lastly, was his talk about trying to get together with Naomi during the move to San Diego. Given that both freeways from Lemoore to San Diego went through or near Bakersfield, finding an opportunity to meet up with Naomi could not be that big of a struggle. Connor's Corvette would need to be driven to San Diego and exiting the freeway even to go to lunch with Naomi was not a difficult task to carry out.

    It was readily apparent that this email was Connor's not-well-thought-out attempt to be gentle in beginning his extraction from contact with Naomi. Naomi re-read the email with both annoyance and relief.

    The reasons for her annoyance were obvious. An email with untruths and incongruities was a slap in the face from a guy to a girl with even the level of relationship she and Connor had shared. His 'see you soon' was obviously just window dressing for his unspoken 'it is going to be tough to get together this next month.' Connor was bright enough to know that Naomi would easily see through this email's meaning. He could have handled this much better.

    At the same time, Naomi had to acknowledge that it was an emotional time for Connor. Losing a parent had to be traumatic, even for a trained warrior like Connor. But, no matter what his emotional state, his avoidance of simply calling Naomi was unmistakable. In fact, it would be logical and natural for him to want to call and talk to her at such a time. Grief or not, Naomi was obviously on the outside of Connor's thoughts.

    Yet, Naomi was relieved to receive this missive—disappointed a bit, but relieved. Connor had been right on New Year's Eve when he had characterized her 'destiny' speech to him as somewhat of a 'Dear John' message. She had been trying to let him know that she had no current intent to get into a long-term relationship leading to marriage. She had wondered at the time whether perhaps his ego was protecting him from embarrassment because he was, in truth, hoping to get serious with Naomi.

Naomi recognized that getting together with Connor had been important for her. That first kiss from Connor had been a transcendent moment in how she felt about being Naomi (and not Mark). And, Naomi trying to be attractive to Connor had taught her much about herself. This was a weird life she was leading since Napa, and the interlude with Connor had provided some answers that she needed to have. At the same time, she knew she was not ready for more involvement of the type Connor probably wanted as a young man with his career in place and his future already plotted out. Like his friend Dennis, Connor was most likely ready to find a wife and start a family. As Naomi had told him, he and she were in very different stages of their life. And, given her bizarre secret, having to deal with a macho Marine directing her life was not a good idea right now. The bottom line being she was relieved that Connor seemed intent on moving on.

Naomi would move on, too.

———

After her first meeting with the college swim team, Naomi had gone home and pulled out her high school annuals. She wanted to find a picture of the tall, black girl who had spoken to Naomi after that first race and seemed to know her from high school.

Ayla Kenton was easy to find; she had been in the photographs of the Centennial High Swim Team. Naomi had not gotten a good look at Ayla when she spoke, but Naomi could now see the stately black beauty was easily a head taller than the rest of the Centennial High girls' swim team. After Naomi found her name, she saw her pictures in a few other clubs and her individual photos. Naomi did not find any autograph signings from Ayla in the yearbooks nor any clubs they had in common, so it seemed they had not been close friends in high school, just acquaintances.

Ayla had been a year ahead of Naomi in high school, so this was Ayla's second year at the college. But, having found her name and a bit about what she had done in high school let Naomi talk to Ayla in later swim practices. They had gotten to know each other better, become friends, and started to hang out together at practice and around the campus. The fact that they were both taking Nursing 099 was a key common ground. Both Ayla and Naomi wanted to be nurses. It gave them something to talk about during the interminable waits between heats at the swim meets. It seemed Ayla was as glad to have a friend as Naomi was.

Naomi and Ayla were thrust even closer to each other right before the swim meet in Ventura County just after Spring Break. The swimmer who usually swam the freestyle in the anchor leg of the Women's 400 Meter Medley Relay pulled a tendon in her thigh. It had been Ayla who had run over to Naomi and given her the word Coach Fentress had inserted Naomi to swim right after Ayla did the butterfly in the medley relay. Naomi would be the anchor swimmer following Ayla in this key team event.

It was a natural place for Naomi with her quick time in the 100-meter freestyle. All she had to do was wait for Ayla to finish her butterfly leg and swim her fastest freestyle for two lengths to finish the relay race. The fact that Naomi had never swum this event with the team did not prevent Naomi, Ayla, and the other two relay swimmers from setting a state junior college record at Ventura College that Saturday in late March.

Ayla was reaching to pull Naomi up out of the pool when Coach Fentress arrived poolside. Jim Fentress had one of the big BC towels for Naomi. He hugged his swimmers as they clustered around Naomi and celebrated.

Fentress told Naomi, "You warned me that first day that you would need practice to do relays since you never swam with anybody else before. What will you gals be able to do after you get some practice?"

Crystal Gilbride elbowed her way past her boss and also congratulated the four women swimmers.

Naomi was still trying to catch her breath as she looked around her. She had won a couple of races on her own earlier in February and March. But, the exhilaration she felt now, sharing this record-breaking moment with her teammates was incredible.

She had her distant memories from Mark of similar occasions, like his big win for San Joaquin Delta College that had put him in line for the university transfer offers, but having won this, as Naomi Donnelley, was special. As she walked back to the team area with her teammates and the coaches, Naomi felt like this was a milestone in her curious path through life. Naomi was a bona fide success in the real world. Naomi's life was real; it was not merely a supernatural prank nor a Twilight Zone episode anymore.

—

Part Three

Chapter 21

Lindy Larche, RN, the charge nurse on the 4-West ward at Memorial Hospital in Bakersfield, watched her nursing intern cleaning up the nurses' station, disinfecting the surfaces and taking the trash to the big trash bin across the hallway by the elevator. She liked Naomi, who was a constant beehive of activity and really bright.

"You're coming up on your NCLEX test soon, right?" Lindy asked.

"Yeah, two weeks, I've put in a time-off request. I have to drive up to some test center in Visalia," Naomi answered.

"They should have it at Cal State Bakersfield. That's where I took mine."

"I've heard of people who did that. I think they've changed since then. Now, you have to take it at a private company's test center. According to their website, the same company does the test all across the U.S. This company has centers up in Visalia and over in Santa Maria."

"So, Naomi will be a for-real RN soon," Lindy said. "Let me give you an advance on that work. The patient in 416 is due to be released this morning. All he needs are the discharge docs from downstairs and a new dressing on his wound. You up for that?"

"All by myself? Sure," Naomi said. "Wait, do you mean…?"

"Yeah, the cute one everyone's been talking about for the last two days. I'll be in to double-check your work. Come get me when you're done. But, I need to warn you about something. You should put the replacement dressing on in exactly the same way as the one he's got now. Doctor Pearson is the surgeon, and he has his own way of telling the nurses in surgery to do dressings—like they don't know. The patient will be going to Pearson's office later this week for a follow-up, and if the dressing isn't the same way it was when he left Pearson's surgery, I promise you Pearson will turn in a quality review report on you for not following doctor's directions. Understand?"

"Got it, no innovations."

"Oh, and here." Lindy handed Naomi a folded camouflage long-sleeved t-shirt. "His buddy came in while our patient, Jesse Manzanares, was talking to the physical therapist and brought him a replacement uniform shirt for the one he got shot through that they cut off him in the ambulance. Give this to him after you finish."

"He's military?" Naomi asked.

"Oh, you didn't hear. He's the Sheriff SWAT team officer who got shot in the credit union heist standoff in Delano."

"So, what should I take in for the dressing?" Naomi asked.

"The wound management tray is on the bottom shelf of the supplies counter. Big, green tray, it's got everything," Lindy explained, as she motioned over her shoulder to the back room. "If there is not everything you need, come back out for it. Don't forget my warning about Pearson's perfectionism. Oh, and here's his take-home meds, 20 Norco standard, take one or two as needed. Give him the standard opioid warning, too." Lindy passed Naomi the bottle.

Naomi smiled and went to get the tray.

"Oh, and Naomi?" Lindy said, waiting to get Naomi's attention, "Take as much time as you need with this one. His buddy hinted he's single."

Naomi feigned not understanding the obvious implication of the older nurse's words.

———

The wide hospital room door was slightly ajar. Naomi pushed it open all the way. The patient did not hear her, as he was bent over, starting to put on his trousers with his back to Naomi. He still had the back-opening hospital gown on. He finally heard Naomi and realized he was mooning someone behind him. He moved quickly to stand up, wincing in pain. His trousers fell to the floor.

"You shouldn't be bending over. You could pull your sutures," Naomi announced, as she put the supply tray, pill bottle, and shirt on the bed table. She pulled a pair of baby blue nitrile gloves on her hands.

"Kinda hard to pull my pants up and put my boots on without bending over," he said.

"Well, Mr. Manzanares, I can help you with that. Best not to reinjure yourself."

"I'm Lieutenant, not Mister."

"Sorr-ee!" Naomi said, a bit too sarcastically.

Manzanares saw the shirt and reached for it.

"Not yet!" Naomi ordered. "I have to change your dressing."

"I just looked at the dressing. It seems fine."

"That's my call, not yours. My rule book says a patient goes home with a fresh dressing, not the one that has the post-op drainage in it. Sit on the edge of the bed, and I'll untie your gown."

Naomi untied the gown and took it off his shoulders. She walked over and dumped it in the soiled linen hamper by the door and pushed the door closed, so the patient was not sitting shirt off, boxers only, with the door wide open.

Naomi turned and quickly took stock of her patient. He was tall and broad-shouldered, quite handsome. He obviously was of some level of Spanish heritage, given his name, dark hair, and light olive skin. His belly had washboard abs, and his chest had a large cluster of curly ebony wool and weight-trained pectorals. In between those two features, he now had a wide band of stretchy, blue gauze wrapping around his chest and a large gauze compress on his ribs under his left armpit.

As Naomi looked at him, and then walked toward him, he let out a slight chuckle.

"What's so funny, Lieutenant?" she asked, emphasizing the 'lieutenant.'

"You can call me Jesse. I was just thinking about the movie *Days of Thunder*. It's one of my favorites. Have you seen it?"

"Yes, it's on cable. I like Tom Cruise, sort of. You can call me Naomi."

As Naomi started to unwind the gauze strap around his chest, Jesse explained, "What I was thinking...? In *Days of Thunder*, the race driver's crew set up this practical joke when they hire a beautiful model to act like she is a highway patrol officer who stops them along the highway. She gets kind of rough with him when she frisks him, and then his crew starts laughing. He finally gets the joke, but later on, when another really beautiful woman appears, supposedly as a brain surgeon, he thinks they are setting him up again and acts accordingly, you know, teasing and flirting, with the neurosurgeon. But, it turns out the neurosurgeon, played by Nicole Kidman, is real. Remember that?"

"Yes, I know it well," Naomi answered. "Cute scene."

"Well, I was thinking. Here, I've got a beautiful woman, who could be a fashion model, who comes in my room in a nurse's uniform with a shirt my SWAT crew obviously brought to the hospital. It could have been just like the set-up in the movie."

"So, should take it as a compliment that you think I am too beautiful to be a **real** nurse?" Naomi asked. She threw the bundle of used gauze in the bio-hazard bin.

"Well, not too beautiful, but... you know, you're not...." He stopped when he saw no way to talk his way out of the corner.

"Control is an illusion, you infantile egomaniac!" Naomi declared, quite harshly, and with a stern expression.

"What?" Jesse seemed shocked.

Naomi smiled sweetly, and explained, "Also from *Days of Thunder*... That's the great line Nicole Kidman says to Tom Cruise, trying to give him a reality check. It became a kind of a meme after they broke up as a couple in real life."

Jesse nodded and looked at Naomi with what she thought might be a bit of newfound appreciation. The pretty nurse could quote lines from his favorite movies.

She told him, "I need you to keep your left arm up while I get the dressing off. Maybe grab your right shoulder with your left hand. Move slowly."

He followed orders.

"This may hurt a little when I pull the dressing off. This is the part in the movie where the pretty nurse gets rough with the action hero. Turn to the right a bit."

He smiled at this and turned. Naomi gently and slowly pulled the dressing off. She saw that he did not flinch, even when he probably ought to. *Tough guy.*

When she saw the wound, she said, "Ah, in and out wound, and you're lucky, it missed your ribs, right in between. A little different angle and the bullet would have stayed inside your chest, and not come back out."

"That's what the doc said, too," Jesse said. He turned his head down to try and look at what she was doing.

"I thought you guys wore bullet-proof vests to prevent this."

"We do. I had mine on. But, the Kevlar is mostly in plates on the front, back and sides. The perp's bullet apparently went in the strap attachment seam where you buckle it on the side."

"This shouldn't leave too bad of a scar," Naomi noted.

"Considering all the others, a couple scars on my ribs aren't a problem."

"All the others? What do you mean?" Naomi asked.

"You didn't see my back when you came in?" he asked.

"No? Well, I saw your backside, but I wasn't looking at your back. I had never seen camouflage boxers before." She gave a little smile at that.

He motioned with a tilt of his head for her to go look at his back. She walked around the bed and saw the lower third of his back was covered with a wide wavy keloid scar area. His normally light olive skin was overlaid by the lighter and sometimes pure white keloid scars from a massive burn.

Naomi walked back around the bed and asked, "How'd you get that?"

"Army."

"No more explanation than just 'Army?'" she asked.

"Not really. Not something I like to talk about," he said firmly.

She went back to work on his current wound. He looked down at what she was doing again.

"I can't work if you keep looking down," Naomi said, as she turned to reach for some cleaning and disinfectant pads, and to rip open their pouches. "Go ahead and look now. Then, keep your head up, so I can work without your body bent."

He lifted his arm out of the way, looked down, and then sat up straight and put his arm back on his right shoulder. Naomi turned back toward him and cleaned the Betadine stain off his skin and applied a bit of wound care ointment over the stitches. As she did, she noticed Jesse turning his eyes down, trying to peek to where she was working.

"<u>What</u> do you keep looking at?" she said, clearly annoyed.

"Nothing. I was just... nothing," Jesse mumbled.

"Relax, I know what I'm doing," Naomi said.

Then, Naomi realized what Jesse had been looking at. He was trying to see her hands, not his wound. She gave a little chuckle and stood up straight.

"Is this what you were trying to see?" she asked. She lifted her left hand up in front of Jesse's face and stretched her semitransparent glove tight to show her ring finger to him. "No ring on my finger. Just like you. Satisfied?"

Jesse just smiled and nodded. Naomi smiled also and went back to work.

Naomi checked the old dressing and fashioned a new one in precisely the same shape and thickness as the old bandage. Doctor Pearson would be happy. She dumped the old dressing in the bio-hazards bin.

When she was done with the dressing, she wrapped his chest again with the wide stretchy blue gauze, just like the old dressing. If it had not been for Nurse Larche's warning to match the old dressing precisely, she probably would have put a regular athletic wrap around his chest.

When she was finished wrapping, she reached for his shirt. She started to unfold it and put it over his head.

"I can do that," Jesse objected.

"No, you can't!" Naomi ordered. "The way that bullet went in and out, it had to injure your intercostal muscle under the ribs. That is a key muscle for body movement. Something as simple as pulling a shirt over your head, or reaching down to put on your boots, could rip up Doctor Pearson's work and set you back. You need to be careful dressing, maybe get somebody to help for the next several days."

She heard Jesse mutter, "Yeah, like that is going to happen," under his breath.

"Well, all I can do is warn you," Naomi said, pulling down his shirt to his waist. She smoothed out the wrinkles with her hands. He had a very firm tummy and back. She knelt and put each trouser leg over his feet. Then, she pulled the trousers up.

"Tucked or untucked?" she asked.

"Tucked," he said.

Jesse did not resist it when she carefully tucked the back of his shirt in his pants, so he did not have to stretch his arm around. He tightened his belt himself.

Naomi reached down by the bed stand to where he had his green mesh combat boots with his socks inside. There was dried blood on the toe of the left boot. She got another sterile wipe and removed the blood. She started to undo the laces. He sat back down on the bed. She saw the SWAT lieutenant smirk at her, but he did not argue about Naomi kneeling, and putting his socks and boots on for him.

—

"It's kind of rare these days that I can sit down to a regular meal with you," Naomi said to Ray and Janet Morrison, as they sat down for dinner on Thursday evening.

Janet was serving beef stew, one of Ray's favorites. After the initial servings were distributed by Janet, she answered Naomi, "Yes, indeed, you've been rather busy, what with finishing up your courses and doing the internship at the hospital. Are things going to settle down now that you've got your RN license?"

"Well, I haven't got the RN license yet, I'm just taking the national nursing licensing exam. I still have to go through all the application bureaucracy in Sacramento to get the actual license," Naomi said, and then taking a bite of stew, before continuing. "But, as to your question, no, things won't be settling down. I'm just switching from Bakersfield College to Cal State Bakersfield. I need to get my bachelor's degree in Nursing to get better jobs in nursing.

"The CSUB program to give RNs their Bachelors' degree is a fifteen-month program that is pretty hectic itself. It is a mix of classwork, online study, and clinical programs. I wanted to talk to you about my plans for that."

Naomi looked to both Janet and Ray. She had their attention with talk of plans. She continued, "Both my friend Ayla, you've met her, and I have been accepted to do our clinical program for the CSUB degree program at Memorial Hospital. That means we will be rotating through different nursing jobs at Memorial and could be put on some really strange work schedules. Ayla's mother is a nurse, and she recommended to us that living close to the hospital will be the best set-up to get us through the hectic schedule for the next fifteen months."

Both Janet and Ray frowned a bit. They sensed what was coming.

"Ayla's mother knew a couple who work at the hospital who were getting ready to give notice to their landlord that they were moving to their new house. Their old apartment is only a block west of Memorial hospital. Ayla and I coordinated our lease application with that couple's 30-day move-out notice, and we are going to be able to rent a two-bedroom apartment together that is perfect for us. Really safe area, close to work.... So, ... I'll be moving out early next month."

Ray and Janet were both nodding. Ray said, "We've known for some time that your days with us were numbered. We've talked about it. We're really going to miss having you around."

Naomi's eyes were moist as she said, "Like I've told you both probably a thousand times, what you two did for me was nothing less than life changing. I'm where I am today because of you two. You couldn't have done more for me if you were my real parents."

It was Janet's turn, "Having you with us has been a godsend. It is not too much to say that your presence here these last few years filled a hole in my mortal soul. I think I can say the same for Ray."

Ray nodded, but kept his usual silence.

Naomi looked at both of them and said, "But, it is not like I'm moving to Timbuktu. I expect we are still going to be seeing a lot of each other. I am probably going to have some big decisions coming along, and I will still need your advice. I'm only going to be a couple of miles away."

Ray now spoke, "Anything you ever need, please know that you can ask us. Anything."

Naomi had a tear on her cheek, "Thanks."

———

Naomi came back from her lunch break and went to put her purse and sweater in the back room. When she came back out front, there were seven nurses clustered around the nursing station counter, both the other four nurses from here at 4-West and three others she knew were on duty across at 4-East. They all seemed to be watching Naomi as she walked up.

Naomi looked, questioningly, between several faces, and said, "What's up?"

Lindy moved to the side, and Naomi could now see the there was a slim crystal bud vase on the counter. There were three large red roses in the vase, and a small envelope was tied to the vase with a red ribbon.

When Naomi did not say anything, Lindy gave a wave of her hand, indicating the vase was meant for Naomi.

"What's this? I don't have anybody who…." Naomi stammered.

Lindy said, "Well, you obviously have somebody. The envelope reads 'Naomi, 4-West, Bakersfield Memorial Hospital.'"

Naomi walked up and fingered the ivory envelope. The flap had a red foil seal embossed with a heart, which had kept its contents secret from the hovering crowd of nurses. She opened the envelope and pulled a tri-fold ivory card out. It also had the red heart seal on its flap. She broke the seal with her thumbnail and unfolded the card. There was a business card inside.

Lindy made a triumphant fist pump gesture and shouted, "Yes!" when she glimpsed the green and gold business card with a seven-pointed star on it.

Naomi frowned at Lindy's histrionics and read the note inside the card to herself, 'Dear Real Nurse, Please call me. With Fond Regards, Your Infantile Egomaniac.' The business card was from Jesse A. Manzanares, Lieutenant, Kern County Sheriff's Department. The card listed both an office phone and a cellphone.

"Is that card from who I think it is?" asked one of the other nurses.

Naomi looked at her and nodded.

"What's the note say?" demanded Lindy.

"You wouldn't understand it," Naomi explained.

"Try me. I was the one who assigned you to him. I deserve to know the fruits of my labors."

Naomi gave a little sigh and handed Lindy the card, "It's really an inside joke. You won't get it."

Lindy read the card, shrugged and passed it to the other nurses, "You're right. I don't get it. It doesn't sound very romantic, except the 'fond regards' part and the heart on the seal. You weren't in there long enough to be exchanging secret inside jokes."

Naomi smiled coyly and said, "It seems some things don't take that long."

———

Chapter 22

"He's picking you up at 7:00?" Ayla asked, as she kicked off her white nurses' loafers and headed for the refrigerator.

"Yup. He says we'll be going out to eat, so we can talk and get to know each other," Naomi answered, as she started stripping off her green scrubs and getting ready for her shower.

"I guess when you're going out with a cop, you don't have to worry about meeting him somewhere else for the first date, so you don't have to give a stranger your home address."

"Well, he's not exactly a stranger, and I didn't give him my home address."

"Where's he picking you up then?"

"Right here. When we had resolved that he was going to pick me up at 7:00 PM, I was getting ready to give him my address, and he said, 'you're in Apartment D-4, right?'"

"How'd he get your apartment number? We just moved in here," Ayla sounded concerned.

"I wondered about that, too, but I already changed my driver's license address, to make sure that it was right for my RN license application packet and background check. He's a cop, he can pull up my driver's license information on his cellphone, probably."

"That's a wee bit spooky, but maybe not for a cop. Watcha gonna wear?" Ayla punctuated her question with the snap-fizz of her Diet Pepsi can.

"I think the first date with a guy who has only seen me in scrubs calls for my clingy crepe Little Black Dress. Figure-hugging and shows a little bit of leg. And, it lets me wear heels, so he doesn't totally tower over me."

"I've never had that problem. Mine is usually the opposite — finding a guy tall enough, so I'm not towering over him if I wear heels."

"Yeah, I suppose some guys have an ego thing about that," Naomi shouted from the bathroom as she turned on the shower.

"You think?" Ayla shouted back.

———

Now that she had her own apartment, Naomi had moved the furniture from the old self-storage company she still maintained with all of her mother's stuff in it. Over the past year or so, she had weeded the pile of stuff down, and now that she had moved the furniture to the new apartment, she had moved the rest to a smaller storage space. The old Naomi's life with her mother and its baggage train was becoming less of a thing. But, the furniture from her mother's apartment had saved Naomi and Ayla from buying stuff for their new residence.

Now, she sat at the mirrored vanity dresser of Naomi's mother, putting the final touches on her 'look' for the first date with Jesse. She had finished dressing, and the black dress, stockings, and heels seemed perfect. She had carefully curled under the bottom of her bob with a heated curler she had borrowed from Ayla. It was the make-up she was not sure about.

Naomi had gotten much better with her make-up and grooming in the last two and a half years. She thought she was doing well, considering she had started in Napa with a zero skill level in such things. She realized her widely set big green eyes, and her gull-winged brows lent themselves to dramatic enhancement, but she was not sure of herself still. She would get a second opinion from her roommate.

Ayla was lounged out on the sofa in sweatpants and tank top, watching television. Her lanky figure filled the couch. Naomi flipped on the light switch and turned to face Ayla.

"Ayla, I need a quick second opinion. How do I look?" Naomi asked.

Ayla muted the television and stood up. Her face brightened when she got a good look at Naomi. She shook her head and walked over to Naomi, "My God, girl! This poor guy tonight is toast. I don't think I've ever seen you in full warpaint before. You look awesome."

"Warpaint, huh? Too dramatic?" Naomi sounded unsure.

"Too dramatic? You've got to be kidding. That shimmery gold eyeshadow under your brows is killer. And, many women would kill to have those cheekbones." Ayla held Naomi's arm and moved her toward the light. "Nope. You shouldn't change a thing. That's new perfume, too. Isn't it?"

"Yeah, I hit Macy's make-up and perfume counter last night after work."

"I wondered where you went. It was worth whatever it cost. Big night, huh?" Ayla went back to sit down.

"I hope it is a big night. I'm kind out of practice at this," Naomi admitted.

"That's a shame because you're obviously an expert at it," Ayla said, as she unmuted her show. "You need anything from me? Can I help with anything?"

Naomi shook her head and raised her voice over the television, "No, I put your curler back in your room. Jesse should be here soon."

"When the doorbell rings, I'll hide in my room. I don't want my sweats outfit to interfere with your aura," Ayla added.

Naomi felt better about herself now that she had the enthusiastic judgment of her new roommate. She was not quite sure what it would be like for the handsome hunk to be 'toast,' but Ayla's comment empowered her.

—

As he bent over to open the car door for her, Naomi noticed that Jesse was dressed in a blue suit that was perfectly tailored to his muscled physique. She thought about saying something about the excellent cut of his clothes but deferred it because he had just given her a compliment on the way to the car, and she didn't want to appear to be 'me-too'ing him. She would mention it later.

Naomi got into the metallic red Ford Taurus, and Jesse shut her door. As she looked around her inside the car, she finally realized she was in a police car. A large radio and computer console jutted out from the middle of the dash, and two thin banks of emergency lights hung on each side of the upper windshield. Some sort of clamp arrangement jutted up where the center console normally would be. Seeing the trigger guard and lock mechanism, Naomi realized this was an empty shotgun rack.

Naomi buckled up, and Jesse got in.

Naomi could not resist asking, "Is this the car you normally drive? Even off duty?"

Jesse started the engine and turned to explain to her, "This is one of my cars. Lieutenants, commanders, and above are all assigned county vehicles for their regular use that can be used to respond to an emergency if need be. We all have our own cars, too. But, we are allowed to use the department vehicle even for off duty use, inside the county. If I get called out for a SWAT team deployment or some other emergency, the trunk has all my gear in it. I could flip on the light, siren, and haul ass." Jesse now smiled, "Of course, I'd have to dump you on the curb somewhere first." When Naomi timidly blinked at his joke, he added, "Jus' kidding.

"I'd probably use my own vehicle for something like going out to eat, usually. I have an extra set of my SWAT gear in it, and I have a magnetic flashing light to stick on the roof." Jesse headed toward downtown. "I didn't think my personal vehicle was a good idea for tonight, though."

"Why is that?"

"My vehicle is a lifted 4x4 Ford F-350 Super Duty. I figured you'd be in heels and a dress for a date, and my running board step on the truck is about thigh-high for you. My choice was either drive this or grab you and manhandle you in and out the truck."

"Good choice," Naomi said. She was amazed that yet another big Ford pickup truck had entered her life. The first one on the freeway offramp was not a good memory. Now, Jesse drove the same vehicle as Ray.

"So, Naomi, I scoped out a couple of options for our dinner tonight. First choice is a steakhouse. Great place downtown, called The Mark. It is close to the Jail, and lots of Sheriff's people, including me, think it is great. The second choice is…."

"Stop there," Naomi interrupted. "You had me at 'steak.' I am always up for a good steak. But, I should warn you—I don't do lady's portions on steak. Bigger, the better."

"Then, steak it is," Jesse said.

Naomi saw a little smile on his lips.

———

They had just walked into the restaurant when the young *maître d'* said, "Good evening, Jesse. Right this way."

They were led to a nice table for two near the main aisle through the restaurant. Naomi sat with her back to the wall, and Jesse sat by the aisle.

"Wow, immediate service and first name basis with the *maître d'*. This must be one of your favorite places," Naomi commented.

"It is one of my favorite places, but I have a secret. The *maître d'* is my cousin."

"Oh, that's cozy."

"Not unusual, though. I have lots of cousins, and other kin. There are many members of the extended Manzanares clan in the Central Valley."

"I see."

They both opened their menus and were still looking when the waitress came for their drink order. She tapped the wine list with her finger and raised her eyebrows.

Jesse answered first, "No wine for me. I'll have an iced tea. Naomi?"

"None for me either. Do you have lemonade?"

The waitress said 'yes,' and Naomi nodded to her.

After the waitress left, Jesse explained, "I never drink more than a single beer when I have to drive, especially in a department vehicle. At home or at a party when I've got a designated driver, yes, but otherwise never—one of my unbreakable rules. But that needn't stop you from having some red wine if you are a steak eater."

Naomi shook her head, "I never drink any alcohol, period. My strongest drink is a Classic Coke or my lemonade."

"Not even a good strong coffee?"

"No."

"Why is that?" Jesse asked.

Naomi had not expected the Mormon Church and their Word of Wisdom to rear its head quite so quickly in the conversation. She now thought of how she wanted to phrase this on her first date with a non-Mormon. She figured she would be a little circuitous until she had a better feel for Jesse's character.

"The couple who took me in after my mother died my senior year of high school are devout Mormons. Living with them, I just naturally gravitated to following their Word of Wisdom. No alcohol, no coffee, and no tea."

Jesse asked, "So, you're not a Mormon? Just them?"

This cop was a good interrogator, Naomi's intentionally circuitous answer was already a bust.

"Well, yes, I am. I was baptized when I was a little girl. But, I hadn't followed the Church rules until I moved in with them. I just moved out this month."

Jesse nodded. "If you're following the Word of Wisdom, doesn't it also say you should limit your eating of red meat to just what is necessary? I thought you were a big-time steak enthusiast."

Naomi stared across the table at Jesse, "How do you know that about the Mormon Word of Wisdom?"

Jesse folded his menu and said, "My kid sister, Lucia, met a Mormon guy when she was going to the University of California, Merced, married him, and joined the LDS Church. She told me all about the Church."

Naomi knew how to answer Jesse's question, she just did not want to sound like she was preaching Mormon doctrine to him, but then, he had asked the question. She explained, "There are two parts of the Word of Wisdom about red meat. One verse says it should be eaten sparingly. The other says it should be eaten only in winter, and times of cold or famine. The key thing is those verses were advice on how to live healthily in the middle 1800s. Red meat for many of the pioneers was a rare delicacy, cattle were a valuable resource, and red meat in summer months rotted easily. It was good advice to eat red meat sparingly and not slaughter it or eat it in times it might be spoiled in the heat before they had refrigeration. There is a big difference between the health advice that every Church member should follow as their own conscience and personal situation dictates, and the outright prohibition against drinking alcohol and hot drinks. My eating, in the 21st Century, a sirloin steak from a commercial meatpacker that has been brought here in a refrigerated truck is a lot different from my great-great-great-grandfather killing the family cow in the summer heat of 1845. However, there is not so much difference when it comes to drinking a shot of whiskey or a glass of wine, as your personal drinking rules seem to agree."

The waitress came with their drinks and asked for their orders, cutting off this line of discussion. She hoped.

Jesse deferred to Naomi ordering first.

Naomi defied Jesse's inquiry into her steak-eating, and ordered the 16-ounce New York steak, medium rare, with sautéed onions, along with the garlic and thyme sauce. The waitress turned to Jesse.

Jesse shook his head and smiled at his date, "I really don't believe you did that, Naomi. That is what I order every time I come here. I'll have the same." He grabbed both menus and handed them to the waitress.

After the waitress left, Jesse continued his inquiry, "I suppose it is a coincidence that my sister Lucia's explanation, when I challenged her after she mentioned the red meat thing, is almost verbatim the same as your explanation, including the line about the family cow."

Naomi gave Jesse a critical glance and said, "No coincidence at all. LDS Sunday School lesson plans come in a published loose-leaf binder. It sounds like your sister listened in class just like I did. The real question is, why does Jesse feel the need to challenge his sister and me on our personal beliefs."

"My philosophy professor at Fresno State taught me that challenging an assertion by one party makes the understanding of both parties clearer when the assertion is defended."

Naomi thought for a minute and then said, "Philosophy class at Fresno State. Sounds like a good introduction to giving me your life story and getting to know each other. That was our plan for this evening. You from Fresno?"

"Nope, born here and grew up in Oildale, near north side of Bakersfield. My mother came from Fresno. My Grandma O'Herlihy still lives there. And, I've got dozens of cousins, aunts, uncles, nephews, and nieces spread all throughout the Central Valley. My cousin working at this restaurant wasn't a one-off thing. I have similar family connections at dozens of places from here to Merced."

"O'Herlihy isn't Hispanic," Naomi said, realizing as she said it that it was stating the obvious.

"Only my Dad's side is Hispanic. Half of those cousins I mentioned are Scotch-Irish. O'Herlihy family came to California from Oklahoma in the Great Depression. Grapes of Wrath era migrants."

The waitress delivered their salads and the appetizer tray.

As they started eating, Naomi did not want Jesse to get off the hook, so she asked, "Mother and Father? Brothers and sisters, besides Lucia?"

Jesse gulped down his bite of stuffed mushroom and continued. "My father, Manuel, worked in the oilfields until he saved enough to buy his first oilfield service truck, a water tanker. Yes, they call him Manny Manzanares. He's been doing that line of work for as long as I can remember. One day he was driving his tanker to dump a load of dirty oil well brine at Kettleman City, and he saw a car broke down on the 99, south of Pixley. He stopped to help, and the driver was a pretty would-be kindergarten teacher from Fresno going home from a job interview in Bakersfield. Adele O'Herlihy got the teaching job in Bakersfield, and Manny Manzanares got the job as her husband. They eventually had three kids, Jesse, Pedro, and Lucia, in that order, and raised them in a tract house in northern Bakersfield, in the middle-class ghetto called Oildale."

"What do Pedro and Lucia do?" Naomi was determined to keep him talking as long as possible.

"Pedro, we call him Pete, runs a big auto parts store here in town. That being another of my key family business contacts, especially in outfitting the aforementioned Ford 4x4. Lucia has become a very proficient baby-maker for her chiropractor husband, Jeff Cooper, the Mormon guy. They currently have two little Coopers. They live up in Merced."

Naomi washed her salad down with some lemonade and said, "So, this philosophy class in Fresno, how did that take you to a career as a SWAT officer?"

"Wow, that is a pretty broad question—like, my whole adult life. Don't I get to know a little about you in this process?"

"We started this conversation out with challenging my religion. Remember? You'll get your chance."

"Okay, philosophy. Don't get the impression I studied philosophy in depth. That class was a one-shot elective to satisfy the required courses for my degree. My major at Fresno State was actually Pre-Med."

"Pre-Med. Really?" Naomi interrupted.

"Yeah, I had this dream of going to medical school, probably planted in me by the O'Herlihy women. I heard the military had a program of sending their top officers to the Armed Services Medical School to get their MD degree tuition-free, so I also took Army ROTC to get a commission. I figured if I didn't get the military medical school, I could just serve my country and get out to go to a regular med school on the GI bill. Remember, this was in the post-9/11 years, and a lot of guys my age thought that they ought to be doing something by joining the military."

Naomi nodded, remembering the same thoughts by Mark at that age.

"It turned out I graduated with damned fine grades in Pre-Med and accepted my commission as an Army officer. With the idea that I needed to do my best as a junior Army officer for a couple of years to get accepted into the Medical Corps program, I went the full-on gung-ho route, and went to Infantry branch and Ranger School."

Jesse interspersed his story with the last of his mushroom. Naomi waited.

"Ranger Lieutenant Manzanares got sent to Afghanistan during one of the worst times to be there. You saw the result of that on my back at the hospital. Turns out, I had plenty of contact with the Army Medical Corps, but as a patient, not as a doctor. My dream of spending my life working in a hospital went up in flames, to employ an awful pun. I no longer wanted to be a doctor. I came home, looked around for something worthwhile to do. It turned out the Kern Sheriff's Department thought my Ranger training was more important than my Pre-Med degree that was somewhat extraneous to their needs. I finished a short police academy course and joined the department. My background in the Army and a BS degree gave me a quick bump up in rank, and my training was perfect for SWAT. I moved up in rank quickly. Trying to be a valiant leader of the SWAT team got me sent to your hospital room, which brought us to tonight. End of story. Your turn."

Naomi pushed her empty salad plate back and asked, "Are questions allowed?"

Jesse shrugged, "I guess you could ask questions, except in two areas. First, you've heard about as much as you are going to about Afghanistan, I don't like to talk about that. Second, you can't ask what was in my stupid head when I gave that armed robber who hit the credit union up in Delano a clear shot at me. That is both because the answer is embarrassing, and also because my SWAT team can shoot straighter than that perp. Thus, his death is deemed an officer-involved shooting and is before a review board still. So, 'no comment.' I'd rather give you a chance to talk about yourself."

Naomi found Jesse's feelings about Afghanistan rather odd. She had Mark's memories of being there, too, and she would not have any qualms about talking about it. Well, most of it. That is, if she could talk about it to anyone other than Doctor Partridge. Her own reasons for not talking were unique, but she gave Jesse the benefit of the doubt that he had a good reason, too. He had suffered a dreadful injury.

Naomi's thoughts about questions were interrupted by the arrival of the platter-sized *entre* plates of New York steaks and side dishes.

They both started in on their meals while Naomi thought of just how she would present her life story. It was a delicate task since she was talking to a native of Bakersfield and a trained interrogator, plus she still had a distinct lack of knowledge about her own life. Not to mention the fact that the old Naomi's life story had some very obvious minefields in it, considering she was trying to impress a law enforcement officer.

Jesse spoke first, "Since I don't hear any questions, I guess that in between bites, you can start out with father, mother, and siblings."

Naomi nodded and finished chewing a bite, "No siblings unless my real father has kids I don't know about. I haven't seen him in like fifteen years. He lives in Utah someplace. That's where I was born. I know nothing about him, except I've got his last name, and this blonde hair isn't from my mother."

Naomi had gotten the easy one out of the way and celebrated with a bite of yummy sautéed onion and garlic-thyme sauce. She continued, "My mother, Elizabeth, died in May of my senior year of high school. She had a vicious form of pancreatic cancer. She died a few months after we found out. She was from Utah, too. She worked as an accountant for a business services company in downtown Bakersfield. We lived in an apartment out on Fruitdale."

Naomi took a rest and had another bite of steak. Jesse was chewing and intently staring at her.

The waitress appeared and asked if everything was alright. They both said it was perfect.

Naomi knew the next part might draw questions, she tried to think of the way to limit them.

"My mother had remarried, so I had a stepfather. He had a temper, and he put the two of us in the emergency room the August before my senior year. When he realized the Bakersfield PD was looking for him after the ER turned in its report on the battered wife and child, he left town in a hurry. He managed to have a run-in with the cops, ran from them, and is now enjoying a few years in prison. I'm going to assert the same thing you did about Afghanistan and tell you I don't want to talk about my former stepfather."

Jesse set his fork down on his plate quickly upon hearing this part of her story. She looked over, and he was staring at her with his mouth open a little bit. They looked at each other for a long moment.

"Problem?" Naomi asked.

"No problem, but I absolutely have to ask a question about that," Jesse bit his lip, knowing that he was going against Naomi's stated wishes.

Naomi rolled her eyes and said, "Okay, but if I decide your question isn't absolutely necessary, then I reserve the right to open up questioning on Afghanistan."

Jesse frowned, but asked her, "Your stepfather didn't happen to be the guy who pulled the gun on a Park Ranger and tried to run a roadblock north of Kernville, coming south out of Sequoia, was he?"

Naomi gave a deep sigh when she remembered the part that Doctor Partridge had mentioned about a SWAT team when he told her about her stepfather. Already guessing the answer, she asked, "How would you know about that?'

Jesse answered, "I was a Sergeant back then. I was driving the Sheriff's armored assault vehicle that your stepfather rammed into when he tried to get by our roadblock."

Naomi waited a long time before speaking, "You arrested my stepfather?"

"No, I didn't do the arrest. The Highway Patrol did that because they had jurisdiction since they were handling the chase. I was asked to go up to the federal court in Fresno to testify, since he had intentionally hit the vehicle I was driving."

Naomi again waited, wondering what to say next. She decided, "Well then, I guess all I have to say is 'Thank you from the bottom of my heart.' Getting that sleazebag out of her life at least made my mother's last months free of his hateful presence."

Naomi was totally unsure of what she should be saying since her entire knowledge of this stepfather they were discussing came from a couple old reports Partridge had given her and a few papers she had found in storage. However, she had become a pretty decent actress when it came to adlibbing about old Naomi's past.

Jesse seemed at a loss for what to say next. He finally said, "What a coincidence!"

Naomi was an expert at coincidences. She gave her best try at a smile and said, "Bakersfield isn't as big a place as its residents want to believe. Let me put a bit more of this luscious meat away, and I will get you back to today in my story. Not much more."

Both Naomi and Jesse filled the silence with bites of steak.

After a bit more pregnant pause, Naomi looked over to Jesse and said, "If this were a movie, this would be the place where the awkward silent *repartee* between the leading man and lady is interrupted by the sidekick running in and telling them some important news about what the villain is doing."

Jesse smiled and said, "That's right, I forgot you are a movie geek, just like me."

They both smiled and ate a bit more. The silence was ended when Jesse again laid his fork on his plate. Naomi looked at him to see him staring with a perplexed expression at the front door of the restaurant.

"What?" she asked.

"My boss just walked in with his wife. They're coming this way."

"Boss?" Naomi asked, but Jesse was already putting his napkin on the table and starting to stand up.

A fifty-ish man in a dark suit was walking up. He had seen Jesse, too. He was holding the hand of a well-coiffed woman with ginger hair in a red dinner dress who was probably quite a bit younger than the man. The 'boss' was much shorter than Jesse with balding sandy-gray hair and a matching bushy mustache. He looked more like a jovial professor than someone who would be a SWAT officer's boss.

Jesse reached toward the man to shake hands, "Good evening, Sheriff."

"Good evening, Jesse," the Sheriff said. "How are you doing? Glad to see you are up and around."

"I'm doing well. Still on light duty, but that should end soon. Like I said when you visited me in the hospital, it was just a glancing shot."

The Sheriff turned to the woman with him, "Dear, you've met Jesse Manzanares. He's our SWAT officer who got shot, up in Delano."

Jesse took her hand when she offered it. He said, "Good evening, Mrs. Oldham."

"And, who is this stunning young lady?" the Sheriff turned to face Naomi, who still sat behind the table.

"Sheriff, this is Naomi Donnelley. She is one of the nurses who treated me in the hospital. This is a kind of thank you dinner."

Naomi stood, and the Sheriff took a step around the table and took Naomi's hand when she offered it. The Sheriff made a gesture toward his wife and said, "Miss Donnelley, this is my wife, Sariah Oldham."

"Pleased to meet you," Naomi said. Mrs. Oldham smiled and nodded. Neither of them moved to shake hands as they were on opposites sides of the table, and the Sheriff and Jesse were in the way. Naomi sat back down.

The Sheriff stepped past Jesse and retook his wife's hand. "Well, we don't want to keep you two from your dinner. Jesse, I'm glad you're doing so well. Miss Donnelley and her cohorts seem to have done their job well, as your team did, up in Delano."

The Sheriff started to walk off, but his wife stopped, pulled his hand for him to stop. She turned back to stand next to Jesse, and said, "I may be out of line to mention it, but I simply have to say… You two make about the most perfect couple I have seen in a long time. I trust the thank you dinner will not be your last together."

She gave them both a broad smile and turned to follow her husband. Naomi and Jesse smiled back, and then looked at each other.

Jesse sat back down and said, "So, my boss' wife likes Naomi."

Naomi added, "…and Jesse… together."

———

Chapter 23

"I was going to tell you earlier that the tailoring on your suit is about the best I've ever seen. It really looks good on you," Naomi told Jesse, as he walked her from his car up to her apartment.

"I can't take any credit for that, at all. My little brother, Pete, asked me to be his best man last year. My mother heard I was planning on wearing my old business suit to the wedding, and she demanded that she go with my brother and me out to Fino's. She picked out my suit, oversaw the fitting and tailoring. If the suit looks good, it is totally to the credit of Adele Manzanares."

"Fino's? That's out by my high school?" Naomi asked. Naomi was finally learning her way around Bakersfield and wanted to give that impression.

"Yeah, that's it."

Naomi added, "I think the great physique of the guy inside the suit has a bit to do with the overall look. Your mother didn't do it all."

Jesse smiled, "Thank you. You know—we are going to have to do this again. Go out, that is."

"Yes, you wouldn't want to disappoint Mrs. Oldman, would you?"

"Oldham. There might be some other good reasons for us to keep in touch, too." His arm brushed Naomi's as they walked, and he took the opportunity to take her hand.

"Right, Oldham. Maybe we can take in a movie, and I can investigate whether your claim to be a card-carrying cinema geek is true."

"Sounds like a good idea. When?"

"Can I call you after Monday? We are starting our new clinical rotation at the hospital this coming week, and we won't know our schedule and assignments until the Monday morning meeting."

"That's fine. What's a clinical rotation?"

"I told you about my B.S. in Nursing program. Part of that is rotating through all the possible nursing assignments at the hospital for training."

"Ah, we do the same for rookie deputies." Jesse slowed as they got to Naomi's apartment door.

Naomi turned her back to the door and faced Jesse, "I had a wonderful evening. And, I think Mrs. Oldham is a very wise woman."

Jesse smiled and said, "Sheriff Oldham was right, too."

When Naomi looked puzzled, he said, "The Sheriff thought you were 'stunning.'"

They looked into each other's eyes. Jesse put his right hand on Naomi's arm. He bent to give her a kiss. As the kiss continued, Naomi moved her free hand toward his body, but remembered his wound on that side and moved her hand to his arm, too.

It seemed to Naomi that the kiss was more than a first date called for, but she had no complaint about that. At last, they parted, and another long look ensued. Finally, Naomi reached for her purse and fumbled for her keys.

All that was said in parting were silent 'Good Nights.'

Naomi closed the door behind her and flipped the deadbolt closed.

Ayla was apparently waiting for that sound, as she popped out of her bedroom in her pajamas and turned on the hall light, "Long night for just dinner."

"We had a lot to talk about. He is a good conversationalist."

"Looks like he was a good kisser, too," Ayla remarked.

Naomi squinted at the comment, "How…?"

Ayla reached out with her forefinger and wiped a lipstick smudge off the edge of Naomi's lower lip.

Naomi smiled and said, "Yeah, good kisser."

"Can I get an after-action report?"

Naomi shook her head, "Maybe over breakfast. I'd kinda like to go to bed with just my thoughts."

Ayla persisted, "How about at least an overall impression, besides good kisser."

Naomi thought a moment, and then said, "Well, you were right."

"Right about what?" Ayla asked.

Naomi raised her eyebrows and tilted her head, "He's toast!"

———

As they went through the clinical rotation period of their degree program, Naomi and Ayla were often able to schedule their assignments for the clinical rotation together. A four-week rotation in neonatal care, a fun assignment, followed by internal medicine, rehab, and other departments. Now, they were starting their rotation working in the Memorial Hospital Emergency Room. Their first week was on the evening shift. It was about 10:30 at night.

For the most part, they were doing follow-up work and gopher duties — go for this, go for that. Now, they stood by as the charge nurse and one of the ER physicians, Doctor Schulz, were handling an elderly lady who had come in from a nursing home in an ambulance with a possible stroke. The old woman, Mrs. Ferguson, had a severely diminished level of consciousness and response to stimuli. The nursing home had called the woman's family, so there were two of her family members standing nearby. An IV and oxygen were started, and tests had been ordered. Ayla had dutifully copied the EMT's notes to the hospital chart. Naomi and Ayla were assigned to handle the bloodwork, blood pressure, temperature, and other routine matters, while the nurse and physician ran to deal with another incoming accident victim.

Ayla and Naomi followed the protocol they had been given in the briefing for the ER and checked the woman's body for bruising or evidence of any problems, other than the possible stroke. They pulled the sliding curtain to give some privacy from the watching family members. When Ayla unbuttoned the elderly woman's nightgown to check her abdomen, she found a Fentanyl patch on the woman's chest wall. She announced to Naomi, "Fentanyl patch, with date and time for 6:00 P.M. this evening."

Ayla pulled the Fentanyl patch off. Just then, Naomi found another patch on her opposite thigh.

Naomi announced, "I've got another Fentanyl patch here. Same date, but the time is 7:30 P.M." Naomi pulled this patch too. They checked the dosage information on the patches, both were '50 μg/hour.' They entered the dosage and date/time entries on the third 'notes' page of the patient's chart.

Both young nurses realized the problem. The frail, elderly woman had been double dosed with the powerful opioid patches. But, whoever had put the second patch in place had not followed procedure to check for other patches when they placed the second patch and wrote the date and time on it. Without letting the waiting family members in on the problem, they knew the physician needed to know about the overdose.

"I'll tell the Doc," Naomi announced, in a whisper, as she hurried to find the physician.

Naomi found the physician and the nurse in another cubicle of the ER dealing with a bloody car accident victim.

"Doctor Schulz, we just did a body check on the possible stroke victim, and we found she had two different Fentanyl patches on her, both dated earlier this evening. They are both 50 microgram per hour patches."

The doctor looked at Naomi, shook head in disgust, and said, "Give her Naloxone 2 mg IVP Stat. I'll be down there as soon as I can break free here."

Naomi hurried to the medicine cabinet and asked the nurse at the desk to open it since she did not have a key to the restricted medicines supply. She hurried with the injectable Naloxone bottle and syringe to where Ayla was waiting.

As she inserted the syringe in the bottle's diaphragm, Naomi told Ayla what the doctor had said. She measured 2 milligrams and removed the air from the syringe.

When the family member saw the hurried activity, they asked what was happening. Ayla responded. "This will help her."

Naomi followed the 'five rights' rule and did the unnecessary, but mandatory task of checking the woman's nametag, before she put the syringe into the needle port of the intravenous tube and injected the Naloxone, a powerful antidote to opioid poisoning. About fifteen seconds later, the elderly woman took in a very deep breath, opened her eyes, and looked around the ER cubicle, mumbling a question about where she was. Her family members rushed over to her.

Naomi stood at the woman's side, did some basic alertness and eye-tracking tests, and made entries on the paper chart used for ER patients who were not yet in the computer system. She and Ayla looked at each other with satisfied smiles. While Ayla stayed with the patient, Naomi walked down to the other cubicle to report to Doctor Schulz that Mrs. Ferguson was awake, alert, and did not have a stroke. Mrs. Ferguson's nursing home had a problem though, Doctor Schulz would probably make sure of that.

———

Dinner and a movie had become a favorite date routine for Jesse and Naomi. Both of them had, indeed, proved to each other their mettle as cinema geeks, although Jesse tended toward action-adventure 'shoot em ups' and Naomi toward sci-fi and pure drama.

In the months they had been dating, despite the difficulty of matching their schedules, Naomi felt things were really going well with Jesse. Contrary to how she had felt dating Connor, Jesse did not put any pressure on Naomi to move on. If anything, the opposite was true. Jesse seemed enamored by the *status quo* and was downright hard to get to talk about future plans. Naomi did not push things on this with Jesse, as their relationship, in all departments, was going well for the time being.

The dinner and a movie format also allowed them to accommodate Naomi's rotating work schedule and Jesse's chaotic schedule and call-outs with little notice. Tonight was the exception, with both of them being available for a traditional Friday evening night out.

Naomi and Jesse had just left the refreshment counter when Jesse thrust the large popcorn bucket into Naomi's hands. He turned toward and hugged a heavyset Hispanic woman who was standing with an equally portly Hispanic man.

After the hug and a handshake with the man, Jesse turned to put out his arm towards Naomi, who walked over to where the three stood together.

Jesse put his hand on Naomi's shoulder, "Let me introduce my girlfriend,

Naomi Donnelley. Naomi is a nurse at Memorial Hospital. Naomi, this is my Aunt Estella and her husband, Joe Quiñonez. Estella is my father's sister."

Naomi shook the hands of both aunt and uncle. Aunt Estella and Uncle Joe both gave Naomi a thorough but quick visual inspection.

Aunt Estella concluded her look at Naomi with more of a statement than a question for Jesse, "Donnelley, that's an Irish name like your mother."

Jesse just nodded his head.

Estella now turned to Naomi, "How'd you two meet?"

Naomi looked quickly at Jesse, who flicked his eyes toward his aunt, giving the okay to tell her. Naomi said, "Last year, when Jesse was in the hospital, I was his nurse."

This caused Estella to react, grabbing Jesse's arm, "Yes, Jesse, I haven't spoken to you since then. I heard about that. Joe saw the report on the shooting on TV and told me. I called Trina, and she said she had heard from your mother that you had been shot but were going to be okay."

Jesse shrugged, "Yes, I'm fine. It was just a grazing shot. No big deal. I went back to work a few weeks later. Naomi did a great job bandaging me up."

"Oh, Jesse. No big deal?" Estella said. "You need to be more careful. Such a horrible job you have."

Joe Quiñonez touched his wife's arm, "We need to get in there. Movie's gonna start."

There was an exchange of 'Nice to meet you' from both Naomi and the couple. Jesse got another hug, and they parted.

Jesse took the popcorn bucket back, and they headed into their assigned theater. Naomi took stock of the meeting with the aunt and uncle. Jesse had declared her to be his 'girlfriend' to a key member of his close family. Considering their months together, that was actually a milestone. And, his aunt had immediately noted Naomi's ethnicity was the same as her sister in law, Jesse's mother. Naomi assumed that both of those points were good. They had been going together a long time, she wondered when she would meet others in his family.

Jesse led Naomi to his usual seating choice - center, middle of the house with Jesse on the aisle seat. After the previews had run and the international intrigue themed movie started, Naomi moved the popcorn bucket from his lap to hers and looped her arm through his, interlocking their fingers. Jesse was a little slow to do things like take her hand. Such hesitancy matched his personality, and Naomi did not mind providing a little nudge. Taking a Jesse's hand was definitely a holdover from old Naomi's portfolio, old Mark would be aghast at grabbing this guy's hand. Naomi thought about that from time to time, but less and less as she got more comfortable with who she was.

———

The Cal State Bakersfield program Naomi and Ayla were in was set up for nurses like them, already licensed but needing more training and certain courses to qualify for the Bachelor in Science degree. It was a combination of a few classroom courses, some online coursework and a structured rotation in various fields. A licensed nurse got 25 credits for having passed the NCLEX license. The prerequisites for a bachelor's degree were mostly covered by the earlier associates degree, but there were a couple schedule opportunities to take electives. Ayla chose to take a pair of Spanish for Medical Professionals courses and Naomi chose to also take a language class but building on Mark's old skillset she took a couple of online Farsi language classes at CSUB. Naomi had no good answer for Ayla when she asked, "Why Farsi?" Studying the language of much of Afghanistan and Iran seemed to connect her to her old self and his interest in language he had developed in Afghanistan and later at BYU.

Naomi had finished her basic rotation in the clinical part of her program. She had rotated to Surgery after her time in the ER. Ayla had gone to Internal Medicine for her next rotation. Now, they were in more traditional schedules, working a regular shift at the hospital and doing their class credits mostly online.

Naomi had done a couple weeks in a surgical setting for her course at Bakersfield college and four weeks more in the CSUB rotation, but those had mostly been watching from the viewing window of the operating room and doing work outside the operating room. Now, in her follow-on work at Memorial Hospital, Naomi had scrubbed in and been in the operating room for open-heart surgery. She was still, for the most part, a bystander, regular surgical nurses needed the specialized training and experience to handle the critical jobs. But, she had participated in moving the patient from the gurney to the table, collecting trays of used surgical instruments, clearing away bloody refuse, and replacing the patient's gown after the operation.

"What'd you think?" the surgical nurse asked Naomi, as they stripped off the gowns, masks, and booties after they left the operating room.

"Really interesting. Very intense in there," Naomi tried to temper her excitement as she replied. "As a practical matter, what is the best route of getting into a job like you have?"

The nurse replied, "It really varies. Since a surgical nurse makes more than a lot of other jobs you can have in nursing, it is a sought-after assignment, as you obviously know. Of course, it would help if you can get yourself into an actual surgical nursing training program, but those are both tough to find and get into for the most part. A good recommendation from a surgeon helps. Lots of people get into true surgery through the ER route. Show your stuff in surgical-related ER cases, and then move on to the operating room. By 'stuff' I mean, a clear head, calm in the intense activity, no trace of queasiness, trustworthy, that stuff. Why, you think you might like to do this yourself on an ongoing basis?"

Naomi thought and answered, "Yes, it seems to me I might be good at this."

"Well, Naomi, you seemed to do well in there just now. Keep it up."

———

"So, what is the occasion that I get a home-cooked meal from Naomi before we go out?" Jesse asked.

Naomi pulled a pan of biscuits out of the oven and said, "I thought I would introduce you to the concept that there are other things you can eat on weekdays besides Mexican food and pizzas."

"Now, you sound like my mother. I can remember as a little kid when my mother tried to get my father to eat corned beef and cabbage. He swore that it tasted like the cabbage had already turned, and I sided with him. Besides, pizza is the lifeblood of modern America. Our society would collapse without pizza," Jesse said, standing at the kitchen counter in her apartment, watching her cook. "Are those biscuits from one of those cool paper tubes that you hit on the edge of the counter, and they have that satisfying 'Ploop' sound when they open?"

Naomi gave Jesse a mock angry stare and sarcastic response, "Did you hear any 'Ploops' coming out of my kitchen? NO! You didn't. These are fresh-mixed baking powder biscuits. I did the dough before you got here."

"As you said to me in the hospital, those many months ago—sorree!"

Jesse waited as he watched Naomi stir something in a pot. Then, he asked, "Ayla working tonight?"

"Yes, now that we are done with the semesters where we did regular job rotation to supplement our online studies, we have been doing more varied work. Ayla has been looking to neo-natal and obstetrics work, and I am trying to get work where I can get assignments that will enhance my ability to get into surgical work once I get my BS degree. Ever since that, we have been on different tracks. In some ways, it is nice. When we are off work, we have the apartment to ourselves, like we don't even have a roommate." Naomi used her tongs to pull a second golden batter-covered oval out of the Fry Daddy and slid it onto a plate.

Naomi pulled silverware from the drawer and handed it to Jesse, "Put this on the table, please. I'm almost ready. You sit down at the end. Oh, and these, too." She put salt and pepper shakers next to the silverware.

Naomi walked to the table with a platter of golden biscuits and a butter dish. She followed that up with glasses of ice and Cokes. Then, she brought two plates and sat one in front of Jesse.

Naomi sat at the table and announced, "My All-American Fare for tonight. Chicken fried steak, garlic mashed potatoes, from scratch, no instant, and country gravy. Biscuits and Janet's home-made peach jam. I think you will find it preferable to corned beef and cabbage, although I can make that next week if you want, and you can compare it with your mother's"

"I'll pass on that."

Jesse ate several bites of steak and potatoes in silence, and then he said, "Jeesh, girl, this is good stuff. Where did you learn to cook like this?"

Naomi could not explain to Jesse how she had learned to cook, as Mark, in his parents' restaurant in Stockton, so she said, "All of us Utah girls are good cooks."

"Yeah, I keep forgetting you are from Utah."

After a few more bites, Jesse said, "I stopped by my folks' house last Sunday on the way to work, and my mother had apparently gotten a full report on you from Aunt Estella. She asked me how long we had been dating, and when I told her she really chewed me out for not having introduced you to her earlier. That was enough to set her off on her favorite rant by saying, 'You're not getting any younger. You need to settle down,' and she basically demanded to meet this girl I'm dating. Correction, she specifically said 'this Irish girl' since Estella had reported everything in detail. Then, she reminded me how old I am, to the year and month, and that I am her only child who hasn't provided grandkids, considering that Pete's wife has a bun in the oven...."

At this, Naomi jumped up from the table and said, "Just a sec...That reminds me...." She ran to the kitchen and switched off the oven.

Naomi thought about what Jesse had said. His mother seemed to be in tune with some of Naomi's own thoughts.

"Sorry," Naomi said when she sat back down, "Continue from the part with your mother griping about not meeting me and wanting grandkids."

Jesse gave a little frown and continued, "So, I thought I would humor her and get you to meet my folks."

"So, I'm not really in serious consideration, just someone to **humor** your mother?"

"I didn't say that, well, yeah, I did, but it's not what I meant. Darn it, you're a tough one.... I'm as serious about you... as I can be."

"Well, that's not exactly a commitment and not very romantic, but I'll take what I can get."

Jesse frowned again at this and continued, "I thought of how we can kill two birds with one stone. You mentioned you wanted to meet siblings and some cousins. The whole extended clan gets together every spring for a kind of a reunion. I thought you might like to come this year. It's the week after next.

And it is potluck. Now that I know you can really cook, I can buy whatever you want me to, and you can cook it, something that is definitely not my forte."

"I'd love to. Let me know the time and date, and I'll give you a shopping list."

Naomi would have to thank Aunt Estella someday; she seemed to have started the process to get Jesse to move forward *vis-à-vis* Naomi.

———

Chapter 24

"Tell more about what is going on today. You said something about a combination reunion, graduation party, and wedding reception. A bit odd," Naomi said, looking out the big truck's window at the scenery along Highway 99 north of Bakersfield.

"Well, yes, but more. In a family this big, there are lots of cousins, and four of them from different families, you know, subfamilies, graduated from high school this year. Instead of making people and especially our grandparents, that's the great grandparents of those cousins, come to several graduation parties, my Mom and all my aunts plan something like this each year. Those aunts, you know, the Manzanares sisters, like Estella, and the sisters-in-law, like Mom, are like a military staff when it comes to organizing weddings, parties, and the like. High school graduation is a big thing in the Chicano culture, the same with *Quinceañera*. Then, there have been two weddings in the past few months. And also, one of the cousins, Selena, is graduating from the University of California, Santa Cruz.

"And now, since I told Mom you were coming, she and Estella have announced that Jesús, that's what the family call me sometimes, is bringing a girl who, you know, might be more than just a girlfriend. The Manzanares Aunts' Mafia is already pushing you for a candidacy that you and I haven't actually talked about much, yet. Just so you know."

Naomi laughed, "Jesse, you do realize that you can actually talk to me about our future, you know, like in a real conversation. Every time you mention the concept of marriage, it is in some vague hint or innuendo. I don't think I have ever heard it called a 'candidacy' before."

"Something you should know about me. I tend to freeze up in a serious, personal conversation. I seem to be really good at hints and innuendo, because you seem to catch the drift every time I drop one."

"Right, I'll keep that in mind. It's not like I haven't noticed. So, where is this family reunion?"

"The McFarland City Park. Reserved just for us."

"The Manzanares clan requires a whole city Park for a family get together?"

"Yeah, my dad has seven brothers and sisters, and my mom and dad, with only three kids, is the smallest family among that generation. Then, you have all the cousins and the other half of the families, the in-laws."

"Yeah, you told me about all of the cousins on our first date. I've been waiting for most of a year to meet more of them. And, the city park has a pool, hence you telling me to bring my swimsuit?"

"That's right. Bikini?"

"One piece. You said your grandma would be there."

"But, my grandpa will be there, too," he wiggled his eyebrows.

Naomi huffed at this, but then snickered and added, "My only swimsuits are racing Speedos. Your grandpa will be okay with it."

Jesse took the freeway exit in McFarland. After the turn, he pointed out the high school, "You've probably been up here before. But, if not, that's the high school where they filmed the Kevin Costner movie, *McFarland USA*."

Naomi remembered the movie, knew about when it came out, and she decided to create a backstory about it, "Yeah, *McFarland USA*, about an Anglo coach with an attitude coaching a down and out Chicano cross country team to win the state title. We watched it in gym class in high school, on a rain day."

"High school? Darn it, girl, you just made me feel really old all of a sudden."

"That's what you get when you mess around with young stuff. I don't know much about the town, though. Is McFarland as much of a pit as the movie made out."

"Naw, not really, the story was set like thirty years ago. The city has grown up a lot since. You'll see. Pretty decent city park."

Jesse turned into the parking lot of the city park. There was an official-looking sign saying, 'Reserved for Private Party.'"

"I was going to ask; how does one go about reserving the whole park?"

"They do it for other things, too, like Little League end of season parties. But, in our case, it helps to have a Manzanares cousin as the city parks and recreation director."

"Aha!"

Knowing that Jesse would try to run around to help her out of the lifted truck before they got out, Naomi said, "I can handle the climb down. You get my pans from the back seat. Don't forget the serving spoons."

Naomi ran around to the other side of the truck, "I'll take one pan."

"These smell good. What is it?" Jesse asked, sniffing the foil-covered pans.

"Noodles Romanoff and fresh garlic bread rolls. I couldn't find my corned beef and cabbage recipe." Naomi took the over-stuffed bread pan, covered in foil, from Jesse.

Seeing Naomi only had her purse and the pan, Jesse asked, "You gonna bring your swimsuit, or come back and get it."

Naomi patted her bright red nylon jogging suit and said, "I've got it on underneath. I do need my towel, though. I brought one for you, too, if you didn't bring one. Did you?"

"Nope."

Naomi smiled, "Can you grab them?" Naomi saw him fold his trunks with the towels.

After dropping off the food on the potluck tables, the first fifteen minutes were filled with Jesse dragging Naomi around to introduce her to relatives. It was quickly apparent that Aunt Estella had already passed the word about Naomi around the womenfolk. Jesse's grandparents were the cute elderly Hispanic couple she had envisioned, but many others, especially Jesse's mother, did not fit into what Naomi had presumed from the Manzanares clan.

Meeting Jesse's parents gave Naomi insight into where his looks came from. His father, Manny, had a stocky, muscular build that came from a lifetime of laboring in the oilfields. Adele, on the other hand, was a couple inches taller than her husband and reminded Naomi of a fifty-ish Kendra, with a pretty face and curly light brown hair that was probably dyed to keep it so perfect in her 50's. When Jesse brought Naomi up to meet them, Manny had his arm around Adele. Jesse could learn from his father. Or, maybe Naomi should learn some training tips from Adele.

Pedro "Pete" Manzanares was younger than his brother Jesse but had the same looks with a bit less height and muscles. Pete's wife, Silvia, was a dark-eyed, olive-skinned Hispanic beauty who was showing about a fifth-month baby bump. Jesse's sister, Lucia Cooper, looked more like her mother than her brothers did. Her blonde chiropractor husband had sired two little blond Coopers with Lucia that looked like their father.

After running the Manzanares family gauntlet, Naomi was thankful when Jesse, at last, announced he was hungry and headed to the food tables. Naomi noted that Jesse diplomatically loaded his plate first with her Noodles Romanoff and garlic bread rolls, before piling tamales and enchiladas on the plate. Naomi carefully piled a wide selection of foods on her plate. At the drink table, Naomi watched Jesse refuse a beer handed to him by his brother and take a Mountain Dew instead, so did Naomi.

Jesse routed Naomi to the same table where his parents, and Pete and Silvia were eating, and they commenced their feast.

———

When everyone had their fill of food, all of the family news updates and Naomi's background story had been cautiously completed, Pete turned to Jesse and said, "So, how about it big brother, are you ready to take me on in a down and back swim race? Pool looks fairly empty right now."

Silvia looked at her husband, "Aren't you supposed to wait for a half-hour after eating to swim?"

Adele added in, "Yes, a half-hour is what they always say."

Naomi was ready to jump into the conversation when she stopped herself just in time. She had been going to say that the half-hour before swimming rule was an old wives' tale. It did not seem diplomatic for her to accuse both of Jesse's female relatives of being 'old wives.' She thought of how to gently reword her argument.

"That wait for a half-hour after eating before you swim rule is what we were all taught, but I learned in the safety class in nursing school that there really isn't any scientific basis for that advice. If you are otherwise healthy, there is no reason why swimming should cause you to cramp up. Swimming is no different than any other exertion, and lots of people eat a hearty meal before they go to do a hard job. I say, let's go watch the race." Naomi hoped her response was okay.

Everybody seemed to buy her comment as they all moved toward the pool. Naomi took the towels with her, handing Jesse his trunks. Everyone waited for Jesse and Pete to go into the men's room to change into trunks. Several other relatives gathered around to see what was happening by the pool. The Coopers and their kids were among them.

The two men came out and stood by the pool. Naomi noticed Jesse had a black t-shirt on along with his trunks. He was obviously covering his scarred back.

They waited while Jeff Cooper ran down the side of the pool to get two kids out of the way for the race. There were no lane buoy ropes, but the two lanes at the side were clear of people down and back the Olympic size pool. The two brothers stood in their starting positions, not regular racing positions, just bent over and leaning toward the pool.

Jeff was the starter, giving 'mark' and 'get set' commands. He brought his hand down and yelled, "Go!"

Both men leaped forward in a semblance of a racing start, but both made huge splashes. Without any underwater surge, they each started their crawl strokes. At the far end, both men just touched the wall and turned around to continue swimming, with no quick underwater flips for them. It was clear to Naomi this was a purely amateur race between siblings who had never raced competitively.

They seemed to be even for much of the race. At the very end of the return stretch, Jesse's greater strength showed itself, and he won the race by a body length. Jeff and Naomi helped the two swimmers out of the pool.

"So, Jesse, good job. Now, you want to race me?" Naomi asked. "If you do, we can give you some time to rest first."

Jesse looked at her, astonished, "You really want to race me?"

"Yup."

"Okay, but I don't need a rest. Let's go."

"Whatever," Naomi said, starting to strip out of her jogging suit and matching red t-shirt. She felt Manzanares family eyes on her as she revealed her shiny silver Speedo underneath.

Naomi did three jumping jacks to limber up, again drawing attention. The crowd around the pool was growing.

"Should we have a handicap?" Jesse asked.

Naomi turned to him with her hands on her hip, "You think I should give you a head start just because you refused to take a rest first?"

"Not for me, for you...", Jesse stopped when he realized Naomi was teasing him.

"Take your marks," Jeff announced.

Jesse took his same half-crouch as before. Naomi bent down to a full racer's start on tiptoes, legs bent, hands resting all the way down on the edge of the pool. Naomi could not resist looking over to see Jesse's reaction to her competition stance. His forehead wrinkled.

"Get set," Jeff announced, waited, and then, "Go!"

Naomi leaped far out over the water. She heard Jesse's big splash before she hit the water. After her usual smooth entry and lengthy underwater dolphin-kick, she came up to start her stroke. She knew she would be well ahead of Jesse, even now.

At the far end of the pool, Naomi did her underwater flip turn and came to the surface a couple body lengths away from the edge. Jesse was only now passing this point, on his way to the turn. She was ahead by several lengths.

Naomi could not resist doing her best on the final stretch to the end. When she reached the end, instead of staying in the water, Naomi grabbed the edge of the pool and launched herself up out of the water to stand on the cement. Jesse's relatives gave her a big cheer. It seemed the female voices were loudest. Jeff gave Naomi her towel.

Jesse was still several lengths out. By the time he finished, both Naomi and Pete were poolside, ready to give him a hand out of the water. He took Pete's hand.

"Hey there, big brother, I think you just got snookered—big time," Pete told him.

Pete and the other relatives were now gathered close, congratulating Naomi and listening to the conversation between Jesse and Naomi.

Jesse was out of breath. He looked at Naomi, was not out of breath, and asked, "What was that?"

"What do you mean? I gave you fair warning," Naomi said with her cutest smile.

"What warning was that?"

"I told you that the only swimsuit I had was a racing Speedo," Naomi said.

Jesse shook his head, "You had more than a swimsuit in your favor."

"Yeah, when your brother challenged you to a race, I realized I had left out something when I gave you my life story. I was so concentrated on telling you about my nursing that I forgot to tell you that when I went to Bakersfield College, I also did some swimming. And, I happen to be a co-holder of the current California state junior college record for the 400-Meter Medley Relay. I swam the anchor leg."

The Manzanares relatives murmured cheerfully at this news. Jesse shook his head.

Naomi said, "Pete was totally correct. I snookered you. I am a total ringer. But, boy, was that a lot of fun." She gave Jesse her brightest smile.

Jesse grabbed her by the elbows and gave her a quick kiss, "Enjoy the fun now, girl. Paybacks are hell."

Jesse got a light "Boo!" from his relatives for this playful threat.

Naomi pulled her jogging suit, t-shirt, and sneakers back on. Jesse and Pete went to change out of their trunks. Naomi walked back over to the picnic tables with Adele, Silvia, and Lucia. They had lots of questions for Naomi, but everything seemed to be on a familial level. It seemed Naomi was being accepted by Jesse's womenfolk.

After the swimming interlude, a few cousins struck up a decent Mariachi band. Jesse smiled when Naomi went to the food table for another selection of Manzanares family treats. She shared her empanadas with Jesse.

Naomi was still finishing her plate when Jesse's cell phone went off right beside her, causing her to jump. It gave off a loud warbling tone she had never heard from his phone before. Jesse pulled the phone out of his pocket and walked a few steps away from Naomi to answer it. He spoke for a moment, and when he finished, he did not come back to Naomi. Instead, he trotted quickly to the other end of the table to whisper in Pete's ear. Pete nodded, 'Yes' to something.

Jesse now came back to Naomi. "Nomy," he used the nickname he had christened her with but had never used before except in private, "My SWAT team has been activated. Bakersfield PD SWAT asked us to augment them. They have some active shooter situation going on downtown. Pete will drive you back home. I'll let you know as soon as I can. Sorry." Jesse turned to Adele. "Bye, Mom," He gave a wave to all the other family at the table.

Jesse gave Naomi a quick kiss and ran to his truck. Behind the door to his truck, she saw him pull on his SWAT camos on over his shorts. Before he left the parking lot, he attached a flashing red globe to the top of his truck. When he pulled onto the road, she heard a siren start blaring.

Naomi turned back toward the table and gave a shrug to Adele.

"Don't worry, Honey. He'll be fine. He's really careful," Jesse's mother said.

Naomi shook her head, "Nice try, Mrs. Manzanares. Did Estella tell you what I was doing when I met Jesse?"

"Call me Adele. No, Estella just said you met on the job."

"Your sister-in-law was being gentle with Jesse's mother. The first thing I ever did with Jesse was to pull a bloody piece of gauze off two bullet holes in his chest. It doesn't matter if he is careful. I know precisely what might happen when he heads out like he just did."

—

Chapter 25

"Nomy, I need to use your bathroom before we leave," Jesse announced. "But, we need to hurry. My truck is unlocked. I'll meet you there. I'll lock your front door."

"Okay," Naomi said as she headed out the door of her apartment.

Jesse shouted down the hallway, "Don't forget your coat. It's really windy." The door slammed. He had missed her. The mid-October weather was getting chilly.

Jesse finished in the bathroom and headed for the front door, thinking she might pop back in to get her coat once she felt how cold and windy it was outside. He put his green Sheriff's parka on since he had just gotten off work and was still in uniform. When Naomi did not come back in, he reached in the front closet and grabbed the nylon parka he found there. He did not remember Naomi wearing this before, but it was Naomi's size, not big enough for her roommate Ayla.

—

Naomi sat waiting for Jesse in the covered parking area of her apartment. She was used to the climb to board the big black truck. She thought about going back in for a coat, but she knew they were semi-late, and she did not want to be blamed for more delay. Her ribbed-knit turtleneck sweater would probably be warm enough.

Jesse jumped up into the driver's seat and handed Naomi the red jacket, "It's cold out there. Windy and probably raining by the time we come home. Put your coat on."

"Not this old thing. I haven't worn it in a long time," she said.

"Why do you keep it then?" He asked as he turned out of the parking lot and south on the boulevard.

"Lots of memories tied up in this. But, it is not my style."

"Why'd you buy it then?"

"I didn't. It was a gift."

"From whom?"

Naomi did not have any quick thoughts on how to explain where the coat came from, so she just said, "Long story."

She put the red quilted jacket on and said, "So, tell me about this party tonight."

"Promotion party. Two guys that I'm really close to made sergeant, plus a couple others. One guy is on our SWAT team, and the other guy was my training officer when I first came on the force."

"If he was your training officer, why is he just making sergeant when you are already a lieutenant?"

"Promotions aren't automatic and don't really revolve around time of service in the Sheriff's Department. Lots of great guys spend their whole twenty years, or more, and never get past senior deputy, let alone sergeant. It is not an 'up or out' thing like the military. They need to keep people in the department even if they aren't promoted. They figure just being a solid peace officer is plenty. Then, there is education and being in the right spot to get top eval marks. I had my degree when I joined the Department, and I got service credit for my time in the Army, and because of that, I got a starting bump to senior deputy when I completed probation and my first year. Then, I got put on the SWAT team and moved up quickly."

Jesse turned the windshield wipers on to clear the first drops of rain from the windshield.

He continued, "Hal, the new sergeant on the SWAT team is moving up quickly just like I did. Gene, the older guy who was my training officer, is a great guy but never pushed the promotion envelope. He's been around long enough, he may be thinking about retirement and a bump to sergeant for his final few years will be good for the final pay level for retirement."

"How long will this be?" Naomi asked, and then she added, "Will there be anyone else like me there?"

"It won't be long. Some people like me will be just coming off work and in uniform. We can't drink much. There may be some who stick around and sip a few more frosty ones, though. There are usually wives and girlfriends in attendance. Plus, we've got many women in the department now. Promotion parties aren't like retirement parties that last into the wee hours, and half the people there need rides home and help walking out."

Naomi acted out writing on an invisible note, saying, "Naomi's note to self: Avoid Sheriff's retirement parties."

Jesse turned his truck into the parking lot.

When she saw where he was parking, she asked, "It's at Lengthwise? The brewery?"

"Yeah, probably in the back room. They have a meeting room for special occasions."

"But a brewery, that sounds like trouble even for sheriff's deputies," Naomi concluded.

"Nomy, I know you don't drink. I understand. Actually, I kinda like that. But, don't hold it against people who do." He turned off the truck.

"I don't hold it against anyone. I've done my share, just not anymore. I just don't like to be pressured to have a drink, and lots of people are bad about that at parties. That is what I dread."

Jesse put his green baseball cap on. Naomi zipped up the red jacket. Jesse hopped out and was around the truck in time to offer his usual hand for Naomi to get down.

They were directed to the rear room in the brewery. There was considerable loud conversation coming from behind the sliding folding-curtain partitions. Inside, a crowd of probably thirty or forty people were standing in groups and sitting at tables. Most were not in uniform, but several, like Jesse, were. A large green and gold three-striped sergeant's chevron made from crepe paper had been taped on the back wall, below which most of the people were congregated.

Naomi could tell the SWAT guys by the unique clothing worn by some of them. The SWAT guys were mostly off to the right. Jesse took Naomi's hand and pulled her through the crowd toward them. She knew a few of his team already, and Jesse made a decent effort to introduce her to a few others.

"We need to go up and congratulate the new sergeants," Jesse said, as he grabbed Naomi's hand again, heading for the cluster of people under the chevron.

Naomi could see the promotees were surrounded. Several women and children stood next to husbands and fathers. On the way toward them, Jesse took time to introduce her to a young female deputy named Milly, who was wearing a motorcycle patrolman's high boots, leather uniform jacket, and the tight-legged riding pants. Then, Jesse plunged on into the crowd with Naomi in tow.

Jesse walked up to and congratulated, Hal, the new SWAT sergeant. He was one of the men Naomi had met before, so she just shook hands and congratulated him, too. Naomi had already met Hal's wife. The two women shook hands and smiled at each other.

Jesse continued to talk to his friend, and Naomi turned to look toward one of the other new sergeants, Gene, who stood with his wife and several people engaged in conversation. By the time Jesse turned around to head toward Gene, Naomi had already left his side approaching Gene. Naomi had never heard his first name before, but she remembered his last name.

When Naomi walked up in front of Gene, he broke into a broad smile and spread his arms to embrace Naomi. She put her arms around the new sergeant and tucked her head into his chest. They gave each other a long, obviously heartfelt hug. When they finally stopped, Gene grabbed Naomi's shoulders and held her out at arm's length.

Jesse was next to them now and heard Gene say, "You know, girl, that is truly a fine jacket you've got there. Did you wear that for me?"

Naomi laughed, "You wouldn't believe me if I said anything else, would you?"

Jesse turned to Gene's wife and asked, "Clara, do you have any idea what is going on between my girlfriend, Naomi, and your husband?"

Clara shook her head, "Not a clue."

Jesse asked, "Naomi? You two know each other?"

Naomi turned and gave him a sarcastic lift of her eyebrows, "You think? Maybe?"

Jesse said, "You're right. Dumb question."

Gene started to say something, but Naomi cut him off with a waving finger and said, "Sergeant Buehler and I had a wonderful adventure together once upon a time. But, it is a secret. Our lips are sealed. Our cover story is that I went to high school with his daughter."

Naomi highlighted this with a little fingertip wave at the young woman standing next to Clara. Naomi assumed that was Connie, the Buehler's daughter, whose picture she had found in her Centennial High School yearbook.

Jesse frowned, "What's this about the jacket?"

"That's part of our secret adventure," Naomi smiled at Gene.

"Gene…?" Clara added.

Gene Buehler put his arm around his wife and said, "Sorry, Dear, when a lady tells a gentleman he needs to keep her secret, he should follow her wishes, especially if it's his wife who is asking the questions."

Naomi and Gene laughed again. The others joined in as though they knew some of the joke.

A waitress was walking around collecting empty beer mugs on a tray. Gene Buehler waved her over to him and said, "I'm the guy running Tab #2. I want you to bring two more of those trays of your house draft beer out and… You sell those root beer floats here, as I recall. Right??"

The waitress nodded.

"Okay, I doubt if you have Rocky Road Ice Cream at a brewery, but I want two of those Root Beer Floats, with whipped cream, and I want five cherries on each one. One float for Naomi here and one for me."

He turned to Naomi, "Did I get that right?"

"Perfect!" Naomi smiled broadly. She was impressed Buehler had remembered her restaurant order from Stockton, from so long ago. And, he remembered from her court testimony that she was not supposed to drink alcohol, so he was giving her cover with the float. He was special.

Buehler turned back to the waitress, "That's it, and there is a big tip in it if you get the five cherries on the top right. Okay?"

"You got it," she said.

When the waitress left, Jesse said to Naomi, "Nomy, you realize you are going to have to give a little bit more background on this, what with the jacket and root beer floats, and all."

Naomi shook her head, vehemently, "Sorry, Honey, that ain't gonna happen."

Sergeant Buehler now spoke up, "Lieutenant Manzanares, you'd be wise to back off and do as the little lady says. You need to be **really** nice to her. I happen to know she has a wicked take-down move that will have you on your ass before you know what hit you."

Naomi and Sergeant Buehler had another quick laugh. As she laughed, Naomi gave a quick sideways glance to Jesse, seeing how he was reacting. His brow was furrowed.

—

Jesse pulled up into the parking space outside Naomi and Ayla's apartment complex. He started to get out, to escort her in, and Naomi reached over to hold his arm. She took in a deep breath, looked toward Jesse, and then straight ahead.

"Jesse, there are some things I need to tell you about," she said.

"Is this about whatever was going on with Gene Buehler tonight?"

Naomi nodded her head, "Yes. It's that, and more."

"Nomy, don't feel pressured to tell me something you don't want to divulge. I was just kidding when I said you **had** to tell me."

Naomi looked over to Jesse and smiled, "No, Jesse, I need to talk to you about this. I realized tonight that there are some things about my past that you, especially since you are a cop, need to know about. It doesn't make sense that Sergeant Buehler knows, and you don't. So, sit back, relax, and listen to a big chunk of my life story that may surprise you.

"Jesse, you know that I am very strict about not drinking, and you probably think that it is because of my living with the Morrison's and trying to obey the Mormon Word of Wisdom. But, it is a lot more than that, and a lot more serious. When I was a teenager, culminating in my disastrous senior year in high school, I had a real problem with drinking. My bastard of a stepfather was a factor in that. He'd let me steal a bottle of hard liquor and never say a thing to me. He thought it was cute or something. And then, I got involved in drugs, some pretty bad drugs. Then, in my last months of high school and with my mother's illness and death, I basically fell apart. I got kicked out of high school, locked up in the county mental treatment clinic, which I escaped from, and then was diagnosed, incorrectly it turned out, to have mental illness. The court ordered me into the state mental hospital up in Napa. Just before that, I had been arrested at the crash pad of a drug dealer, locked in the bathroom, and I apparently swallowed three little bags of drugs— shrooms, meth, and opiates."

Naomi had been staring straight ahead, out of the truck's windshield. She looked over and saw Jesse with his gaze locked on her. She nervously looked back forward and continued, "By the time they moved me to Napa State Hospital, the drug baggies had clogged up my gut and were leaking. I nearly died, but instead, I went into a coma and was unconscious for months. When I finally came to, I had a really great psychiatrist who took charge and determined that I really wasn't insane, didn't belong in a mental hospital, but I actually had a really, horrible substance abuse problem. That psychiatrist and another female doctor reported their findings to a Kern County judge who released me from the mental conservatorship and gave me a clean bill of health, clearing my record of everything and giving me a new chance.

"A big part of that had to be my absolute avoidance of any alcohol or drug use forever, for the rest of my life, which I have stuck to. Having gone through that horrendous medical problem, I decided I would dedicate my life to caring for others. There is a bit more to that dedication, which is personal to me, that you don't need to know about. But, after meeting back up with Gene Buehler tonight, I realized that if you and I have any hope of building a future together, you need to know this important stuff that goes to the heart of who I am and the destiny I feel drawn to live."

As Naomi paused, Jesse reached over and touched the red jacket, "I didn't hear how Buehler, or this jacket, or the root beer floats fit into that story."

Naomi smiled and looked over to Jesse, "Oh, yeah, there's that. Buehler drove me home from Napa in the Sheriff's van when I was released. It was a cold October morning, the Sheriff's van was cold, and I didn't have a jacket. He stopped and bought me this one at a Walmart. Then later, on the way down here, he took me to eat at a little restaurant in Stockton, where I ordered a root beer float, just like he described. On the drive from Napa to Bakersfield, he heard my whole story, and he kinda sympathized with me, since I really had gone to high school with his daughter. He was there in court with me when the judge cleared me of my bad court and criminal record and told me to build a new life."

"And this 'wicked takedown move' Gene mentioned. What's with that?"

"Yeh, this story keeps having loose ends, huh?"

Naomi told him the story of the insane guy with the scalpel at Napa and her reward for stopping him. Naomi finished with, "I had told Gene about it in the van coming down here form Napa, and then he heard that the judge probably gave that story, which she read in the hospital records, some importance in her going easy on me in her ruling on my case. I still have that nice little plaque the state hospital gave me, but I can't show anybody without having to explain how I got inside an insane asylum."

Now, Naomi looked over at Jesse, "So, now you know the deep, dark secrets of this woman you thought you knew all about. Well, some of the secrets." She smiled meekly at this.

Jesse slowly nodded, and then said, "Thank you for telling me all of that. I think it is good you did. You need to know that nothing you have said makes any difference in how I think and feel about this beautiful, kind, endearing woman I have known for these past two years. If anything, it makes me admire her strength of character. There are not many people who could have gone through all that and come out like you have."

Naomi's eyes were moist as she looked over at Jesse. She was glad she had told him this part of her secrets. She still wondered how she would ever be able to tell him of the real underlying story of who she was, the story that only she and Doctor Partridge knew. If Naomi was going to spend her life with this man, she knew she had to find a way to tell him everything about herself. This part was a good step, though.

Jesse ended the talk with Naomi in the truck by leaning over to her and embracing her. Their kiss went on and on.

———

Naomi saw the signs about the Career Expo in the Student Rec Center at Cal State Bakersfield. She had no need to go to the Career Expo since she already had two competing offers from local hospitals, once her B.S. in Nursing was official in December. Besides, a public job fair was probably not going to have many nursing or medical job opportunities. But, she had nothing better to do and was curious, so she headed over.

The Expo was well-attended, both with jobseekers and employers. Many of the booths and tables had gifts, and trinkets to attract attention. Naomi accepted the Real California Cheese mug offered to her by a model in a plaid and denim farm girl outfit. The employer tables and booths were a mix of high-tech companies, retail firms, a couple agricultural conglomerates, and various financial and business service companies. The crowd seemed to be a mix of both CSUB students and older people looking for work.

Naomi was on her way around the back aisle of the Expo, ready to leave when she saw something that stopped her in her tracks. As though it had been placed there to attract Naomi's attention, there was a large poster sitting on an easel announcing, "Surgical Nurses Needed – We Train — $30,000.^{00} Bonus."

Naomi stared at the bold letters of the poster for a moment, and then she noticed that the font and green color of the letters on the poster matched the large banner above the booth, "U.S. Army Reserve." The booth had several oversized posters of soldiers in various military jobs, and to one side was a full-sized stand-up cutout of an Army nurse in surgical scrubs standing next to her twin in a camouflage uniform and Army field gear. On one side of the booth, a male staff sergeant in a dress uniform was talking and trying to hand out a brochure to a couple of young men, and on the other side, a female officer was working with a video monitor and laptop.

Naomi had already resolved that her hope of working her way into a nursing job in the surgical area might take a few years, so she found it hard to resist getting some information about this offer. Once before in her life, back when she was in Mark's life, a conversation with an Army recruiter had been a turning point. She wondered if it might be again.

The two young men had accepted the brochure and walked on by the time Naomi walked through the crowd to the booth. She walked up to the staff sergeant.

"Yes, Miss, may I help you?" he asked.

Naomi pointed to the sign on the easel, "Info about the surgical nursing program?"

The sergeant gave a mock look of disappointment, "Just my luck. Not my area. You're already a nurse?"

Naomi nodded, "Yup, I graduate in December."

He nodded and said, "I can't help you with that. Major Dunleavy?" He motioned to the female officer.

The female officer across the booth turned toward them. The sergeant pointed to Naomi.

Major Margot Dunleavy walked over and introduced herself. Naomi did the same and explained her interest in the surgical nurse program.

"Yes, I'm a nurse myself. I'm with the 7305th Medical Training Support Battalion in Sacramento. We need nurses in our unit and a couple of other medical reserve units in our Army Reserve region. We realize that with the general shortage of nurses all around these days, that we must have something special to get young nurses to sign up. So, they came up with both the sign-up cash bonus as well as guaranteed surgical specialty training." The major pointed Naomi to a couple of folding chairs at the back of the booth. "Would you like to have a seat? Let's exchange some information and see if we may have something to offer each other."

Over the next few minutes, the major gleaned the information that Naomi was at the end of her Bachelor of Science in Nursing program at the university, already licensed, single, healthy, and interested in being a surgical nurse. Naomi learned about the $30,000.00 bonus, paid over three years, the four to six month active duty period for training, and the fact that the Army would give her credit for her nursing work back to when she was first licensed as a registered nurse after she finished her associate degree at Bakersfield College, so she would have a couple years of advanced rank if she signed up.

Naomi smiled and said, "And the only catch is that if things go bad like they did in Iraq and Afghanistan, the nice Weekend Warrior nursing duty in sunny California becomes active duty in God knows what hell hole."

The major smiled and said, "Well, as a recruiter, I would leave off your last few words there, but yes, the whole point is to have qualified medical reservists when the need arises."

"Yes, that's the tradeoff," Naomi surmised.

"Does it sound like it might be something you'd be interested in?"

"Well, yes, for me, the surgical training is what draws me to it. My boyfriend might not be too happy about it."

The major gave a little frown, "He's not too keen on the military?"

Naomi shook her head, "Not really that. Not at all. He was an officer with the Rangers in Afghanistan. He had a pretty bad time of it. He has some things he still isn't talking about. He might have a cow if I say I'm considering a commission as a nurse."

"You two planning on marriage?" the major asked.

Naomi laughed, "Yes, I think that is on the minds of both of us, but Jesse is just a little tough to pin down on details... At least so far."

"Guys are like that," Margot Dunleavy conjectured.

Naomi thought for a minute and asked, "If I wanted to move ahead on this idea, what would be involved?"

"First, there'd be the paperwork to make sure you are qualified. From the sound of things that is pretty certain. Then, you'd need to go up to the Military Entrance Processing Station, we call it MEPS, in Sacramento to do the physical and some tests, and while you are up there, you'd interview with the senior medical officers at the 7305th Medical Training Support Battalion, which, as I said, is located at Sacramento. They who would be the ones to approve you for one of the surgical nurse slots we have."

Naomi smiled at this, she had visited the Sacramento MEPS years ago, as Mark. "How long are we talking for the process? Do I have to wait until I graduate in December?"

"No, we could get things moving whenever you want. I could even give you the first forms to fill out today, and you can get back in touch with me when you are ready. Or, we can have you come up to our reserve unit in Sacramento to see what things are like? Oh, and once you are in the Reserves, you don't necessarily have to do your once a month weekend duty in Sacramento, there are other Reserve units closer down here where you can attend. The other Army Reserve and National Guard units around the state like to have our medical people stop in for their weekend drills."

With Mark's background and memories, Naomi did not need any introduction to the military or the reserves. Mark had stayed in the National Guard after his active duty tour, while he was in community college in Stockton, and at BYU, for extra cash. Naomi just needed to make sure this was the right thing for her. She had a gut instinct that it was. The same sense of destiny she had felt when she had led herself toward nursing now urged her on this path. It just seemed right.

Naomi took a deep breath, "Give me the information and the forms. Let me think about it. I think this might be right for me."

———

"What?" Jesse's voice was too loud for the restaurant they were in. His one-word question sounded as if it bordered on anger.

Naomi gave him a quiet "Sshhh!"

Naomi had somewhat expected this, sort of, based on his experience. She assumed it was his Army experience that gave him this attitude. She stared at him for quite a while before she finally said, "You heard me."

"But why? I thought your degree in nursing was what you needed to get your career started. Why would you even think of getting involved in the military?"

Naomi continued her stare for a moment, and then answered, "I got into nursing because I felt I could make a difference in people's lives. I don't want to spend a career taking temperatures and changing colostomy bags. Just like you don't want a career running the county jail. You know what you are good at and what your destiny seems to be. It seems to me the opportunity to be a certified surgical nurse, so early in my career, is a good choice. I could be waiting years for a slot to open up in a regular hospital. It is a plum job for a nurse—important work, extra pay, critical skills."

"But, you'd have the reserve commitment tying you down for years. It would interfere with family life, even if you just consider the weekend reserve duty, let alone if you get called up to active duty. Think about being married and having kids, and then getting pulled out to head for the next war they start overseas."

Naomi thought carefully about her response to that, as she did not want to further anger Jesse. She figured he needed to be cut down a bit, "Given that those words come from a guy who has scrupulously avoided any serious discussion about actually having a marriage and kids, except in your cutesy side references to it, I'm not sure you get to make those 'family life' arguments against a good career choice for me."

It was now Jesse's turn to stare silently at Naomi. At last, he said, "Nomy, you have to realize that having you called up to go on active duty to a foreign war zone somewhere is getting pretty close to Jesse Manzanares' worst nightmare. No, let me just say it… it is my greatest fear. I am not sure how I could handle that."

Naomi took a deep breath and looked Jesse in the eyes, "Jesse, you never really have discussed with me what is behind that nightmare of yours. But, I'm guessing it is pretty close to the terror I have already had to endure seeing you head out with lights and siren going, and knowing you were going into an active shooter scenario. Your own career choice has some pretty dire impacts on 'family life,' assuming you ever actually get in the mode of discussing that plan for family life. Or, hadn't you ever thought of that?" After finishing a bite of her enchilada, Naomi finished off with, "It seems to me that my thought of signing up as an Army Reserve nurse is nowhere near as dangerous to marriage and family as you having a job where your routine job, your daily duties, call on you to stand up to crazies with guns and who-knows-what, whose fondest desire is to kill you. Have you ever thought about how that nightmare impacts someone like me?"

They looked across the table at each other in silence. The stress was palpable. Finally, Jesse said, "I guess we can talk about it. We need to get going. I really hate to be late for the movie."

As Jesse looked down at his plate to finish his meal, Naomi saw the muscles in his jaw and down the sides of his neck were standing out, tensed up. Jesse was not joking about how Naomi's decision was freaking him out. She wished she knew why Jesse felt this way. It must be his injuries overseas. Combat service left many good men with PTSD. Mark Kelleher had been lucky on that, but unlucky in other ways. Naomi had a passing thought of whether her nightmares about Mark and burning vehicles was Naomi's PTSD.

———

Chapter 26

Naomi could not help but feel a queasy dose of fear and angst, as she approached the building she had once been held captive in. She pulled into the parking space and turned off her car. Doctor Partridge had made sure they knew Naomi was coming.

The guard checked her ID and gave her the visitor's badge. He asked if she needed directions to Partridge's office. Naomi smiled and shook her head. She crossed the street from the Admin Building at Napa State Hospital. She walked to the right-hand entrance, to the entrance for Unit A-1 and the medical staff offices.

She told the guard at the outside entrance to the huge Program 4 building where she was headed and went inside the lobby. Naomi suppressed the urge to open the door to A-1 and look inside her old living area. She knew that Tiara had long since been discharged, so the only person inside she might want to see was Mindy, if she still worked there. But, Naomi pushed the button on the old elevator and headed upstairs.

Naomi walked down the hall to the same counter she had once been delivered to, locked in a wheelchair, years ago. Nothing really had changed. She even recognized the nurse.

"Good morning, Becca," Naomi said. "I have an appointment with Doctor Partridge."

Becca smiled at her, "Yes, Miss Donnelley, Larry told me you would be visiting. It is nice to see you after all this time. It's kind of nice to see a successful alumna, so to speak. He's waiting for you."

Naomi smiled and walked toward Doctor Partridge's door. She knocked.

Doctor Partridge opened the door, smiled, and started to offer Naomi his hand, and then changed his mind and spread his arms to hug her. Instead of sitting at his desk, like they had so many times before, he motioned her over to the armchairs.

"You certainly are looking lovely this morning. This must be your interview outfit," Partridge said, indicating Naomi's dark blue business suit.

Naomi smiled, "Thank you. Yes, I finished the administrative and medical processing at the military MEPS office yesterday, and it seems I passed, so I have the interview with the Medical Corps colonel after lunch today. This gave me just enough time to drive up here this morning and meet with my Svengali, or maybe my Professor Henry Higgins is a better moniker for you."

"I'm afraid either of those characters gives me too much credit. I was really just a bystander in whatever miracle took place with your life."

"Ah, Doctor, you give yourself too little credit. If not for your wisdom, help, and direction, I don't know where I'd be today. You helped me figure out who I was and helped me get out of this place."

Partridge shrugged, "So, from your phone call, it sounds like your life is really coming together. B.S. in Nursing under your belt, thinking about getting surgical training in the Army, and you have a guy who cares enough about you to give you a hard time about joining the Army. And, that's a different guy than the pilot you told me about when we talked a few years ago. Right?"

"Yes, that other guy, the LDS pilot in the Marines I told you about, went in another direction with his life. I was not ready for what he wanted back then."

"And, mentioning that he was LDS, are you still active in the Church?"

Naomi gave a nervous shrug, "Not anything like Bishop Partridge would like. I was plenty active when I lived with the Morrison's, but only occasionally now. My life is pretty busy. I am sticking with the Word of Wisdom strictly. Your warning to me was fully absorbed. My new guy, Jesse, has a younger sister who married a Mormon doctor, a chiropractor, so I guess you could say the path is still open for us. Huh?"

Partridge smiled, "Yes, I glad you are happy in life. You need to forge your own path. You will find the right path through life in your own time."

Naomi now looked directly into Partridge's eyes and asked, "Speaking of my path through life, have you had any more thoughts about what happened to me. Does either Doctor Partridge or Bishop Partridge have any better idea about the miracle, for want of a better word?"

Partridge took a deep breath and thought for a moment, "Well, first off, I can tell you without a doubt that Doctor Partridge has no answer as to what happened. From the standpoint of medical science, what happened to Mark Kelleher and Naomi Donnelley, simply could not happen based on our understanding of science. All the scientist can tell you is that a young woman woke up one morning with some really strange memories and thoughts, and she inexplicably was able to know things that logic could not explain how she knew. So, psychiatry, logic, and science are not much help in finding an explanation.

"However, Naomi, I can tell you that the other guy, Bishop Partridge, and Larry Partridge, the ordinary man, have thought about what happened to you more times than I can count. Of course, like we talked about back then, there are a couple of choices of what happened spiritually. Maybe that the young woman messed up her life so badly that she had wiped out her own mind and memories while in the coma and with her drug use. Then, perhaps the thoughts and memories of the young man, Mark, were given to her as the raw materials for her to build a new life. The other explanation, which I kind of favor, is that this fine, young man was killed in the prime of his life. And then, he was given the young woman's life to rebuild and enjoy the blessing of life that was so wrongfully taken from him. A Karmic kind of thing. Either way, it is pretty clear you had a really unique method of being 'Born Again.'"

Partridge put up his hands in a questioning motion, and continued, "Of course, I'm guessing that with time, you probably have a better picture of what you think happened than I possibly could."

Naomi nodded, "Amazingly, I have come to terms with what happened. I'm not that old Naomi. My soul is Mark's. However, I do think your old theory and the warning you gave me that I am working within the parameters of Naomi's body and brain are correct. My emotions and reactions to things are the product of Mark being impacted by the deep essence of the female self that Naomi once had. In my nursing education, I took a couple psychology classes, and I now realize that the concepts of what they call Depth Psychology are at work inside me. I have all of Mark's thoughts and memories up to his passing, but when I come up with some issue like sexual response or thinking about having children, or my own self-image, or even just plain things that make me happy or inspire me, at those times my thoughts, feelings and emotions are often disconnected from what Mark would be feeling. Down deep inside me, my internal essence is reacting like Naomi, and Mark has decided that it is not a bad thing, all else being considered. Despite all her problems, there are some things that Naomi was better at than Mark ever would be. When I am being embraced by my boyfriend, my internal function is 100%, female, in spite of having Mark's memories of the exact opposite. And, I have never gotten any sense that this Naomi, myself, might like girls like Mark did. I get a kick out of dressing up and looking as pretty as I can, and the old Mark would be freaking out, you know, embarrassed, about the ramifications of that."

Partridge was smiling, "So, Naomi is feeling good about life and seems to have it under control?"

Naomi now smiled, "Yes, pretty much so."

"So, you wouldn't mind if I finally did my psychiatric journal paper on your case? I'll have Freud turning over in his grave." Partridge quickly added, "Just kidding! Your secret is safe. But, if you ever put out your own memoir, you will be the world's foremost authority on interbody soul transfer. You could write whole new chapters in our Depth Psychology textbooks."

Naomi shook her head at his joke and his retraction, "Nope. My story is too implausible for anyone to believe. Besides, even if we tried to tell this story, the key point that made you believe me and helped convince me that I wasn't crazy, would be missing for the reader of that story. Even in a tell-all memoir with a foreword by an eminent psychiatrist, it would never fly. Heck, I still have my own doubts. I lay in bed at night and wax philosophical, wondering if it all is real."

———

Naomi poured a bit more water into her glass from the plastic water bottle they had provided her. The flimsy plastic crackled in her grasp. She felt good about the answers she had given the three Army officers on the other side of the table. They had been thorough in their questioning of her goals and motivation for wanting to join the Army Reserves. They had also been open and honest in answering her questions.

The officer in the middle, Daniel Latimer, was a full colonel, the medical doctor who commanded the reserve battalion. The other man was a major, a younger surgeon. Major Dunleavy, the nurse who had been Naomi's recruiter, was the third officer on the interview panel.

The colonel gathered up his papers in front of him and said, "Ms. Donnelley, if you have no further questions, I think that just about covers it."

Seeing that he was expecting her to answer, Naomi said, "No, I don't have any questions."

"Well, then, Major Dunleavy can show you where you can wait. Let us discuss things, and someone will be with you shortly." The colonel stood and offered Naomi a handshake across the table.

Major Dunleavy showed Naomi to a waiting room down the hall.

Naomi did not have to wait long. Major Dunleavy came in after about five minutes and invited Naomi across the hall into Dunleavy's office. There was a name placard on the desk, "Margot Dunleavy, M.S.N., R.N, Major, U.S.A.R."

Once they were seated, the major asked Naomi, "I didn't bring it up in the interview, but I was wondering if you resolved things with your boyfriend, you know, about whether he opposed your joining up."

Naomi looked at the major and said, "Yes, we had a long talk, actually several long talks. In the end, he left it up to me to decide. I pretty much leveled with him that anyone with as dangerous a job as he has, can't really complain about a far less perilous job as an Army nurse."

Margot Dunleavy gave a questioning look and said, "He has a really dangerous job? You mentioned he had been a Ranger. Is he still in the reserves? What does he do now?"

"Oh, no, he got out after his active duty. Now, he is a SWAT team leader for our County Sheriff. I actually met him while I was bandaging up a bullet wound in his chest. Hence, he cannot complain to me about my wanting to be an Army nurse being a dangerous choice."

Margot and Naomi laughed at this.

Naomi asked, "Why do you ask about my boyfriend?"

"Well, because that seemed like that had been the only thing holding you back from making a decision. After your perfect performance in our interview panel, all that is keeping you from being an Army nurse is whether you want to raise your right hand and take the oath. Colonel Latimer gave me his approval. Your background check came in from D.C. without a hitch. Your physical and tests at MEPS yesterday were fine. Cal State Bakersfield's Registrar certified you are complete on your degree requirements. If you want, I can get our Personnel technician to work on the paperwork, and we can send you home to Bakersfield this evening as an Army Nurse — 2nd Lieutenant Naomi Donnelley, Nurse Corps, USAR."

Naomi sat for a moment, looking across the desk at Major Dunleavy. Naomi really did not have to think much about the decision, as she had gone over and over the choice she had to make for weeks. She had a firm belief that this was the right way for her to proceed. She still had the old recurring thoughts that there was some destiny she must pursue, a reason underlying the bizarre miracle that had so changed her life at Napa, and this decision was now clearly part of that pursuit. And, as opposed to many things that she did these days, this decision seemed to be coming from the part of her that was her core essence, her soul, as Mark. And, Mark was going back into the Army, this time as Naomi.

Naomi gave a smiling nod to Major Dunleavy, "Let's get the paperwork going. I'm ready to raise my hand."

———

Jesse was helping Naomi pack her car for the trip to Texas. A spring cold front was passing through central California, and Naomi was pulling on her CSUB sweatshirt for her car trip. Jesse was in uniform, ready for work, so he wore the green parka with the Sheriff's star over the pocket and the bold 'SWAT' across the shoulders. He shook his head and smiled at the suitcases Naomi had sitting in the apartment hallway.

"What's so funny?" Naomi asked.

"A lot has changed from when I went to Officer's Basic. My ROTC instructor required us to have a duffel bag and taught us how to pack it. No suitcases for us," Jesse hefted the bags to emphasize his words.

"The introduction pamphlet says they give us a duffel bag when we get there, for our field gear. And, thank you for helping me get my uniform stuff purchased ahead of time. I'm glad I get to take my car. I packed extra stuff in the trunk that I wouldn't be able to if I had flown. If I've forgotten anything, I thought maybe you could bring it with you when you visit like you promised in between my courses."

Jesse smiled at Naomi.

"What now?" she asked.

"I'm not used to seeing you in glasses. And, that short haircut on your beautiful blonde hair is a crime."

"Yeah, they don't let you wear contacts for the field training part of the initial course down there. I thought I'd get used to wearing my regular glasses again for a while. And, I'll have plenty of time to grow the hair back when it isn't getting in the way. Ayla and Janet said they like my pixie cut."

"Unnecessary," Jesse said, shaking his head in disagreement. He picked up the suitcases. Naomi grabbed her vanity case and held the door for Jesse.

Naomi had traded in her mother's old Toyota Prius for a new red Honda Accord. Jesse packed the suitcases in amongst the boxes Naomi had already put into the trunk.

"Nomy, I'm really going to miss you," Jesse said, setting the last suitcase in the trunk, so he could put his arms around Naomi.

"Me, too," Naomi stood on tiptoes and nuzzled her face into Jesse's neck. The two of them stood for a long time, without words.

"Take care, and don't be too much of a hero out there. I won't be here to patch you up for a while," Naomi told Jesse.

"You, too. I can't believe I actually said it was okay for you to do this."

Naomi gave Jesse a little frown and shook her head without words.

"I need to go," Naomi said.

"Yeah, I know. Let's see if we can do a kiss that will last us until I come down to see you in San Antonio at the end of May," Jesse suggested.

"Let's try…." Naomi turned her face up to meet Jesse's lips.

———

Chapter 27

Naomi had gone to a couple of her reserve unit's drill weekends while she waited for her active duty class to start in San Antonio. She had spoken to two people who had recently gone through Fort Sam Houston's Army Medical Department & School (AMEDD) Basic Officer Leadership Course (BOLC) for reserve medical officers, so she knew what to expect upon her arrival. The Reserve Officers' Basic course was held in concert with the final weeks of the active duty officers' course, which was longer to accommodate more military oriented subjects than the reservists needed.

Naomi was amazed at how different her experience as a young nurse was from what Mark had gone through in enlisted Basic Training at Fort Jackson, South Carolina, years before. She drove onto the sprawling Fort Sam Houston military base mid-morning. The building number listed on her Army orders turned out to be a Holiday Inn Express. Then, after a quick, efficient check-in and document inspection at a table in the hotel labeled "TacO, BOLC," she was told to go to another on-base hotel, the Candlewood Suites, where she would be staying. She was also asked to report in duty uniform, if possible, at some helicopter on display nearby at 1530 hours. She was free until then, and they told her she could get her lunch at some 'Rocco' building, also nearby, if she showed her orders and ID card. Naomi's first day in the Army was far different from Mark's.

Following the directions given by the enlisted soldier helping the TacO at the Holiday Inn, she managed to drive by both the helicopter out front of the AMEDD headquarters and the Rocco dining hall across the intersection from the Candlewood Suites. Naomi checked into her room and discovered it was a typical commercial hotel room; queen bed, wi-fi, mini-kitchen, and she had no roommate. Her window overlooked a fairly decent swimming pool in the hotel courtyard. Given Mark's contrary memories of a forty-man open bay barracks, this was starting to feel odd.

After unpacking her things and using the iron and ironing board to fight the wrinkles from packing, it was approaching lunchtime. Since she had to report to the helicopter in uniform mid-afternoon, Naomi figured she could get into uniform to go get lunch.

She had tried on all of her online uniform purchases back in Bakersfield as they arrived from the mail-order company. It was, however, kind of a cathartic moment when she finished donning her Army Combat Uniform and checked out how she looked. The supply sergeant in Sacramento had already supplied her with the unit patches for the 7305th, and all of the other patches, rank, and embroidered tapes were in place, so her uniform was proper. She had stayed overnight at a Super 8 Motel near Interstate 10 in Kerrville, Texas, and had put on minimal make-up that morning. She had already cut her hair, and she was wearing plain, tiny gold balls for earrings, so Naomi figured she was ready to go.

She put her ID card, wallet, a folded copy of her orders, and a little memento Jesse had given her in her pockets. She wondered how her classmates were handling this first day. Maybe she could meet some of them at lunch.

Naomi exited the Candlewood Suites lobby and started across the parking lot toward the dining facility when she heard a group of women exit behind her. She turned to look and saw that they were three young women, in civilian clothes, about her age, and they were each carrying a single page of paper. That page was probably the orders they needed to get lunch at the dining facility. Naomi turned and walked back to them.

"Excuse me, are you three in the Basic Officers course?" Naomi asked them.

All three stopped in their tracks, arms at their sides, and one of them said, "Yes ma'am."

Naomi was a bit startled at the reaction. Then, she smiled and held up her hands, palms toward them, saying, "Relax, I'm one of you. Just trying to find someone to go to lunch with."

The three women laughed at themselves. All four introduced themselves; Melanie Kirk, Jillian Brown, and Kara Campbell, plus Naomi.

Jill asked Naomi, "Are you prior service or something since you are already in uniform? My recruiter said to wait until they told us to wear it."

Naomi shook her head, "No, brand new – well a couple months in my reserve unit. But, the guy where I checked in said to be at the helicopter in uniform, if possible, at 3:30 this afternoon. So, I figured why not."

The four continued across the parking lot and down the sidewalk toward the mess hall. At the intersection, Naomi saw a tall, black soldier crossing the crosswalk, headed toward them. She pushed her glasses up on the bridge of her nose, trying to make out the rank patch on the front of the soldier's combat uniform. He had the black three-tiered chevron with a single rocker bar of a staff sergeant centered on his chest.

Instead of meeting the approaching soldier in the crosswalk, she told the women with her, "Wait here a second, ladies."

Kara, Jill, and Melanie all stopped and looked at Naomi questioningly.

Naomi stood and waited for the soldier to step up on the curb in front of her. He brought his arm up in a snappy salute. Naomi returned the salute and checked his nametag.

Before the soldier could move on, Naomi said, "Just a second, Sergeant Jennings."

Naomi reached in her pocket and pulled out a large silver coin. She handed the coin to Sergeant Jennings. As she did, she had a thought that he seemed vaguely familiar.

Sergeant Jennings smiled at Naomi, "So, I'm your first, huh, ma'am?" He looked down at Naomi's nametag.

"You are, indeed, Sergeant."

"Glad to be of service, Lieutenant Donnelley," the sergeant said, saluting again.

Naomi saluted back and added, "Hoo-ah, Staff Sergeant Jennings!"

He smiled and continued on his way. Naomi watched him walk away, with the odd thought that she knew him from somewhere.

The women continued across the street, and Melanie asked, "What was all of that?"

"Old tradition, the Silver Dollar Salute. First enlisted soldier to salute a new officer gets the silver dollar," Naomi explained.

"Are we supposed to know that?" Jill asked.

Naomi shrugged, "Maybe not, it is an old tradition; they really follow it at the military academies. That staff sergeant sure knew about the tradition, didn't he? My boyfriend reminded me of it before I left, and he went to a coin shop to buy me the silver dollar. I think he was kind of proud his gal was going to be an officer." Naomi finished off, declaring, "My guy was a lieutenant in the Rangers in Afghanistan. I'm proud of him, too."

———

Naomi and the other medical students in the Basic Officer Leader Course (BOLC) had been wearing their camouflage Army Combat Uniforms (ACU) to class for the first few weeks. For the first time this morning, the young officers had been ordered to dress in the impressive Army Green Service Uniforms, called the "pinks and greens" after the old World War II nickname. The Pink was an odd old name for the lighter khaki-colored shade of parts of the uniform. They had stood in formation for uniform inspection before they started classes for the day. This was new for Naomi. When Mark had been in the Army, it had been during the short period when the Army had worn the blue service uniforms that looked like the old blue cavalry uniforms. Then, in 2020, the decision had been made to go back to the Army's historical green uniform roots. Wearing the uniform that was a throwback to World War II gave Naomi a good feeling like she was part of something special and connected across the years.

After the uniform inspection at MacArthur Field, the 150 or so student medical officers filed into the AMEDD School's largest theater-like classroom. This was a mixture of both the reservists and active duty officer classes. As usual, the seats in the back of the large auditorium filled up first. Naomi finally found a seat on the left-hand aisle close to the stage.

All these students in their new uniforms, whether medical doctors, nurses, dentists, or medical service specialists, wore their Army officer branch designation insignia on their lapels. For the medical officers, the collar insignia was a golden caduceus symbol with coiling snakes and wings. Nurses like Naomi had a large 'N' emblazoned on top of the caduceus. All of them also had the historic officer's service hat with the gold Army seal on the front. The announcement for the inspection had specified the service hats, instead of the berets or garrison caps that could also be worn with this dress uniform. As Naomi sat, she balanced her service hat and notebook on her knee.

With her credit for time as a registered nurse after her graduation from Bakersfield College and the time she had waited to get her Army orders to active duty, Naomi's time-in-rank credit was now well over two years. Thus, her shoulders showed a silver bar of her rank, First Lieutenant, or 1LT as it was written on her ID card.

Many of Naomi's fellow students with prior service had various qualification badges and rows of service ribbons above the pockets of the uniforms. Seeing this, Naomi remembered that if she were still Mark, she would have had a Combat Action Badge and two full rows of ribbons with a Bronze Star in the spot of highest precedence on the upper right. Naomi had no service ribbons. Like the other brand-new officers, she would be awarded her first two service ribbons when she completed this Basic Officer Leadership Course.

Many students were standing around, conversing, when two senior officers, also in their green service uniforms and a staff sergeant in camouflage ACU uniform with a Smokey the Bear hat, walked down the far-right aisle of the auditorium. The two officers climbed the steps onto the stage, and the drill sergeant took a cordless microphone off of the stage edge and sat in a folding chair below the stage facing the audience.

Most of the students finally sat down, but a few still stood and talked, oblivious to the officers' entrance. One of the officers on stage, the Special Forces lieutenant colonel who was the head of the military operations faculty at the school, went to the lectern and tapped the microphone.

"Seats!" was the lieutenant colonel's simple but effective command.

After everyone quickly sat down, the colonel spoke, "I want to say I thought you all looked fantastic in your new uniforms out on the parade ground this morning. I hope you take great pride in the honor you have to wear that uniform."

He continued, "As you all have completed the first few weeks of orientation to the military, Army customs, military law and all the rest, we now move into the phase of your education where you will be taught the basics of the various military operations that you might experience in the modern Army. You will experience field conditions at Camp Bullis. You will be taught about weapons, field equipment, Army vehicles, aircraft, and various types of military operations like amphibious, special operations, civil pacification, urban warfare, field infantry tactics, and the like. The linear battlefields of the past have disappeared, and Medical Corps officers of today need to be prepared to face the tactical challenges of the full spectrum environment on today's asymmetric battlefields, while preparing for the future Joint Operating Environment and the unique threats it will bring."

The colonel cleared his throat and continued, "Today, we are lucky to have Major Jonathan McMurtry with us as a guest lecturer in airmobile and air assault operations. Air assault is the movement of ground-based military forces by vertical take-off and landing aircraft—such as the helicopter—to seize and hold key terrain which has not been fully secured and to directly engage enemy forces behind enemy lines. These operations are a key capability of the U.S. Army to project power against the enemy on a fluid battlefield. Airmobile operations played an essential part in the Iraq War, and they have been the primary mode of fighting in the bulk of operations in Afghanistan.

"Major McMurtry is a highly decorated infantry officer holding, among other decorations, a Combat Infantryman Badge and the Silver Star medal for service in Iraq, where he has deployed on four different occasions. He has also taught Air Assault tactics at West Point. He comes to us today on temporary duty from Fort Hood, where he is currently serving as the Deputy Commander of the Sustainment Brigade of the legendary 1ˢᵗ Cavalry Division.

"Before Major McMurtry takes over, I will remind you that this is a very big room, and to make sure any questions are heard by all, you need to stand and wait for Drill Sergeant Moskowitz to bring you the microphone. As we've said around here many times, there is no stupid question, except the one you do not ask. Major McMurtry, please." The colonel left the stage and took a seat in the front row.

The students gave perfunctory applause to welcome the major.

Major McMurtry set his stack of papers on the lectern and picked up the audio-visual clicker from the podium.

"Uh, if I could have the staff pass out my syllabus handouts... and please turn the lights down about halfway, so everyone can see my PowerPoint presentation."

As several enlisted soldiers came down the aisles to distribute handouts and the auditorium lights dimmed, he started, "I am delighted to be here with you today. You will be joining a great Army Team and all of the soldiers you will serve with truly value the Medical Corps. I hope I can shed some light for you on Air Mobile and Air Assault operations, which are really much the same thing these days, but with a bit of historical differentiation."

Naomi shifted in her seat and tugged at the snug, tailored waist and bodice of her new uniform jacket to make sure it did not wrinkle while she sat.

The major began with a history of what he called 'Army Air Ops,' starting with Vietnam and describing in detail the Battle of Ia Drang Valley in Vietnam in 1965. He also mentioned the limited medical use of helicopters in the Korean War. He then launched into a detailed lecture with a myriad of photographs and maps projected on the screen behind him.

Naomi struggled to stifle a yawn several times during the major's lecture. She was not alone amongst the students. There were no questions.

At the end of what was obviously a lecture he had given many times before, the major straightened his stack of papers and paused. "Since I am speaking to a room full of Medical Corps officers, I have been asked to put air operations in perspective with how it can impact your medical mission."

There was a rustling of paper in the auditorium as everyone turned to the Medical Ops page in the handout.

"Of course, the primary impact on battlefield medicine from Korea and then, more so, in Vietnam forward has been the ability of airmobile assets to rapidly bring casualties from the battlefield to the rear for medical assistance. I will address that in much more detail in a moment. But first, I want to address an impact of air operations on the modern battlefield that can significantly lead to a high level of mass casualties that was not a major factor in earlier conflicts. With the increased passenger capacity of large helicopters such as the CH-47 Chinook and the CH-53 Super Stallion, we have found that hostile fire incidents or accidents can lead to a higher level of injuries to the real combat soldiers at the front lines or further out, inside enemy territory, that your medical troops will need to deal with in their position in the rear areas."

The major stopped abruptly when he realized he had misspoken and implied that medical troops were not 'real' soldiers. The lieutenant colonel had also caught the major's verbal slip, as Naomi saw his closely cropped head tilt back, and although Naomi could not see his face, she could imagine that his eyes were rolling toward the ceiling in consternation.

The major quickly said, "Sorry, that is not what I meant to say. I apologize. Let me rephrase that…."

Please do! Tell us about the 'real' soldiers. Naomi was pretty sure her thought was shared by the other doctors and nurses, particularly the prior service officers.

The major thought for a moment and continued, "What I meant to say was that with the recent advent of very large aircraft, like the CH-47 Chinook and the CH-53 Super Stallion, capable of carrying large numbers of troops into forward areas and even to deliver them directly into distant, hostile territory that the possibility exists for a single incident to generate a large number of casualties, which the Army medical team will need to deal with. Let me give an example."

"The highest number of casualties from a single enemy action in the post-9/11 era occurred in Kuhner Province, Afghanistan in August 2011, when 38 Army Rangers died when a Chinook helicopter was brought down by enemy small arms fire. That number is exactly double the number of deaths that resulted from the infamous 'Blackhawk Down' incident in Mogadishu, Somalia, in 1993. And, of course, the 19 dead associated with the Blackhawk Down crash included a number of casualties from on-the-ground fighting after the helicopter went down."

Naomi immediately knew the major was wrong.

Without thinking, Naomi raised her hand, and the sergeant below the stage stood and told the major, "Question!"

The major pointed at her, "Yes, please stand and identify yourself when we get you the microphone."

As the drill sergeant walked to her, Naomi was getting cold feet, but she stood when she was handed the microphone.

"Yes sir. Lieutenant Naomi Donnelley, and it is not a question. It is a correction."

"Oh really, a correction?" the major said, sarcastically.

"Yes, sir, you got the casualty incident you mentioned mixed up with another one. There was another deadly Chinook crash that did happen in eastern Kunar Province…," Naomi corrected the major's pronunciation of the place name by using long vowel sounds for both the 'u' and 'a.' "But that one was way earlier in the Afghan War in 2006 when 16 Navy Seals died in a Chinook helo shootdown. The deadly August 2011 shootdown you spoke of was actually in <u>Wardak</u> Province west of Kabul, and the 38 troops that died were, indeed, being deployed to support the 75th Ranger Regiment operations in Wardak province, but the casualties weren't Rangers. Seventeen of those dead in 2011 were also Navy Seals. Five, the aircrew, were Army Reserve and Army National Guard. Three were Air Force Special Tactics guys. Eight of the dead were with the Afghan National Guard. And, there was also an American military working dog casualty on the Chinook."

The major blinked at Naomi for a moment before he, with a hint of sarcasm, said, "You seem to be pretty damned sure of yourself, Lieutenant."

"I am, Sir."

There was a murmur from the audience. Naomi saw the lieutenant colonel tip his head back in his seat. She could not see his face, but she could guess he was again rolling his eyes to the ceiling.

Naomi saw that the lieutenant colonel stand and head up the steps toward the instructor on the stage. The major waited. Naomi gave a little sigh, worried she was getting in trouble. The colonel walked up to the major and motioned that he wanted to say something to him, away from the microphone. The instructor stepped away from the lectern and the colonel whispered something into the major's ear with a cupped hand. The major whispered back to the colonel something which seemed to be 'You're sure?' The colonel nodded firmly and turned to go back to his seat. The major stepped back to the lectern.

Major McMurtry turned to face Naomi, "Well, I have been told that you are exactly correct in what you told us. How do you happen to know all of that, Lieutenant?"

Naomi had been certain of the facts, because, as Mark, she had been ordered with other Army truck drivers to the scene of that crash to help the Rangers collect bodies and wreckage, and truck it back to Kabul. And, that horrible crash and the earlier similar crash had been hot topics in Mark's barracks in Kabul for some time afterward. Plus, the *Stars and Stripes* newspaper the troops read in Kabul covered the crash and the history of such helo crashes in depth. The aftermath of the Wardak crash had been traumatic to see, and the details were etched in Mark's memory, and now Naomi's remembrance. She thought quickly on how to explain how she knew the details of something that Mark knew from experience, but which had happened when Naomi Donnelly was probably in middle school.

Those listening could hear Naomi's voice crack with distress as she said, "Someone very important to me… was involved in that crash."

Naomi handed the microphone to the drill sergeant and quickly sat down.

The major said, "Thank you for your contribution, Lieutenant. The class should note the correction on my handout."

Naomi's friend, Melanie Kirk, who was sitting next to Naomi closed her fist to give Naomi a fist bump but kept her hand out of sight to everyone except Naomi in the darkened auditorium. Naomi bumped fists.

Medical students—1, surly Infantry major—0.

—

After the first few weeks of training, the new medical officers left the main Army Medical Department & School (AMEDD) campus on Fort Sam Houston and went to the site for their field training, Camp Bullis. Camp Bullis was an old Army training site from the two World Wars that the many training programs for the military services at Joint Base San Antonio used for field training. The sprawling site was northwest of suburban San Antonio. Living in the Bullis' twelve-person tent-like hutments was more like the Army of Mark's day. Having lived through worse as Mark, Naomi was not prone to the griping most of the women in her tent did in their time at Camp Bullis.

The three weeks they spent at Camp Bullis were full, morning to night with weapons training, familiarization with field operations, long hikes, and military training operations, both night and day. The Army assigned various trainees as leaders for the field camp. Naomi had not been chosen for leadership, not having any prior service nor anything else to clearly differentiate her from her peers.

Late in the afternoon on Thursday of their second week, their trainee platoon leader stuck his head in the canvas flap of the hutment she lived in with eleven other nurses and shouted, "Donnelley, the TacO wants you to report to him ASAP. You can follow us to dinner if you're not finished when we go to chow."

Naomi gave a surprised expression and looked at her roommates.

Kara Campbell said, teasingly, "Uh oh, Naomi is in trouble."

"Either that or the major wants to get her phone number for when Camp Bullis is over," said another roommate. Most of the women laughed at this. Major Ben Williamson was a hunk. He was the Infantry officer who served as the officer in charge, or the "Tactical Officer – TacO" of the Camp Bullis field training for the Basic Officer Leaders Course.

Naomi put her ACU field cap on and left the hut shaking her head.

The TacO's office was in one of the other hutments, at the far end of the row, with a large sign "AMEDD TacO" above the door.

"1st Lieutenant Donnelley reporting as ordered, sir!" Naomi said with a salute.

"Stand at ease, Lieutenant. I just had a couple questions for you," said Major Williamson, as he returned the salute.

"We've been going over the performance grades for the first two weeks out here. I spoke with Drill Sergeant Jennings about you. He mentioned he was your Silver Dollar salute. We have a question. You don't have any prior service on your record. How have you done so well in the grunt fieldwork we've given you here? You fired Expert Marksman on both pistol and rifle first test. Sergeant Jennings saw you showing a group of the long course trainees how to field strip an M-4, and he says you did it like you'd done it hundred times. Your classroom scores on the military subjects are near perfect. Your orienteering team finished first, and the prior service captain on your team told me you were the one who did that for them. How do you do that? You are a brand new nurse, only here a few weeks, and in the short Reserve course, at that, yet you act like a combat veteran, and you make our roughest training at Camp Bullis seem like a walk in the park," Williamson left his hands open to gesture his question.

Naomi knew she had to think on this. She did not want to make something up to cover up for her having Mark's soldiering skill set. At last, she said, "I guess I just take to it naturally. And, my boyfriend is an ex-Ranger. He made sure I was ready for this. He told me a lot of stuff. And I've watched him field strip his M-4."

Williamson perked up at this, "Oh really? Ranger huh? What unit and where did he serve?"

"He was with the 75th Rangers in Afghanistan, in 2011 and 2012, I think."

"No kidding! Me, too. What's his name?"

Naomi was getting a bad feeling about this. She answered, "Jesse Manzanares."

Williamson seemed a bit shocked. "Really, Jess is your boyfriend? I haven't seen him since he left Benning when we got home. What's he doing now, since you mentioned he has an M-4?"

"He's a SWAT team leader for our Sheriff's office in Bakersfield."

Williamson just nodded his head at this, "That's a good job for Jess. I was disappointed he decided to get out of the Army. One of the finest officers I ever served with, and I've seen more than a few. We were fellow platoon leaders with the 75th. We were all proud of Jess when he got his Silver Star. Nobody ever deserved it more."

Naomi tried not to seem surprised at this. Jesse had never mentioned having been awarded a Silver Star medal. He never spoke about his Army service. She had wrangled his unit, the 75th Rangers, out of him once when he could not avoid answering a direct question in a conversation that one of his SWAT buddies had started at a barbecue party they all attended. Knowing she had to say something, she said, "You are probably right, he is a good fit for that job. But from my point of view, that is probably one of the few jobs he could do that is more dangerous than being a Ranger."

Williamson nodded and continued, "So, I guess that information answers my question a bit. But, Jess must have done a Vulcan Mind Meld on you to get you up to speed for this training. Good work. And, if we don't talk again, give Jess my best. Dismissed."

Naomi did her departing salute, performed her best about-face, and left.

She had one more piece of the puzzle that was Jesse Manzanares, or 'Jess' as his friend from the old days called him. A Silver Star.

———

<h1 align="center">Chapter 28</h1>

Naomi pulled her Honda into the parking space at the Powless House Holiday Inn at Fort Sam Houston. She looked over at Jesse in the passenger seat.

"What's wrong?" she asked.

"Nothin' wrong. It was a long trip," Jesse unbuckled his seat belt and started to get out.

"Wait, Jess. We've been together long enough for me to be able to read Jesse's body language. Things were great at the airport and halfway here, and then you got silent. Clammed up on me. Now, you've got a look on your face like somebody shot your puppy dog."

Jesse took a deep breath and looked over to Naomi, moving his eyes toward her, but not turning his head, and she could see his jaw muscles tense up. After a moment, he said, "Sorry, Nomy. I thought I would be better at this. I hadn't counted on you getting me a hotel room within sight of that." He gestured out of the car window to the northeast of the hotel.

Naomi looked over to where he pointed to the huge, eight-story, red-brick building that filled the eastern horizon, and Naomi asked, "Brooke Army Medical Center?" She looked at Jesse, and then a look of realization came across her face. "Gosh, Jesse. I'm sorry. I didn't think this out very well. After the Basic Course, they moved me over to the housing nearer the Center, where a lot of my training will be. I figured it would be best to have your hotel room close since they have their silly no-friends-or-family in student's quarters rule. I never thought about your connection to BAMC... and the Burn Center."

Jesse nodded. "Yup, I spent the two worst months of my life in that building over there. Screaming in pain, drugged out of my gourd, and then worrying about whether I'd ever recover. I promised myself I would never return. That's what kept me from trying for my dream of medical school through the Army. Only the thought of being with my Nomy for 72 hours got me anywhere near this whole damn city. Let alone, in the shadow of that place."

"Sorry, I already checked you in, earlier this afternoon, but we can get you someplace else."

"Right, you are going to find a new hotel room on a military base the Friday afternoon before the Memorial Day weekend. You told me weeks ago how you'd been lucky enough to reserve a place for me on base for the long weekend. Another room? Not gonna happen. Besides, I am over the worst of it already. Let's drop off my bag, freshen up, and go find some food. I'm starved."

"You sure, Hon?"

"I'm sure. What you got planned for us this weekend?"

"Food's going to be big. San Antonio is one of the few places in the country to challenge the San Joaquin Valley for Mexican vittles. And, of course, Texas is a steak lover's paradise. I've got tickets for a concert you're gonna love tonight. It's a surprise. No fair using your smartphone to peek at who is playing. Then, I think we can think of some things to do together, without much trouble. San Antonio is a big place, some pretty romantic spots, so I hear."

"Sounds like a plan."

They got out of the Honda, and Jesse took his bag out of the back seat.

As they walked in, Naomi took a key card folder out of her purse and handed it to Jesse, "Your room is on the top floor, overlooking the pool, opposite side from the hospital building."

"Good," was all Jesse said.

Jesse held the hotel door open for Naomi, but Naomi saw Jesse looking back at the huge red-brown monolith as they entered the hotel lobby.

———

"As near as I can see from the freeway signs, we've left San Antonio city and are heading for Austin," Jesse said. "I would have thought it was a little easier than this to find a good Tex-Mex restaurant in a city the size of San Anton'. My airline snack lunch six hours ago is seeming a long way off."

"Don't worry. I have this all planned out. Great little restaurant, recommended by the locals, real close to the concert venue," Naomi said. "I promise you. It will be worth the wait."

"Concert venue in Austin?"

"No, have patience. We're close," Naomi said, as she turned on her blinker to take an exit at New Braunfels.

———

Jesse and Naomi were taken to their table in the Dos Rios Mexican Bar & Grill in New Braunfels, Texas. As they waited for their server, Jesse and Naomi looked around the restaurant.

Jesse gave his verdict, "As far as the atmosphere goes, these people have what I think of Tex-Mex down to a 'T.'"

Naomi started to reply, but she was interrupted by a pretty ginger-haired waitress handing her a menu. She waved off the menu, saying, "We won't need a menu. Bring us the Plato Comal. And, I'll have a lemonade. Jesse, what'll you have to drink? I'm driving tonight, so feel free to order whatever you want."

Jesse smiled, "Ah-ha! Nomy takes charge. I'll have the house draft."

The waitress serving them wrote the order on her pad, smiled, and left with the menus.

Naomi explained, "I asked some locals where to eat in New Braunfels and what to order. They said this place is best, and the Plato Comal is a fantastic mixed platter for two really hungry people, or a merely great choice for three or four people without a big appetite. Having seen Jesse devour food when he says he is hungry; I figure it will be just right for us tonight."

A huge, frosted glass of lemonade and an oversized mug of beer arrived.

Jesse took a long gulp of beer and turned to Naomi, "So, Nomy, time for a detailed report of what you've been up to so far. Your emails and phone have been good, but I need a complete recap."

Naomi put her drink down and gave a little grin, "Can I start out by bragging?"

"If you've got something to brag about, have at it."

"Yesterday afternoon, at the graduation ceremony for my Basic Officer's Leadership Class, I was top in my class."

"Wow, top in your class. Out of how many?" Jesse asked.

"Hundred fifty or so."

"Good work, Nomy. I'm proud of you," Jesse said.

Naomi looked at Jesse and wondered if she should mention that the TacO had written her up for the top in class honors was an old friend of Jesse's from the Rangers. Given Jesse's mood when he saw the hospital, Naomi thought that anything else to bring up repressed memories might not be welcome.

"It felt good to finish up the Basic Course on a high note yesterday. Then, I got moved out of the old room near AMEDD to my new place nearer the hospital. I have 16 weeks of that, then I get to come home. It'll be both classroom work, and then an internship in surgery at the hospital."

The waitress started bringing plates of various foods, starting with appetizers.

"So, Nomy, after your first few months of this… you still happy with your decision? Is that surgical qualification worth all this military garbage they are putting you through?" Jesse asked, before chomping a scorched green onion shoot.

Naomi laughed, "Jesse, on our first date, you explained to me how you had volunteered for Ranger School to look good in a future application for the Army, sending you to medical school. And now, that same guy is asking if all the 'military garbage' is worth it for my nursing career."

Jesse smiled and nodded, "Point taken."

"And, how have things been back home? I haven't heard a lot out of you about your work."

Jesse shrugged, "It has been fairly slow. Just the usual. Nothing big. But, oh, I didn't to tell you yet, since you are going to be gone all summer, the Sheriff nominated me for the FBI National Academy at Quantico in Virginia in July through September. I got accepted, and so we'll both be students at a military base this summer. My FBI Academy ends just before your training here."

"Hmm, sounds interesting. I'm all for anything that gets you promoted, and out of the Kevlar vests and active shooter responses," Naomi said, sorting through the meat platter.

"Uh, Nomy, that is kind of an oxymoron. Handling the active shooters and dodging bullets is what gets guys like me promoted <u>and</u> sent to the FBI Academy."

"You know what I mean, Jess. When you make Sheriff commander, you'll be telling some other lieutenant and his SWAT squad to flush out the bad guy with the AK-47. Promotions of their guy out of the line of fire is the fondest dream of all the SWAT wives I have talked to so far."

Jesse said nothing to this but gave a slightly annoyed, yet quiet, growl.

With that, the conversation took a back seat to the consumption of scrumptious non-Vegan food.

—

It was a short drive from the Dos Rios restaurant to the public parking lot in downtown New Braunfels. Dusk was falling, and the streetlights were coming on. Jesse helped Naomi put a sweater on for warmth. The heat of a Texas day was getting chilly.

"When you mentioned the concert venue, I had thoughts of a stadium. But, this looks decidedly small town, not a stadium. Who we gonna see and where?" Jesse asked.

"Remember when you told me you had concert tickets at the Kern County Fair, and you were so upset when you got called out on a touchy domestic abuse case and missed the concert?"

"Yeah, I was pissed. I missed Lorrie Morgan and Pam Tillis."

Naomi pointed her finger at Jesse triumphantly, "No, Pam Tillis this time. But, you are getting your Lorrie Morgan concert."

They rounded the corner of a building, and Naomi pointed at the impressive, neon-lit, marquis of the Brauntex Theater and its announcement, "Lorrie Morgan in Concert."

"No kidding? Wow, she's one of my favor…."

Naomi interrupted, "Duh? Anyone who has ever heard your cellphone playlist knows that. I thought this would be fun."

Jesse put his arm around Naomi and squeezed her, "Thanks, Nomy. You're the best."

—

Naomi could not believe it was Tuesday. The Memorial Day weekend had gone too quickly. Her last evening snuggled with Jesse and, then, their embrace at the entrance to the airport TSA check-in line was still on her mind. She was following the instructions in an email to go to her new unit, Company C, 188th Medical Battalion, to register for the rest of her coursework at Fort Sam Houston. That unit handled nurses in professional training, such as Naomi's Perioperative Nursing curriculum. Her new classes would be in the large Professional Training building across the street from Naomi's new residence in a different Army hotel, Building 1384.

The good thing was that she was no longer a newbie 'trainee.' The Perioperative Nursing course was an advanced course for Army nurses. A few of her fellow students might be new to the Army like her, but many would also be experienced Army nurses, honing their skills with further training. This course was why she joined the Army Reserve.

At Company C, Naomi was directed to a room where two sergeants stood behind a counter labeled 'In-Processing' to handle the morning's incoming nursing students. One nurse, a tall brunette in the ACU uniform like Naomi, was already at the counter.

Naomi had a large manila envelope that she had brought from her previous unit over at the main AMEDD campus where she had done the Basic Course. She handed the envelope to one of the sergeants, a young Hispanic woman.

The other sergeant told the nurse ahead of Naomi, "Ma'am, you're all done for now. You can wait in the Dayroom until your class leader comes to brief your class. Dayroom is across the hall."

Naomi's sergeant went through her envelope. She asked Naomi, "Are you all checked in at Building 1384?"

Naomi answered, "Yes, I've been there since last Thursday."

"Any leftover problems from BOLC, like payroll, uniform issues, medical profile, or anything else?" the sergeant repeated the question like she had said it a thousand times. She probably had.

"No, as far as I know, everything is fine."

"Okay, give me a minute, so I can look through all this," the sergeant said. As she shuffled through the paperwork, occasionally pulling out something to set aside.

"Lieutenant Donnelly, congrats on your FLPB. You got a 2/2 score. AMEDD S-1 sent your change form into DFAS, and your new FLPP of three-hundred a month should start next period."

Naomi blinked at the sergeant, after a moment she said, "I'm sorry, the acronyms slipped by me there. Could you translate that?"

The sergeant laughed, "Sorry, ma'am. I guess that was a big dose of alphabet soup. You got a qualifying score on your FLPB language test for Dari that you took during your Officer's Basic. You qualify for the Foreign Language Proficiency bonus of $300 a month."

Naomi was surprised. She had not thought much about the checkmark she made on the form she had filled out at BOLC about language use. Years before, as Mark, she had spent some of her free time in Kabul, taking an online class in Dari, the Afghans' common language, which was almost the same as the Farsi language spoken in Iran. Mark had thought it might be handy to know the local language while driving and working with Afghans in his truck driving duties. Then, at BYU, Mark had taken two years of college Farsi to cover his foreign language requirement for graduation. Naomi had taken the placement test in Farsi at Cal State Bakersfield, followed by two online courses of Persian/Farsi language there to cover her electives for her BS degree in Nursing. Naomi could read common Farsi or Dari, written in Arabic script, reasonably well, and spoke either dialect well enough to get by in a simple conversation. The afternoon of language testing, while she was at BOLC, had gotten her out of a boring military customs class. Naomi had not realized it was connected to a bonus in her Army paycheck. Her records would now show 1LT Donnelly was a speaker of Afghan Dari/Farsi. She wondered how many Army nurses fit in that category; probably quite a few after twenty years of war in Afghanistan, she assumed.

The sergeant nodded, "Okay, ma'am. Please fill out this personal notification card with your cell phone, room number at Building 1384, and AKO address, plus civilian email, if you use it more often than your AKO email. When you are done with that, you can wait in the Dayroom with your class members. You got here fairly early, so you may have a bit of a wait."

Naomi filled out the form and handed it in to the sergeant.

The Dayroom for Company C was more of a waiting room or classroom than the kind of 'dayroom' Naomi remembered from Mark's enlisted days. A traditional Army dayroom was a place where troops could hang out and pass the time without leaving the company area. A television, foosball and pool tables, and a magazine and book lending library had been common features. This dayroom had a television, a coffee pot area, and a couple of couches, but it was mostly classroom-type chairs and a podium. Naomi figured that Company C, with mostly officers assigned to it and officers who did not live in traditional Army barracks, really did not need a dayroom to pass the time in.

There were only two people in the room, the brunette Naomi had seen at the counter and a dark-skinned man. Naomi walked up to the brunette to introduce herself.

Holding out her hand, Naomi said, "Hi, I'm Naomi Donnelly."

The woman stood to take Naomi's hand, "Hello, Angelina Bethune. Call me Angie."

Naomi saw Captain's bars on Bethune's rank patch on her chest.

The man, also a Captain, saw the introductions and walked over to join the two women. "I'm Ted Gilly."

After they all shook hands, Naomi saw that both of the other two had maroon berets in their hands. "Both of you are Airborne. I'm outnumbered."

Angie gave a little laugh, "Only just barely for me. I graduated from Jump School last Friday. When my detailer told me about the opportunity to transfer from Fort Bliss, Texas to the Pacific Northwest, she never mentioned that my new unit, the 250th Forward Resuscitative Surgical Team, was an airborne unit."

Ted added in, "Yeah, detailers are notorious for missing little things like that. My home unit is the 173rd Airborne Brigade in Italy."

Naomi said, "Me? I'm just a measly weekend warrior. My unit is in Sacramento."

The three nurses sat and exchanged background stories. They were soon joined by several more classmates.

———

Chapter 29

Naomi and her fourteen classmates were watching the PowerPoint presentation on various preoperative complications checklists that a surgical nurse should be aware of in practice. They were in a darkened room watching the various slides on the screen, while Major Fortenoy, one of their Perioperative Nursing instructors, gave her lecture. It was typical of the type of classes they now had at the midway point of their sixteen-week course.

"It is not necessarily a serious complication, but surgical staff should be aware of the status of a patient with any form or level of diabetes. Things to check for are...."

The classroom door opened, and a figure appeared in silhouette in the doorway. The room lights were flicked on, and the class and instructor saw a full bird colonel in the Army Service Dress, 'pink and green,' uniform standing there. Major Fortenoy and most of her students recognized her boss' boss, the Deputy Commander of AMEDD, who ran the Professional Training Branch.

"Atten-Hut!" Major Fortenoy announced. The class jumped to their feet.

"At ease, seats," the colonel countered. Everyone sat down again.

"Sorry to interrupt you, Major. You have a First Lieutenant Naomi Donnelley in your class." It was a statement, not a question.

"Yes sir," came the joint answer of both Major Fortenoy and Naomi, who jumped to her feet.

The colonel took a moment to take stock of Naomi, as she stood at attention by her desk. "Lieutenant Donnelley, unaccustomed as I am to running errands, I have been personally requested by the BAMC Commander, Brigadier General Conroy, to make sure you get delivered for scrub-in at Operating Room Four over at Brooke, Stat! They are apparently in critical need of your specialty."

Naomi looked over at Major Fortenoy with a wide-eyed look. Fortenoy asked the obvious question on Naomi's behalf, "Uh sir? Might I ask what specialty the colonel is referring to here?"

The colonel nodded, "A reasonable question. Brigadier General Conroy tells me an Air Force Medevac flight is on final approach to Randolph Air Force Base. They have a VIP patient on board with critical thoracic and burn injuries. Given the combination of internal and burn injuries, as well as political considerations, they opted out of taking the VIP to Landstuhl Hospital in Germany and flew her directly from Kabul, Afghanistan, to Randolph, and now Brooke. The Air Force Flight Surgeon on the flight reports a serious problem with communicating with the patient, the daughter of the Vice-President of Afghanistan, who only speaks Dari or Afghan Persian."

Naomi's slight nod at this showed her understanding of what was in the works.

The colonel continued, "The Air Force medics recommend finding a surgeon or surgical nurse who speaks Dari to be available when the helicopter transports the patient from the flight line at Randolph to Brooke in about fifteen minutes. The personnel people say there is only one person who can fill that bill on this base right now. Lieutenant Donnelley, your Perioperative Nurse internship just started a few weeks early. Please follow me, I have the shuttle van waiting to take you over there."

Naomi and Major Fortenoy exchanged glances. Naomi quickly stuffed her notes and laptop in her backpack and put her ACU field cap on. The colonel held the door open for her to go out ahead of him.

The colonel smiled at Major Fortenoy, "Sorry for the interruption, Major. As you were. Please make sure Lieutenant Colonel Crosby knows I took Donnelley out of class and make sure her grades aren't impugned by this interruption in her classwork. I'm guessing she may be away for a good bit."

"Yes sir."

———

The van had dropped Naomi off at the Emergency Room entrance. She followed an E.R. nurse's directions to Operating Room Four.

"Anybody using this locker?" Naomi asked a man in surgical scrubs standing in the dress-out area just outside the scrub room. He shook his head and motioned for Naomi to feel free.

Naomi stuffed her backpack, boots, and ACU top in the locker and grabbed a set of surgical scrubs, booties, and clogs from a cart. The women's dressing room had two women in there already. One was a nurse about Naomi's age, and the other was a woman with silver hair cut military short. The silver-haired woman took off her Army Service Uniform, which showed full colonel's insignia, rows of ribbons, Combat Medical Badge, and Nurse Corps lapel insignia. A very senior nurse was scrubbing in for this surgery. Naomi quickly changed out of ACU trousers and t-shirt, looking to the other two women to see if they took off their socks before putting on the scrub booties and clogs. They did not. Back at her locker, she stuffed the rest of her clothes inside. Her backpack made the locker hard to close. She followed the other two women into the scrub room.

Inside the scrub room, an older man was in partial scrubs and holding a clipboard. He was checking in the operating room staff. He nodded to the silver-haired woman, wrote something on his clipboard and said, in greeting, "Colonel Everitt." He raised his eyebrows to the next nurse in an unspoken question. She responded with "Minsky, Carla, Captain, nurse anesthetist, anesthesia assistant." He nodded, wrote something on his clipboard, and then gave Naomi the same raised eyebrow.

Naomi told the clipboard guy, "Donnelley, Naomi, First Lieutenant, I was told to scrub in. Brigadier General Conroy told my commander you needed a surgical nurse who speaks Dari."

Before the clipboard guy could say anything, another man across the room said, "Great, thank goodness, we've been hoping they'd find somebody. Yes, scrub in, but you need to go out to pre-op. That's where they'll bring our patient."

The man came over to Naomi and put out his hand to her, "Hello, I'm Major Cesar Del Rio, the Air Force Medevac Liaison here at Brooke."

Naomi shook his hand, "As I said, I'm First Lieutenant Naomi Donnelly, uh, from AMEDD." She had a feeling nobody wanted to know she was still a student.

"I'm really glad they found you. The flight surgeons on the flight have been screaming for someone like you. It is hard to treat a critically injured patient with whom you cannot communicate. I'll show you where they'll bring her in."

"Wait," said the clipboard bearer. "Before you go, how do you spell your last name, Lieutenant?"

Naomi spelled it for him.

"You familiar with the layout here?" Del Rio asked.

"Not at Brooke, no." The only surgery layout Naomi knew yet was back in Bakersfield.

Major Del Rio waited for Naomi to do a wash-up, get gloves, and get a cap on her hair. Then, the Air Force officer took Naomi out of the back door of the scrub room.

He pointed to double swinging doors nearby, "That's the patient prep room, you'll accompany her in there. You can re-do gloves, gown, and mask in there before going into the surgery arena."

Naomi saw several more people standing near one of the patient pre-op stations. Del Rio took her over there.

"This is our pre-op team. They'll check all the basics, do labs and get her ready to go into the prep room. Your job will be to explain everything to our patient. She is apparently terrified of what is happening to her, and she is in a world she does not understand. You need to be her guardian angel, stay right with her, be aware of any cultural problems she has and deal with them. You are the only one who can do that for her. And, translate everything the staff says to her. Assuming she's conscious, of course. Reports from the flight surgeon say she is going in and out of consciousness. And, they had to anesthetize her for an emergency procedure mid-flight."

The distinctive flutter, far-away, of Blackhawk rotors could be heard and felt by the medical team around Naomi. The Air Force Medevac chopper was arriving on the BAMC helo pad after the cross-town flight from Randolph Air Force Base.

"Sounds like showtime," said one of the men standing nearby.

Another tall man in full scrubs, surgery-ready, came through the Prep Room door and stood nearby. His expression was solemn, and he was not talking to anyone. Naomi assumed this was the primary surgeon, come to see his patient arrive.

"I understand this is the Afghan President's daughter. Right?" asked one of the pre-op nurses.

Del Rio was talking on his cellphone, and since nobody else answered, Naomi said, "I was told she is the Vice-president's daughter. They have two vice-presidents. It is a very important office in Afghanistan. The vice-presidents hold the country's ethnic factions together." Mark had been an information junkie about such things, and Naomi made use of that.

"CNN reported a Taliban attack last night in the capital, Kabul. Must be this," said another nurse.

Major Del Rio was off his phone and now spoke, "Yes, we heard she has serious lower abdomen and leg injuries and bad burn injuries. IED hit her father's car—assassination attempt. Her parents were not injured badly. Their bodyguards and driver are dead. Flight surgeon actually took out one piece of shrapnel near her kidney while in-flight over the Atlantic. He thought it was causing excessive bleeding and decided it couldn't wait."

The first man who had spoken now said, "Wow, they call them flight surgeons, but I didn't know they did full surgeries like that, in flight."

Del Rio responded to this, "She was onboard our best C-17 Globemaster, out of Charleston. It is better equipped than many ground hospitals. They flew her direct from Kabul, refueled in-flight over Greenland."

Their conversation stopped as several people pushed through the swinging doors on the far wall. Del Rio signaled them where to go. Four people in Air Force flight suits wheeled a gurney toward them.

The man Naomi assumed was the surgeon, and one of the men in a flight suit seemed to recognize each other and stood, heads together, apparently talking about their patient.

One by one, the Air Force people handed off responsibilities to the Army staff, and the Air Force team backed off. The patient was moved from the flight gurney to the hospital gurney by lifting the blanket under her. She screamed in pain.

Naomi had watched the process until she heard a young woman's voice scream, *"KamKam Kan! Men kaja histam?"*

Naomi elbowed through the crowd by the gurney and stood near the patient's head. The patient was a young woman, no, a girl, in her teens. She had a few small bandages on her face, and her left wrist was wrapped in gauze, but it was clear most of her injuries were lower. She had a bloody white towel covering her head in an improvised hijab. A blue and white USAF blanket covered her body.

Naomi bent over the girl and tilted her head to look straight into the girl's eyes. Naomi spoke in Dari, *"You will be good now. We are taking care of you."*

The girls' eye widened, and she reached up to grab Naomi's surgical smock. *"Where am I? I was on an airplane."*

As Naomi answered, the Army surgeon and his Air Force peer took their places on the other side of the gurney from Naomi. *"You are in America. Texas. This is a big hospital in America."*

"America?" she sounded awestruck at this.

"Yes, America. My name is Naomi. What is your name?"

"Tarjiila."

The pre-op crew worked on Tarjiila as Naomi spoke to her.

Naomi looked at the surgeon, "What's your name? I need to tell her who you are."

"Lieutenant Colonel Paul Westover."

Naomi motioned from Tarjiila to Westover, as she said, *"Tarjiila, this is Colonel Paul Westover. He is your surgeon. He will help you,"* Naomi hoped she was saying things right. She had used the English word for 'colonel.' She remembered a joke from Persian class in Provo that the word for 'surgeon' was almost the same as for 'giraffe.'

"How bad am I? I hurt so bad," Tarjiila said through clenched teeth.

Naomi looked over to the doctor and said, "She wants to know how bad things are?"

"Tell her the worst is over. She is here now, and we are the best doctors on Earth," Westover said.

Naomi could not help but give a little smile at the humility of the surgeon. She told Tarjiila, *"Doctor Westover says you will be fine now. They will make things better for you."*

Westover now announced, "Let's get her into Prep."

As the gurney started to roll, Tarjiila moved her hand from Naomi's smock to her gloved hand, Tarjiila said, *"Stay with me, Sister."*

"I promise I will not leave you. My job is to stay with you."

The movement of the gurney caused Tarjiila to moan in pain and squeeze Naomi's hand tighter.

Inside the prep room, Naomi bent low and whispered to the girl, *"I need to let go for a moment, I need to wash my hands and get ready to help the surgeon."*

Naomi washed up in the sink next to the Doctor Westover. An assistant helped them both get into new outer gowns, gloves, and masks. Naomi got back to the patient's side just in time to intercept the male orderly, starting to remove the patient's blanket and gown to put a surgical drape over her. Tarjiila grabbed the blanket and rebelled loudly at this.

"Hold on, she's not used to this kind of thing. I'll do it." Naomi told the orderly. "I'll need two drapes and another female to help me."

The orderly shrugged and handed Naomi another drape. Colonel Everitt, in full surgical scrubs and mask, stepped forward to help.

"Colonel, say something, so she knows you are female," Naomi told Colonel Everitt.

Everitt nodded, bent toward the patient, and said, "You are going to be fine, Dear."

Naomi said to Tarjiila, "*This is our head nurse. She will help me get you ready for the doctors.*"

Tarjiila tried to say something but winced in pain. Naomi had done basic surgery prep in Bakersfield, and she had finished the Army class in it a few weeks before. She hoped she remembered everything since she had pushed aside the orderly who usually did this. Naomi had stepped in for the orderly to follow Major Del Rio's orders to take care of the young Moslem girl's fears and cultural angst. She hoped she was up to this.

Naomi stretched the first drape over the patient, and then she and Colonel Everitt carefully took the blanket underneath away and took the girl's remaining gown off under the drape. Naomi and the Colonel laid the girl's arms up on top of the drape. Naomi took Betadine sponges from the orderly's cart and swiped the exposed skin surfaces, above and below the drape. The colonel did the same on the other side. Then, Naomi finished by laying the second drape over the top and pulling the bottom drape that had touched the dirty clothing off of the patient while Everitt held the top drape on her.

Naomi grabbed an elastic hair wrap from the hands of a nurse waiting nearby, reached for the towel/hijab of Tarjiila's head.

"*I need to replace your hijab,*" Naomi to Tarjiila and put the hair wrap on her, stuffing Tarjiila's long black hair inside. The orderly Naomi had replaced grabbed the soiled drape, blanket, gown, and towel headscarf, and stuffed them in the refuse hamper.

Naomi used an alcohol wipe to disinfect around the hairline and the face. The patient was now sterile and fully shielded for surgery, except for the dressings on the wounds, which were the surgeon's responsibility to remove, not the prep nurse. Naomi nodded to Colonel Everitt, who nodded back, giving Naomi a thumbs-up sign. Naomi shook her head and motioned with her head to the colonel that the senior nurse should announce their work complete.

Colonel Everitt announced in a loud voice, "Patient is prepped and ready!"

Naomi turned to the orderly and lifted her hands in the air. "We need new gloves."

The orderly quickly pulled the two nurses' gloves off and pulled new ones on for them.

Naomi returned to Tarjiila's side and told her, *"You are ready. God will be with you."*

Tarjiila tried to smile, *"I will be fine, as God may will it. May God be with the doctor and guide him."*

Naomi looked over to the door to the surgical arena, where Westover stood waiting, gloved hands aloft. Naomi announced, "Colonel Westover, our patient just said a prayer for you. She asked God to go with you into surgery."

"Good, but make sure he scrubs in," Westover replied.

A gentle murmur of laughter went through the Prep Room at this. An orderly pushed open the door to surgery for Westover. Naomi held Tarjiila's hand as the gurney was pushed through the door into the surgical arena.

Naomi could see why they called it a surgical arena, instead of a mere operating room. It was quite literally an arena. It was two stories tall and twice the size of any operating room Naomi had ever been in before. Three rows of theater-like viewing seats were behind glass on two sides on the floor above them. Naomi looked up and saw a couple of the flight-suited Air Force team watching along with several other persons. Brigadier General Conroy was recognizable there. There were not that many black generals around the hospital.

Naomi was still at Tarjiila's side to help the surgical team move Tarjiila over to the surgical table. The move was painful, as they had to physically pick up her body, burns and all.

A boom microphone was moved directly over the table. Two video cameras, each with an operator in scrubs, were also set up away from the table. That was new to Naomi.

The lead anesthetist came over, and Naomi translated his questions and instructions to Tarjiila. Naomi became a bit worried about this. If they were recording this, Naomi's possibly faulty Dari translations were going to be clear for posterity. At last, Captain Minsky, the assistant anesthetist, brought the syringe of milky white Propofol over to give to Tarjiila through her IV port.

Naomi bent low to Tarjiila and explained, *"You will feel warm, moving like a cloud over you, then you will sleep."* Naomi moved her free hand in the air over Tarjiila's body to show the spread of warmth, from arm to chest to head. Minsky nodded when she saw how Naomi was explaining what the patient would feel. Naomi knew the feeling well; Propofol was similar in effect to the Fentanyl Naomi knew so well from her first evening at Napa.

Tarjiila tried to smile and nod to Naomi, who nodded to the anesthetist and the Propofol was injected.

As Tarjiila's thick, black eyelashes fluttered closed, Naomi backed away from the table and stood next to one of the video cameras by the wall. Her job was done, for now, until the patient woke up. Naomi Donnelly had become an Army surgical nurse today. It had not been in the way she had planned or could have foreseen. Then again, it seemed she had been in the right place at the right time today. The unique circumstances of Naomi's curious life had come together for a remarkable and important outcome. Hopefully, it would be successful. It seemed this was part of the destiny Naomi had felt pulling her, but there had to be more than just this.

———

Jesse Manzanares' FBI Academy graduation in Quantico, Virginia, had been on Thursday in late September. He had just enough time to hop a flight to see Naomi's graduation on Friday morning in San Antonio.

Naomi had already introduced Jesse to several of her friends who would be graduating with her. The graduation ceremony in the big auditorium would be combined with a few other professional classes graduating the same week from the AMEDD School. All the graduates were in their full Army Service Uniforms. Naomi had her two new service ribbons above her left breast pocket. Jesse thought Naomi looked fantastic in the throwback 'pink-and-green' uniform. He had never really seen it up close before. With her well-tailored waist of the jacket, Naomi looked like a model ready for a recruiting poster. It was better than the sharp blue dress uniform he had worn when he got out off of active duty in the Army, or the somewhat-ugly old gray-green uniform they had worn when he started ROTC and was first in the Army. The historic 'pink and green' uniform was a vast improvement.

Jesse sat in the friends and family area behind the graduates. The graduates were just getting ready to follow the lists to take their seats in the correct order when Jesse saw a stocky, bald-headed soldier with command sergeant major stripes walk up to Naomi and say something to her. Naomi seemed confused and said something to him. The sergeant major said something else, and Naomi followed him to the stage area, where he had a chair for Naomi at the edge of the cluster of chairs for the senior AMEDD faculty and speakers. Before the sergeant major let Naomi sit down, he pointed out something for her on the stage area near the podium, as though he were giving her walking directions. Jesse could tell Naomi was ill at ease sitting with the senior field grade officers on the stage. Jesse wondered what was going on with all the formality. Before the graduation ceremony started, Jesse saw a colonel walk up to Naomi, who stood up. The colonel shook Naomi's hand. Something interesting was in the works for Jesse's girlfriend.

The colonel who had spoken to Naomi stood at the podium and introduced himself as the Deputy Commander of the Army Medical Department Center and School. He announced and welcomed several dignitaries, and congratulated the various student classes for their achievements in their medical education at AMEDD Center and School.

After the colonel finished with his preliminaries, he turned to the audience and said, "Before we have our usual graduation and academic award presentations, today, we have a special honor to bestow on one of our students. To do so, I am honored to introduce Colonel Gwyneth Everitt, Chief of Nursing Services for Brooke Army Medical Center. Colonel Everitt holds the Distinguished Service Medal for service in Operation Enduring Freedom and wears the Army Combat Medical Badge for service in Afghanistan and Iraq. Colonel Everitt."

A woman with silver hair and far more decorations on her Army Service Uniform than just the Distinguished Service Medal that was mentioned came to the podium. She carried a blue folder and a smaller blue box. She cleared her throat and spoke, "I am particularly honored to be here today, as I had the opportunity to work beside our honoree today. I got to meet and work with a young Army nurse, who exemplifies the skills and service all of our graduates today should strive for in service to the country.

"In early August I was in my office at Brooke Army Medical Center, when I got a phone call from our commanding general informing me of a situation that started with an assassination attempt on the life of the vice-president of Afghanistan. The vice-president and his wife had survived, but several others had not, and the vice-president's young daughter had been horribly wounded and burned by an improvised explosive device. A U.S. Navy field medical team had responded to the incident, along with Afghan medics. Due to the serious injuries and burns suffered by the vice-president's daughter, she was transported for treatment at the U.S. military medical facility at Bagram Air Force Base. A decision was made to get this young woman, whose father has been an essential ally of the United States throughout the Afghan hostilities to the finest medical care possible. Because of the severe nature of her injuries, in particular, her burns, it was decided to medevac her to our Burn Center at Brooke Army Medical Center. She was put on an Air Force C-17 medevac flight that was re-routed from its normal destination at Landstuhl Germany, to here, in San Antonio. The commanding general told me he was calling his Chief Nurse and Chief Surgeon to ensure we were directly involved in getting this important young woman the best medical care possible. Even though it had been a number of years since I had personally scrubbed in as a surgical nurse, the general's call made it clear he wanted my personal attention to this case.

"While we waited for the flight, we got word the young woman's situation was so dire that the Air Force flight surgeon in charge of the flight had decided to undertake the unusual action of actually conducting surgery on the girl while airborne to remove shrapnel from her abdomen that was endangering her life.

"While I was scrubbing in outside the operating room, I happened to notice a young Army nurse walk in and announce to the Surgery NCOIC that she was the surgical nurse who spoke the Afghan Dari language, that the Medical Center Commanding General had ordered to be ready since our young patient did not speak English. This young nurse scrubbed in and made ready to assume her duties as surgical nurse and translator.

"A few moments later, this young nurse accompanied the patient into the Surgery Prep room, translating for the patient and the other medical staff. When she realized this young Moslem woman was severely uncomfortable having a male surgical orderly disrobe her and prep her for surgery, this young nurse immediately took charge of the situation and started presurgical preparations of the patient. She asked for another female nurse to assist her, and I stepped forward. To my mind, this young nurse did an outstanding job, establishing a sterile field for the patient, cleaning her up and dressing her for surgery under a surgical drape, all the while consoling the young women in her native language. I watched and followed the directions of this young surgical nurse who did her job prepping the patient as though she had done it a thousand times. In the end, she signaled me she thought the patient was properly prepped, and I concurred, announcing it to the chief surgeon. Just before we went into surgery, this nurse told the chief surgeon that the patient had just told her she was praying for the surgeon and that the Afghan girl had asked God to be with the surgeon as he operated. The surgeon told the nurse to make sure God had properly scrubbed in."

The audience laughed at this, as did Jesse. He now realized that the young nurse they were talking about was probably his Naomi, but he was confused… *How did Naomi know how to speak the Dari language?*

Colonel Everitt continued, "The nurse helped get our patient into the surgical arena and explained what she could expect with the anesthesia. As the anesthesia took effect, the nurse backed away from the table, and let the various surgeons and their teams do their jobs. She waited on the periphery for when the patient would be awakened after surgery and would need her language services, again. But, given the severe injuries to the patient, internal shrapnel wounds, orthopedic trauma, and severe burns, there were at times three different surgical teams at work around the table. Eventually, this nurse and I were called on to help with the clearance of used tools and other assistance for the three teams of surgeons. The burn surgeon apparently assumed this young nurse who appeared at his elbow was there to assist him, so he gave here various tasks to perform and asked her to bring things forward for him.

At one point, this burn specialist asked this nurse to be a third set of hands for him holding forceps as the surgeon and his primary nurse removed charred skin from the girl's burned leg. I saw her move in when asked to assist the burn team, professionally and competently, as though she was a part of it. Three hours later, when the surgeons' work in the operating room was complete, the burn specialist told this nurse that she 'could leave now' and she told him she had to stay for the patient to wake up. For the first time, the burn specialist apparently realized that the surgical nurse who had been assisting him was actually in the room to be the patient's language translator.

"I next saw this nurse several hours later, when I visited the patient's room with the commanding general. She was standing bedside, translating for the staff and the patient, and the patient held tight to her hand like the nurse was her sister. The Army nurse had truly become this young girl's guardian angel. When I stopped by the following morning, this nurse was still beside the patient's bed; she had apparently slept in a chair in the room, always ready to speak for and to the patient as there was nobody else who could do that for her. I immediately called the hospital OB-Gyn department and ordered an Iranian/American perinatal technician, who spoke a bit of Farsi/Dari, to report to the patient's room to let this valiant young nurse get some well-deserved rest.

"Then, when I asked if this nurse needed a ride to her housing, she finally informed me that she was a temporary resident in the Army hotel across the street, since she was, in fact, just a student in the Perioperative Nursing class here at AMEDD." Some in the audience chuckled at this. "I was shocked to realize that this competent surgical nurse whose lead in prepping the surgery patient I had followed and assisted was only in her ninth week of surgical nurse training. She had been amazing.

"That brings us to today. The young woman from Afghanistan is back home, fully recovered. I understand the vice-president of the Islamic Republic of Afghanistan is grateful for the medical services provided to his daughter. The Secretary of Defense has acknowledged that efforts of the initial Navy medical team on the ground in Kabul, the Air Force Medevac and Flight Surgeon team who brought the patient to America and the Army surgery team here at Brooke Army Medical Center were truly a Joint Service operation in the truest sense and has ordered an appropriate recognition of the work of the various people involved. With that, I turn this over to AMEDD Command Sergeant Major Kinsey."

The sergeant major, who had taken Naomi to the stage, now went over to Naomi and walked her to a spot near the podium. Naomi stood at attention and faced the audience. Jesse was impressed at how she looked up there. Colonel Everitt and the AMEDD deputy commander stood next to Naomi.

The sergeant major went to the microphone and said, "Please stand." He waited as the faculty onstage and the audience stood up. He continued, "Attention to Orders."

He read from a blue folder on the podium.

"By order of the Chairman, Joint Chiefs of Staff, U.S. Department of Defense;

"1st Lieutenant Naomi Lynne Donnelley, United States Army Reserve, 7305th Medical Training Support Battalion, distinguished herself by exceptionally meritorious service while on temporary duty at Brooke Army Medical Center, during the period August 9th through August 17th of this year. Called upon on very short notice to assume the duties of both surgical nurse and translator during emergency treatment of a family member of a senior leader of the Islamic Republic of Afghanistan, Lieutenant Donnelley, carried out both her life-saving duties as a surgical nurse and her duties as a translator of the native language of her patient with extreme competence and efficiency, thus allowing a joint team of surgeons, nurses and medical personnel to treat and save the life of their patient, and bring credit upon the Armed Forces of the United States of America. Lieutenant Donnelley's tireless efforts and steadfast dedication to her duties as a nurse over a critical eight-day period reflected the highest level of service to her nursing profession. The performance of Lieutenant Donnelley, in conjunction with the work of her colleagues in the U.S. Navy, the U.S. Air Force, and the U.S. Army, through her and their distinctive accomplishments, reflected credit upon herself, and the Department of the Defense."

When the sergeant major finished reading the award of the Joint Service Commendation Medal, he handed the blue folder and blue box to Colonel Everitt, who opened the box. She pinned a blue, white, and green striped ribbon with a golden eagle hanging below it to Naomi's pocket. Colonel Everitt closed the box as she gave Naomi a salute. Naomi returned the salute. Naomi was directed back to her chair on the stage, and she was given the box and folder. The audience broke out in applause, and Naomi's classmates cheered.

When quiet was returned, the graduation ceremony continued with nurse anesthetists, nurse practitioners, psychiatric technician specialists, pharmacists, and the other professional classes each having their students called up onstage alphabetically to accept their diplomas. The last person called in most classes was the Honor Graduate, the top student, which, in almost all cases also earned an Army Achievement Medal.

Finally, Naomi's Perioperative Nursing class was announced. Jesse noticed that the 'D' in the alphabet was passed without 'Donnelley' being called. When the last of Naomi's classmates had received her diploma, the colonel from AMEDD announced, "I'm sure that those of you who have been paying attention will note that I have not called the name of our surgical nurse who received the Joint Service Commendation Medal earlier. But, yes, in spite of missing the better part of two weeks of classes, Lieutenant Donnelly is our honor graduate for the perioperative nursing curriculum, and she gets an Army Achievement Medal to keep her Joint Service Commendation Medal company. So," he paused, "1ˢᵗ Lieutenant Naomi Donnelley, the honor graduate for this class of MOS 66E, Perioperative Nurse."

Naomi stood up and crossed the stage to get her diploma, and another box and folder. This time the folder and box were Army green, not Defense Department blue.

After Naomi had received her diploma and award, the colonel announced the ceremony was over, "Godspeed to our graduates."

Jesse had to wait to get close to Naomi and congratulate her. He was not the only one proud of Naomi this day. He would get to tell Naomi what he thought of her on the car trip back to California tomorrow. Jesse's concern when Naomi had announced her intention of becoming an Army nurse seemed to be overblown. This was going to be alright.

Her Army Reserve active duty for training was at an end, and Naomi was coming home to California. However, Jesse still wanted to know where and when she had learned the Dari language. There were a lot of strange pieces to put together in this puzzle that was Naomi.

—

Part Four

Chapter 30

Naomi had only met the young x-ray technician who had sub-rented Naomi's spot in the apartment with Ayla once, back in the spring. Now, six months later, Naomi and Jesse got a chilly glance from the girl as she carried out her stuff to vacate the apartment now that Naomi was back in October. Jesse was helping Naomi move back in, and the x-ray technician apparently did not want her residence a block away from the hospital to end.

"Wow, if looks could kill," said Naomi to Jesse.

"You can't really blame her. Moving is a big hassle, and this location is prime for you medical types – walking distance to work," Jesse said, as he balanced a box and opened the apartment door with his other hand.

Ayla was running the vacuum cleaner in the bedroom the temporary roommate had just vacated.

"Ayla, I can do that," Naomi protested.

"Naw, I got it. I'm so glad to have you back, Naomi. Little Miss Mood Swings and Leave-it-Where-You-Used-It really made me appreciate Naomi. She really got sort of bitchy when I reminded her she had to leave in October. When she started to suggest maybe you could find another place, I pointed out to her the bed she was sleeping in, not to mention the couch and the TV, and, you know… were all Naomi's."

"Where is she going now?" Jesse asked, as he set the boxes in Naomi's bedroom.

Ayla said, "Not quite sure. Don't care. Just glad Naomi is back."

"Naomi, can you wait to unpack 'til later. I have someplace I want to go now, with you," Jesse said.

"Someplace to go at noon on a Sunday. You already ate. Where you want to go?" Naomi asked.

"Just someplace… I'll tell you when we get there."

Naomi looked at Ayla and raised her eyebrows, "Sure, Jess. Whatever. Am I dressed right to go to 'just someplace?'"

"You're fine. I'll get that last box from the truck."

———

The big pick-up truck continued out of town on the Westside Parkway.

"You're awfully quiet. Where we going?" Naomi asked Jesse again.

"If I had wanted to tell you, I would have told you when I asked you to come with me."

"Why can't you tell me?"

"Because if I told you, you'd ask me all kinds of questions, and we would be all talked out by the time we get there. This way, at least, there is a bit of suspense."

"So, this is a surprise?"

"No, not a real surprise. Not yet. Just something new to do and think about for us."

Seeing where they were heading, Naomi asked, "We're not going to Ray and Janet's are we."

"Nope," Jesse said, and he put on his blinker to exit the Westside Parkway, a mile before the turn-off to the Morrison's. He headed south.

Naomi now added, "We are headed out into the boonies."

"Nope."

Jesse turned west after a couple miles. Naomi saw they were driving by a new housing development. She thought Jesse might be taking her to look at homes, but he passed the model homes and their multiple flapping flags on poles. Jesse turned into a freshly paved street in an area filled with construction equipment, partially completed new homes and stacks of lumber.

Naomi saw Jesse pull a Post-it note off his speedometer screen and checked something on it, before wadding up the note. He stopped in front of one of the lots that only had a foundation poured and nothing else built. It had a sign in front of it saying, 'Lot B-118, Model IV, Elevation 1 – SOLD.'

Jesse stopped the truck and turned off the ignition. "Let's look around."

Naomi hopped out of the truck before Jesse could get around to assist her. Jesse jumped over the freshly poured curbing and put out his hand to help Naomi over the rough ground heading up to where the foundation was poured.

With no information coming from Jesse, Naomi started her questions, "What is this? You didn't buy a house, did you?"

Jesse looked at her like she had just said an off-color joke, "No, of course not." Jesse waited a bit before continuing, "This is where Pete and Silvia, and the new baby will be moving in January. He called me to let me know their mortgage got approved."

"Hmm, little brother has a new baby and a mortgage. I bet your mother will be hassling you over that, huh?"

Jesse gave Naomi a look that rivaled the 'if looks could kill' expression she had gotten from Ayla's interim roommate.

"You know Jesse, you've got your VA loan you haven't used, with your salary you wouldn't have any trouble getting out of that little apartment of yours."

Jesse gave Naomi another 'look' and said, "Duh? Let's go look at the models now."

—

Naomi and Jesse had spent the afternoon looking at model homes. They went through seven different models of the two builders in the area. They shared their thoughts about "this is nice" and "small bedrooms" with each other, but much of the banter came for Naomi. Jesse was his usual quiet self. Only once, when he mumbled something about 'plenty of room for swing sets and stuff,' did he approach any discussion of what his motivation for this housing tract review was. Naomi was annoyed but held her tongue. She knew who she was dealing with, but she had not yet cracked Jesse code for getting him to talk about their future together. Naomi realized that the simple act of bringing her out here with him was a jump for Jesse.

On the way back into the city, Naomi was thumbing through real estate brochures. "What did you think of the different lots?" she asked him.

Jesse thought for a moment, and then answered, "The Elevation 5 for the big house, the last one on the row, at the first place we went to was nice."

Naomi turned to that page. "The one with the RV parking? You planning on getting an RV?"

"Dunno, maybe."

"Or, you could just park your SWAT Team's Bear Cat there. That would be handy, huh?"

Naomi got another 'look' from Jesse. "I wasn't thinking about the RV parking, I liked the five bedrooms and a big back yard."

"Five bedrooms, sounds like Jesse has some expansion plans in mind." Naomi tried pushing the conversation.

"Dunno, maybe."

Naomi gritted her teeth. She relented, pulled her cellphone out of her purse, and said, "I guess I ought to call Rusty's Pizza for carryout on the way back, huh?"

"Sounds like a plan," Jesse answered.

"The one by your place or mine?"

"Yours. You still need to unpack."

Naomi looked over at Jesse. She realized she had gotten all she would out of him. She saw he was biting his lip and nodding his head minutely with a slight curl at the corner of his lips. He was having good 'Jesse' thoughts. Someday, Naomi would figure out how to get him to tell her those thoughts.

———

The morning's schedule of four arthroscopic surgeries was complete. Naomi considered such operations to be the easiest to handle. Less mess, very little needed in the way of dressings, and fewer potential complications. She dumped her surgical clothing in the hamper and got her street clothes out of the locker.

In the months since she got back from Texas, things had gotten into a groove. Her time with Jesse was good, in all respects. They were both happy together, but Jesse had not followed up on the idea about the house or anything else about making future plans. She did not press things, as her life was fairly full right now.

Naomi checked her iPhone for messages.

Her iPhone showed the little green dot on the icon that a voice message was waiting. She assumed it was either Jesse or the nursing coordinator giving her the schedule for tomorrow. However, when she looked, it was from an area code she did not recognize. *253?*

The iPhone voice mail app had done a transcription for her, which she read instead of listening, "Hello, this message is for Naomi Donnelley. This is Major Robert _____, calling from Joint Base Lewis McChord in Washington. I need to speak to Lieutenant Donnelley on a matter of some urgency. Please call me back at 253-_____47."

Naomi shook her head at the transcription. The app never really seemed to get the whole message right. She listened to the recorded voice to clarify the man's name and the full phone number. She made a new contact entry of Major Robert Brightman's name and phone number. She would call him at lunch.

———

A young man's voice recited very rapidly, "This is the 62nd Medical Brigade. This is a non-secure line. How may I help you, sir or ma'am?"

Naomi had to stop and think for a second, after that introduction. She replied, "This is Lieutenant Naomi Donnelley, returning Major Brightman's call."

"One moment, ma'am. I'll see if the major is in."

Naomi waited on hold for several minutes.

"Lieutenant Donnelley?"

"Yes sir."

"Sorry about that delay. I was in the middle of another important call, and I had to get all the information before I could get to you. Thank you for calling back so promptly."

"Yes sir. How can I help you?"

"Well, let me introduce myself and explain why I'm calling, and then you'll probably have some questions.

"I'm Major Rob Brightman, the S-1 with the 62nd Medical Brigade here at Fort Lewis. One of the units under our Brigade here is the 250th Forward Resuscitative Surgical Team or FST. Are you familiar with our unit or FSTs in general?"

Naomi answered, "Yes sir. In general. Angie Bethune, ah, Captain Bethune was in my class at Fort Sam Houston, and she told me about being assigned to the 250th."

"Yes, Angie told me about having met you there. That is how I knew to call you."

"Call me about…?" Naomi asked.

"Yes, I'm getting the cart before the horse a bit here," Brightman seemed to pause, and then proceeded, "Angie mentioned you had gone through the surgical nursing class with her and that you happened to know the Dari language. Our brigade has just been informed we are getting tasked with a short term and short notice deployment to Afghanistan of an FST to fill in for a manpower shortage amongst the NATO contingent there. The 250th will be the FST sent over, and due to the needs in-country, the 250th will be augmented with some extra personnel beyond those normally assigned to an FST. We are running short of active duty people to fill the needed slots without impinging on other units' deployment plans or repeat deploying people. Army HRC has given us permission to call reservists to see if you would be interested in deploying with the 250th to Bagram Air Base for a six or seven-month deployment."

Naomi struggled with words to respond, "Well, I…,you know I am so new in the Reserves that I really don't know how such things work. You sound like you are asking me if I want to do it, and I didn't know getting called up for deployment was a voluntary thing."

Brightman gave a little chuckle, "Well, you are right about that, but not in this particular case. This isn't a matter of calling up a whole reserve unit to go on active duty and deploy. That would be involuntary for the entire unit, but it would also require orders for the call-up of the reserves with orders on the level of the Army secretary. What is happening here is a special deployment of an active duty unit, and we are trying to see if we can augment that active-duty unit with reservists. And, reservists can volunteer to be called up to fill a necessary active duty slot.

"Also, for a separate reason, this would be a matter of volunteering. The 250th is an Airborne designated unit, and any personnel assigned to it for foreign deployment should be airborne qualified. Army Jump School is a voluntary thing, for most people."

"Ah, yes, Angie told me about going through Jump School just before she got to San Antonio," Naomi said.

Brightman continued, "Right, the current people assigned to the 250th are all airborne qualified. We have a couple of people from other active-duty units who are getting qualified and will be assigned to the 250th. We are still short a couple people, hence my call to you. Let me explain in a bit more detail.

"An FST typically includes 20 staff members: 4 surgeons, 3 RNs, one or two who are perioperative trained, 2 certified registered nurse anesthetists, 1 administrative officer, 1 detachment sergeant, 3 licensed practical nurses

(LPN)'s, 3 surgical techs and 3 medics. The team is meant to be attached to other forward-deployed medical units, like a medical company or hospital unit, to provide the surgical expertise not found in the normal unit. The idea arose out of Viet Nam to get the surgeons as close to the action as possible, to be able to provide care in the critical first hour after the injury. In the present case, they are supplementing the existing joint service and NATO medical detachment at Bagram, and it is estimated they need three extra nurses and three surgeons beyond the normal FST. We were hoping you would be interested in being one of the RNs."

"So, you are asking me to volunteer for three weeks of Army Jump School and for a seven-month deployment to Afghanistan?"

"Yes, and Army HRC says that even though this is a short deployment that it will count as a deployment for any reservists, so you would be credited with having deployed should any future situation come up where reservists are called upon to deploy. You would then be last in line if you wish. You could avoid a long twelve to fourteen-month deployment if there is a major deployment of reserves in the future."

Naomi commented, "Major, that carrot you are holding out doesn't sound that attractive."

"And, of course, there is the fact that a junior officer reservist who has deployed is virtually guaranteed early promotion to captain and major when the time comes. The bottom line is that you would be coming back in six or seven months with every ticket punched that a young Army nurse could hope for at this stage of their service. You would have a line on your nursing resume second to none. You will have served in the most critical job in nursing, a forward-deployed surgical trauma nurse."

"When would this be happening?" Naomi asked.

"I am not exactly sure what happened to cause the shortage, but they say they need the 250th at Bagram by mid-February. With the whole unit doing pre-deployment workups at Fort Benning in early February, we would have to get you to Jump School in the first class after the New Year. We have a spot set aside for you if you want it."

"When would you need to know my decision?" Naomi was worried about the answer to this query.

"HRC says that if I cannot get a reservist to bite, they will be assigning an active duty nurse who is airborne qualified and already deployed a short while back, and they need to let her or him know a month ahead."

"So, I have to tell you in a couple weeks or so? First weeks of December?"

"Preferably sooner. We have to get this through Washington and your current reserve unit."

"One question. Don't you have a number of perioperative nurses in the reserves? You seem to be focusing on me."

"Lieutenant Donnelley, we are putting together a cadre of qualified surgical professionals to send to Afghanistan. It would be nice to have someone on the team who can speak the language, and I understand you do."

"Ah, yes. You did mention speaking Dari earlier. Should have figured that one out without your help." Naomi tried to think about what else she needed to know. "Major, as you can guess, this is going to be a tough decision. My significant other is going to have a cow that I would even consider this, uh, volunteer opportunity. Do you think you can have Angie Bethune call me? She probably has some good perspective to give me on the unit and what she knows."

"Certainly, and I will send you an email to your AKO account, giving you some other things you need to know if you are going to be accepting these orders."

"Thank you, Major, and I am probably going to have other questions once I get a chance to think about this."

"Sure, call me at any time. I'll put my cell in the email. And, you are right, talking to Angie will help you make the decision, but from the way she talks about you, she probably has a vested interested in convincing you to go over there with her. She speaks very highly of you. I hope to hear back from you shortly."

"Yes, Major, I understand. Let me think about this."

Naomi ended the call and put her cell phone away. She had, of course, known that a call like this might come to her in the Reserves. Jesse had warned her of just this, repeatedly. But, this was not the impossible-to-avoid deployment in a national emergency. This would be Naomi volunteering to leave home and Jesse. This was an opportunity to fulfill the urge, no, the destiny she had felt was pulling her, ever since she had started to put together the pieces of this crazy life that had been handed her. The hardest part was obvious, talking to Jesse about this. Discussing this with the guy who had been opposed to her Army nursing career and who had a dark cloud over his psyche with 'Afghanistan' written on it was going to be awful. Naomi had to think about how to do that. There was no good way to do it. Naomi wished she knew more about Jesse's hostility to her being in the Reserves. She wished she could tell him about herself, the real Naomi. Someday, maybe.

———

SMS Text:

JAM4614: Nomy, you are probably still in surgery, so I thought I would leave a text with this. I will be in field training exercise out by Kernville this afternoon, so bad cell service. My Mom wants to know if you and I could do Thanksgiving at her place this year. Lucia and her crew will be down from Fresno, and Pete and Silvia, too, since their house isn't ready, yet. Whole Manzanares brood will be there. I know it is short notice, but....

Later:

Naomi.Donnelley: Jess, Sure, it sounds nice. I was going to call you about Turkey Day. Ray and Janet are going to Colorado to be with their son and his family, so it works perfectly. Ask Adele if I can bring something to contribute to the meal. What time would we get there? I need to know about my food dish ASAP, so I can pick up makings after work.

JAM4614: Mom says we can bring some dessert or munchies for watching the football games. I can get stuff if you are busy. Tell me what to buy.

Naomi.Donnelley: I will buy TG stuff myself. Usually get my best ideas standing in the grocery aisle at Ralph's. CUL8R.

—

Adele and Manny's little ranch house was packed with people. A folding card table sat near the regular dinner table. After the big feast was over, Silvia, Lucia, and Naomi had pushed Adele toward the overstuffed chair, and they had taken over the cleanup. Manny, his sons, and son-in-law were in the living room watching the Detroit Lions lose to somebody. The little Cooper kids were using a new Google handheld video game to entertain themselves. Silvia had put her baby to bed in the bedroom Pete and Jesse had once shared.

After the initial cleanup was finished, Naomi took the munchies tray she had put together out to the living room and put it in front of the football-watching men. They initially groaned at not being able to eat anything else, but Naomi saw them start to nibble as soon as she set the tray down.

The seating in the living room was full, so Naomi sat in the end chair at the dining table and watched the game. Lucia was seated on the arm of the armchair her husband sat in. Adele and Silvia had disappeared in the direction of where the baby slept. Naomi got up and went to the sliding door that looked out on the back yard. She saw the picnic table on the patio was clear and the weather outside was nice. She decided she would ask Jesse to go outside with her to talk about the call from Washington state. She was not sure that having an intense discussion with him in this locale was the best place, but it had some advantages. He probably would not totally 'blow up' in front of his family. She went into the living room and whispered in his ear. Jesse followed her out to the picnic table after grabbing a few more of her munchies.

Naomi patted the picnic table across from where she sat down. Jesse sat, facing her, with a questioning look on his face. Naomi reached forward to take one of Jesse's hands and took a deep breath before she began talking.

———

Adele Manzanares came to the kitchen to warm her grandbaby's Gerber's Apricot Mixed Fruit jar in a bowl of hot water. She looked out the window, and saw Jesse and Naomi sitting together on the patio. At first, Adele just saw the two holding hands and thought the couple was just having an intimate conversation. But, she saw the look on her son's face, and then he pulled his hand away from Naomi's grasp. Adel could not remember having seen Jesse angry like that—not in a long, long time. Adele turned away from the window so that she was not caught spying on the couple. She wondered what the problem could possibly be. Naomi had been with Jesse for nearly three years now. Adele assumed this argument was about her son's obvious slowness to commit to Naomi and their future. Adele wished Naomi well if that were the case. Naomi would be an excellent addition to the family.

———

The ride home from Jesse's parents' house had been in silence. Jesse pulled into the parking space at Naomi's apartment and turned off the truck. They both sat in the truck in silence.

Finally, Naomi broke the silence with, "So, that's it? Silence from Jesse?"

Jesse looked straight ahead, out of the windshield as he spoke, "I'm not sure what else you expect from me. You knew before you said anything what my reaction would be. This is exactly what I didn't want to happen." He paused, and then added, "No, it's worse than that. This isn't the Army doing it to you, this is you telling me you want to volunteer. You want to volunteer yourself into my worst nightmare."

"I don't really know why it is such a nightmare. I'm gonna be at a hospital on the biggest American base, near the capital city. It is a lot different from back when you were there, and it is not out on the front lines like you were."

'Nomy, I don't think there is much else to talk about here. I realize you really weren't telling me this to get my opinion on your decision. You obviously decided you were going to go before you ever told me. This is all part of some big plan of yours that you have only been half honest with me about. You decided to join the Army Reserves when it did not really seem necessary, at least to me. When I asked why you had taken Farsi in college, your answer sounded half-baked. Now, you volunteer to go to a war zone. And, you give me that crock about having to fulfill some destiny. This isn't destiny; this is Naomi coming up with some wild plan for her future that she couldn't level with Jesse about. It is about Naomi's plans, not Naomi and Jesse's plans."

"Jesse, that isn't the way it is. Not at all."

"Naomi, it is the way I see it."

They sat in silence again.

"Let's both think about this and talk again," Naomi suggested.

Jesse waited, and then said, "Okay, when do you need to tell them?"

"Next week."

"I don't suppose there is anything I can say that will change your mind. The way I am reading this, you are going to say yes, no matter what I say. Right?"

"Maybe."

"'Maybe' is Nomy-speak for 'yes.'"

More silence.

Jesse asked, "What if I told you I planned on buying the 5-bedroom house we looked at, and I want to elope to Vegas right now."

Naomi gave Jesse her best attempt at a dirty look and said, "I'd tell you we went house-hunting almost two months ago, in October. You're a bit late, it's December next week. And, that attempt to bribe me was insulting. That is not the way I want to get proposed to for marriage."

"I had to try. I'm getting desperate."

"Sounds like it. Kind of sad that you have to be desperate to ask me about marriage," Naomi picked up her purse, indicating she was ready to get out. "Jesse, I think you are right. I'm planning on telling them yes. And, that will give you seven months to work on your proposal technique. If you are still interested, when all this is done."

"I'm pretty sure I will be."

"Good."

Jesse walked Naomi to her door, but their goodnight kiss was missing something.

Chapter 31

It was a cold, blustery January day. The sun was nearly down in the west. On the way out to Lawson Army Airfield, Naomi and her fellow trainees loaded the buses at the Airborne School across the street from the two 250-foot Jump Towers they had mastered the week before. The olive-drab Army buses were poorly heated, but few noticed that fact. It was their second trip of the day. They had already done one jump that morning. The high winds the previous day had precluded the night jump, and they were doing it now, late on Thursday, their last day of training. They would graduate tomorrow. Hopefully.

Naomi exited the bus and headed into the hangar. She did her best to hide the limp she had developed after the Wednesday morning jump. The jumpmasters could pull you from the stick if they thought you were injured. Naomi was not the only one hiding sore muscles or sprained ankles.

As with their previous four jumps, they assembled in the hangar, donned their chutes, and then were checked and re-checked by jumpmasters before going into the Ready Room to wait for boarding the C-17 aircraft they heard roaring to life out on the tarmac. This time, the hangar had red lights on to help the jumpers preserve their night-vision for the jump.

At a whistle from the head jumpmaster, the first stick lined up at the door to go board the plane. As they waited, Naomi felt a tap on her shoulder from behind.

She turned to see an Army Field Artillery captain, who towered over her, one of her fellow trainees. He shouted above the noise from the C-17 outside, "Lieutenant, mind if I ask you a question?"

"No, go ahead."

"At the risk of sounding like a troglodyte or misogynist, what in the hell is a woman with your looks doing here. You ought to be wearing Gucci pumps, not jump boots."

Naomi gave a little laugh, "Captain, you're right about sounding misogynistic, would you believe my fiancé is a Ranger, and he wants our children to be pure-blooded Airborne."

"You're kidding."

"You're right. I am kidding. The truth is my country needs somebody in Kabul who knows how to put broken bodies back together, and you can't do that very easily in Gucci pumps. Hoo-ah, Captain."

Naomi abruptly turned around and ignored the captain as they waddled in their heavy gear out to board the C-17. Naomi adjusted the heavy elastic headband on her black Army-issued glasses. You did not want to lose your glasses during a jump. As she had been taught, she covered her left eye with one hand to keep one eye away from the glare of floodlights on the tarmac. With her night vision preserved by the red lights, her left eye would still be able to see in the dark.

The C-17 also had red lights on inside the cargo bay. It was a very short flight from Lawson Field south to Fryar Drop Zone. The C-17 circled once to gain altitude and leveled off at 1250 feet, Course 180. They were given the command to stand up and hook up their ripcords on the overhead cable. Everyone checked the gear of the person in front of them. The assistant jumpmaster ran down the stick for a final check. The green light went on, and Naomi followed the others and jumped out of the starboard side door into the dark, night air. It was a totally different experience than the day jumps. She could barely see her chute unfurl above her in the partial moonlight, but she saw nothing else but darkness. At the last second, she saw the grassy ground of Fryar Field coming up to meet her. She hit the ground and rolled as she had been trained. Her ankle complained mightily, as did her buttocks.

The blustery wind made deflating and gathering up her billowing chute difficult. But, she did it without having to disengage the quick-release buckles. She dragged the bundle over to the rally point, bagged it up, and waited for the next stick to land. They had done it. She had done it. Four day jumps and a night jump. Her three weeks at Jump School were a success. First Lieutenant Naomi Lynne Donnelley was a paratrooper—Airborne.

———

Naomi and the two other reservists slated for the 250th finished Jump School on Friday were the first to arrive at the Overseas Deployment Center (ODC) at Fort Benning. The rest of the 250th flew in from Seattle on Friday night, and the unit ODC briefing started Saturday morning. The group meeting at ODC was Naomi's first opportunity to meet the people with whom she would spend the next seven months in Afghanistan.

Angie Bethune gave Naomi a hug when they saw each other. Angie then went around, introducing Naomi to the other people. Naomi tried to remember the twenty-plus names but knew it was hopeless. She would have to remember their names as she got the know them.

"This is Captain Evans, one of our surgeons," Angie said, as the person she was introducing turned to meet Naomi. Captain Evans was a blonde with the same Pixie haircut as Naomi, standing nose to nose with her.

Naomi blinked in surprise and recognition. It took her a moment to remember the woman's first name, "Lindsey?"

The young Army surgeon was also having trouble remembering names. She pointed her finger at Naomi and said, "You're... You're..."

"Naomi," she reminded her. Immediately, Naomi got worried. This doctor knew things about Naomi that she did not want to be common knowledge in the Army. Naomi's days as a patient at Napa State Hospital were... well, no longer part of her being.

Captain Lindsey Evans now remembered, "Yes, Naomi from N..."

Naomi cut her off, "Yes, back home in California. I can't believe we meet again like this."

From her expression, Naomi realized Lindsey Evans knew why Naomi had cut her off.

"Naomi, you are our new surgical nurse?" Evans asked, a bit incredulously.

Naomi thought, and answered, "Yes, and I have you to blame for all of this. If you will remember, you were the one who gave me that first nursing magazine."

"I had forgotten about that." Lindsey shook her head at the irony, then smiled, "We'll have to compare notes. It seems like we'll be spending a lot of time together in the coming months. We have lots to catch up on." The last sentence was spoken as though it had hidden meaning.

"That is for sure." Naomi now had yet another weird coincidence in her life to remember. Doctor Lindsey Evans, one of the first people she had met as Naomi, was back in Naomi's life.

The instructor from ODC was up at the podium. "If everyone could take their seats. We have a lot to cover to get you ready for deployment next week."

———

The commander of the 250th Forward Resuscitative Surgical Team, Lieutenant Colonel Darren Kazinsky, had asked everything to get together at an on-post restaurant, Zaxby's, to build some camaraderie and get to know each other after the first day of pre-deployment briefings at Fort Benning. There was even one new member of the unit who had just arrived that Saturday evening, Sergeant Mitzi Riordan, an LPN, the last member of the deploying team, who had been given scant notice.

Kazinsky made a short speech, welcoming Mitzi and the other new members, like Naomi. Everybody was still in their ACUs. Naomi liked the group she would be living with for the next months of the pending deployment. They tried their best to make the new people feel at home.

While everyone was talking, Naomi's cell phone went off. She answered, started to get up, and leave the table. She replied, "Hi, Jess, I'm in a restaurant, let me go outside... No, wait, ... I can easily... I understand... Call me whenever you get done. I'll be worrying if you don't call. It doesn't matter how late. Love ya."

Instead of going outside to take the call, Naomi sat back down and slapped the cellphone onto the table with obvious frustration.

Angie was sitting next to Naomi, "Your guy calling?"

"Yeah, we had said we would talk tonight. Now, he calls me to tell me he is just starting a surveillance stakeout of a drug cartel warehouse, and he doesn't want me to be worried when I can't reach him. Doesn't he know that information is more worrisome than just not reaching his cell."

"He's a cop?" Mitzi asked.

"Yeah, SWAT officer," Naomi replied.

"Wow, you two are kind of a power couple, an airborne nurse, and a SWAT officer. Kinda intense in your world, huh," Mitzi suggested.

"Prior to being SWAT, he was a Ranger, so he is slightly improving. But, you are right, I'm not helping it much. My ex-Ranger was not too keen on me deploying. As a Ranger with a Silver Star from Afghanistan, he thinks he has the answers."

Several people around the table nodded and indicated they understood.

When they broke for the evening and headed back to their rooms at the on-base hotel, Lindsey Evans let Naomi know she wanted to talk to her. They broke free of the others and walked together.

"Okay, Naomi, you have to explain how you pulled this off. The difference between where I last saw you and where you are today is mind-boggling," Lindsey said.

Naomi was nodding, "Think about it from my perspective when I saw you standing there. Seeing you kind of knocked my bearings out of whack. It was a long time ago I first met that young intern at Napa. Let me try to explain. You'll remember that when you first saw me, I had just come out of a drug-related coma. I'd been in a total coma for two and a half months."

"Yes, I recall. You were all trussed up in restraints, and it freaked me out, looking at you. I thought you looked enough like me to be my sister. That's still true. We are even dressing alike now," Lindsay laughed.

"Yeah, it turns out that I had been admitted to Napa based upon a wrong diagnosis of mental illness. In reality, my problem was three baggies of drugs that I had ingested. Once I came to, and the psychiatrists checked me out, they gave me a clean bill of mental health and sent me home with a diagnosis of substance abuse. The court that had ordered me to Napa released me, and then cleared my record, both civil and criminal. All I needed to do was keep myself clean from drugs and alcohol, and I would get a new chance at life. I took the opportunity and ran with it. This young doctor I met at Napa had given me a copy of a nursing magazine to read, and I had gotten a free copy of a nursing manual, Lippincott's. I read them while I waited to get released and decided that is what I wanted to do with my life—nursing. I finished my BS in Nursing and cleared the Army background check. Then, Army perioperative nurses training and **voila**, here I am. Like I said, it is all your fault."

"My fault, huh. I'll have to think on that one. But, I heard from Darren that you were also our linguist who knows the Afghan language. Where'd that come from?"

Naomi had gotten good at answering this one, "Nothing except me picking a language to take at college. French and Spanish seemed boring. It just happened that I seemed to be good at Farsi and its cousin Dari. I wanted to study something exotic, and look what it got me?"

"And, of course, you want to make sure I keep quiet about where we met up. Right?"

"Uh, yeah, I'd obviously prefer that."

"So, what's our story."

"I Googled you on my cell this afternoon and saw you went to UC Davis for medical school and apparently grew up in Sacramento."

"Yes."

"I'm from Bakersfield. So, let's just say we met in California the summer after you were in med school. That's the truth. Nobody should ask for any details. We can talk about where we each grew up, compare notes, and put something common together."

"Ok, I guess so."

"Alright, now my turn for a question. When we last met, you were getting ready to head out for your residency in psychiatry. And now, you're here as a trauma surgeon. What happened?"

Lindsey laughed. "I got halfway through with my residency and thought about spending the rest of my life in someplace like Napa and got really depressed. I saw an advertisement for the Army needing surgeons, and I jumped at it. The Army sent me to a surgical residency at Walter Reed. And, here I am."

Naomi laughed, "Yup, the big poster that said, 'Surgical Nurses Needed, We Train" got me."

"Yeah," Lindsey laughed with Naomi.

"So, Lindsey, instead of working at a place like Napa, you're heading for Afghanistan. Is that an improvement?

"We'll see. Both of us will see."

—

SMS Text

Naomi.Donnelley: Jesse, no cell answer on your end. We are getting on our plane in Atlanta. One stop to change planes in Europe, then Bagram. Probably no cell service on the flight. I'll contact you when I figure out comms in Bagram.

———

Naomi and the rest of the 250th exited the Airbus airliner that had no marking except the registration number, and they were escorted to a nearby building. An Air Force sergeant told them to pile their bags in the back of a room that looked like a classroom, and they could take their seats for their welcome.

An Air Force lieutenant colonel arrived, and she went to the podium. "Welcome to Bagram Air Force Base and the Heathe N. Craig Joint Theater Hospital. I am Lieutenant Colonel Kathryn Marks, Deputy Medical Director. I cannot tell you how happy and excited we are here at Craig to have our own in-house forward surgical team. Of course, we already have an exceptional cadre of surgeons, surgical support and specialists here at Craig, and two other Forward Surgical Teams are operating at other sites in Afghanistan to provide the all-important surgical services in the 'Golden Hour' after a battlefield wound is suffered. The idea that brought about your deployment at this time is that having an augmented FST available for on-call service in the field will be a great benefit to spreading the usefulness of an FST to more field units. But, unless there is a specific and obvious need for your services in the field, we will be using your specialized surgical expertise to augment our own staff here at Craig. I am told that there will be a review of the success of your deployment at Craig. The results may change the future manpower allocations of FSTs both here and elsewhere in future conflicts."

Kathryn Marks continued, "So, we welcome the 250th Forward Resuscitative Surgical Team to Bagram, and we are happy to announce that as the new guys on the block, you will be assigned to our latest staff quarters, freshly constructed of the finest pre-fab plywood known to mankind. I joke about it, but our new staff quarters are a world of improvement from what was available in the past at Bagram. I see a few faces in this crowd that are familiar to me from my past deployments here, and those veterans of Bagram can let you know how much better things are, this time around. We hope.

"On behalf of the 455th Expeditionary Medical Group, your hosts and landlord, welcome to Bagram. Get yourselves settled in, and we will be posting a duty roster faster than you would think humanly possible."

The colonel left the podium and shook hands with Darren Kazinsky. Then, the sergeant with a female airman at his elbow reappeared, "If you could grab your bags and follow me out the rear door, I'll show you to your quarters. Airman Conway has your initial billet assignments on her magical clipboard. Bribes are appreciated but will probably be ignored."

Angie Bethune turned to Darren and asked," So, that is the plan, they're gonna deploy us out of here around the country?"

"Angie, that is the first I have heard of that. Word to me was we are augmenting this hospital. I'll talk to somebody to get clarification. But, if that is the plan…?" He threw up his hands in an unanswered question.

———

051219362

From: Naomi.L.Donnelley@OC.US.Army.mil

To: JAM4614@Sheriff.Kern.Ca.gov

UNCLASSIFIED Non-Secure Channel

Subject: Arrived

Dearest Jesse,

Finally arrived. The flight was so long, as you well know. The last leg of the trip, the flight from Germany, was on a contract flight with most of the passengers being German *Bundeswehr* troops deploying here with NATO. The Germans broke into song as the approach to Bagram was announced. It was kind of with mixed emotions that we Americans flew into a war zone with half our airplane's passengers singing *Panzerlied* and stomping their boots in march-step. My seatmate told me that old WWII *Wehrmacht* song has been banned by the German Defense Minister. We assumed that was an unauthorized performance by the enlisted troops. But maybe not. I did not see any officers try to stop them.

One of the women on our team only had 48 hours' notice she would be deploying. The LPN she is replacing found out she was pregnant just before she deployed, and her replacement, SGT Mitzi Riordan, was notified on Friday to start deployment briefings on Saturday.

They have brand new quarters here for us. Nothing very fancy, but new and clean. Better than the quasi-tents you guys had 8-10 years ago. Angie Bethune, you met her in Texas, will be my roommate.

You never did tell me how your stake-out of the warehouse went, except to tell me there were no injuries. You get those bad guys?

Say hello to everyone for me. I will write again when we know more about the work we will be doing.

I'm told there are Skype booths here to call home on, but the patients get priority. I guess that is fair. I hope you've figured out the Skype app on your cellphone. When I have some news worth telling you, I will figure that process out.

I love you, Jesse. I am feeling very far away. Keep safe for me.

Love, Naomi

———

Naomi heard Angie come into their room. Without turning on the light, Angie flopped onto her bed.

"Bad day?" Naomi asked.

"There's been worse. Three SEALs from the Pakistani border. SEALs are the worst patients; they never want to admit how bad they are hurt. You have to interrogate them about where they are hit."

"Yeah, I've noticed. Sorta the same with Marines," Naomi added. "You eat yet?"

"No, I thought I would just hit the rack. But, now that I'm here, I realize I need to unwind a bit."

"Why don't we both go and have an anniversary dinner together. I go on duty at 20:00," Naomi suggested.

"Anniversary?"

"Yes, two full months here," Naomi said, as she sat up to put on her boots.

"Wow, time flies. Not!"

"Yeah, I totally lost track of time. I got a Happy Easter card from Jesse's mother. I had to look at a calendar to figure it out. Easter was last Sunday. I totally phased it out."

Angie sat up, also. "Me, too. By the way, what day is it?"

"Wednesday, I think."

———

042119362

From: Naomi.L.Donnelley@OC.US.Army.mil

To: JAM4614@Sheriff.Kern.Ca.Gov

UNCLASSIFIED Non-Secure Channel

Subject: Happenings

Dearest Jesse,

Things are going well here. As well as could be expected, all considered. I got a nice Easter card from your Mother. Janet sent a Care package; she must think they don't feed us over here. I gave some of the candy Janet sent to my patients yesterday.

I had a bad day the day before yesterday. I can tell you about it now that it has passed, and everything worked out alright in the end. I think it will help me to tell someone about it.

It all started a little after midnight. I was on the night shift, as usual, in the ER. Two Marines were brought in by ground vehicle, which was unusual for Bagram. They had apparently been with an Afghan Army patrol north of Kabul and were hit by an IED and gunfire. One Marine, a sergeant, had a bad leg wound that required immediate surgery. The other Marine, a PFC, came to my ER station. My surgeon, Major Kerry, the AF guy I told you about, did a nice quick job sewing up this PFC's upper arm and shoulder wound from the IED shrapnel. I assume it was shrapnel. Local Anesthetic. Nothing major. He was in decent shape physically, probably able to return to duty soon, but he seemed to be out of it mentally. We gave him meds to stave off shock and calm him down.

At that hour of the night, we did not have a hospital bed ready for this Marine, so we moved him into the Standby Room, a kind of staging area with multiple beds across the hall where we put patients who are done with the main ER work, but either need something else, more extended period of observation or like this guy, waiting for room elsewhere. I checked on him a couple of times and the LPN who watches that Standby Room said he was constantly agitated and did not sleep, even though it was the middle of the night, and we had medded him up. I stayed with him for a while as I didn't have anything going on in the ER at the moment. He told me his fears that he was going to die, that the Afghans he worked with were out to get him and that kind of really paranoid stuff. He asked me if his wound was enough to get him sent home. I lied to him and told him, "Maybe, we'll see." I got my surgeon to prescribe a stronger med to put him to sleep. I noted his apparent paranoia in his ER chart and made a referral for psych eval when he got his room in the morning.

A little after 0500, we heard a gunshot in the hallway. The Air Force Security Force people ran through, and we were told one of our patients from the Standby Room across the hall had taken the sidearm off of an SF guard in the hall and shot at him, but missed, before barricading himself in the surgical supply room down the hall. The LPN told me it was my patient—the Marine PFC. An Air Force captain was assembling his SF equivalent of a SWAT team to rush the patient in the supply room and overpower him.

I stepped in and argued with the Air Force captain that this was not the way to handle things. I knew what the problem was with my patient, and I thought it was stupid to even think of rushing a wounded Marine with a 9 mm pistol at close quarters. The AF captain said they would go in with a flash-bang grenade and overpower him. My surgeon warned him about using a flash-bang in a room with stored oxygen bottles and flammable supplies like ether and alcohol. I said I should go in and try first. My surgeon backed me up, and since he outranked the SF officer and it was in a hospital, the captain finally relented and let me try to talk to the guy, instead of going in guns blazing.

My surgeon gave me a syringe of Fentanyl that I put in my trouser leg pocket. I looked at the chart to make sure I had the PFC's first name right, and I knocked at the door to the supply room. The kid really was afraid of letting anyone in, but I told him my name was Naomi, the nurse he had talked to, and he could trust me. I promised I was the only one who would come in. He finally let me in.

I saw that he had made a pretty good bunker out of medical supply crates. He would have creamed the Air Force SF response team if they had come in that door. He was on edge and wide-eyed with fear, clearly psychotic.

I sat on a big crate of surgical masks and talked with him. I was just wearing my ACU t-shirt, so I had no rank insignia for him to see. We talked for probably twenty minutes. I got his life story. He had enlisted in the Marines from Story City, Iowa. He was just twenty years old. I had him tell me about the problem with the Afghans. It really didn't make sense; he was clearly imagining dire threats that didn't exist. At least, so it seemed to me.

Given his shooting up the hospital, my earlier lie about whether he would be sent home was now the truth, so I talked to him about how I was sure I could get him on a plane to the States. I finally got him to accept a plan to have me give him an injection and take him out of the room on a gurney, so the SF force wouldn't shoot him. I promised him he would be on a medevac flight soon. He set his 9mm aside and let me give him the Fentanyl.

The Standby Room LPN rolled a gurney down to the supply room, and we put the snoring PFC in a separate room under guard. My surgeon signed an emergency Evac order on a direct flight to Joint Base Charleston a few hours after that.

My shift was over, but the SF officer said I had to come to his office after breakfast to sign a statement. I checked with the AF JAG first about what a medical officer had to say about a criminal act that occurs in her presence, given doctor/patient confidentiality. Apparently, doctor/patient confidentiality isn't a big thing in the military.

So, my darling Jesse, my life at Bagram is getting close to yours back home, what with AF SWAT teams and active shooters. Whodathunkit?

A little over four months to go.

I Love You,

Naomi

—

Chapter 32

Even this early in the morning, the July heat walking between buildings was oppressive. Naomi had finished a night shift in the ER. There had been heavy casualties from attacks out west in Herat, but the 274th Forward Resuscitative Surgical Team in Herat had done an excellent job with the casualties. They were all properly triaged, marked, and ready for the ER to send to surgery, critical care beds, or prep for medevac on the usual early evening flight to Landstuhl. Of course, there was still a lot for the ER staff to do, but the value of a forward surgical team was obvious. The night shift in the ER also had a part in the job of processing the evacuees leaving on the evening flights to Landstuhl hospital in Germany, or the rare flight directly to the States. The ER had direct access to the flight line, so this was often where the Critical Care Evac Teams from the aircraft came to get the evacuees.

This was Naomi's first morning wearing captain's bars. Her time-in-grade for promotion to captain had passed, and as promised in the recruiting phone call from the S-1 at Fort Lewis, as a reserve nurse on deployment, that promotion was virtually automatic. She was now Captain Donnelly.

Naomi was tired and ready to eat. Night shifts were always strange, eating breakfast when you were ending your workday. Understanding this, the mess hall tried to offer dinner meals at breakfast, but it was obvious the dinner offerings were leftovers from the meal the night before. She ordered her usual Denver omelet from the cooks, poured her usual large orange juice, and waited. She did not see anybody else from the 250th in the mess hall. But, in the last six months, the dividing line between the people in her unit, the 250th, and the other medical personnel at Craig/Bagram, many of whom were Air Force, had blurred. They were all now part of the same team. The integration of the extra Army FST into the hospital staff had been a success. Naomi wondered what it would be like here when the 250th left next month.

The cook had just waved Naomi over to the counter to get her omelet when the speaker in the mess hall gave a loud, dissonant squawk, and a man's voice announced, "All emergency and surgical personnel to duty stations, all shifts. Mass casualties inbound. Repeat, All emergency and surgical personnel to duty stations, all shifts. Mass casualties inbound."

Naomi had never heard this announcement before. She had read about it in the emergency procedures manual but never heard the announcement. She gobbled a couple large mouthfuls of omelet, drank her orange juice, grabbed her muffin, and followed most of the other people in the mess hall out the door, back into the heat. It seemed to be even worse than ten minutes before.

Naomi arrived back in the ER that she had just left. It was now crowded. The Air Force colonel who ran the ER had his hands raised above his head, trying to quiet the crowd. He finally used a handheld bullhorn to say. "Please, please, listen up. We do not know exactly what to expect. Bagram flight control just called. They have nine choppers reported inbound with casualties. Colonel Marks has called ISAF HQ in Kabul, and all they can tell us is that we have mass casualties incoming from Kandahar. We have been unable to reach the NATO Medical team at Kandahar for clarification. All we can do is assume the worst."

Several people were reading the red vinyl Mass Casualty Manual. LPNs and surgical technicians were moving fresh supplies out to all the various ER stations. Per the Manual, the usual routine Sick Call area down the hall was rapidly turned into another set of ER bays.

Mitzi Riordan was at Naomi's shoulder after having finished her resupply task. Mitzi was on the day crew now, so she was already on duty when the call went out. It was nice to have someone Naomi knew at her side. Mitzi had proved her mettle as an ER LPN time and again. Naomi was glad to have Mitzi with her. Naomi did not know the Air Force surgeon at their ER station. He was new at Craig. Naomi also noted that the surgeon at the next table to hers was Captain Lindsey Evans.

Lindsey walked over to Naomi's table and said, "Congratulations on your promotion, Captain Donnelley," and shook her hand. After that, they waited.

——

The flimsy pre-fab walls and ceiling of Craig Joint Theater Hospital did not mask the sound of the choppers at all. The experienced ears in the ER heard the first Blackhawk as it approached. They also heard a deeper, louder sound of a bigger Chinook right behind it. Then, other Blackhawks seemed to join the rumbling chorus out on the Bagram flight line. Medics and surgical techs rolled gurneys out of the doors toward the tarmac.

As the bodies rolled into the Craig ER, the differences from the casualties from Herat the night before were obvious. The first few patients only had minimal field dressings on massive wounds, sometimes none. It was clear no one beyond a field medic had seen the casualties.

Then, with the patient who was rolled into the ER bay Naomi and Mitzi were manning, the Craig staff saw that the patients often were wearing medical scrubs, and even surgical masks and gloves, not battle camouflage uniforms. Many of the incoming patients were wounded medical personnel.

A nurse with a leg wound was able to tell the ER staff, in German-accented English, that they were the NATO Medical Team from Kandahar. The reason there had been no pre-triage or wound prep was that the medical team members who had that job were the victims of the attack. News of what had happened spread amongst the staff in the Craig ER, and then elsewhere in the hospital. For Naomi and Mitzi, it was disconcerting to be cutting a surgical gown off a young woman to get to her shrapnel wounds.

The crowd in the ER, the constantly swinging doors, and the hasty construction style of the Craig Joint Theater Hospital combined with oppressive July heat outside to make the ER increasingly and miserably hot. Air conditioning units were overtaxed, and that led to a couple of brownouts of the lights.

Choppers with casualties kept arriving, seemingly without end. At times, the wounded only spent a few moments in the ER before they were wheeled down the corridor toward the surgical teams. Surgery became backed up. At one point, Captain Evans chose to do a thoracic cavity surgery on the gurney in the ER when she could not get confirmation that Surgery was ready and available for her patient.

The wounded were not only NATO medical personnel, but many were also both German and Romanian NATO combat troops from Kandahar with a smattering of Afghan Army troops. Communication became a problem. In one case, a German nurse was brought in on a gurney, and after her minor shrapnel wound and burn were dressed, she got up off the gurney and started helping the ER staff with other patients, translating for the *Bundeswehr* soldier patients who did not speak English.

Towards mid-morning, there was a slowing of the incoming patients. Gatorade, bottled water, and a few boxed lunches were distributed amongst the staff. Bathroom breaks were finally possible.

Just as Naomi looked up to see the ER clock showing 10:38, there was another squawk of the Craig loudspeaker system. Naomi heard, "All members of the 250th Forward Resuscitative Surgical Team are directed to stand down from their current duty stations and report to the Ops Ready Room, Building 412." The announcement was repeated.

"What is that all about?" Mitzi asked as she pulled off her nitrile gloves.

From the next table, Captain Lindsey Evans pulled down her mask and answered the question, "Sounds like showtime for the 250th. Ladies, go grab your Kevlar gear. I bet Kandahar in July is lovely."

—

Angie and Mitzi were sitting on either side of Naomi. Lindsey Evans and Sheri Clifton faced them across the cabin of the Blackhawk. Two German medics returning from escorting wounded to Bagram were in the rear.

No more than six or seven team members were in each Blackhawk since they were also carrying the 250th's airborne-droppable field equipment crates that had sat in a hangar at Bagram since February—unused. Most of the team had not seen their field equipment since they packed it at Fort Lewis in January. Naomi had never seen the unit's field equipment. During the first hour of the flight, Angie had shouted and explained to Naomi and Mitzi what was included in the field gear for the 250th. It was meant to give them full surgical capabilities in a field location. They did not know what to expect in Kandahar, so they brought everything they had in the Bagram hangar.

The briefing officer had told them the distance to Kandahar was roughly 500 kilometers, and flight time to Kandahar from Bagram in a Blackhawk was about two hours. Naomi adjusted the ugly black Army-issued glasses on her nose. Her regular glasses and her contacts were left in her personal gear stored back at Bagram. Army-issue glasses were shatterproof and fit when wearing a helmet. They were told it would be a quick deployment, just temporary.

Naomi looked at the scrub watch Ayla had given her for Christmas. They had to be getting close to Kandahar. The white face and band of the watch seemed out of place on Naomi's current ACU field uniform. She was in the same combat gear she had worn at Jump School, except for no parachute, and her heavy jacket was in the camouflage haversack at her feet. Even at cruising altitude and speed, it was still hot in the Blackhawk.

Naomi shifted uncomfortably in the Blackhawk's fold-down jump seat. The unusual presence around her waist bothered her. Just before each member of the 250th had boarded the aircraft at Bagram, the Air Force Security Force officer that Naomi had confronted in the incident with the Marine PFC had handed each Army team member a 9mm semi-automatic pistol in a holster belt with ammo pouch. He asked them to sign a serial number log for the weapon they had to wear when flying over possibly hostile territory. It was an angst-causing reminder that their mission was serious.

The Blackhawk crew chief pressed his headset to his ear and gave the team members a hand signal for five minutes. The lights in the cabin were turned off. The sun came in the starboard side windows. It was getting late in the afternoon. Naomi was impressed. The 250th had prepared, equipped themselves, and boarded the choppers for field deployment in a little over four hours. Now, they were ready to land in a forward location and set up surgical shop in a matter of hours. It was the way things were supposed to go on paper. The only thing missing for the 250th was that they were not doing the landing by parachute. Thank goodness.

The crew chief gave a one-minute signal and mimicked to everyone to have their helmets strapped on tight. The engine sound changed as the

Blackhawk dropped to the tarmac in Kandahar.

A tall *Bundeswehr* sergeant in tan-brown desert camouflage was directing the landing. He had a work team of Afghans ready to unload the Blackhawks. The begoggled work crew in Afghan native dress seemed to Naomi to be something out of a Star Wars Tatooine scene. Several stretcher-bearers were ready to send wounded back to Bagram on the return flight. A German medic went on the Blackhawk that had the wounded. Three fuel trucks rapidly filled up the Blackhawks. Three choppers landed at a time and the area was cleared before the next three came in to land. The 250th's incoming flight was a total of six Blackhawks. Naomi ran with the other team members and assembled near where their equipment was piled by the Afghan crew.

On the ground in Kandahar, the smoke of buildings on fire was pervasive. The late afternoon sun showed red through the smoke. Several buildings near the aviation tarmac were in ruins. Then, just as the last of the Blackhawks took off, one of the Germans shouted, *"Ducken!"* The newly arrived Americans looked around confused, but the Afghan work crew and the Germans all dove behind crates or vehicles, or merely hugged the ground. Within seconds of the *"ducken"* warning, three mortar shells fell at various spots around the field. They exploded harmlessly, away from anything important, but there was a shower of shrapnel dropping from the sky all around a few seconds after the blasts. The unseen Taliban were welcoming the 250th to town.

After the noise of the Blackhawks and the mortar barrage, relative silence now descended on the 250th. A senior German officer in a tan Mercedes SUV arrived. Darren Kazinsky walked over to meet him. The German seemed to be giving direction and reporting on conditions. Naomi was close enough to hear Kazinsky speaking German with the *Bundeswehr* colonel. Naomi saw Kazinsky nod to the German, salute him and return to where the others waited.

Kazinsky held his arms up to get his team of twenty-nine to gather around. "Well, things seem to be what we expected. That building over there," he pointed to the biggest smoking shell near the flight line, "used to be the NATO Medical Station. It took a couple direct rocket hits. Most of their medical team were inside, on duty. The good news is the Taliban have stopped firing rockets, for the time being, just the mortars you saw. They had several attacks by our aircraft today, both bombers and attack choppers. It may have set the Taliban back, but they obviously are still capable of trouble. The Germans are in charge of the region, they have platoons going after the Taliban along with the Afghan Army. The Romanian Army is in charge of perimeter security for the airport. They are headquartered over across the field," Kazinsky pointed to the eastern horizon that was already growing dark.

"Colonel Reicker, the German C.O., wants us to use this hangar here as our new Medical Station," Kazinsky indicated the large aircraft hangar their gear was stacked by. "Looks like we will be sleeping where we work. They'll send some food over soon. The Afghani work crew will help us get set up. This building apparently was chosen since it still has power. They have a temporary medical aid station in another building. Their medics will be sending the existing wounded over to us."

One of the female medics, Sheri Clifton, asked, "So, we are not really a Forward Surgical Team supporting an existing medical cadre, we are the whole field hospital?"

Kazinsky shrugged, "Seems like, for the time being. Reicker says he is asking NATO for more help. Let's get our stuff inside and get ready to do business. Sergeant Morton, you get things set up like we did last summer during the field exercise. Donnelley, you are straw boss to get the Afghanis to do what Morton says to do. They apparently don't speak English or German very well."

Naomi looked around to try and see which Afghan worker looked like he was in charge. It was anyone's guess.

———

Master Sergeant Hank Morton did a quick survey of the hangar they were assigned to setup. Naomi followed along with a couple of the Afghan workers in tow. There was an empty office area in one corner of the hangar. It wasn't big enough for surgery, but it would make a proper triage and admin area. Morton explained to Naomi that they needed the Afghans to help set up the surgery tents inside the main hangar area.

Naomi could not remember the Dari word for sterile when she had to explain to the workers why they needed tents inside a building. The Afghans moved the 250th's equipment pile into the hangar as directed by Morton and Naomi. Morton and two of the 250th's enlisted technicians set up the first surgical enclosure, and the Afghans quickly got the idea.

A senior German non-commissioned officer, *Hauptfeldwebel* Kopel, made his appearance in the hangar and announced he was the Base Engineer. He laughed at the Americans and the Afghans sweating in the stuffy hangar. He went to the wall and threw a switch, starting the huge intake and exhaust fans overhead on each end of the hangar. After a brief round of dust tornadoes, the hangar quickly sucked in the cooling night air. He also showed them where the main overhead lighting was, as night had fallen. Kopel led the Afghans outside on the tarmac where they could find dozens of orange and white striped cement aircraft tie-down weights that ended the quandary about how to anchor the ropes holding up the surgical tents' endpieces on the concrete floor.

Naomi's usefulness as a translator was bypassed by the German sergeant's presence, so Morton told her he could handle things. Naomi found the rest of the 250th was inside the office area, where a German crew was serving pork steak, potatoes, and strudel with chilled bottled water. As promised, the German medics soon started a steady flow of patients but also brought many cots and general medical supplies. Some of the cots and supplies were slightly charred, having been scrounged from the burnt-out NATO clinic. A couple of German nurses who had not been on duty during the rocket attack were added to the 250th's team. A tall, broad-shouldered *Bundeswehr* officer, *Oberleutnant* Kurzweil, set up a radio and phone line inside the office area, and staffed it with his assistants, who were in touch with the NATO command and flight control.

Hauptfeldwebel Kopel came over to ask how many people they had on the team, counting the German nurses, and ten or so German field medics that had shown up. When he was told, he made a call on his handheld radio, and in a few minutes, two large pneumatic tents were inflated in the far corner of the hangar, and beds and chemical latrines were set up for the American/German medical team's housing. By midnight, with the rows of patient beds in the open area near the surgical enclosures, the huge hangar interior was a decent semblance of a small field hospital. When he saw the patient beds out in the open area of the huge hangar, *Hauptfeldwebel* Kopel quickly added three more bubble tents. The *Bundeswehr* at Kandahar was well-provisioned.

LTC Kazinsky set up a two-shift rotation for the medical teams and let everyone know they expected a flight of four Blackhawks to land at 03:00 to extract as many wounded as they could get ready. It was hoped the night landing on the tarmac north of their hangar would diminish the threat of the Taliban mortars in the hills to the east and south. Word was there might be more medical help onboard the choppers.

Naomi was assigned to the second shift, so she found a cot and blanket in the women's housing bubble and fell quickly to sleep.

———

Chapter 33

Naomi awoke with a start. Her ACU t-shirt was wet with sweat, and her nightmare had been vivid. As she blinked her eyes open, the surreal view of the backlit gray-green vinyl pillows of the inflatable tent's ceiling above her was unrecognizable. She had no idea where she was for a long moment.

As Naomi looked around and got her bearings, she had to laugh at the nightmare. Her dream imagination had fused together old and new memories. She had been dealing with the scalpel-wielding crazy-man from Napa but in the medical supply room at Bagram hospital. She quickly realized why she had been awakened. It had not been from the nightmare. An ominous ground-shaking rumble came from outside the big hangar at Kandahar. She quickly put her boots on and ran across the hangar to the doors on the north side.

She was not the only one who raced outside to see the spectacle of American bombers dropping ordinance across the northern horizon. Many of the 250th and the Germans with them stood near Naomi, watching.

Darren Kazinsky turned to the German lieutenant, Kurzweil, who was their connection to the NATO staff, "I thought this airport was to the south of the main city of Kandahar. Is our Air Force bombing the city? Have the Taliban taken Kandahar?"

Oberleutnant Kurzweil shook his head, "No, *Herr Oberst*, there is a ridge of highlands between the airport and the city. The Taliban and IS forces have infiltrated up the *wadi* to the southwest into the highland ridge. The Afghan Army and our *Bundeswehr* troops have consolidated in the south of the city and here with the Romanians, then called in the American B-52s and the naval bombers to attack the enemy locations on the ridge in between. The *Bundeswehr* will be augmenting our own troops with a detachment of the 26th Airborne Brigade this morning. They will be dropping at a little after 08:00."

"You're doing an airborne drop?"

"Yes, *Herr Oberst*, it will be the first combat paratrooper jump for the *Bundeswehr* since the World War. The rumor is the Taliban want to take Kandahar, so they have a provincial capital in their hands before the peace negotiations, and the German commanders are going to make sure that it is not our province the Taliban take."

"But, this airport is still operational. Why bother with a parachute drop?" Kazinsky asked.

The German nodded, "Things were starting to look bad in the city last evening, about when you landed. I am told the *Luftlandebrigade Sechsundzwanzig* was given orders to deploy, and they didn't know what things on the ground would be like hours later when they arrived here from *das Saarland*. They loaded on the planes at Spangdahlem Air Force Base equipped for an opposed-force parachute jump, and I'm guessing the commanders want to let the paratroopers arrive in proper airborne style."

"I understand. Our airborne troops would feel the same," Kazinsky admitted, with a knowing smile.

Kurzweil smiled.

Sergeant Sheri Clifton waved her hand to get the officers' attention, "If the Taliban are now up there to the north, that means the neat idea of landing helicopters on the north side of the hangar to hide from Taliban eyes is kind of kaput. Right?"

Kurzweil shrugged, "Quite possibly, but that is one reason why that," he pointed to the bombardment, "is happening."

Clifton, Kazinsky, and several Americans nodded.

Naomi and the others watched the ordinance show in the pre-dawn light before they went inside to get ready for a busy day. The Blackhawks that finally landed at 04:00 were just for medical transport to Bagram, with no additional medical personnel onboard. The 250th was pretty much on their own with a few German helpers.

———

Later, Naomi had been able to run outside quickly when she heard the paradrop was taking place. It was impressive watching the German Airbus A400's circle in from the east out of the morning sun and drop a half dozen clusters of a hundred or more paratroopers with distinctive gray chutes. They landed on the far northern side of the main runway. The final four A400s paradropped huge pallets of cargo to the troops martialing on the ground. The view of the mass *Bundeswehr* paradrop was impressive, but not so much so for Naomi, as would have been the case before she had gone to Jump School.

As Naomi turned to go back inside, she noticed the Germans had set up defensive sandbag emplacements at the four corners of their hangar staffed by squads of four or five heavily armed troops. Things seemed to be getting dicey at Kandahar airport.

Naomi and the others went back inside to work with the day's increasing casualty count. Twenty minutes after the jump, three German paratroopers with various broken bones were added to the beds in the hangar.

In late morning, Kazinsky sent word that Naomi should leave the surgical enclosure where she had been working and move to the triage area. The number of wounded Afghan troops coming in was increasing, and most did not speak English. Trucks with wounded Afghans and Romanians were coming at frequent intervals from the eastern side of the airport. Wounds were horrendous, and it was not unusual for dead bodies to be unloaded from the Romanian and German trucks. There was obviously nobody at the Romanian Army headquarters doing much medical aid for these wounded.

In the chaos of the triage area, the only way Naomi kept track of time was when the German cooks arrived in the foodservice area near the triage beds. Her lunch had only been a granola bar and boxed fruit drink, but by the evening meal, she was able to sit down on the crates they used for furniture and eat a ham and cheese sandwich with Lindsey Evans.

"So, Lindsey, after today, is a career at a place like Napa looking any better?"

Lindsey laughed, "You would think so, but really, you couldn't get any job more important or rewarding than helping these people that come through here. It's gut-wrenching but rewarding. And certainly not boring."

Naomi nodded and started to speak when Darren Kazinsky came over and stood by where Naomi and Lindsey sat. He began to say something but had to stop when the sound of a new landing of helicopters outside made it impossible to hear.

When the noise died a bit, Kazinsky said, "I need to get outside for this onload, but I wanted to tell you two that Colonel Reicker has asked that we send a team over to the Romanian Army site to help them with casualties. They are down to just a few field medics, and no actual medical staff for treatment or triage. They've been sending untreated and untriaged casualties over here all day. Since many of them are Afghan, I want Naomi to go. And, I want you, Lindsey, and Riordan and Clifton to go over, too. We'll try to spell you over there with another team in a day or two. Be ready to head over when Reicker gets transport and an escort ready for you. Morton is putting together a couple supply crates for you four to bring with you."

"So, we're gonna be a little Forward Surgical Team for you guys back here at your makeshift field hospital?" Captain Evans asked.

Kazinsky smiled at the irony, "Yeah, sort of…"

"Yeah, a little all-female Forward Surgical Team," Naomi added.

"I hadn't thought of that, but yeah," Kazinsky turned and left.

—

The four young women were back in their full combat gear with sidearms when they headed for the waiting Enok light armored vehicle with the black *Bundeswehr* cross on the door. They left their personal gear behind, as this was intended to be temporary. The Enok had a trailer that Sergeant Morton was loading with two supply crates and a few bundles as they boarded.

The trip across the airport was enlightening, to say the least.

"Hey, those are American choppers, we have an attack helicopter squadron here," Sheri announced. "Why haven't we seen any Americans yet."

"We've been lucky, I guess. You want to see American casualties? I guess the ground troops are all NATO, German and Romanian, plus the Afghans," Lindsey surmised.

As they drove by the Cobra and Apache gunships on the tarmac and under half-tube protective enclosures, they saw the multiple craters that repeated shelling near the attack helicopters had left. One Apache was a pile of smoking rubble. They proceeded down the taxiway on the south side of the main runway. There was quite a bit of activity at the airport. Their view from inside the medical hangar had been skewed and limited.

The Enok passed the nine decorative roof arches of the main terminal building. It had once, obviously, been a showplace. Now, one of the arched sections and many of the facing windows were blown out. No civilian aircraft could be seen. Smoke still rose from the damaged terminal section.

Far to the east, they approached a large cement building out beyond the terminal. It was surrounded by sandbagged emplacements, full of troops in mottled tan camouflage uniforms. This was apparently their destination. A lift-gate was raised, and they entered a courtyard behind the defensive perimeter. Naomi and the team got out of the Enok.

Lindsey used a handheld radio to report, "Two-Five-Oh, this is Two-Five-Oh Alpha, arrived at destination, over." A blast of static and noise, sounding like the *Oberleutnant*, answered.

They were met by a short, stout man in the tan camo uniform with muted red and gold shoulder boards. They saw him rapidly look between the Americans to see their rank.

With both Lindsey and Naomi showing captain's bar, the Romanian officer simply saluted and said, "Welcome, I'm Colonel Alexandru Cristescu." He spoke passable English.

Now that they knew what his shoulder boards meant, the four American women saluted in near unison, and Lindsey said, "Colonel, I'm Captain Lindsey Evans, Doctor Lindsey Evans. This is Captain Donnelly our surgical nurse, and these are Sergeants Riordan and Clifton, a practical nurse and medic."

"Yes, your presence here is very needed, uh, necessary," he signaled that he wanted them to follow him.

Before she followed, Lindsey said, "Colonel, can we have someone unload our gear from the trailer?"

"Yes, of course," Cristescu waved to a group of soldiers standing nearby, who were obviously waiting for the signal. They ran to unload the trailer.

"They will bring your equipment to where we have set aside your medical, uh, location. Please follow me." Cristescu continued to talk as he walked inside. "As you may have seen, we have no true medical capability at our location. We are just getting, uh, used to this new combat mode. Before the Taliban attack on Sunday, we used the German medical clinic for the Romanians, and the Afghans we work with had their own medical people in the city. Now, we are down to just one Romanian field medic, and the Afghans are cut off from their medical people in the city. We were happy to hear the Colonel, Reicker, would be sending you uh… ladies, over to help us." The Romanian colonel was obviously uncomfortable with how to address a group of four female soldiers.

They passed a large shell crater on the way across the courtyard. They entered the main building and immediately turned right into a hallway. Then, they saw a room with multiple stretchers on the floor and a few cots. Several were occupied by patients. Two of the stretchers had bodies on them that were totally covered with canvas tarps. There was one man with a red cross on his tan t-shirt standing in the middle of the room. Colonel Cristescu motioned the man to come to them.

When the man walked over, rubbing his blood-stained hands on a rag, Cristescu introduced him, "This is Sergeant Nistor."

Several mortar shells went off outside.

Cristescu turned to leave, "Nistor will help you with whatever you need. I need to go. Sorry. "

As Cristescu disappeared, Nistor looked at the four women, seemingly in shock. He eventually thought of saluting. Lindsey returned the salute, as was her right as the senior American officer.

The work crew arrived with the crates.

Naomi looked at obviously dead bodies under the tarps. It was going to be another long night.

———

The dead bodies turned out to not be a problem. The work crew that brought in the supply crates took charge of the dead without asking and loaded them into the Enok's trailer to send back to the medical hangar. This explained why the dead bodies had been appearing in the ambulances. The Romanians had no provisions for dealing with the deceased, so they marked the bodies with identification and shipped them for the NATO staff to deal with. There were four living patients on the floor of the Romanian aid station that the four Americans immediately set to work treating.

Sergeant Nistor spoke virtually no English but knew the words for most medications and was a master at Charades. Mitzi Riordan and Nistor soon had a good rapport going. When the sun started to set, and light became poor, she asked Nistor about electricity, and he nodded, climbed through one of the broken windows, and started a gas engine generator outside the window that powered the aid station's lights.

Lindsey and Naomi were working on the four patients. The Enok had left before they could triage the patients at the aid station. Three had significant bullet or shrapnel wounds, but were not critical. One, a Romanian sergeant, had a chest wound that indicated only one lung was working, the other probably collapsed or in full pulmonary edema from bleeding. He needed immediate surgery, but it was not something they could handle at the aid station.

Lindsey got on the radio and contacted Kurzweil, "Two-Five-Oh, this is Two-Five-Oh Alpha." She waited for the response, then said, "We have four patients for immediate transport, one critical. Recommend prep for immediate chest surgery. Over."

"Two-Five-Oh Alpha, Roger, standby, over."

Kurzweil's voice was replaced by LTC Kazinsky's, "Two-Five-Oh Alpha. This is Two-Five-Oh Six, we received your last two 'patients.' What is up over there? Over?" Colonel Kazinsky used the radio-talk nickname for the unit commander, 'Six.'

"Six, we have no possible morgue space here. We have eight beds total, four of those on the floor. You have to take the, uh… failures, over."

After a pause, they heard, "Roger, Alpha, understand, your ambulance is dispatched. Are your conditions adequate there?"

Lindsey looked at Naomi before answering, "Six, Alpha, a roof over our heads and generator power. Lots of Romanians doing their best. The Romanian Six is glad to see us. We have not seen the menu yet, we'll see. Over."

"Roger, out."

Lindsey set down the radio, and Sergeant Nistor walked over to her. He had been listening to the radio call and asked, "*Menui?*"

Lindsey said, "Uh, yeh, the menu?"

Nistor did his best 'charade' of eating, and Lindsey smiled and said, "Yes, food."

Nistor chuckled and said, "*Menui,*" a couple more times. Apparently, the joke worked in Romanian, too.

He started to leave the room when Lindsey said, "No, wait." She pointed to the men on the floor and made her own 'charade' motion of 'driving." Then, she held five, and then ten fingers, pointing toward the west, hopefully indicating the ambulance was coming soon. She made the motion to get the patients out to the loading area.

Nistor nodded and left to find the work crew. They quickly came in and loaded the four stretchers out the door. Clifton went with them. Lindsey again shouted, "Wait!" She tried to indicate she needed the stretchers back. The men nodded that they understood.

Nistor came back a short time later, with his answer to the *menu|* joke. He had a large box filled with American Meals-Ready-To-Eat (MREs) and bottled water. The freeze-dried and plastic pouched MRE rations would be all that was on the menu. Apparently, the Romanians could not match the German cooking staff.

———

Sergeant Nistor disappeared in the middle of the evening and reappeared with his work crew carrying three more stretchers, with two Romanians and one German who seemed to be a paratrooper. He also brought a German medic with him. The medic was surprised to find the four American women there.

When Naomi stood up to face the German as he walked in, he saluted her, "*Unteroffizier* Kalb, *Kapitan.*"

Naomi saluted back and pointed to Lindsey, "Captain Evans is in charge."

Lindsey was already looking at the wounded German on the floor. She looked up and asked Kalb, "You speak English."

"Yes ma'am."

"You staying here or just passing through?"

"My company is digging in across the runway from here, down at the end to protect the road to the city. The Taliban are moving this way. Headquarters said there was a medical aid station here. I did not know you were Americans. We did not know there were any American ground troops in Kandahar." Kalb saw what Lindsey was doing and knelt to help her remove the coat from the wounded paratrooper. "I am supposed to help out at the aid station and coordinate the transport of any wounded troops from *Die Sechsundzwanzig*, the 26th, my Brigade." He tapped the radio on his belt to indicate how he would coordinate.

"You are a paratrooper?" Naomi asked.

"Yes ma'am," the *unteroffizier* proudly proclaimed, taping his insignia, "*Fallschirmjagerbataillion* 261."

"Good, so are we!" Naomi turned her pocket to Kalb and pointed to the black wings above her 'US Army' patch.

"Did you jump into Kandahar, like us?"

"Unfortunately no, we had to take a helicopter," Naomi answered, but Kalb did not seem to understand her comment was in jest, as he shook his head sadly and mumbled, "*Schade.*"

———

Lindsey set up a two-shift, four-hour rotation with Naomi, Riordan, and Nistor, followed by Evans, Kalb, and Clifton. Another ambulance run near midnight temporarily cleared out their wounded. But, that was short-lived as two more wounded soon arrived via Kalb's comrade airborne medics.

When she awoke the oncoming shift for the 03:00 shift change, Naomi noticed Sheri Clifton was shivering and sick. She admitted to being under the weather. Lindsey came over to check her out. The doctor discovered Sheri had a high temperature to the touch and had cold sweats. When they finally found the electronic thermometer in the supply crate, they found she had a temperature of 103°. Before they could get a blanket around her, Sheri ran to the window and vomited out the window, on the generator. As she turned around, Sheri fainted. Kalb caught her.

"What do you think is wrong with her?" Mitzi Riordan asked Captain Evans.

"Really no clue. There are lots of bad bugs over here. Some are deadly. But, we have no way of dealing with it here. We don't even have any electrolytes to prevent dehydration. We need to get her back to the 250ᵗʰ," Evans said, reaching for the radio.

"Two-Five-Oh, this is Alpha Team, over." They had to repeat the call several times.

It took a long time for the answer in the middle of the night. It sounded like Master Sergeant Morton, not Kurzweil, "This is Two-Five-Oh, Roger, over."

"Is Two-Five-Oh Six Actual, there?"

"Standby, over." There was a pause, then another voice, Kazinsky, spoke, "This is Six Actual, over."

"We need a vehicle for evacuation of two wounded and one of our Team, Stat, over."

"Six here. Is your team member wounded? Over."

"Negative, team member seriously ill. Needs immediate attention, over."

"We are on our way, over."

By the time the Enok arrived, Sergeant Sheri Clifton was unconscious. For once, a 250ᵗʰ medic was riding in the vehicle to escort Clifton back. The Enok also brought a supply of empty stretchers and some more medical supplies. They loaded Clifton and the two Germans in the Enok, and returned to their main building.

As Lindsey and Naomi turned to walk inside, they heard intense automatic gunfire and explosions from far across the runway. The Taliban had run into the *Bundeswehr* paratroopers. That was probably a problem for the Taliban, but their mere presence that close to the airport presaged that the situation was getting worse.

As Naomi and Lindsey walked back into the building, they saw Colonel Cristescu heading out of the building with a Kevlar vest and helmet on.

As Cristescu passed them, he said, "You need to turn off your lights. The lights can be used to target the building."

———

Nobody slept, even if they were off duty. Naomi found herself standing at the window looking to the north with little to see except an occasional light streak of an incandescent tracer round across the sky. Four more German paratroopers came in on stretchers before dawn. The routine started over again. Check the wounded, do initial triage and treatment, if possible, stabilize and call for transport. Nistor had found several battery lanterns to use in the darkened aid station.

Just after dawn, there was a different sound outside. The sound of multiple helicopters rattled the Romanian HQ. Lindsey and the others joined Naomi at the window to watch as a flight of multiple attack helicopters, Marine Vipers, flew in and took station on the far side of the runway, orbiting and facing toward the enemy to the north, waiting.

The object of the Vipers' wait appeared. Twelve V-22 Osprey vertical takeoff and landing transports arrived in waves over the runway and dropped loads of Marines and their equipment off on the runway. The Vipers were covering for the landing of a Marine battalion.

High above, the roar of jet engines crossed over the Kandahar airport. Six F-35 attack aircraft started a bombing run on the hillside across the runway to the north. Like the German paratroopers had done the day before, the U.S. Marines had arrived to put on a show for their NATO allies at the expense of the hapless Taliban. Naomi, Lindsey, and their medics watched from their window.

To the west, on the Kandahar airport flight line, not to be outdone by the Marines, most of the U.S. Army attack helicopters took flight heading north. Farther north, the unmistakable rumble of the bigger bombers dropping their ordinance joined the thunder.

Outside of the window, on the defensive perimeter of their building, the Romanian troops cheered the quasi-showboating of their allies' arrival. It was impressive.

———

Chapter 34

The arrival of the Marines did not change the duties of the Alpha Team of the 250th. The Marines rapidly headed to the northwest to engage the primary Taliban incursion toward downtown Kandahar. The Romanians and the German paratroopers were still engaged with the Taliban moving south along the road from town. The wounded kept coming into their triage station.

Naomi and Mitzi were loading six wounded into a German truck in the courtyard when an officer in Marine camouflage and full battle gear walked up with Colonel Cristescu. The two Americans continued loading their patients as the Marine colonel watched.

When they were done, and the truck departed, Naomi turned and saluted the Marine.

"Good Morning, Captain. Seeing you here is a bit of a surprise. Until Colonel Cristescu mentioned you were here, we thought all the American medical team was back with the Germans. We had no idea your team was here with the Romanians. Are you in charge? By the way, I'm Colonel Heath, the QR Force commander."

"Uh, no, sir. Captain Evans is inside. She's our senior officer, our doctor. Do you want to meet her?"

"By all means. I see both of you are airborne," Heath said as he followed Naomi and Mitzi inside. Heath put his hand on Naomi's shoulder as he walked next to her.

"Yes, sir, the 250th Forward Resuscitative Surgical Team is an airborne unit."

"And, I understand you got sent in here when the German medics got hit bad."

"Yes sir."

"Well, let's see if we can get you folks pulled back outta here. I have a full Naval field hospital loading on *USS America*'s Ospreys as we speak. They will replace your team this afternoon. So, I'm told."

"Sounds good, sir, here is Captain Lindsey Evans, our officer in charge," Naomi said, as she knelt to take over from Lindsey with a bloodied Romanian patient on the cot. The Marine colonel did his introduction again with Captain Evans.

———

With the arrival of the Marines, things actually got worse for the Romanians and Germans. As the Taliban were pushed off the highlands and out of the east of the city, they came south, toward the airport. By afternoon, there were a dozen wounded NATO troops with just the one doctor, two nurses, and a few field medics to handle them. There was occasional gunfire, plus mortar and RPG shells from the Taliban on the nearby road and the open country to the east.

"Two-Five-Oh, this is Alpha Team, over," Naomi called, then she repeated, "Two-Five-Oh, this is Alpha Team, over."

There was no answer for a long time. Then, they heard, "Alpha Team, this is Two-Five-Oh Six, we are in the process of turning things over to Navy. You should be, too. You should be here to transport out. Over."

"Commander, we have no Navy medics here. It is just Alpha Team. We have multiple serious casualties to evacuate. Nine in all, several are in critical need of air transport to offshore or Bagram. Over."

"Roger, let me get word on what to do from Navy here. Standby. Out."

Naomi was back helping Lindsey with a sucking chest wound on a Romanian soldier when Nistor motioned that there was a call on the radio. They answered it.

"Two-Five-Oh, this is Alpha, over."

"Yes, Alpha, this is Six Actual. We have been ordered by QR Force commander to onload with wounded to Bagram. Navy is sending a relief team to your location. You are ordered to stand by for Blackhawks at your location in fifteen, that's one-five minutes. They are medical transports to Bagram. Turn your duties over to the Navy, load the wounded, and depart when they arrive. Over."

"Roger, Out."

As they waited for the Navy medical team to arrive and for the Army Blackhawks, things got progressively worse around the Romanian HQ. Shelling and stray gunfire were common. Twenty minutes passed without any sign of the Navy doctors that were promised. But, two Army Blackhawks appeared in the northern sky, one closer than the other.

The first Black Hawk came in and landed in front of the Romanian HQ. With no sign of the Navy doctors and with ten wounded, four Romanians, five Germans, and now one Marine, Lindsey now had to decide on what to do. The main 250th Team had already left, and Alpha Team had no contact with the Navy replacements. She decided to load the wounded onto the helicopters that the American team was supposed to use to go to Bagram. That would clear out the aid station of patients in preparation for the missing Navy medical team to be located and come take over.

Unfortunately, the Blackhawks were not the medical evac choppers that had been expected. They were regular troop-carrying aircraft. There were only two flight crewmen and no medical personnel on the first chopper that landed. Given the prospect of the two-hour flight to Bagram, Captain Evans made the decision to load the worst patients who were ready for evac on the chopper. Captain Lindsay and Mitzi Riordan would go with the five more serious patients on the first Blackhawk. Naomi would go with the more ambulatory patients on the second Blackhawk that was on its way.

The Romanians helped move the patients out to the Blackhawk, and Captain Lindsey Evans and Sergeant Mitzi Riordan boarded. Lindsey shouted to Naomi over the rotor noise, "See you in Bagram in a couple hours."

Naomi nodded and gave the thumbs-up signal. She ducked and shielded her eyes from the rotor wash as the Blackhawk lifted off. She ran back to the building to get the last patients ready to board the incoming Blackhawk. Nistor, Kalb, and the Romanian work crew carried the stretchers out, and Naomi guided the two patients who could walk to the landing area.

The next Blackhawk landed, and it had one Air Force pararescue medic on board to assist on the flight back to Bagram. They started loading the stretcher patients. Naomi ran over to get the last two walking patients. As she did, she saw three stretchers being carried on the run by German paratroopers heading toward them across the runway. Naomi ran to meet the stretchers.

The Germans on the stretcher were in bad shape, victims of an RPG blast with open wounds in several places. They were not ready to be loaded on the chopper, and there was not room enough on the chopper for three more stretchers. Just then, the presence of the Blackhawk out on the open taxiway had become too much of a target, and a couple of mortar rounds went off, but short of the Romanian building area. Naomi looked at the Blackhawk, and the crewman was frantically making a pumped fist signal that they had to hurry and lift off. They needed to get the aircraft out of the line of fire.

Naomi made the split-second decision to stay with the wounded who had just come in and let the patients on the chopper who had a medic with them head to Bagram. There was little room left on the Blackhawk. Naomi gave a thumbs up to the crewman and did her best to signal they should lift off. The Blackhawk door slid closed, and Naomi was on the taxiway with the German stretcher-bearers. Kalb and Nistor were looking at her like she was insane.

Naomi directed the stretchers into the building and started to work. She had barely begun when two Romanians, severely wounded, arrived.

Where is the Navy medical team?

Sometime later, Naomi had lost track of time, she was working to stem bleeding on one of the Germans when she saw Kalb motion to look behind her. Colonel Cristescu and Colonel Heath were standing in the doorway to the aid station. Heath had his arms crossed and a scowl on his face. Naomi showed Kalb where to press on the German's leg to slow the bleeding.

Naomi stood up and turned around to face the colonels. She held her hands up, at an angle, chest high, to keep the blood on them from dripping down her arms. She had taken her blood-soaked ACU shirt off, leaving only her now-bloody t-shirt.

"Captain, I asked the NATO Commander in Kandahar to send two Army helos in here that you were supposed to be on. I ordered your team to turn things over to the Navy and get back to Bagram. I just got a SATCOM call from ISAF HQ in Kabul, demanding to know where their missing captain was. It seems the chopper pilot radioed you had stayed behind." Heath was pissed.

"Sorry, Colonel, I don't see any Navy medical team around here." Naomi made a dramatic wave of her arms around the Romanian aid station. "I had three badly wounded Germans, two critical Romanians and nobody to care for them. More casualties arrived just as the Blackhawks landed and the Taliban started shooting at the chopper. I had to make a quick decision and I made it. My duty is to save lives. I loaded the ambulatory wounded that could be transported onto the chopper, and I stayed with my critical patients. If you will excuse me, Colonel, I have important work to do, a brave paratrooper is bleeding out on the floor. You could help by finding out where the damn Navy medics who were supposed to relieve me are."

With that, Naomi turned and dropped to her knees beside the hemorrhaging *Bundeswehr* paratrooper. She did not see Colonel Heath stomp out of the aid station, nor Colonel Cristescu's slight smile.

A while later, Sergeant Nistor notified Naomi that they had a truck with enough room for four of the critically wounded to be driven to the medical hangar across the field. With the two recent additions to their patient population, that would leave three patients for Naomi, Kalb and Nistor to deal with. She had not heard anything about whether the Navy medical hospital was up and running yet, but she had to assume so since the 250th had left and the German Enoks were still arriving. She told Nistor to ship off the four most critical patients. Her call on the radio to 'Navy Medical' went unanswered.

An hour passed. Naomi's current patients were stable. She waited for the truck to return from across the airport, so she could load more. The patient number was back up to six. She was cleaning the blood off her hands with bottled water and gauze patches. She had run out of sterile gloves and other supplies were low.

Kalb got word on his radio that more casualties were inbound. Naomi, Nistor, and Kalb did their best to get ready to send the existing patients to the

Navy at the hangar. They desperately needed help.

Outside, the same intense noise Naomi had heard early that morning returned. It was the sound of a Marine Osprey VSTOL aircraft landing in front of the Romanian HQ. In a few moments, a figure in Marine camouflage appeared in the door to the aid station. It was a Hispanic woman with her black hair tied back in a short ponytail.

Since she could see no nametag or rank on Naomi's blood-soaked t-shirt, the woman asked, "Captain Donnelley?"

Through her blood-spattered glasses, Naomi could now see a bronze maple leaf rank insignia and a 'US Navy' on the woman's uniform, a Navy lieutenant commander wearing a Marine combat uniform. She had a name ribbon reading 'CONTRAREZ.' Naomi answered, "Yes ma'am."

Contrarez announced, "I am here to relieve you."

Naomi's conversation skills were numbed by the day's events, and all she could think to say was, "It's about time. I missed my ride."

Contarez smiled, "Yes, Colonel Heath let my C.O. know that, in no uncertain terms. There was some confusion as to exactly where the Romanian Headquarters was and who was doing what."

"No kidding. Are you a doctor?"

"A nurse practitioner. Trauma specialist. I'm Detachment OIC. We have two surgeons with us. One will be going with you on this Evac flight to Bagram. Another will be on the next flight incoming. I have six corpsmen who are unloading our gear."

"So, you're sending this Osprey to Bagram?"

"Yes, with any patients who are ready for Evac, and **you,** onboard. I have been ordered under penalty of court-martial to make sure you are on the flight. Word back on *USS America* is that you refused to obey Old Man Heath's order to leave."

Naomi smiled, "That's not quite the way it was. I had no room left on the Blackhawk, and five critical casualties just arriving. I didn't have much choice but to take care of my patients. Since the promised Navy detachment was a no show."

Contrarez smiled, "We figured that was the way it was. You want to brief me on the situation?"

Naomi nodded and turned to the patients on the stretcher and cots. "As you can see, we have six current in-house. We have two of each flavor, that is, two Romanians, two Germans and two Marines. No Afghans coming in today. All are relatively stable, but need surgery. They could be evacuated, especially if you're gonna have a surgeon onboard. But, the Romanian has light shrapnel wounds that your other surgeon could probably handle here, and after a rest he could be returned to his unit. If you are planning on using the Osprey to evac them fine, but we have been sending them over to the main medical hangar. Your decision.

"Operationally, the Marines who landed this morning are fighting to the north. There is a ridge between here and the city where the Taliban were. The Romanians have a depleted battalion protecting the airport. The German paratroopers, a light brigade, landed yesterday, or maybe it was the day before yesterday, I forget. Many of them and some Marines are down here now, fighting with the Romanians against the Taliban coming down the road from the city to the airport here to the south. From the casualties we have seen, the Romanians took the brunt of the early fighting. It has evened out since then. We are in the Romanian battalion HQ here; the main airport and the medical hangar are a couple thousand meters west. That is where your main naval hospital group should be. Anything else?"

Lieutenant Commander Contrarez looked around the bloody, dystopian medical station and turned to face Naomi. She gave Naomi a crisp salute and said, "Ma'am, I relieve you."

Naomi was surprised at the salute but recognized the Navy's traditional 'Taking over the Deck and the Conn' ceremony, where an officer in command is relieved by his or her successor. She responded with the appropriate return salute and, "Ma'am, I stand relieved."

"You have anything you need to take with you for the flight?" Contrarez asked.

Naomi looked around, adjusting her glasses. She realized her haversack with her personal gear had been left at the 250th's hangar when the Alpha Team had deployed. She hoped someone had collected it for her. Naomi poured water on her bloody hands, put on her camo field cap and strapped on her 9mm pistol. She picked up and held her blood-soaked ACU shirt and field jacket away from her body. "This is it. Airborne travels light."

As she left, Naomi passed the corpsmen dragging their gear crate from the Osprey. The Navy medical crates looked identical to the 250th's gear. Near the front gate to the Romanian compound, someone in a Marine combat uniform was taking pictures. The photographer took a picture of Naomi and saluted her as she passed him. Naomi returned the salute, then held her hat on and ran to the rear ramp of the Osprey. Naomi waved hello to the surgeon, a very young-looking lieutenant who was getting the wall-mounted medical stretcher stations folded down.

Since they were on the ground in a war zone and an active battlefield, the pilot kept the Osprey's engines running, ready to take off at a moment's notice. In that noise, there was no way to talk inside the plane. The surgeon directed Naomi forward to the fold-down seats. With thick vinyl padding, they were far more comfortable than the Blackhawk's seating.

Lieutenant Commander Contrarez apparently had decided to send four of the six patients Naomi had turned over to her to Bagram, as the corpsmen returned to the Osprey with four stretchers and put the patients on the wall racks. One corpsman stayed onboard with the surgeon, and a Marine crewman raised the rear ramp.

The engines and the huge rotor/propellers on the Osprey added power. The aircraft took off in a forward-rolling upward lurch. As they gained speed, Naomi could see out of the side porthole the engine nacelles and rotors roll forward into propeller position, and the Osprey sped into forward flight.

Naomi's July sojourn in Kandahar was at an end.

—

Chapter 35

United Express' Embraer short-haul airliner landed smoothly at Meadows Field Airport in Bakersfield. Naomi was exhausted. This flight from San Francisco to Bakersfield was the last of five flights that had been needed for her return from Afghanistan. It had been offered that she stay overnight at Joint Base Lewis-McChord in Washington state where she and the rest of the 250th Forward Resuscitative Surgical Team had in-processed early that morning from their deployment, but Naomi had chosen to get home as soon as possible.

As the airliner taxied to the terminal, the cabin speaker clicked on with an announcement, "Good afternoon, ladies and gentlemen, this is your pilot, Captain Ridgley. On behalf of United Express and your flight crew, I want to welcome you to Meadows Field, Bakersfield and the Central Valley of California. Local time is now 6:12 PM. While we finish our taxiing, I wanted to let you know that my cabin crew informs me that our flight has onboard several U.S. Marines and one soldier who are returning from a combat deployment overseas. It has always been my policy of recognizing the service of our valiant troops by allowing them to deplane first. So, if the rest of you would kindly keep out of the aisles when we come to a stop to allow the uniformed military to go first, I would appreciate it."

Naomi realized the 'soldier' announcement from the pilot referred to her. She had already retrieved her uniform jacket and beret from the overhead compartment before they had started to land.

When the Embraer lurched to a stop at the gate, Naomi stood and got her black carry-on bag from under the seat, and then started buttoning the uniform jacket she had folded in the seat next to her. She adjusted her beret on her head. Around her, the other passengers in the front of the plane obediently stayed near their seats. The other people in the 250th had switched to the Army Service Uniform and maroon beret for the trans-Atlantic flight home, and so had Naomi. After months of wearing the ACU's camouflaged field cap, the beret felt odd to wear, but they wore the beret home with pride. The petite white-haired lady across the aisle from Naomi caught Naomi's eye and said, "Thank you for your service."

Naomi smiled at her, "You're welcome, it was an honor."

They heard the sucking plop of the cabin door opening ahead of them. Naomi picked up her carry-on and turned to leave. Four Marines, coming up from the back of the aircraft, were nearly up to her seat. The Marines were all in the formal dark blue dress uniform of the Corps with the shiny black Sam Browne belts and white saucer caps.

The front Marine of the four saw Naomi and abruptly stopped in the aisle. Naomi had not looked closely at the lead Marine until she saw the bill of his white saucer hat tip up. He looked at Naomi's uniform, her beret, and then her service ribbons on her chest. Naomi, almost unconsciously, did the same to him and saw the captain's bars, pilot's wings, and service ribbons. Then, she looked him in the face and saw the smile.

When he recovered from the surprise of seeing Naomi, Captain Connor Holloway crisply saluted with a touch of his fingers to the shiny black bill of his hat and said, "Semper Fi, ma'am."

Naomi smiled back, returned the salute, and said, "Hoo-ah, Gyrene."

Connor motioned for Naomi to go first.

The five service members exchanged greetings with the pilot and crew as they left the airliner.

Connor caught up with Naomi in gangway to the concourse. Connor said, "Of all the gin joints in all the towns in all the world...."

Naomi smiled. "Yeah, I'm guessing you'd never expect to meet me like this."

"I'm not so sure about that. You'll remember that I was on the receiving end of your 'I Have a Destiny' speech. From those rows of ribbons, the combat medical badge, and the silver wings, I'm guessing you found part of that destiny."

Naomi smiled and nodded as they walked. "And, you. What brings you back to Bakersfield?"

"My wife and children are waiting for me inside. They stayed with her folks in Visalia while I was deployed. You?"

"So, you married a local Central Valley girl after all. My guy is a SWAT officer with the County Sheriff. He'll be out there, too."

As they walked, Naomi looked over at Connor and asked, "Connor, you're just returning from deployment like me. You didn't happen to be at Kandahar last month, did you?"

Connor looked at Naomi, "Yes, why do you ask?" Then, before Naomi could answer him, Connor added, "Oh my God, you're her, aren't you?"

Naomi looked confused, "I'm who?"

"Captain No, from Kandahar! The Army nurse who refused the Marine QR Force commander's order to evacuate Kandahar. You're famous."

Naomi's eye rolled up, and she shook her head in disbelief.

Connor stopped walking and motioned for the other Marines to stop, also. "Gentlemen, hold up a second. All of you will probably want to shake the hand of 'Captain No' from Kandahar."

Connor was correct, each Marine took Naomi's hand. One said, 'I thought you were kind of an urban legend."

Another Marine said, "The Media Office on the *USS America* had a picture of you when you finally left Kandahar, they made it into a poster they labeled 'Captain No,' the nurse who told our colonel to take a flying leap."

Naomi was clearly embarrassed, "Well, I did not know that, but in reality, your colonel seems to have forgiven my insolence. And, thank you all for helping at Kandahar. The Taliban almost had NATO on the ropes before the Marines arrived. But, let's keep moving, I've got an ex-Ranger waiting for me in the terminal, and I haven't hugged him in many months."

Connor led the Marines in saluting Naomi, she reciprocated. She turned, followed by the four Marines.

Naomi and Connor were in the lead when they rounded the angled turn in the Meadows Field concourse. She saw a large crowd assembled beyond the security checkpoint. A raucous shout went up as Naomi's impromptu phalanx was seen by the crowd. "There they are!" A huge red and gold banner "Welcome Home Marines" was held aloft.

"Good to see you again, Connor," Naomi shouted above the noise.

"You, too, Naomi."

As they passed through the security turnstile, the crowd surged forward, cheering, slapping backs, and hugging. That Naomi's uniform was not Marine blue did not seem to matter. Naomi was embraced by the joy of the crowd, given several handshakes, and one hearty group hug from two old men in Veterans of Foreign Wars caps. Naomi stood on her toes in the crowd, trying to see the face she sought.

Naomi did see a beautiful woman with shoulder-length blonde curls in a bright red dress with a toddler in her arms embrace Connor. Two little twin girls, perfect clones of their mommy, with red ribbons in their hair hung on to each of Connor's legs.

At last, Naomi saw the handsome guy in a Sheriff Deputy's green dress uniform waving at her above the crowd. She quickly moved through the crowd.

Jesse and Naomi ran to each other. Naomi dropped her bag. Jesse grabbed her in a bear hug and swung her around, and then set her down, and kissed her, long and passionately. The crowd of well-wishers for the Marines surrounded them. People in the crowd patted Jesse's and Naomi's backs in congratulation. Jesse finally drew Naomi out to arm's length and looked at her, before giving her one more kiss.

"Welcome home, Nomy."

Naomi just smiled and nodded. She noticed Jesse looking up at her beret, and then down to the pocket of her dark green jacket.

"Let's get out of this crowd," Jesse suggested.

"Okay. Are you it? I thought the Morrisons...."

Jesse leaned close to be heard in the noise, "I talked to them. We agreed I would come to get you. Janet is making a Welcome Home dinner for you. My folks are there, too. My brother and his family, too. And Ayla. It seems Janet and my Mom have become best buddies while you were away. A mutual interest in Nomy. Mom got a Blue Star banner for Janet to put up on the front of the Morrison's house, to show a member of the family is deployed overseas. Janet said my Mom should have one too, but Mom said you weren't officially in her family yet, because Jesse had not done a change of command ceremony."

"Wow, another rather blatant hint and innuendo about marriage from Jesse, or rather Jesse's mother."

"Have patience, I'm doing things my way."

"I see... have patience, he says. Well, family dinner sounds good. I've got to pick up my baggage."

Jesse smiled and helped her push through the crowd. He kept his arm around her all the way to the luggage carousel.

Jesse took Naomi's duffel bag and suitcase and led the way to his vehicle. Naomi did not see the black truck. Jesse clicked a key fob, and a white Ford Explorer chirped and flashed its lights in welcome.

"Jesse got a new Explorer?" Naomi asked.

"Yes, I decided Jesse needed to grow up and get a vehicle Naomi didn't need an assist to climb into every time."

Jesse threw both big bags and Naomi's carry-on into the Explorer's back hatch. Also, in the back of the Explorer, Naomi saw a kelly green footlocker with a large golden star decal. Jesse's SWAT gear was waiting, if needed. Jesse moved to open the passenger door for Naomi.

"Wait," Naomi turned to face him and put her hand on his arm. "What's wrong? You didn't say a word all the time we were waiting for my bags. You sure don't seem as happy as I am to be with you again. What is wrong?"

Jesse looked into her eyes and said, "I am happy, gloriously happy, but...."

"But what? I can still read your face quite well."

Jesse gave a half-hearted smile and said, "You disobeyed orders."

"Huh?" Naomi gave an incredulous squinting expression.

Jesse took in a deep breath and said, "That day that you left, I specifically told you to stay safe, keep your head down and come back to me. My exact words, I told you it was a direct order, as I recall."

"I did. I'm here."

"You obviously didn't do your best to stay safe nor keep your head down. And, your lovely emails seem to have left out a hell of a lot."

"What...? What do you mean?"

Jesse held Naomi out at arm's length, holding her by her shoulders, and then pointed with his finger as he spoke to her. "First off, there's this and this," pointing to her beret and silver wings on her chest, "You left in a uniform hat like any soldier and come back in a maroon Airborne beret with a flash on it that shows you are assigned to some airborne unit I don't recognize. And, I had those silver wings myself. When did you go Airborne, jumping out of planes?"

"Well, I...."

"Wait, I'm not done. By a long shot. And then, there is this," Jesse said, pointing to the silver badge below the silver wings, "That's a Combat Medical Badge, as in COMBAT, ground combat. You don't get that in a Kabul hospital. And your three rows of ribbons. I see a Bronze Star, but not just any Bronze Star. It's got a 'V' and an Oak Leaf on it. That means 'Valor in combat' and multiple awards. I missed that in your emails. And, I don't even know what these other two medals below that are. But, I'll bet you didn't get them for keeping your head down."

Naomi stared into Jesse's eyes, and then spoke, "You want me to explain all of that while we're standing here in the parking lot. Can't you at least let us sit in the car?"

"You started it, but yeah, get in." He opened the door for her.

Naomi watched as Jesse got in the driver's seat and buckled up, turning to look at her. Instead of buckling up, too, she turned in the seat and moved her knees over next to the gear shift console.

"You want an explanation?" she asked.

"Please."

Naomi began, "Well, first things first, as to your accusation of me disobeying orders. Lieutenant Manzanares, if you will look at my shoulders you will see Captain's bars. I outrank you. So, I cannot be guilty of disobeying your orders."

"Captain Donnelley," Jesse nearly shouted this. "I may be a lieutenant in the Sheriff's Office, but I never resigned my inactive status in the Army Reserves. It would literally take an Act of Congress to get me called up from the deep reserves, but I'll have you know that I am Major Manzanares, U.S. Army Reserve. I will forgive this one incidence of your insubordination and disobedience, but don't make it a habit."

"Sorree! Major. It won't happen again. Maybe.... However, I understand I am being called on the carpet by you for not being fully forthcoming about my time in the Army in Afghanistan. And, this is coming from a guy who is expert at giving one-word answers or going silent whenever the subject of his own time in Afghanistan comes up. And, now, I guess I can add, keeping your true military status secret. You've done a pretty good job of teaching me not to talk about what happened in Afghanistan."

Jesse started to speak, but Naomi cut him off with a finger in his face and a firm, "Shhh!"

"You want an explanation from me. Here it is." She took off the maroon beret and hung it carefully on his Explorer's gear shift handle. "Yes, that is indeed an Airborne trooper's 'red' beret because the unit I was assigned to for my deployment, the 250th Forward Resuscitative Surgical Team...."

Jesse gave a quick look of surprise and furrow of his brow when she mentioned the unit. His expression was downright dark.

"Something wrong with the 250th?" she asked.

Jesse thought a moment, and he said, "I knew some people in that unit a long time ago. And, you didn't have that on your mailing address. Your orders were issued by the 62nd Medical Brigade. You told me you were assigned to the hospital at Bagram."

"That's because, for most of my time there, the 250th was augmenting the hospital at Bagram, near Kabul. APO Mail service was to the hospital. Can I continue now?" Her voice signaled her irritation.

Jesse nodded.

"The 250th Forward Resuscitative Surgical Team is an Airborne designated unit, part of the 62nd Brigade. Their normal assignment stateside is to support an Airborne Brigade. Everybody on the team that deployed was parachute qualified, except us reservists they added at the last minute. You knew my unit was sent to Fort Benning for pre-deployment briefing and training. You and I were on questionable conversation terms those last few weeks before I left. In the mood you were in, I intentionally did not mention that I had volunteered to go to Fort Benning three weeks early so I could be airborne qualified like the rest of my unit. That was required to deploy with an airborne unit. I was assigned to that Airborne unit for a deployment, so yes, I get to wear the maroon beret. I wear the silver wings of a paratrooper because I earned them. Just like you did.

"Next, the Badge. Yes, the Combat Medical Badge does certify its wearer performed medical duties while engaged in ground combat operations. But, the story behind the three medals you asked about explains the Combat Medic Badge.

"I, in fact, did tell you about the way I got the first award of the Bronze Star, I just did not mention the Medal. I sent you an email telling you in detail about the young Marine who shot up the hospital office at Bagram, and I kicked the Air Force security force guys out who were sent to get him out and maybe shoot him, and I went in the room he was barricaded in and talked him down myself. Remember that email?"

"You don't get a 'V' for that. The "V" is for valor in combat against an enemy force, not a shell-shocked trooper in a supply closet."

"You want to hear this or argue?"

Jesse bit his lip and gestured for her to proceed.

"That was the first Bronze Star, a plain Bronze Star. The other Bronze star, represented by the Oak Leaf dillybob and the 'V,' is really for the same thing I did that the other two medals below it are for, just from different commanders involved.

"The middle of last month we got word that the units at Kandahar, down south… you know where it is…. Anyway, the NATO troops in Kandahar, down south, were under heavy mortar bombardment and probing ground attacks by the Taliban forces in the hills around the city. You probably saw it on the news. The Taliban wanted to take back at least one provincial capital before the big peace talks got underway. They tried at both Herat and Kandahar.

"The NATO Medical Aid Station at the Kandahar Airport took a direct rocket hit, actually a couple, and almost all of their medical personnel were casualties, either wounded or dead. They medevacked the injured and dead medical personnel, and the 250th Forward Surgical Team, me included, was sent in to do our primary job, provide surgical and medical support to forward areas. We were the only medical unit readily available to go in right away. We only had like an hour's notice; no time to send any message home. It was never meant for an extended stay, just an emergency fill-in.

"The 250th flew into Kandahar in Army Blackhawks." Naomi saw Jesse's brow crease at these words. Naomi continued, "We landed there and found the Medical Building to be a smoking ruin. The German NATO troops, who were the main force at Kandahar, helped most of the team set up shop in a Hangar. It was pretty rudimentary, just the basics, no internet to get word out of where we were. Then, a few of us - a doctor, two others and me, after a couple days were sent over across the airport to the headquarters for the Romanian NATO troops whose job it was to guard the airport. They had lots of casualties and couldn't deal with them alone. So, we found ourselves dealing with dozens of casualties. We only had one Romanian and a couple German medics to help us. Those medics were spending a lot of their time going out and bringing in more wounded. When we got a chance, we were supposed to send our wounded across the airport to the main medical station in the hangar. However, crossing the open runway tarmac, at times, was like running a Taliban gauntlet. They could see the flight line from the hills to the north and liked to take potshots at us.

"The next day, the situation in Kandahar got so bad that the brass in Kabul got serious and sent in an augmented battalion of Marine Quick Reaction Force off of a Navy LHA ship stationed out in the Arabian Sea, the *USS America*, and the F-35 air attack planes and the strategic bombers that go with that. All Hell broke loose on those Taliban in the hills. It was like that scene from *Apocalypse Now*, there in Kandahar. The Taliban responded by lobbing more mortars and rockets our way, trying to get the aircraft when they landed. The main 250th contingent was sent back to Bagram when a Navy field hospital arrived. The NATO Commander in Kandahar arranged for the evacuation of the 250th. They sent a couple of the Blackhawks to land over by the Romanian HQ and evacuate the wounded and our remaining medical people, being me, Dr. Evans, and a practical nurse, Mitzi Riordan. The fourth person in our original group had already been evacuated. The idea was that the Navy medical team that came with the Marine Quick Reaction Force would replace us, but no Navy medics came to our side of the airfield.

"The Blackhawks that arrived on our side were just regular troop carriers not medical equipped, and it was a long flight to Bagram. At that point, the decision was made to have Dr. Evans and the other medic go in the first helo with the worst wounded and me to go in the second with the others, the less critical wounded. We loaded the last of the wounded onboard with the Marines and Germans moving in around us to join the Romanians in the defense. The helo with Dr. Evans left. The last Blackhawk was nearly full and the Marine force commander, a colonel, had ordered me to take it. Just when it landed, the German field medics came in with other soldiers carrying more critically wounded Germans, and then a couple of Romanians. More mortar rounds were falling, and the Blackhawk crew was anxious to get out of there. I made the decision that until the Navy medics from the LHA got there, I had to stay to deal with these new critically wounded. I helped the NATO medics load some of the wounded Germans in the last spots on the Blackhawk and told them to lift off. I took the new wounded NATO troops back into our aid station. When he found out I had not taken the Blackhawk flight he had sent in, the Marine colonel in charge of the Quick Reaction Force was pissed at me, but eventually got over it.

"Apparently, the Romanian colonel in charge of the Romanian Army troops guarding the airport had overheard me telling the Marine colonel I wouldn't leave the Romanian wounded without medical care. So, I was still there, huddled in the Romanian HQ, treating wounded NATO troops and Marines. Just me, one American nurse, and a couple NATO medics. A pretty wild experience. And finally, I went out with the last wounded when things had calmed down, and an Osprey with the long-awaited Navy/Marine medical team came in from the LHA offshore. I was the last member of the 250th to get out of Kandahar. My people were frantic about me back in Bagram. All they really knew about me was what they heard from the Army door-gunner who had helped me get the last German wounded on his Blackhawk, and I told him to take off. I have since found out the Marines nicknamed me 'Captain No' for having disobeyed the landing force commander's orders to leave.

"And so, about the medals. The Romanian colonel had to send a report to Bucharest explaining all of those Romanian dead and wounded. He gave Bucharest an explanation of what he had heard me do, that is, disobey the order from the senior American and refuse to leave the side of the wounded Romanian troops in battle. The Romanian Ministry of Defense sent a medal citation to the Romanian ambassador in Kabul to be given to me.

"The German brigadier general who was NATO commander in Kandahar region, and the guy who ordered the helos I was supposed to get on, also wrote me up for an award from NATO. That's this one down at the bottom. The American general in Kabul, not to be outdone by the Germans and the Romanians, listened to the Marine colonel who had changed his mind about my disobedience, and ordered me to get the Bronze Star with 'V' Second Award for bravery while engaged in combat against an enemy force.

"So, one day at Bagram airfield just last week, Captain Naomi Donnelley got a NATO Meritorious Service Medal, this pale blue one, this Bronze Star with 'V' and this red and yellow one, they call it *Emblema de Onoare* in Romanian. That translates to Medal of Honor. And when he pinned it on, the Romanian ambassador kissed me on each cheek, quite European it was. And, that's your explanation. I've been so busy in Bagram and getting ready to come home to you that I really have not had time to write anything about it. I mistakenly figured you'd like to hear about it when I got home."

"You have a Medal of Honor?"

"Ehh, sort of. That's their award for honorable service in combat with the Romanian Army, pretty much the same thing as the Bronze or Silver Star for us. Not like our American Medal of Honor, you know, valiant service beyond the call of duty, usually given posthumously."

"Well, even so…" Jesse shook his head.

Naomi stared at Jesse with raised eyebrows, "Now, is this interrogation over? Can you take me to get something to eat and to sleep for a couple days?"

Jesse carefully took the maroon beret off his gearshift and set it in Naomi's lap. He held Naomi's hand for a moment before starting the SUV. Naomi leaned across the seat to give him a kiss.

"Buckle up, Captain Donnelley," Jesse said, "Welcome home."

As they left the airport, Jesse could not resist singing a slightly modified parody of the old Barry Sadler song from the '60s, "Put Silver Wings, on my girl's chest. Make her one of America's best…."

Naomi punched him in the shoulder, gently.

—

Chapter 36

Naomi and Jesse sat next to each other on the sofa in the living room of his apartment. Jesse pointed the TV remote at the television and clicked it off. He tossed the remote on the almost empty pizza box on the coffee table. He leaned back, put his feet up on the coffee table, and lifted his arm around Naomi, leaning back with his other arm on the back of the sofa. Naomi snuggled closer. She raised her left hand and admired the new diamond solitaire on her engagement ring finger.

"Well, Nomy, great movie. You always do a good job picking them. What now?" Jesse said, leaning his head to touch hers on his shoulder.

Naomi thought for a long time and answered Jesse, "Well, with your very wise move of finally popping the question and giving me the ring, I have something very important to tell you about."

"Oh! That sounds ominous."

"I truly hope it is not 'ominous.' But I guess that is up to you. I̲f̲ you don't believe me, it gets ominous. It is extraordinarily important to me, and I need to tell you the correct way. I have thought about this for a long... a very long time."

Naomi got up and moved the coffee table out of the way, setting her soda can on the table. Then, she moved the ottoman over in front of him. Jesse started to put his feet up, but Naomi pushed his feet off the ottoman and sat down. She scooted forward until her knees interlocked with his when she squared her shoulders to face him. She leaned forward.

Jesse said, "You did say you intended to 'talk' to me right. It looks like you are getting in position for somethin' else. Thumb wrestling, patty-cake, or...."

Naomi giggled and said, "No, this is my look-him-in-the-eyes serious talking position."

"I guess I better sit up then," he said. He sat up straighter and faced her.

"Yeah, that's good," Naomi reached forward to take his hands in hers.

Naomi looked into his eyes for a moment, gently cleared her throat, and began to speak, "Now, I told you all about my time at the mental hospital, my hitch in Juvenile Hall and the problems that got me there, right? Well, I...."

He cut her off and said, "Hey, Nomy, I don't need any kind of confessional of your past from you. You have turned out to be such a great woman, your teenage probs don't matter. I know who you are now, and I am happy with that. That is all I ever need. I love YOU."

She closed her eyes and lifted her hand away from his, motioning him with an open palm to be silent. When he got quiet, she opened her eyes and took his hand back in hers. Her eyes glistened with moisture.

She smiled gently at him. "This isn't a confession, at least not about the kind of stuff that got Naomi in trouble."

He gave a curious curl of the corner of his mouth when she spoke of 'Naomi' in the third person.

After a short pause, she continued, "No, this is more of me needing to tell you the full story of who I really am. Where I really come from. If I am going to marry you and spend my life with you, which I really want to do, I decided there is no way I couldn't come clean with the whole story of my deepest secret. Yeah, deepest is a good word for this, a secret that goes deep down to the very soul of who I am."

Naomi gave her little smile again and said, "The problem is I have been struggling to figure out how to tell you this secret. I realize that my story is so strange that if you tried to tell me a yarn like this, I would have trouble believing you, no matter how much I love and trust you. My secret is so bizarre that I have only ever told one other person in the world about it. I've kept this secret from everyone, but now I need to share it with you."

He cut in to ask, "That other person, was he the shrink at the hospital you told me about?"

Naomi nodded, "Yes, I told Doctor Partridge. When he believed me, that helped me believe it myself. I realize he only believed me because of a little factual connection that really couldn't be explained by anything other than my story being true. Doctor Partridge was able to check on something I told him that there was no way for me to know right then other than my story being true. My problem now is that I don't have any magical proof for you to make you believe me. I just have to look my big, green eyes into yours and try to convince you my bizarre story is true."

"Okay, try me," he said with his own little smile. "I get it… Naomi is going to tell me the honest truth about her deep, dark secret that is truly unbelievable and unprovable."

"Yeah, that's about it." She took a deep breath and continued. "You remember I told you how, when I woke up from my coma in the hospital, I was crying and screaming at the top of my lungs, fighting against the nurses, and I kicked so hard I broke an orderly's nose?"

He smiled, "Yes, I have done a bit of wrestling with you, I fully believe you could break a guy's nose with a kick."

"Shush!"

"You asked me a question."

"Yes, but it was rhetorical, don't interrupt my story, this is hard enough already." She reached over and took a sip of her soda. He reached for the last piece of pizza, and she playfully swatted his hand away from it. "No, you pay attention to me. You get the last piece after you tell me you believe my story.

"Well, I told you about my waking up like that, but I never have told you what I was screaming and crying about. When I went in to talk to Doctor Partridge, like, you know, the second morning after that episode, he had already been told in the incident report what I had been screaming about. The hospital orderly strapped me to the wheelchair in front of Partridge's desk, and the doctor and I talked about what had happened. He knew from the incident report that I had been screaming about the orderlies and nurses trying to pull my arms and skin off, and that I was crying about being burnt."

Jesse's expression darkened instantly when he heard Naomi speak of being burned. His face seemed to show fierce emotion far beyond what she thought her story would evoke, at least so far. She was confused by his reaction. *Was he angry? Afraid? For Naomi? Was he thinking about his own burns?*

She continued, "Well, I told Dr. Partridge about why I was screaming those things about pain and burning, I told him about a horrible accident, that ended in fire and death that I had been in. I explained a few of the details. I had him do an internet search for a name I gave him, that is, I told him to do an internet lookup of news about that name I said. He quickly found a blog post with a video from a San Francisco TV station from the night of my incident in the hospital. I had him read the article to me."

Jesse was still openly glaring at Naomi when she continued. She was confused by his almost hostile reaction so far. It was not what she had expected, she continued, "Doctor Partridge read me the article about how a drunken, wrong-way driver had entered the Interstate 80 freeway at an exit close to that hospital and drove into oncoming traffic causing a multi-car wreck. Several people were injured, and one person died while they were using the Jaws of Life to extricate him from the burning car. The name of the dead driver he read to me was the name I had just told him to search for, Mark Kelleher. I nodded and told him 'Yes, that is what I was screaming about.'" Naomi saw Jesse's scowl intensify as she said this.

"Partridge realized I had been strapped to a bed and locked in a hospital room without any outside contact for the entire time since that fiery wreck. I had no possible way to know about that name and what happened to Mark Kelleher. He asked me if I thought I had somehow channeled that poor guy's thoughts as he died, and I told him 'No,' that I was that guy, not this sick drug addict girl he had hobbled to the wheelchair in his office. It was me, my memories, and everything, ... my soul, not her anymore."

Jesse's face was contorted in confusion, and some sort of pain or anguish, Naomi did not understand. He started to speak, "You thought you were him...?

But, Jesse stopped abruptly, and Naomi could see him mouthing the name… *Mark Kelleher.*

Now, Jesse's expression of confusion remained as he asked her, "You're talking about Mark Kelleher. The guy who drove an Army truck in Afghanistan."

It was now Naomi's turn to give a furrowed-brow, perplexed look and say, "Yes, that is right, but how do you know about the truck?"

After a moment's thought, Jesse's expression abruptly changed to full anger. He had only once shown such anger; when he first heard about Naomi's deployment. He jerked his hands away from hers and pushed back into the couch away from Naomi. He was almost screaming when he said, "Look, Naomi, I was trying really hard to go with you on this. Trying to believe you. But, … but, I really don't know what this game is all about here. I was damned serious when I told you I didn't want to talk about what happened to me in Afghanistan."

Naomi was shaking her head in confusion, reaching toward him she said, "No, Jesse, dear, I wasn't talking about you in Afghanistan. I was talking about me in my former life. It is something I remember. I really need you to explain what you are talking about, and how you know about Mark Kelleher."

Jesse looked into Naomi's eyes for a long time in silence. Neither of them blinked or spoke. Finally, the tension and tightness went out of his shoulders and arms, and his angry expression changed.

"Naomi, you are serious… aren't you? This isn't some kind of trick to get me to talk about…." He pressed his lips tightly together after he said that.

Naomi nodded and wrinkled her chin into a dimple, "Honey, I have never been more serious, or honest in my life. I really need to know how you know about Mark… me…."

"Alright," he said, softly, as he shifted his weight on the sofa and pushed himself to his feet, bumping Naomi with his knees as he stood. He gently grabbed Naomi's upper arms and pulled her to her feet as he shoved the ottoman out of the way with his foot. Jesse turned and pushed past her, heading for the hallway. She followed.

Jesse flicked on the hallway light as he passed and opened the hall closet door. He pulled a cardboard file box from the top shelf and sat it on the floor. He reached under two folders of papers on top and pulled something from underneath. Naomi saw that it was a thick, green leatherette folder with the United States Army seal embossed in gold on the front. She knew exactly what it was. Mark used to have one of those, and Naomi had several of them.

Jesse thumbed the folder open. With his other hand, Jesse pulled two loose papers from the folder, so he could show the inside of the folder to Naomi. The bottom panel inside the folder was a color lithograph of a military medal, a purple ribbon with a purple enamel heart pendant, and an ivory profile of

George Washington on it. The top panel was a printed page entitled 'Citation – Purple Heart Medal.' Naomi could make out the top line of the writing, '*1ˢᵗ Lieutenant Jesse A. Manzanares* ….'

Jesse spoke softly, with a catch in his voice, "I was Platoon Leader for a Ranger team that was escorting a convoy of trucks…" Jesse hesitated when Naomi took in a sharp breath and put her hand up to her mouth, "…from Bagram Air Base, out west, through Bamyan Province when an improvised explosive device, an IED, blew up. I was in the second Humvee in the column, and we took the brunt of the blast. The Taliban had learned to pick out the command vehicle because of the extra tall antenna. All hell broke loose, an ambush, and the remaining Rangers and the transport troops returned the hostiles' fire. Two drivers from the front five-ton truck in the column ran up and tried to get to us in the Humvee. They got two of us out… out of the wreckage and the fire." Jesse stopped and closed his eyes for a moment. "But, many of my men did not make it. I heard they never even found most of the gunner's body who had been standing in the turret. Several others were…." Jesse broke down and could not speak.

Naomi put her hand on his arm. "You don't have to go on… I know…."

Jesse shook his head and said, "I need to finish… After the fighting was over, they medevacked the two of us to Bagram. My radio operator lost part of his leg, but I only had a concussion and the burns. I had the burns you have seen on my hand, arms, and back, and elsewhere." He tried to smile at this, but the smile was a failure.

"Before they put me on the hospital plane to Germany, I was able to ask them to find out who had pulled me out of that burning carcass of a Humvee. I assumed it was a couple of my Ranger team. The Air Force chaplain at Bagram managed to get me a set of copies of the citations they had drawn up to award those two truck drivers for valor for rescuing the two of us from the burning vehicle in the middle of a hot firefight. I wanted to remember their names… and I have."

Jesse set the two loose papers from his hand back into the folder. They were photocopies of Bronze Star (with V) citations. Jesse looked at one, and then flipped the other one to the top. He pointed to the top line of this citation and started to read it to Naomi, "Mark R. Kelleher, Specialist Four, United States Army, with conspicuous valor and at risk to his own life, did, on 24 September …."

Naomi put her hand over Jesse's hand to interrupt him and said, "You don't need to read it, Jesse. I've read it before. A long time ago. I can't believe I didn't put this together before now. It's like I was hiding from the same memory you were. Keeping such an important thing locked in the past."

Jesse stood silent for a long time, staring down at the citation. He gently closed the Purple Heart folder and carefully restored it to its place in the box, above another folder just like it.

"Is that other folder in the box your Silver Star?" Naomi asked softly.

"How'd you know about the Silver Star?"

"I never told you because I didn't want to pressure you to talk about… you know. But, my TacO at Fort Sam Houston was Ben Williamson," Naomi told Jesse. She saw that he recognized his Ranger comrade's name.

"Did Ben tell you the details?"

"No, he wrongly assumed that someone with a Silver Star would have told his girlfriend about it."

He turned to face Naomi and looked down at her. He could see the tears on her cheeks.

After another long pause, he put his hands on her shoulders and said, "So, you're telling me that you're really Mark, not Naomi?"

Naomi quickly shook her head, "No, Jesse, I am Naomi, the only Naomi you have ever known. But, I'm just not the Naomi that grew up as a little girl out in Utah. Or the one who went to high school here in Bakersfield. I have no memories of hers. I'm the Naomi that woke up screaming in that mental hospital. I'm the Naomi that, unbelievably—No, miraculously—was given a new chance at life by stepping into the shoes of a drug-addict mental patient, and who somehow managed to pull her life together, and made it here to find you and hopes to spend her life with you. It is just that this Naomi talking to you happened to start out life as a little boy up in Stockton and grew up to join the Army and drive a truck…."

Jesse cut in to add, "… and then saved a Ranger by pulling him from a burning wreck on the other side of the world…."

And Naomi finished, "… and then died in a fiery crash on the freeway up in Vallejo at the same instant that a near-dead Naomi woke up screaming in a mental hospital."

Jesse gazed into Naomi's eyes. He, ever so slowly, shook his head from side to side, not with disdain, but with gentle astonishment. He moved his hands from her shoulders up to either side of her face. With his thumbs, he wiped the lines of tears from her cheeks.

"Darn it, girl, you sure can spin a fantastic story! You do realize how unbelievable all of this sounds, right?"

Naomi gave a coquettish smile, dimpled her chin, and shrugged. *What could she say?*

With his hands still at the sides of her face, Jesse bent and gave Naomi a long and fervent kiss.

When he pulled his face away from hers, Jesse said, "I think we need to go back and sit down on the couch together, and you need to go over everything, from the start, all the details."

Jesse looked down at the box, and then at Naomi. "About my Silver Star. We can talk about that…, but maybe tomorrow. I think I am ready to tell you that story. It explains one of my deep secrets. Right now, we have your story to talk about before we can take on mine."

Jesse put his arm around Naomi's shoulder, and turned toward the living room, but stopped and looked down at Naomi, "Oh, and I've earned that last piece of pizza. I believe you. How could I not believe you? Nobody could make up a lie like that."

—

Chapter 37

Naomi entered the apartment door as Jesse opened it. She walked in, holding her McDonalds' bags up. She announced, "As promised, I brought food."

She looked at Jesse standing behind the door in his sweats. "Jess, you spent all day Saturday in sweats?"

Jesse closed the door behind her and followed her into his kitchen. "Yup, Costco doesn't have a dress code. You look nice and fresh after a full day at the hospital. I was kind of disappointed you had to go in to work. I was looking forward to a full day together."

"Me, too. But, that is the way it works. I just got back into town and, for now, I am filling in on the surgical team rotation. So, if they have an unexpected surgery, I get called, like this morning." Naomi sat the bags on the table and went to Jesse's refrigerator, extracting a beer can and a Perrier bottle.

Jesse sat at the dining table and said, "Since you brought burgers, I assume that is your signal we spend Saturday night at home. No movie theater tonight?"

Naomi looked at Jesse, "I seem to recall a promise last night that you would follow up my epic disclosure with your own story hour. I'm not going to let you off the hook."

Jesse nodded and opened his Double Quarter-Pounder box. "I assumed as much. I'm ready for you. Evidence is ready and sitting by the TV."

Naomi looked over to the glass, video equipment hutch and saw a green leatherette folder sitting on the DVR unit.

Naomi smiled, "Good boy, Jesse. Your training is coming along nicely. I'll have you ready for the Big Day soon." She wiggled her engagement ring for emphasis.

Jesse gave a playful frown.

"How do you want to do this? Eat first, interrogation later?" Naomi asked.

"I think I can eat and talk at the same time," Jesse said, bringing the stack of items from hutch over to the dining table. "Just don't get any ketchup on my citation."

"Heaven forbid," Naomi said.

Jesse saw Naomi start to open the beer for him, and he said, "Just a sec Naomi. Let's forego the Heineken, can I have one of your Perriers?"

"Sure," she said, going back into the kitchen. Jesse rarely drank Perrier, her drink of choice for meals. She put his beer back in the fridge.

Jesse was already halfway through his Double Quarter Pounder when Naomi got back to the table. She sat down and poured her fries into the lid of her grilled chicken sandwich box.

Jesse started to speak, "Okay, Nomy. You said last night that you had thought for a long time about how you were going to tell me about your life. Well, I did too. Only I was planning on telling this story to a nurse from Bakersfield, not to someone who had been to Afghanistan, not just once, but now, it seems, twice. So, excuse me if I over-explain things. If I get through doing this with you, I probably ought to tell it to Pete, Lucia, and my folks, too. They have been waiting for me to talk about it for a long time."

Jesse opened his green water bottle and took a sip. "I'm going to tell you first about my going to Afghanistan. Then, I'll let you read my citation for me, and I will explain why I have acted the way I have.

"I got to Afghanistan in early 2011, several months after Mark Kelleher got there, it seems. That was the big ISAF Surge that was meant to change things in Afghanistan. I was a platoon leader in the 1st of the 75th Rangers. You met Ben Williamson; he was leading another platoon. We roomed together for a time. Things were hectic. Both the Taliban and other Afghan factions were causing trouble. Iran was surreptitiously sending arms into the country, supporting anybody that was opposed to the U.S., NATO, and the Afghan leaders. Osama bin Ladin was killed in May across the border in Pakistan. Bombings, assassinations, and worse were happening every day in Afghanistan. I know I'm preaching to the choir on that….

"You and I both know what happened to me in September of 2011, since you, or Mark, played a role in that. But, my getting injured is the start of my real story. After Mark Kelleher and Eddy Jennings pulled me out of that burning Humvee, I…."

"Jennings, Oh My God, yes… Jennings!" Naomi shouted joyously.

Jesse squinted at Naomi, "Yeh, Eddy Jennings, the other guy. What, you forgot his name?"

"Yeh, I guess you could say that. That one time, in Bamyan, was the only time I drove with Jennings. He was usually a staff car driver in Kabul. I really didn't know him and I guess I forgot his name, even when I met him at Fort Sam." Naomi was shaking her head in wonderment.

"You met Jennings at Fort Sam Houston?"

Naomi looked at Jesse and said, "Sure did. He got my Silver Dollar. He's a Staff Sergeant now. I thought I recognized him but I didn't put things together."

"Jennings was your Silver Dollar Salute and you didn't recognize him?"

"Yeh, I guess you and I are alike in letting memories of Afghanistan get hidden. Jennings was also out at Camp Bullis and I kept thinking I knew him from somewhere, but... You know how that feeling goes."

Jesse gave a little laugh, "Yeh, I know what that feeling of strange connections and coincidences is like. It happens a lot when a person is around Naomi."

Naomi smiled and said, "Sorry, don't let me interrupt your story.

Jesse took a drink of Perrier and continued, "Ok, after the attack I was transported to our headquarters and the field medical team there, and it just happened that the nurse who was on duty was someone I had known and had flirted with a bit in the ramshackle Officer's Club at our base. She was an Army nurse named Kathy Willoughby. She was assigned to a medical team that was supporting the medics in the field with my unit the, 75th Rangers. She was with the 250th Forward Surgical Team."

At this, Jesse looked into Naomi's eyes, "Yeah, that is why I was so surprised to hear you mention the 250th. But, there is more on that, later.

"Kathy Willoughby was a brunette, about your height, icy blue eyes. She came from Twin Falls, Idaho. She had taken her nursing courses at BYU Idaho."

At hearing this, Naomi quickly glanced at Jesse's face. He did not seem to recognize the significance of this nurse's alma mater.

Jesse continued, "But, I knew most of this about her from before I came in on that helo from Bamyan. I was in no shape to flirt with her when I was on the gurney, and it was her job to cover my burns with Silvadene ointment and keep pumping the pain killers into me. I can just remember feeling so odd that this beautiful woman I had lusted after in the O Club was the one keeping me alive, while we waited for the medevac flight. I can still remember her smiling down at me and my feeling like she was an angel watching over me.

"I was flown out, and at Landstuhl Hospital in Germany, they decided my burns called for me to go to the Burn Center at Brooke in Texas. Like I said, I spent almost two months there. The worst time of my life. They did skin grafts and god knows what else to me. I really don't remember a lot of my time at Brooke, all drugged up and all. But, they knew their stuff, and by mid-November of 2011, they declared me fit for return to service.

"Then, I did something that only a Ranger or other Special Ops warrior would understand, and instead of taking a transfer to a nice, cushy stateside assignment to rehabilitate, I demanded that since I was technically still assigned to the 75th Rangers, I wanted to return to my unit, and finish our deployment with my fellow Rangers. Since I had been declared fully ready for duty, they decided to let me have what I wanted, and I got back to Afghanistan just after Thanksgiving 2011.

"I took a helo flight out to the 75th out west in Herat, I found Kathy

Willoughby and thanked her for helping me back in September. I remember her chewing me out for asking to be sent back to Afghanistan. But, she said she was glad to see me again, and she gave me a big hug, being careful about where she put her hands on my back since she knew the intimate details of where the burns had been. Oh, before I had left for Herat, I also tried to find Jennings and Kelleher at Bagram, to thank them, but their unit had already spent their year in-country and were back in the states, I was told."

Jesse saw Naomi smile and nod at this memory.

Jesse finished his burger and continued, "So, Jess is back 'in-country,' and his old platoon already has another lieutenant leading it, so Jesse gets assigned as OIC of the field reconnaissance team for the 75th. We'll fast forward to the New Year 2012 after the 75th has spent a miserable Christmas in northwestern Afghanistan. Nomy, can I ask you to read the Citation out loud. I think you would be better at reading it than I would."

Jesse opened the green folder and handed it to Naomi. She set her drink aside, wiped her hand on a napkin, and took the folder. She read, "Silver Star Medal,

Citation:

The President of the United States of America,

authorized by Act of Congress July 9, 1918 (amended by an act of July 25, 1963),

takes pleasure in presenting the Silver Star to

First Lieutenant Jesse A. Manzanares, United States Army,

for gallantry in actions against an enemy of the United States during combat operations in support of Operation Enduring Freedom, on 13 January 2012. At 1600 on 13 January 2012, 1LT Manzanares while acting as Officer in Charge of the Regimental Reconnaissance Detachment, 75th Ranger Regiment, in the field in Badghis Province, Afghanistan, was notified by radio that an American HH-60M helicopter carrying U.S. Army medical personnel assigned to the 250th Forward Surgical Team (Airborne)..."

Naomi stopped at this, took a deep breath, and looked at Jesse. He was looking down at the table. She went back to re-read that part,

"...an American HH-60M helicopter carrying U.S. Army medical personnel assigned to the 250th Forward Surgical Team (Airborne) had been shot down by Taliban insurgents near his Detachment's field location. 1LT Manzanares ordered his unit, consisting of two lightly armored vehicles and 12 men, to proceed to the reported site of the crash. Upon arriving at the scene 1LT Manzanares and his men located the downed helicopter in rough terrain approximately 500 meters from the road in a valley inaccessible by the vehicles. They determined that there were multiple survivors of the crash who were, upon arrival of 1LT Manzanares' unit, still engaged in small arms fire with enemy fighters estimated at 40 men. The enemy fighters occupied the high ground on three sides of the crash site and initiated an attack on the Rangers immediately upon their arrival. The Rangers engaged the fighters, and 1LT Manzanares and two of his men, SGT Matthew Carruthers and SSG John Kalkowski, set out through the rough terrain, under heavy fire, to try and reach the crash survivors before darkness fell. At this time, the Rangers on the road and the three heading into the valley were under fire by small arms, rocket-propelled grenades and were vastly outnumbered. Upon reaching the crash site, 1LT Manzanares determined that all 8 persons aboard the downed HH-60M had survived the crash, although four were wounded, two of those were grievously burned in the crash. 1LT Manzanares, by tactical radio, told his men on the road to request air support to suppress the enemy fire from the surrounding high ground, but he realized they needed to try and make it back to the road and the other Rangers prior to darkness. So, without air cover and only with the cover fire of the nine Rangers on the road above, 1LT Manzanares ordered SSG Kalkowski to lead the unwounded survivors and ambulatory wounded through a ravine up the rocky hill to the road, and SGT Carruthers and 1LT Manzanares would man carry the two seriously injured as the medical litters onboard the aircraft had been destroyed in the crash. Prior to leaving the crash scene carrying the wounded medical officer, 1LT Manzanares destroyed the crashed HH-60M with grenades to deny it to the enemy. In the climb up to the road, one of the crash survivors and SSG Kalkowski were wounded, but were still able to proceed. 1LT Manzanares carried his injured crash survivor through the heavy fire and led all 8 survivors and his three men to rejoin the Rangers 500 meters away on the road. Still under fire, now from all sides, 1LT Manzanares ordered his Detachment to drive several miles to the closest allied base with the wounded and crash survivors since the enemy fire, rough terrain, and nightfall made aerial evacuation dangerous. Throughout the intense 3-hour battle and rescue operation, 1LT Jesse Manzanares inspired his Rangers and reassured the wounded and crash survivors. Thanks to his bravery and leadership, all of his men and seven of the crash victims survived the ordeal.

By Order of the President,
Raymond T. Odierno
Chief of Staff, United States Army"

Naomi closed the citation folder and pushed it across the table to Jesse. She could see him staring straight ahead. He put his hand out on the citation folder.

Jesse's voice was gravelly when he spoke, "It wasn't until I set off the grenades in the chopper and went to carry my survivor up the hill that I realized who it was I was carrying. The uniform on the body was partially burnt, and the other medics had tried to bandage the worst of the burns on the face and upper body. When I hoisted the body over my shoulder, I saw that the body I had to carry was Kathy Willoughby's. I had to duck down to avoid the blast coming from the chopper as it burned and the firing from the Taliban in the hills above. When I finally got the body over my shoulder and started to run up the ravine, I could hear Kathy screaming in pain.

"That trip up the ravine and climbing that hill seemed like an eternity. My men did a great job laying down covering fire. An armed British Lynx helicopter eventually made it to our location and laid down a barrage of heavy machine-gun fire on the Taliban on the hilltop. We finally made it to the road just after dark.

"We decided to drive to the nearby NATO base at Qala I Naw. It was crowded in our Stryker vehicles with both my men and the survivors. I actually had Kathy in my arms, with one of their surgeons treating her as we raced to get out of those hills. In the light inside our vehicle, I could see that the side of Kathy's face was badly burned, as was her hair. About the only thing really recognizable was those intense blue eyes. About half-way to Qala I Naw, I noticed Kathy was no longer screaming in pain. She was still looking up at me, but without sound. Then, just before we entered the town, she closed her eyes, and the surgeon couldn't find a pulse. She died before we got her to help. She died in my arms. My citation talks about the people who survived that battle. It doesn't say much about the one who did not."

Now, Jesse turned to look directly at Naomi, "So, Naomi, when I got so angry when I heard you wanted to become an Army nurse, or later, God forbid, that you were going to that hell-hole of Afghanistan, I wasn't angry at you. I was angry at the horrible world that burned the skin off that beautiful nurse's face. When I refused to talk about Afghanistan, I wasn't being quiet about my own problems, I was remembering the angel who had died in my arms in that Stryker. I dealt with my own injuries just fine, and even asked to go back and finish my tour of duty with my unit, but I couldn't handle that I was not able to save that Army nurse, who had helped save me a few months before. When I cringed at you telling me your story about being burned in that car accident, I was not cringing about my own burns, but about Kathy's. Having another beautiful nurse, you, speak about horrible burns and pain, just... I couldn't handle it. When I heard you tell me that you had flown into battle in another Blackhawk as a nurse for the same unit, the 250th, I could not believe the nightmare... the possibility...."

Naomi got up and walked around the table to stand where Jesse sat. She cradled his head against her body and hugged him, stroking his hair with her hand.

"I understand, Jesse. I think I am finally figuring things out." Naomi paused, and then said, "I love you, Jesse."

"And, I love you, Naomi. I love you more than life."

———

Chapter 38

The Manzanares' white Ford Explorer sped through the mid-morning heat of southern Utah. The traffic was sparse on this Saturday morning. Jesse was driving, listening to Country music on the radio with the volume low. Naomi sat in the back seat, with her blouse open, cuddling her baby and holding him to her breast.

"How we doing?" asked Naomi.

"I just saw a sign that we are approaching Cedar City. It is still a way beyond that," was his answer. After a moment, he continued, "Ya know, Nomy, I really am glad you are finally getting in touch with your father. Everybody needs family."

"You've provided me with lots of family in the Central Valley."

"You know what I mean, your blood relatives. Tell me again, what made you change your mind? When you first told me about him, you made him sound like a troublemaker, who had a court order to keep him away from you and your mother."

"I told you I looked him up on the Internet. I found one news article that David Donnelley, who owned a local construction company, had been a candidate for mayor. Another blog mentioned that he had been appointed as a counselor to the bishop of the Mormon ward there. It didn't seem like a businessman, politician, and church leader would be a dangerous troublemaker. So, like I said, I called the number I found. I got hold of his wife, Laverne, and she was charming, sounded glad to hear from me. He called back, all excited to finally talk to his daughter. He offered to drive out to meet me, but after you and I talked... well, here we are."

Naomi saw her son's tiny eyelids flutter and felt his fervent sucking stop. Naomi gently burped the baby, carefully strapped him in the car seat, and reached forward to touch Jesse's shoulder, whispering, "I think he is going to sleep now, turn off the radio."

Jesse obeyed his wife's instructions.

Naomi leaned forward, closer to Jesse, and whispered, "Ya know, Jess, I just thought of another little road trip we could take."

"Yeah, where?"

"Up to Stockton to see Mark's parents."

"Wait, you wouldn't...?"

Naomi chuckled, "Tell them about me? No never. That would be tough for me and impossible for them. What I do think is that it would be a really, sweet thing for the guy whose life was saved by Mark, to go up and tell his parents… tell them how much…" Naomi's voice cracked, "…how much he did for you and ultimately us. They'll probably get a kick out of how the girl who knew Mark married the guy he saved. I think that would make them feel good. I would really love to see them again. It'll probably take a little preparation to get our story straight, though, especially my story."

"That's right, you said you had stopped in once, with Gene Buehler. Sure, Nomy. If you want. Let's talk about it. We can think about the idea. It's is kind of funny that you have two sets of parents, Mark's and Naomi's," Jesse whispered. "Now, why don't you lean back and take a nap while the baby's asleep. We had an early morning leaving Vegas."

———

Jesse followed the Explorer's navigation screen through the little Utah city's bustling downtown and turned up a side street. He had to slow for a group of kids playing kickball in the residential street.

Naomi looked up as Jesse turned into the driveway of a large, white Victorian house and stopped. She pulled the anchor release on the baby's car seat, opened the door, and pulled the car seat out behind her. Jesse closed the car door for her as she saw a man open the screen door of the house and look out. He seemed to shout something inside before stepping off the porch and striding toward them.

The man was tall, broad-shouldered, and lanky. He could not be called elderly but was a bit beyond middle age and had silver showing in his light-colored hair. He wore denim jeans and a plaid shirt with long sleeves rolled up above the elbows. A woman now came out of the door and raced to catch up to the man. She was a pretty brunette, quite a bit younger than the man. She wore a cotton house dress and apron.

When David Donnelley neared Naomi, he spread his arms wide, obviously intending to hug her. Naomi quickly passed the car seat to Jesse and was enveloped in a powerful hug.

David said, "God, Nomy, it has been so long."

Naomi was surprised when her father called her the same nickname Jesse had chosen for her.

When David finally released Naomi, his wife moved in for a lesser hug and kiss on Naomi's cheek. "I'm Laverne, we talked on the phone."

Naomi smiled and said, "Glad to finally meet you."

David and Jesse introduced themselves and shook hands firmly.

The woman was trying to ask Naomi something when they heard a squeal from the porch, and a young girl with long blonde hair crossed the lawn in a full run. Just like her father had, the little girl spread her arms wide as she neared

Naomi, but her enthusiasm turned the hug into a leap into Naomi's arms.

"Whoa, Bebe, be careful!" said David.

When Naomi finally tried to release the hug and set the girl on the ground, she looked up into Naomi's eyes and said, happily, "I'm your little sister, Belinda. But, you can call me Bebe."

Naomi said, "Yes, I see." The other adults all laughed, but Naomi was quickly counting the years since the tragic death of the Morrison's daughter and comparing it to the probable age of her newfound little sister, Belinda. *Another odd connection in my life?*

The Donnelley family seemed big on hugs, which did not surprise Naomi.

"And, everyone, this is Jesse, Jr." Naomi motioned to the baby in the car seat.

"Ah, my first grandbaby!" Laverne cooed, as she leaned to get a close look into the car seat Jesse held.

Naomi was surprised her young-looking stepmother seemed so anxious to assume the role of grandmother.

"Everybody, let's go inside," David invited.

The big, high-ceilinged front room of the house had a sofa, loveseat, and two matching armchairs arranged facing each other. So, there was plenty of room for everyone.

David took the center armchair, with an air that it was his usual spot. Jesse followed Naomi's hand signal to put the baby's seat in the middle of the couch next to where she stood, and then he sat in the loveseat.

When Bebe started to sit beside the baby, Laverne said, "Bebe, can you sit with your brother-in-law on the love seat. I want to sit with my grandbaby."

"I've got a brother, too?" Bebe plumped down close to Jesse, beaming.

Before she sat down, Naomi touched Laverne's shoulder and whispered, "I love this room. You've decorated it fabulously."

Laverne shrugged, "I studied interior design in college, but with the cards life dealt me, I only have one house to decorate. So, I do it right."

"Well, you have an open invitation to visit in California. Aesthetics is not my forte. I can use some help," Naomi whispered, before sitting on the couch, nearest her father.

David started off by asking, "So, Jesse, how was the trip. I understand you were going to stop in Vegas?"

Jesse nodded, "Yes, that broke the trip into two manageable bites. It's only about 500 miles total so I could have done it all in one day, but with the baby...."

"Yeah, when I was driving trucks for Walmart, I used to make the run to California, one day out, one day back."

"Oh, you drove for Walmart, huh?" Jesse asked.

"Yeah, they have big warehouse center in St. George."

"I saw that on the way through. Just off the Interstate. Big place."

"That's where we were living when Nomy was a little girl, St. George. Living there made it a little easier with all my time on the road. But, eventually, time apart took its toll; that's why Nomy's mother left with her."

Laverne decided to change topics. "So, Naomi, what do you and Jesse do. I mean unless you are lucky enough to be a stay at home Mom."

Naomi answered, "I get to spend a little time at home on maternity leave, but I'll be back at work when he stops exclusive breastfeeding. When I am at work, Little Jesse will stay either with Jesse, if he's off, or with his mother, she lives near us. She loves to take Jesse, Jr. for us. My usual work schedule and Jesse's have variable hours, so we should be able to move things around.

"Jesse is a lieutenant with the Kern County Sheriff's SWAT team. I'm a nurse practitioner at a hospital."

"What's a practizhoner?" Bebe asked.

Naomi smiled, "We like to say it's like a super-nurse. A nurse practitioner is allowed to prescribe medicines and order treatment for patients just like a doctor does, with a few differences."

Bebe and David both said, "Wow!" at the same time.

Laverne decided to continue her conversation management, "How did you two meet?"

Naomi smiled over at Jesse, who rolled his eyes at the ceiling. Naomi answered, "Well, Jesse is the leader of a SWAT team and managed to take a bullet in the ribs when they faced a barricaded shooter. It wasn't a really bad wound, but enough to put him in the hospital. Before he checked out of the hospital, he needed a fresh bandage, which was my job. Apparently, he liked my bandaging skills, because I got a vase of roses and his business card delivered to my work the next week."

Jesse raised his hand to be heard, "Wait, wait. Most of that is correct, but I saw it differently. Yes, I sustained a very minor gunshot wound in the line of duty. This pretty, blonde nurse was openly flirting with the valiant law enforcement officer while she had him sitting in his boxers on a hospital bed, while she slowly spread the antiseptic around, and around, and... you get the picture. As she meticulously applied her bandage, not too quickly either, she made it abundantly clear that her feelings would be hurt if I did not reward her efforts once she finally let me leave and begrudgingly gave me my discharge papers."

Naomi laughed, "There is a ring of truth in both stories."

Laverne huffed, "A gunshot wound, I just... wow! What a job to have. Naomi, how do you stand it when he goes to work."

"It's tough. It is what I signed up for, though. You can't say I wasn't forewarned from the moment I met him."

Laverne stood and announced, "Well, I'll let you folks talk and get to know each other. I need to make sure our meal is not burning and get it on the table. You all stay here; I can handle everything."

Naomi had been looking around the room's decoration and found one she was surprised at, "Dad? Gee, it is nice to have someone to call Dad," she smiled at her father. "Dad, I see your Iraq Campaign Medal and Bronze Star in your military decoration frame. I didn't remember you served in Iraq."

"Oh, yes," David said to Naomi, "I was in the Utah National Guard when you were a baby. Something to bring in some extra bucks as a weekend warrior. Walmart was good about letting reservists off for drills. Then, Bush goes and starts a war in Iraq, and I found myself in Kuwait, waiting to head to Baghdad."

"What did you do in the Army?"

"I did the same thing in the Army as I did back home. I drove a truck."

When her father said this, Naomi quickly looked toward Jesse. He was looking at her, shaking his head in amazement. Naomi was more than merely amazed; she was awestruck at the repeated coincidences and connections tying her life together. David Donnelley and Mark Kelleher had both been Army truck drivers, and Bronze Star recipients. She had to ask the next question.

"If I can ask, what is the Bronze Star for? If you want to talk about it, that is."

"Oh, I don't mind talking about it. Kinda proud of it, though it was a long time ago. On the way up to Baghdad, the invasion, the combat teams led the way, but those of us in the service and support units were right behind, you know supplies, medical, communications, transportation, and such. A couple of the units in that convoy to Baghdad got mixed up in the swampland with primitive roads in southern Iraq. They made a wrong turn got off track way out in the boonies. You probably heard on TV of those gals who got taken prisoner. Well, probably not, you were a baby. But, the famous ones were not all that got lost in that mess. Two medical units got separated from the main convoy, and they were getting shot up by some Iraqi units that were hiding out, hoping to keep their heads down and avoid the main American force. Anyway, these medical units couldn't get back with some of their vehicles out of order and a few wounded, so the brass sent my transportation unit and another to get 'em. To make a long story not quite so long, they gave some of us truck drivers Bronze Stars for going and rescuing the lost medics, fighting off some of the Iraqis, and getting the medics to Baghdad."

Naomi could not quite believe it, "You got a Bronze Star as an Army truck driver for rescuing a medical unit in Iraq?"

Naomi again exchanged glances with Jesse.

Her father nodded, and then asked, "But how does a nurse from Bakersfield recognize an Iraqi Campaign Ribbon and a Bronze Star?"

Naomi looked again at Jesse as she explained, "I'm in the Army Reserves. I'm a captain in the Nurse Corps."

It was David Donnelley's turn to be surprised, "My little girl is a captain in the Army."

Bebe interrupted, "I'm your little girl, Daddy. Naomi is your big girl."

David turned to Bebe, "Yes, Honey, you're right there. I have two girls."

Jesse cut in to say, "I can see Naomi is going to be shy about how she really knows what a Bronze Star looks like. Naomi has two Bronze Stars, one with a 'V' for combat valor like yours, plus a Medal of Honor from the Romanian Army, for her service in Afghanistan."

David turned to Naomi, fumbling for what to say, "… Uh… Really, Nomy?"

Naomi nodded. To keep from having to talk about herself, she added, "Since Jesse spilled the beans on my decorations, I guess it is fair to tell you that my husband has a Silver Star and a Purple Heart for Afghanistan."

David was still wordless, except for, "I'll be…"

"Lunch is on! Everybody gather 'round," came Laverne's announcement from the dining room.

As the three adults stood to follow Belinda to the dining room, David put both his hands out onto Jesse's and Naomi's shoulders, and said, "Looks like I get a double helping of war stories from you two over lunch. Can I carry my grandson in for you?"

David started the meal with a prayer thanking the Lord for the blessing of Naomi, Jesse, and baby Jesse visiting them. The hearty 'Amen' at the end of the prayer by everyone except Jesse spooked the baby awake. Food was passed around. David filled his wife in on what she had missed in the living room. Then, he asked both Naomi and Jesse about their Afghanistan service. They gave very abbreviated accounts of their medal exploits, while Bebe and Laverne stared with wide eyes. David was obviously proud of his daughter and son-in-law.

To change the subject after she and Jesse finished, Naomi turned to her father and asked, "Dad, I'd be interested to know, if you remember, the names of the two medical units you helped rescue on the road to Baghdad."

He scoffed, "Remember? How could I ever forget? They were two Medical Detachments, the 274th, and the 250th."

Seeing both his daughter and son-in-law react to his saying this, David asked, "Why do you ask? You two look like you know something about those units?"

After glancing at Jesse, Naomi answered, "Those two medical detachments are called Forward Resuscitative Surgical Teams now. I was assigned to the 250th in Afghanistan, and Jesse served alongside them, too. They were the ones in the helicopter he mentioned."

"What a coincidence?" David voiced his daughter's thoughts.

"Isn't the baby going to eat?" Bebe asked. "Gloria's baby, Mikey, likes to eat taters."

Laverne quickly answered Bebe, "Little Jesse is a lot younger than Mikey, and he is still nursing, it seems."

"Nursing?" Bebe asked.

"Uh, breastfeeding," Laverne said.

Seeing Bebe's quizzical look, Naomi mouthed a question to Laverne, behind her cupped hand, "Can I show her later?"

Laverne nodded and said, "Bebe, your big sister will show you about that later. Something you will need to know about eventually."

David spoke again, "Talking about big sister and little sister, looking at Belinda sitting here today reminds me how much she looks like Naomi did last time I saw her. Of course, Belinda has got her mother's big blue eyes. But both have Grandma Donnelley's blonde hair. And, they sure have the same look and smile.

"Do you really think I look like Naomi, Daddy?" Bebe asked.

"Of course, Honey, I wouldn't say it otherwise."

"Good, because Naomi is really beautiful, and I want to grow up to look just like her."

"You are right at the same age as Naomi was back then. You've just had your baptism, and I had just performed Naomi's baptism before her mother left with her."

"You baptized Naomi?" Jesse asked. He was not familiar with Mormon baptism practices.

"Of course, I did. It is what is expected. You remember, don't you, Nomy? Down at the Stake Center in St. George."

Naomi smiled and nodded as though she remembered. This had been one of her fears coming here. Having to hide the fact she remembered nothing of David Donnelley, or Utah, or anything of Naomi's childhood. She caught Jesse giving a little smile at Naomi's subterfuge.

David continued his recollections, "Yes, that was the summer Nomy turned eight in May. The country was coming out of the Recession, and Wal-Mart was in a big push to build more stores and had us company truckers on overtime. That summer and fall, I was away most of the time, and Nomy's mother just didn't handle it well. I got back in town just before Thanksgiving and found Nomy, her mother, our old Buick and even the family cat were gone with a note from her mother saying she was sorry, but…"

Naomi saw a stern look from Laverne toward David about where this story was going, but David did not see her, so he continued.

"I didn't hear anything of them for a long time, then I got a letter from the Henderson, Nevada police department telling me to pay up for three parking tickets on the family car that was still registered to my address in St. George. They sent copies of the tickets, and all three were for overtime parking on the same block of the same street in Henderson. I hopped in my pickup I had bought since Nomy's mother took the car, and I drove to Henderson. I sat there on that block until I saw her drive up and park the Buick. I couldn't get to her before she went inside an apartment, so I followed her and knocked. This guy answered. I guess he was the guy who eventually became your stepfather, Nomy, and he wanted to know what I wanted there. I said I just wanted to talk to my wife and see my daughter. Nomy's mother tried to come to the door, but this guy pushed her back and when I tried to get to her, he hit me, and then I hit him. Pretty soon, neighbors called the cops and since it was his apartment, I got arrested and warned that if I ever came back there, it would be bad for me.

David finally saw the look from his wife and tried to hurry the story to an end. "Nomy's mother and that guy got a restraining order on me, and eventually filed for one of them quick Nevada divorces. They moved on to California, and I lost track of them. I know this isn't the nicest of stories, but I needed to tell Nomy that I tried to see her, and I'm sorry for not being a part of her life while she was growing up."

Naomi reached over and took her father's hand, "I understand Dad. Nothing much we can do about that except try to be a family now."

David put his other hand over Naomi's, and they looked at each other until Naomi wiped a tear away. Laverne started passing food dishes around the table for seconds.

David still had another question, though, "I know your mother passed away when you were 18, Nomy. Can you tell me whatever happened to that guy, your stepfather?"

Jesse cut in, so Naomi would not have to answer, "He is in federal prison in Lompoc, California. Serving an 8 to 12-year sentence for assaulting a federal officer. Last time I checked, his sentence had been extended for fighting in prison."

"That figures," David said, before piling more green beans and a dinner roll on his plate.

Laverne took charge of the conversation now, "So, after the divorce, David quit Wal-Mart and moved back to town here. That was the same time I came back from college at Utah State to be home to help my mother take care of my father when he had a stroke. David was working with a buddy of his to start their construction equipment business. I caught David's eye at church. He was quite bit older than me, and once while we were dating and had a little fight, I told him I thought he was just interested in me because he was looking for another ex-cheerleader with curly brown hair to replace his ex-wife since I remembered Naomi's mother and I had that in common."

"You knew my mother, too," Naomi asked.

"Oh, well, I knew her to recognize her. I think I was maybe in 5th or 6th grade when your mom was a senior and a cheerleader. Football, cheerleading and all that is big stuff hereabouts. And at that age, I idolized your mother and her friends on the squad, and managed to follow in her footsteps, both on the cheerleading squad and as Mrs. David Donnelley."

It was David's turn to want to move the conversation elsewhere, and he said, "It's great you came this weekend because my mother has her birthday tomorrow, Sunday, and all her kids and grandkids are going to be at my folks' house to wish her happy birthday. Naomi can meet all of her Donnelly relatives."

Naomi glanced at Jesse and told David, "We had only planned on staying the one day before driving back to California. Jesse needs to get back to work by Tuesday. He has to testify in court."

David said, "That would really be a shame since little baby Jesse is your grandmother's first great-grandchild, and we'll miss a great opportunity. Plus, if you stay, you can see your aunts, uncles, and cousins."

Naomi looked at Jesse, who said, "Well, like we were talking about in the other room, taking two days for the trip between here and Bakersfield isn't a necessity. If we get a good early start on Monday morning, I can drive straight through to California."

David clapped his hands for emphasis, "Great, then it's settled. Little Jesse gets to meet his great-grandmother, and Naomi gets to see her grandparents and all of her aunts, uncles, and cousins."

"I've got a question," Belinda said. "If Naomi is my sister and big Jesse is my brother-in-law, what am I to little Jesse, his cousin?"

Laverne answered first, "No, silly, you're his aunt."

Now, it was Belinda's turn to clap her hands in glee, "I'm Aunt Bebe? This is wonderful. Yesterday, I was just me, and today, like magic, I've become a sister and an aunt."

Naomi could not help smiling at her little sister as she realized the same had been true for her. One day she had been someone else, and the next day she had become Naomi.

End

About the Author

Kevin E. Ready

Kevin Ready studied Government and Politics at the University of Maryland, University College in Berlin, Germany and received his Juris Doctor degree from the University of Denver. He had four decades of experience as a US Navy officer, US Army officer and government attorney. He has twice been a major party candidate for US Congress. Kevin E. Ready lives in the Santa Barbara, California with his wife, Olga and children. He is the author and editor of several books.

—

Visit Kevin's website at http://www.KevinEReady.com
Kevin produces a blog on Politics and the Law at
http://www.LawfulPolitics.com and
http://www.Twitter.com/LawfulPolitics

A New Chance

by

Kevin E. Ready

Published by
Saint Gaudens Press

Phoenix, Arizona — Santa Barbara, California

http://www.SaintGaudensPress.com